The Huguenot II

Building the Dream

The Huguenot II: Building the Dream
is a work of fiction.
Names, characters, places, and incidents either are the
product of the author's imagination or are used
fictitiously. Any resemblance to actual persons, living or
dead, events or locales is entirely coincidental.

LIBRARY OF CONGRESS CATALOGING-IN-PUBLICATION
DATA

Force, D.C.
The Huguenot II: Building the Dream: a novel / D.C. Force

Second Edition, 2020

ISBN 978-1-7339762-2-0
eISBN 978-1-7339762-3-7

Published in the United States of America

Book Cover Design by
The Book Cover Whisperer

The Huguenot II

Building the Dream

By

D.C. Force

Books by D.C. Force

The Huguenot Series

The Huguenot*: Flight From Terror*

The Huguenot II*: Building the Dream*

*The Huguenot and **The Tower of Constance***
(an e-book novella)

*The Huguenot and **the Heathen***
(release planned for 2020)

*The Huguenot and **the Heathen II***
(release planned for 2020)

Other Books by the Author

Family: a Century of Blood and Tears
released 2007

Visit our website to leave comments, ask questions, learn about the author, or catch previews of books to come.

www.dcforce.com

This series is dedicated to all the men, women, and children throughout history who have suffered severely and cruelly because of their sincere and non-political beliefs in and love for
our Lord, Jesus Christ.

True love's the gift which God hath given,
To man alone beneath the heaven,
The silver link, the silver tie,
Which heart to heart, and mind to mind,
In body and in soul can bind.

----Sir Walter Scott

"Remember that life is neither pain nor pleasure;
it is serious business, to be entered upon with courage
and in a spirit of self-sacrifice." – *De Tocqueville*

Chapter 1

New Jersey Colony -- Spring 1690

After so many nights of hearing Marie's expressions of pleasure as she and Jacques made love in the next room, Richard could not believe he was being invited to join them. True, he and Jacques had shared almost everything since they were small children. They had even shared a putain *once when they were very young but a wife was a far cry from a* putain *and to willingly share his wife was something Richard had never anticipated, never expected, never dreamed was possible.*

None the less, he was being invited.

She was such a giving person, so passionate, so caring, but she had never looked at anyone but her handsome, blond god.

He could not remember his feet touching the ground but he found himself at their bedside. With Jacques' approval, she was welcoming him with open arms. He was smiling. Richard gladly joined them in their bed. He felt her mouth hot on his skin as she began kissing him, caressing him. The hair all over his body was standing on end. She was so soft, so small, so very, very lovely. Everything a man could want and he had been silently wanting her for years.

She moaned and sighed so innocently as she held each of them close to her. Richard was hard to bursting with his ache for her. He ran his hand down her body, healthy, supple, smooth as silk. Her thighs taut, strong wrapped around him. He could weep. There was no resistance as he slid into her. Was this too much? Had he gone too far? Surely he had not been invited to a feast only to have the pièce de résistance *forbidden to him. He looked to Jacques for reassurance. Jacques, his best friend, had backed away with a shrug. Making room. Marie remained. Richard held her in his arms. He loved her, he wanted her, he needed her, he had her, he would share her if he must, it was better than not having her at all. But now he wanted to hear her cry out with the pleasure he was giving her. He wanted to hear her cry out for him as he had heard her cry out so many times for Jacques, he wanted... he wanted...*

Richard groaned aloud and woke, sitting straight up in bed. A dream! It had only been a dream. Of course, it had only been a dream. The tall, dark young Frenchman cursed softly in the shadows.

Very early in the morning, Jacques-Jean Charte, his wife Marie, and his best friend Richard Bonchance left the log cabin they shared at the edge of the frontier. It sat on a small river running into a harbor and the easiest route to New York Towne was via their square sailed craft. A long day's sailing up the eastern seaboard brought them in sight of New York harbor by dusk. After securing rooms at The Pork 'n' Porridge, they were able to catch up on the truth of the news about the French attack on the old fort. Master Henry Thompkins, the inn's owner, assured them that the town had never really been in danger of martial law although the harbor master had suffered many anxious moments. The limited troops on the navel ships were no match for a furiously disgruntled and armed citizenry numbering in the thousands.

Early the next morning, Marie went over to the Wingate Emporium to arrange for restocking her completely depleted food supplies and trading goods. Richard agreed to sell Marie's own pile of pelts for her and had the task of equipping himself for his first solo trading trip which meant buying a second boat. And Jacques sat down with paper and ink to write two letters both bound for France, one to his parents and one to Denis Dufee.

In his letter to Dufee, he updated the ship owner's son whose office was in Paris, on their progress in the New World. Jacques suggested one of the Dufee merchant ships might come to their harbor to take on a load of timber, free of a harbor master's duties or taxes. Exercising caution in his wording, Jacques did not specifically say anything about avoiding taxes or duties, but it was implied in his request for discretion in regard to the location of the harbor. He did not doubt that Dufee would understand and enclosed a map illustrating the small, over-looked harbor. Both letters were entrusted to a Dutch ship's captain bound for Amsterdam. He agreed to see that they made their way to Dufee in Paris. And Dufee would see to it that the letter for Jacques' parents was sent on to the duke's country estate.

Next, Jacques posted a sign outside a decently reputed tavern near the waterfront. The sign was a notice to all able-bodied men desiring work, especially those with experience in lumber, to gather there on the following day. In the Old World, labor was once again abundant and cheap. In the colonies, labor was a scarcer commodity and Jacques chose to say nothing about pay on his public notice. The prevailing wage for able-bodied men was easily five to seven times as much as they might be paid in France or England.

The following day Jacques went back to the tavern. A scant fifteen men had responded, not an especially large turn out but he remained hopeful.

"Gentlemen," Jacques drew himself up to his full height and spoke with authority as he stood against one wall of the tavern's low beamed room to address the small gathering. The general murmuring immediately ceased. "My name is Jacques-Jean Charte and as my notice states, I am looking for good men with strong backs to come to the frontier."

"Ain't nobody said nothing 'bout no bloody frontier," came a strident voice from the side. "I .."

"Hear me out, please," Jacques spoke importantly. "Yes, the frontier... but the frontier is a vast place. I do not speak of those areas of the frontier deep inland where war parties can be expected any day for dinner," he softened his words with humor. "But of frontier close to the sea, so safe my own wife has lived there several seasons, alone, with only friendly natives as neighbors. I will transport you by boat to do a job, and when the job is finished you may elect to stay or to leave. It is up to you but I will ensure that you get back here if that is your choice. If you have a family, there is cheap land available where we are going. Land on which to build a home of your own if you choose, in a new community. I can pay you no wages now..."

There was a sudden rumble of disgruntled mutterings from the crowd.

"But at the end of the job," Jacques raised his voice above the noise, "you will share in the profits of the harvest of the timber." Suddenly, the mutterings ceased. "How much you will make will depend upon you, the harder you work, the more profit there will be. But I will guarantee a base wage equal to anything you could earn in the same amount of time here."

"How do we eat in the meantime?" called a voice from the back with practical concern.

"Food for the work team and their families will be provided. And your first task will be to erect temporary shelters for yourselves against the summer weather. Are there any other general questions before I talk to you individually?" Jacques stood surveying the gathering.

Another smaller wave of mutterings hummed through the room but no one spoke out in direct response. Jacques walked to a table in the corner and took a seat. With paper and quill at his disposal, he proceeded to call each man up one by one.

The first to approach, with his hat in his hand and awkward formality, introduced himself as William Boot. He was tall, standing close to seven feet, and had to stoop within the tavern to keep from hitting his head on the beams above. His hair was the color of clean hay and his eyes looked like two cornflowers in a broad honest face.

"Please sit," Jacques signed for him to take the chair across from him. The man gratefully settled his huge frame onto the chair and smiled, visibly relaxing as, from his seated position, he could once again straighten his back and hold his head high. "Have you harvested lumber before, Monsieur Boot?" Jacques asked the young giant.

"Yah, it is vhat my family do back in S-veeden, sir."

"I did not realize Boot was a Swedish name."

"Oh, no, sir. I tire of people struggle over my name, say it funny and never get right. So I take English name that vas simple. People do not ask how to spell my name no more."

"Very practical," Jacques smiled. "Well, you certainly have the build for the work."

"I be runt of litter," Boot replied and his earnest face broke into a huge grin. "My brothers call me *wee one*."

Jacques' eyes twinkled at the humor. Wee, indeed. Boot appeared almost a head taller than Richard. "Where are your brothers?"

"One come five years ago, but we get letter he die on ship. The other two are home vit Mama. Now I am here and hope to settle and someday convince the rest to come, too.

"Are you married, Monsieur Boot?"

"Oh, yah, but please, call me Villiam."

"Very well, William, so you are married, yes? Do you also have children?"

"The first is on its way, sir, and I am needing a place of my own for sure. You say we could stay and homestead? That is most likely vhat I vill do if we like the looks of things."

"I am glad to hear that. Since I intend to also build a saw mill, I will have need of some permanent people. Perhaps we shall speak of it later. Your name will be on my 'Accepted' list. You can check the board for future announcements of meetings and when we shall be leaving town."

"T'ank you, sir," the big man said quietly and got up carefully, ducking his head and stooping as he left.

The next man to approach was much smaller in stature but had a powerful presence despite his youth and curly dark hair. He smiled often and seemed quite merry yet there was a certain weariness and reservation in his eyes. He bowed with dignity and took a seat when Jacques gestured for him to do so.

"*Bon jour, monsieur,*" he said easily in French.

"*Bon jour,*" Jacques replied back in French. "Do you not speak English?"

"*Oui,* but poorly. And if you speak French, there is not much need," he shrugged lightly.

"But there is much need," Jacques replied now in English. "If you are to join my crew where everyone is speaking English, and if you are to be part of that crew and get along with the others, you must speak the same language. Have you understood what I have just said to you?"

"*Oui*... ahhh, yes."

"Good. For you and I to discourse in French might lead to suspicion and resentment. 'When in Rome,' as they say. Agreed?"

"Agreed," the man said with a merry twinkle of acceptance, as he struggled to reply. "You ask to suffer, much, monsieur. Zee English I speak bad, many bad."

"It will do," Jacques smiled back, "and it will improve with practice, I guarantee you. We all started with the same struggle."

"Struggle, yes." the young man nodded his head.

"Why are you in the English colony?"

"I am Huguenot, monsieur, like yoo I theenk."

Jacques nodded.

...you do for a living in France, Monsieur Nicholet?"

"...eeth my father, a... how yoo say... a builder of... furniture fine..."

"...raftsman? Why would you want to chop trees?"

"You misunderstand, monsieur," he lapsed into French again and spoke more rapidly. "My father is a very fine furniture maker, but I am not skilled. I helped him, did rough work, lifting, the initial cutting of large pieces. I have no patience for the detail to my father's dismay."

"But you know wood?" Jacques queried, again speaking English.

"Yes, yes, zee wood… I know."

"Good. I can always use a strong man who knows wood. Do you have a wife?" For the first time the man's countenance grew dark, the smile leaving his face.

"No longer, monsieur. I am alone."

Jacques nodded sympathetically. Any number of things could have happened to the former Madame Nicholet. She might have died in childbirth, been murdered by robbers or run off with a lover. He saw no reason to invade the man's privacy.

"You are welcome on my crew."

"*Merci,* ahh..thank yoo, monsieur, yoo regret never," Nicholet smiled again.

And so the interviews continued. In the end Jacques rejected only two of the men. One, because he appeared painfully unhealthy and one because instinctively Jacques summed him up as an untrustworthy troublemaker. And one older fellow politely decided that this was not what he wanted to do. In the final count, Jacques was left with twelve men, solid and sturdy; four were married and would be bringing their wives, three more thought they might want to stay and settle, and five stated they were only signing on for the job and would be leaving when it was finished. Jacques had his first work crew.

That afternoon when he saw Marie, she could tell he was very pleased. He described the events of the day and suggested she would need to quadruple her stock of supplies.

"I am afraid I have bargained your services to feed the work crew," he said holding her hands in a show of public affection. "But you will have other women to help you. Four of these men are married."

"Oh, Jacques," her eyes lit up, "that is wonderful! We are becoming like a little village. And I shall have lady friends." She was as delighted as he had hoped she would be.

He nodded to her and decided for Marie's sake he must bring one of the wives immediately who could help her with the cooking. It might as well be the wife of the young Swede Boot, he thought. He wrestled with the logistics of how to transport everyone.

Even with the assist of the second craft which Richard had procured, transporting twelve grown men plus four wives and baggage, Richard, Marie and himself and all their many supplies in one trip would be impossible so Jacques planned to make a second trip in a week and assigned who would be taken on the first. He would take Boot and his wife as well as two of the single men in his craft with Marie. Richard was able to transport six along with his own trade goods and Jacques decided it would be better to leave the three remaining married men with their wives for the second transporting. It was more important to get as many of the work crew there on the first trip as possible since their labor was needed to erect shelters for the women to come.

Everyone gathered very early the next morning and Jacques disclosed his decisions. The workers who were to remain behind were told to wait patiently, and in exactly one week, weather allowing, he would return for them and the remainder of his supplies. The three remaining couples left the wharf a bit disappointed.

William and Britta Boot boarded Jacques' boat as did Francois Nicholet. Marie saw immediately that Mistress Boot was expecting a baby as Francois gallantly helped assist her into the rocking vessel. The wife of the big Swede was large like her husband, with the same hay colored hair and clear blue eyes. Marie warmed to the young woman instantly and felt very protective of her comfort and safety. With a sharp pang, she was also reminded of her own desperate desire to give Jacques a son.

It was a long trip in the packed vessels; they were crowded and heavy in the water. The winds were at cross purposes and they did not make good time. As the day progressed, Jacques' boat seemed to fall farther and farther behind. Britta Boot became ill within minutes of leaving the calm of the harbor and spent the rest of the voyage retching miserably over the side of the small craft. Marie offered what help she could to the young woman and William watched over his wife with patient concern, holding rags dipped in cool seawater to her forehead.

A privacy corner had to be established on Jacques' boat for the purpose of urinating on board in mixed company. On Richard's craft which carried only men, no such sensibilities inhibited the passengers from streaming over the side whenever they felt the need. Their only inhibition was making certain they were downwind of their fellow travelers.

Francois Nicholet spent much of the day conversing with Marie. He felt relaxed with the attractive wife of his new employer because he could speak French to her whenever he became frustrated with his limited English vocabulary. It was the first lengthy conversation he had been able to have with anyone since his arrival in the New World and his first with a member of the opposite sex in a very long time. Francois could not help but find Marie charming and considerate, as well as intelligent and witty. Although she was the wife of a gentleman she did not look down her nose at the workmen as some might have. But he was very conscious of the way her husband, his new employer, watched them, and he made very certain he neither said nor did anything which might be misinterpreted as an offense.

Marie found Francois' warm Gallic personality very ingratiating and he reminded her poignantly of her homeland and her siblings. With the discriminatory power of the mind, Marie's memories were mellowing, rendered by time into sweet and tender moments of innocent pleasures and bucolic scenes gleaned away from all the harsh, bitter, and cruel realities of her all too short childhood.

Jacques noted that his wife was again playing the schoolteacher helping the newcomer increase his vocabulary as they spoke together. The young husband did not mind this. He had become spoiled to having her company exclusively, he told himself, and it was good for her to speak with others. She would undoubtedly help his new employee immensely in learning the foreign English tongue. Just so long as Nicholet did not misinterpret her kindness. Let no man ever be foolish enough to overstep that line with his dearly beloved wife.

As the sun began to drop into the frontier wilderness to the west, the temperature on the water grew chilly. Jacques was thankful it augured to be a clear night with a moon and stars bright enough by which to sail. In the growing dusk Marie carefully worked her way over next to her husband.

"Jacques, it will be very dark soon. Everyone will be hungry. And where is everyone to go for the night?"

"They should be able to camp out in our open space. You have not planted as yet, have you?"

"But yes, Sheehoo and I did that before you and Richard returned."

"Oh, ah, do not be concerned, we will manage," he gave her an affectionate squeeze of encouragement.

Well after dark, they came at last to the harbor and were guided by the large fires Richard had the men build upon the shoreline.

"Look, they are as we were when we first came to this place," Marie observed, "but I cannot get food to them way out here."

"You are right" Jacques replied and then called to the beach. "How many of you are there?"

A distant voice replied, "Two. We were told to keep the fires going to guide you in."

"Right. Now I must take you with us if you want to eat." A quick reply of enthusiasm for that idea came from the voices.

"I am going to bring the boat closer. Can you see us?"

"Yes. Yes. We see you fine."

Jacques brought the boat in until its bottom scraped. They unloaded a large barrel and a keg, leaving it upon the beach to be fetched in the morning. The two fire tenders scrambled aboard barefoot, holding their boots up and dry and giving the craft a shove back into the water so it could make its way to the river mouth and continued upstream. Before long they saw another fire and found Richard himself tending it to guide them. He had lined the switchback trail with torches. Arriving in the dark was difficult on the newcomers who had no reference for the lay of the land but had to cautiously pick their way over the rough ground and between the trees.

More fires being tended on the cabin level lit the scene and Britta Boot emerged from the boat drained and weak.

"Jacques, I am going to take her to our cabin for the night... if you do not object. Poor Mistress Boot needs to lie down," Marie consulted with her husband.

"Of course, an excellent idea. I will get things organized here. And if you will see to getting some food prepared? Richard and I will come to fetch it." He gave her hand a squeeze of gratitude and kissed it warmly.

She nodded her agreement as she began to escort Britta up the little switchback path which took one from the river level to the cabin higher above. Marie came to a sudden stop. "Jacques? I almost forgot. With what am I to cook?" He turned back to look at her. "Someone needs to carry up a sack of flour and one of the large bags of barley. And, oh, I want that box right there," she pointed.

"Of course. Of course. Just keep it simple since it is already late. I am sure everyone will be pleased just to have something hot in their stomachs." And he turned to direct the closest two workman to pick out the requested food stuffs and follow Marie.

Carrying a lantern, Marie continued to guide Britta up the steep and winding switchback trail to the cabin. After a stop at the privy for both of them, Marie brought the pregnant woman into the cabin and on into the second room where Marie urged her to lie down on one of the narrow beds. Britta filled it with little room to spare.

The flour, barley, and food box had been left at the cabin door and Marie immediately built up a fire in the hearth using the lantern she had carried. After fetching fresh water and setting it over the hearth to heat, she went about lighting a number of candles and tallow lamps. When the water was hot enough she steeped wild mint leaves for a tea effective in soothing a sour stomach. At the same time she started a barley based soup in a second kettle with the now boiling water and began her first batch of pan bread with fresh baking ammonia from the storage box.

When the tea was done she brought a cup in to the ailing girl.

"Oh, t'ank you, Missus," Britta said gratefully, sitting up. "I do not know vhat to say, so embarrassed I am. Being so sick... in front of everybody. I hope you do not hold it against me. I just cannot take the sea and the baby, he helps not."

"Do not be silly," Marie smiled warmly and sat for a moment on the edge of the other bed. "No one can hold it against you. You cannot help being sick. Were you sick like that on the voyage over here?"

The girl nodded weakly, her face pale and drawn.

"And me with the Vikings for ancestors, yah? After a time, I vas better. At least I vas not wretched so. But never good until I vas back on solid ground."

Marie had never heard of *Vikings* but assumed they must have something to do with sailing. "Just keep sipping, stay here and try to rest."

"You are so kind, Missus.

"Please, call me Marie," she invited as she slipped down into the root cellar and found the last sack of onions. She grimaced as she looked at them. She would see what she could salvage.

"A good impression I do not make; I should be doing my share to help."

"Hush, you are going to have a baby. Most women get sick. It is nothing to be ashamed of," Marie soothed as she came back out of the hole in the corner. "When are you to be delivered?"

"He should be here by mid summer," the large girl replied.

"So soon? I did not realize," Marie said in surprise, "why, I thought you were perhaps only three or four months gone. You do not look to be that far along."

The girl smiled wanly.

Thinking that it surely did not do the young woman or her baby any good to be retching all day, Marie was convinced she should be still for a time.

"Rest," she said with some authority, "I want to see the color return to your face before you get up. And you must tell me if the smells of the food bother you. But we must get you fed soon. Let me know when you feel you can tolerate food."

"T'ank you, Missus Marie," she responded softly and drank more of the soothing tea.

Marie worked rapidly to produce a large kettle of thick, grainy soup, rich with homemade sausage, those last pitiful onions, and hardy barley to which she added salt and a number of dried herbs including parsley. While it simmered, she completed the first batch of pan bread and set about making a triple batch to follow the first. Marie felt her own stomach rumble loudly in a demand to be fed. She had not eaten since breakfast and it was way past supper time. With the first pan bread done she asked Britta if she felt she could eat a little. The girl accepted some bread with sweet maple syrup and was soon feeling well enough to manage soup. In a short time, she insisted on rising to help Marie.

The men had built a ring of fires on the land sloping toward the sea and edging Marie's garden plot. They were relaxing within its illumination, warmth, and protection. Jacques and Richard came to the cabin to carry the food pots out along with every bowl, cup and small pot Marie could scrape together. She had thought to buy more bowls for the crew she was now to feed but they had been left in the barrel on the beach.

Marie ordered Britta back to the bed and stayed herself to complete more pan bread. When she was finished she prepared to bring it out to the men and Britta appeared at the bedroom door.

"Please Missus Marie, might I be allowed to see my Villiam? He vill be vorried for me, I know."

Marie looked over at her in surprise. "Oh, of course. I am sorry. I did not even think. Of course you must let him know you are better. Come, you take this lantern; I have the bread. Just watch your step in the dark."

When William saw Britta, he jumped up and ran to her. Helping her across the uneven ground, he brought her to where he had been sitting. The fires lent cheer and Marie made the rounds with the fresh pan bread.

"Who did not get bread before? Jacques, how is the soup? Is there any left? Pass it around to anyone who wants more."

Jacques watched the men eagerly take the bread she offered until her basket was empty. "The soup has disappeared already," he called to her in reply. As she walked over to him, her stomach growled again. He lowered his voice. "Except for this bowl which I saved for the cook. It was quite delicious and I think everyone is content for the night."

Gratefully, Marie looked to her soup. The men began to stretch out on bedrolls. They determined amongst themselves to take turns feeding the fires to ensure their warmth and safety through the night. William Boot led his wife back to the cabin and returned to the others.

"Jacques, since Mistress Boot is staying in the cabin, could we not ask Monsieur Boot as well? Surely Richard cannot sleep there and the bed will go to waste," Marie quietly asked her husband who was carrying the empty soup kettle.

He thought for a moment. It sounded reasonable but he decided against it. To allow a pregnant woman to stay in the cabin was one thing but singling out William from among the other men for special treatment was another.

"I do not think that is wise," he responded and as he led Marie back to the cabin, Richard fell in beside them.

"So, what is this I hear? You have given away my room?" he joked and took the empty bread baskets from Marie.

Marie had one arm linked in Jacques' and put her now freed up arm around Richard's arm.

"Only for the moment, Richard, when you return you will have your room again," she reassured him.

"So, is her husband to come in as well?" Richard asked.

"No," Jacques replied firmly. Marie still did not understand why but she did not question her husband's decision.

"So, a bed goes empty. What a waste! But I do not feel like fighting a husband for the privilege of sleeping in the bed next to his wife," Richard continued with humor. "Especially a husband the size of William. So, are you going to let me sleep beside *your* wife's bed?" he looked over at Jacques with a grin.

"Only because I will be sleeping there as well," Jacques replied easily.

"With Mistress Boot here, we will all sleep with our clothes on anyway," Marie replied reasonably. "You can bring the mattress from the other bed."

"It will be like camping out again," Jacques said with a shrug. "Like when we first came here."

"It will be more like camping out when we first came here than you realize," Richard chuckled.

"What do you mean?" Jacques asked.

"Have you never told him?" Richard looked at Marie.

"Told me what?" Jacques frowned in puzzlement.

"The last time we all camped out you got to cuddle the pretty girl as well!" Richard said teasingly. They had reached the cabin and paused outside.

With a sudden flash of remembrance, Marie realized what Richard was talking about and she blushed slightly.

Jacques looked at his wife. "I hope you will enlighten me. I would have to wait all night for this one to explain," he gestured toward Richard who was still grinning at his private joke.

"Those first nights before the cabin was built, remember how we slept in the boat?" Marie asked.

He nodded.

"The very first night, I did not realize what I was doing in my sleep. I must have moved in next to you for warmth. And when I awoke in the morning you had your arms around me, holding me."

"I did?" Jacques smiled in surprise. "What a pity I did not know this. And were you pleased?" he teased.

Richard opened the door and went in quietly with the baskets lest Britta Boot be already asleep.

"I think I was very pleased," Marie replied softly looking into her husband's handsome face, "but I was also a little frightened perhaps."

"Frightened? But why?" he asked setting the kettle down on the ground and taking her into his arms. "Surely you knew I would never have taken advantage of you," his voice caressed her.

She stood looking up at him in the soft moonlight. How was it possible, she thought in a sudden rush of emotion, that this man could really be her husband? What had she done to deserve such happiness?

"I think I was frightened because I was beginning to realize how very deeply I do love you," she said softly. No answer could have pleased him more. She gave him a long, warm kiss and when they parted he had a twinkle in his eye.

"We sleep with company tonight, my darling," he whispered. "I must assume the discipline of a monk. Anymore kisses like that are forbidden for this evening."

In the early dawn light Richard bid his friends farewell and departed south to the mouth of the Delaware in his square sailed craft loaded with trading goods. From that day forth, their harbor was never quiet from sunrise to sunset except occasionally when it rained. The sounds of axes, saws, and hammers echoed through the valley while the little settlement swarmed with activity. Trees of appropriate size were marked and felled. Rough summer barracks were quickly framed out in which the men could shelter from bad weather while the other construction continued. The men who planned to stay would all need cabins before winter, but the married men would need theirs the quickest. By the first week's end, one cabin was complete and it was decided that all the women would share it until the rest were finished.

As the land on the eastern side of the fast moving stream became denuded, it grew easier and easier to see down the sloping hillside toward the harbor beach. And it was on this freshly cleared land upon which they built.

Jacques divided the men into two work crews; he put Boot in charge of one and Nicholet in charge of the other with Marie as an emergency interpreter. Jacques returned on his own to New York harbor to pick up the last boat load of workers and their wives as agreed. At the last minute, Marie put in a request for yet another large barrel of flour to add to the rest of the supplies left behind.

Son-of-Sky-Hawk came to trade. He knew the mate of She-Who-Battles-On-Bread had returned and that they had left together as was their habit to seek supplies from the large, white man village. What he was not prepared for was the number of whites they had brought back with them this time and the village they appeared to be building.

He had brought his sister, She-Who-Laughs-In-Her-Sleep, with him to speak the white tongue. When they reached the edge of the forest they stood for a time in silent observation, watching the activity they witnessed. It meant the *shëwanàkuxkwe* would never have to be alone again. But if he was glad the white woman would not be left in solitude, he was not certain how he felt about the number of trees being felled, many more than was needed just to build a few shelters.

He scanned the area around the cabin and saw Marie. Mere words could not have said more to the proud Indian than her look of unabashed delight when she saw the two natives meticulously painted up in their bright colors. She smiled and waved enthusiastically before walking toward them. Then she led them back to the cabin insisting they sit outside, drink tea with her and share some freshly baked, crusty bread.

Marie wanted everyone in the settlement to know these Indians were her special friends. There was nothing to fear and they were not to be treated with any hostility or unkindness.

As they sat Marie noticed the interest with which her native guests observed the work which was being done all around them. Allowing time for interpretation she explained slowly to the woman that they were harvesting lumber to be sent where trees were not so plentiful.

Britta Boot, having awakened from a nap, came out to use the privy and came face to face with the native Indians. She stopped abruptly.

"Oh," she gasped.

"Britta, good! I want you to meet some special friends of mine," Marie said quickly with a big smile. "This is Sheehoo and Looking Glass. He is the chief of a local tribe and she is his sister."

"I...pleased I am to meet you," the tall young woman said rather mechanically as she had no idea what else to say. The startled look on her face dissolved into simple curiosity as she stared at all the tattoos and colorful stain.

Sheehoo said something to her brother after which they both nodded in greeting.

"Pardon, missus, but go to privy I must," she pointed and quickly moved on.

"She have baby coming," Sheehoo nodded in the young Swede's wake.

"Yes," Marie confirmed. "but we have no midwife, no doctor, no… medicine man. I am concerned for this woman,"

"No need man for birth, his job done already," the Indian woman grinned displaying her missing teeth. "When baby come?"

"Mid-summer, perhaps two more moons."

"I come back, help," she volunteered and noted none of the other women had any children with them. Sheehoo pondered that white women seemed to lack the confidence to perform the most natural act a woman is born to. If this was so, surely there could not be many whites in the world.

"Oh, would you?" Marie exclaimed with tremendous relief. "That would be wonderful." She had been secretly concerned ever since she had met Britta. Marie was the only one in the lumber camp who had experienced child birth and she had been so young she didn't remember much of the ordeal and preferred not to mention it at all. Her baby had not survived and that hardly instilled confidence.

"When you have baby?" the stout native woman asked bluntly.

Marie felt the blood rush to her face in embarrassment and a touch of shame. She had, in fact, just begun another monthly flow and keenly felt the bitter disappointment of failing to be pregnant… again.

"My husband only just came home," she said, avoiding the other woman's eyes.

"Mmmm," the squaw grunted. She had always been suspicious of what harms might be done sitting in hot water, cooking one's body like stew. It was unnatural.

In less than two months, the sight of several cabins constructed on low land and a pile of logs being stacked near the beach greeted Sheehoo when she returned to the settlement with one of her sons. They quickly constructed a temporary shelter near the Charte cabin where Sheehoo awaited Britta's labor. When it came, all the women gathered to lend encouragement, to help, and to learn. They deferred to the squaw who had had four children of her own and seemed to know exactly what to do to further the process.

While they would have put Britta to bed, the squaw insisted the laboring mother stay on her feet and walk. Round and round the outside of her cabin they walked her, taking turns. The men grew more agitated as the pains came closer together so the women went indoors. Still Britta was made to walk within the small cabin until her water broke flooding the close quarters with the primal scent of life. That was the sign the squaw said and pushed Britta down on her hands and knees upon a mat.

The tall Swedish woman bore down, grunting from her depths and pushing with all her strength. At last with a final gush of amniotic fluid she could feel her child slip from her loins and into the squaw's waiting arms. Once the baby boy was bathed and wrapped, he looked exactly like his parents, large, blond and with big blue eyes.

Labor had not lasted long. The birth was over.

As Sheehoo prepared to burn the afterbirth and bloody rags, she was shocked to see William Boot admitted into the cabin to see his wife and new child. It was forbidden in her culture for a man to come so near after a birth. But it was not her village so she said nothing.

The happy parents rejoiced and inspected their offspring together after which the mother slept for a well deserved rest and the proud father went off to join the men for some celebratory drinking. Marie was handed the baby for the first time by one of the other women.

As she stood with the warm, perfect, and helplessly sweet little being in her arms, Marie felt such a longing within her that she found tears coursing down her cheeks. It was their settlement's first child and it did not belong to her. Marie looked upon the sleeping infant in all his pink and white perfection. She was sharply reminded of her own baby and of baby Bo-Bo whom she had wet nursed for money in the wake of her own child's death, and with what was almost a physical pain she thought again of the sons she had promised to Jacques.

Marie was blinded by tears. Abruptly she gave the child back to one of the other women. Thrusting it away from her, she excused herself and left the cabin quickly. She didn't know where she was going but she had to get away. Randomly she ran up the hill and into the forest, plunging deeper and deeper until in the privacy of the tall green trees in an area which had not yet seen a lumberman's axe, Marie wept loud racking sobs while she pleaded with God to have pity on her.

You have blessed me with so much, Lord, she cried out within her heart, *I know I have more than I deserve but please, please let me have babies... healthy babies, strong babies, sons for Jacques, for my Jacques... oh, please...*

Marie felt a hand upon her shoulder and she jumped in fright. It was Sheehoo. Marie quickly wiped away her tears.

"You ask Great Spirit for baby," the stout little woman said without hesitation.

Marie nodded, ashamed at being caught during what she harshly judged to be a self-indulgent fit of self-pity.

"Sometime woman try too hard, want too much, make spirit inside too strong."

Marie drew a deep breath and nodded, blowing her nose on the edge of her apron.

"Must not think so much. Worry no help."

Marie smiled weakly. It was all well and good to say not to think about it, but in fact, it was almost all she could think of anymore. The nagging doubts were always at the back of her mind now, even when she and Jacques made love. She knew it had nothing to do with their *spirits* fighting. She appreciated Sheehoo's attempt at kindness but it really didn't make her feel any better. Tears were flowing again and she could not stop them.

She had been reading one of the history books they had recently added to their little library. King Henry of England had put aside his Queen in his desire for a son, and when his second wife failed to produce one, he had been far less patient and beheaded her. And in the Bible, Sarah had been so desperate to give her husband Abraham a son that she had finally given him her handmaid. Rachel had done the same for Jacob. Marie had no handmaid to give Jacques, and while she was certain he would never wish to behead her, still how long would he keep her as wife if she remained barren. Was not his purpose in marrying her to conceive legitimate heirs?

Sheehoo gathered Marie to her and rocked the weeping girl gently as women over thousands of years have instinctively done in giving comfort to small children and those who are hurting. From deep within the squaw's throat came a melodic trilling which Marie found very soothing and strangely calming. After several minutes, the tears ceased and a sense of peace enveloped the younger woman during which she drifted into a serene absence of thought. When thought returned, the first which came to her was of her appearance. She could not go back to the settlement looking as though she had been crying. Jacques would want to know why, what had upset her, and she had no heart to tell him the truth, not about this.

Feeling the subtle change in Marie, Sheehoo immediately released her. Marie stood and visibly shook off her melancholia. "I need to wash my face before I can go back," she said, "we must find the stream from here."

"This way," said the squaw and as they walked along in silence a thought came to the Indian woman.

As Marie knelt by the stream, dipping up water in her hands to wash her face and sooth her eyes, Sheehoo began picking leaves off a benign little plant which she knew could be used to make a harmless tea. Sometimes the real medicine was in a person's mind, she thought. Sometimes magic only needed to be believed.

"What are you gathering?" Marie asked as she dried her face on a clean corner of her apron. She was always curious to learn whatever she could of the medicinal qualities of the plants and herbs.

"This for you. After leaves dry, you make tea. You start three days after moon time end, you drink every night. After you and husband share pleasure do not get up, stay in furs. Do not sit in hot water. Do this all winter and in spring you have baby coming," she said with such certainty that Marie did not have a shadow of a doubt.

She looked at the leaves as if they were precious gold or rare jewels. An expression of awe played over her face and she reached out with hesitation to touch them.

"Ohhhh," was all she could utter at first. "I knew it. I knew you would know of something."

Sheehoo maintained her serious demeanor. "Come, we gather more," she said, knowing she must not smile.

When the two women finally emerged from the forest, Marie was relaxed and full of hopeful joy. She believed without doubt that the Indians had a cure for everything. She would drink the tea faithfully and at some point when she and Jacques shared their pleasures together, she was going to conceive their child.

When Richard returned in the late autumn, he brought two pair of sheep with him from the Swedish settlement on the Delaware River. As he sailed into the harbor it was immediately evident that a large section of land had been completely cleared of timber and the process of removing the stumps had begun, readying the soil for the plow in spring. Along the waterfront a long wharf had been constructed to facilitate the loading and unloading of larger ships and a smaller dock stood at their landing farther up the river. Richard soon learned that Dufee's ship had come and been successfully loaded to capacity with prime timber. As per Jacques' word, the money had been shared with the men who reaped a year's worth of wages for only four months work.

Finding Jacques Charte a very reasonable taskmaster, all twelve men decided to stay on although several stated that it would only be for the winter. They were now employed with monthly wages to continue construction on the sawmill as the weather permitted. The two temporary barracks had been improved upon with a huge fireplace built into a wall now shutting up the north-end of each building while clay daubing plastered up the cracks and chinks in the timber walls. The buildings were ready for use through the winter by the bachelors while four neat cabins stood in a row defining the first street of the settlement. The married couples lived in those cabins.

The ship had not arrived empty but by Jacques' request had delivered much to the tiny settlement. They had received a full compliment of books. Some were *belle lettre*, novels and poetry for pure amusement and enjoyment printed in French, along with French works on wine, cheese making, and cooking, but most were extremely practical reference guides in English, spanning every subject in the natural sciences including animal husbandry, modern methods of farming, health and healing practices, construction, geography, history, and law. They also received the iron and steel works necessary for the construction of a sawmill as well as a healthy compliment of tools and plow blades to supply their needs in the absence of a blacksmith.

Richard also found a new barn housing a population of four legged residents including a bull and three pregnant milk cows, two pair of pigs, several goats, two plow mules, a pair of cats intended to breed and keep down the growing rodent population, and a pair of puppies who promised to grow into fine hunting dogs. Chickens roamed about feasting on insects and at dawn he was to hear a rooster wake them. Richard laughed as he added the sheep to the menagerie and reclaimed his room in the cabin, a room that was going to get a long overdue fireplace before winter.

On this solo trading foray, Richard had enjoyed much better luck than he and Jacques had had the year before. He had easily found guides amongst the Indians they now knew. His expedition had been without incident, but he was not as pleased with his haul of furs. Compared to the ones they had gathered from farther north over the winter, they were a disappointment. After several discussions with Jacques before the toasty hearth during the long winter evenings, Richard decided the next season he would go back up the Hudson.

"As you have said, I do not have a price on my head, *mon ami,*" Richard reasoned. "I can travel all the way up the Hudson to *lac de Champlain* and portage over to the river *Saint-Laurent*. I can travel amidst the French and trade with their Indians. None need know I live in English land. The Hudson is closer and the furs from around the Great Lakes are better. It makes good sense."

Jacques nodded his agreement.

Winter had been short and moderate and the construction of the sawmill at what they had begun to call "Chartes Landing" was completed through the long malingering autumn. With the first early greening of spring, the three companions, this time in separate crafts and with a few extra passengers, again returned to New York Towne where Richard gathered his supplies to head back toward the Great Lakes Wilderness via the Hudson River route.

Jacques and Marie accompanied Richard back to the wharf. As they said their farewells, he gave them each a bear hug, winked and whispered something into Marie's ear to which she grew pink in the face. He climbed into his craft and pushed off.

"I will see you in the autumn," was the last thing he called out to them, grinning ear to ear at Jacques as though he knew something Jacques did not. As the wind filled the sail, the boat pulled swiftly away from the wharf.

They waved to him then turned to go about their business. Jacques looked at Marie and when she glanced up at him, she gave a quick smile and looked away hoping he had not noticed the heightened color she could feel in her cheeks.

Having their own supplies to purchase, they set about their business. Marie no longer cooked for the crew but the trading post was busier than ever as the settlement grew. The lumbermen now looked to it for their personal supplies as did the farming families. Marie was in charge of getting the staples she would need for the store, things like flour, sugar, tobacco, salt, musket powder, axes, hoes, shovels, hammers, nails, and spices. She also decided it was time to add to their own supply of eggs and purchased two more crates of laying hens. And she selected trade goods such as bolts of calico, iron cooking pots, small hatchets, sturdy knives, small mirrors, flints, and traps. They arranged for everything to be loaded onto their boat by early the next morning.

Jacques and Marie always stayed at The Pork 'n' Porridge when they came to town but this trip they had found the inn completely full. They had to find another hostelry for respectable folk where they secured a sleeping room for the night but at the end of their busy day they went back to their favorite inn out of habit to eat supper.

They stepped into the comfortably large dining room and Marie was very aware of the smells filling the warm and crowded space. The odor of people, some quite ripe with acrid body sweat, filled the tavern already exuding the combined scents of powder, talc, cosmetics, and colognes. It all mixed with the more expected smells of cooked food, wine, and ale. The waxy sweet essence of beeswax candles, the aroma of fresh wood construction, and the more robust fragrance of the wood fire were laced through it all.

Master Thompkins, smelling of soap, onions, roast lamb, and spices, approached them when they arrived.

"Welcome, welcome," he smiled cordially. "How very good it is to see you again. You both are looking most well. I trust things have been going smoothly for you at the frontier."

"If not *smoothly*, at least busily," Jacques replied pleasantly. "The settlement grows."

Marie nodded. "We are in town again for supplies. And Richard has just left to go back into the big lakes region for more furs."

"The trading post prospers?"

"It grows too. More and more people are coming to the area," Marie replied.

"Most all the lumbermen have decided to stay and I now have a sawmill to run," Jacques added proudly.

"Indeed, no wonder you are giving up the trading treks," Thompkins nodded to Jacques with an approving look of respect. "Congratulations!"

The tavernkeeper showed them to a table by the window. "I saw the Wingates not long ago; they asked about you," he added.

"Oh, we have spent much of the day at their store, ordering up supplies. It was very good to see them, and in such good health. And you as well... and how is Mistress Thompkins?" Marie asked warmly.

"Busy in the kitchen, as usual," he grinned. "Our sons are growing up and they help more and more to run the place so we are building on as I'm sure you noticed. Our rooms are always full to bursting and so we decided to add a new wing. It will give us eight more rooms when finished," he said proudly, "four above and four below."

"Indeed we did notice," replied Jacques, "we were here yesterday evening when we first arrived and spoke to Hank. We tried to get a room but there was none to be had with privacy."

"I am sorry," Thompkins apologized sheepishly, "but please try again next trip, we'll see if we can't put you up in one of the new ones."

"Of course, we shall look forward to it," Jacques responded congenially.

"And this evening? Can I offer you a very good roast leg of lamb... or do you prefer fish?"

"The lamb sounds delicious," Marie nodded, "fish, we have often on the frontier."

Jacques nodded in agreement.

"And wine? I believe I have a bottle of the French red you like in the cellar." Thompkins prided himself on remembering his steady customers' favorites. Jacques nodded again.

"I think I would prefer ale," Marie said abruptly. She had a sudden taste for it. "And one of your wife's large pickled cucumbers, please."

"Of course," Thompkins responded agreeably although more than a little surprised. He could not remember Marie having ever ordered ale before and vinegar bathed pickles were no special compliment to lamb.

"And how are the Van Hootenaugs?" Marie could not help asking about the family she had worked for when first arriving in the New World.

Master Thompkins smiled. "She is always looking for a nursemaid. They now have seven children, you know."

"Seven? They waste no time," Jacques laughed. "Do they intend to populate half of the colony themselves?"

Thompkins chuckled. "One other bit of news – Brother Robert has left our church to start one of his own."

"Oh," Jacques and Marie both looked up in surprise.

"Yes. He is calling it the Huguenot Church. I didn't realize there were so many of you folks here in New York Towne. I'm not sure where they are meeting. They haven't a building yet." Thompkins added, then excused himself and returned quickly with their beverages.

"So Brother Robert now has his own church," Marie mused. "I am happy for him." She giggled. "Remember that ugly pineapple printed coat we dressed him in? He looked so silly." Jacques nodded. "And remember that first winter, Jacques?" she reminisced. "How you would rescue me from the Van Hootenaugs each Sunday, and we would spend the day here?"

"The three of us," he added, "Richard was always here as well."

"Yes, the three of us," she murmured in agreement. "We would talk for hours. I would bring those primers and we would practice our English together. You have no idea what those days meant to me."

The Thompkins' youngest son, George, brought their food while his older brother Hank served their drinks.

"George!" Marie exclaimed in delighted surprise. "You have grown as tall as your pa-pa! By next year you will be taller and catching up to your brother."

"Yes, Mistress Charte," the lad beamed and gave her a huge smile, trying not to trip over his feet as he set out the food and withdrew.

Marie's smile lingered watching the lads and disappeared again as she stared quietly at her food for a long while. She drank her ale and tried to stifle a sudden belch. "It seems so long ago," she said softly and began sucking on the large pickle taking an almost irrational delight in the vinegar brine.

Jacques was completely spellbound for a moment, fascinated by her technique; he cleared his throat. "Does it?" he asked, slicing into his roast.

"Does it not?"

"Perhaps. When you think of all that has happened since and how much we have accomplished."

"I guess we have accomplished much," she agreed looking at him wistfully.

"Of course, we have. But there is still much more to do."

"Jacques," Marie said after a pause, slipping the pickle from her mouth. "I think I need a building for the store. It is too crowded to keep all these goods and pelts in the cabin. Besides it is not the way one runs a true store, having people barge into the middle of your home. Perhaps we can hire some of the lumber workers to help in the construction."

"Hmmm," he replied chewing thoughtfully, noncommittally considering and trying not to stare at her continued dealings with the pickle.

"Besides," she added removing the pickle from her mouth again, "if we had a building for the store, we could have a room in the back where Richard could stay."

"But he already has a room."

"But the cabin is very small..." Marie said hesitantly and poked at her food. The lamb had sounded so good but now that it was setting on her plate, she had lost her appetite for it.

There was a silence.

"What did he say to you this morning?" Jacques asked with practiced nonchalance after taking a swallow of wine to wash down his meat. He carefully wiped at his moustache with his napkin.

"Who?"

"Richard, who else?"

"When?"

"I think you know when." His voice sounded oddly strained.

Marie looked at him blankly.

"He whispered to you when he left."

"Ohhh. Nothing," Marie looked down at her plate and returned the pickle to her mouth, running her tongue along its length and sucking fiercely to extract the vinegar.

"I did not know you two had secrets." There was a strange edge to Jacques' voice now. He expected honesty from his wife and she was prevaricating... and she was publicly putting on a very erotic display with that pickle. He looked around quickly, glad to see no one else seemed to notice.

Marie looked up into her husband's face and saw something there she had never seen before. "Jacques... we have no secrets," she replied earnestly, putting the large pickle down again. He continued to stare at her and it made her uncomfortable. "Surely you can not think anything indecent of your best friend..." she half-whispered.

"Has he made advances to you?" Jacques' eyes had darkened. "Are you hiding something from me? Is that why you want him out of the cabin?"

"No, no, Jacques... Richard is your *meilleur ami,* your best friend."

"I had thought so," he replied stiffly. "And you are my wife. The combination has been known to go afoul before."

Color rose in Marie's cheeks as full comprehension of what he was implying struck her. She looked her husband straight in the eye. "Yes, I am your wife," she replied, lifting her chin slightly. "Is it possible that you could be jealous?"

"Is it possible that you could play me for a fool?" he spit out in anger.

Marie's heart was pounding in her chest. This was a Jacques she did not know, he was unpredictable and angry and it scared her.

"Please," she begged quietly, suddenly sensitive to their public surroundings. "I do not understand. What is it? Why? How have we come to such angry words? I do not even understand what we are talking about. And I certainly do not understand what has suddenly made you so angry." Her words were greeted with another hard stare. With a sudden flush of indignant anger of her own, she threw her napkin upon the table and stood. "Do you think I would ever forget that I am your wife? Now, by your leave, monsieur, I feel great need of some fresh air," and abruptly she left the tavern just as her stomach revolted to all the suffocating smells around her.

Outdoors, Marie took a deep breath and staggered slightly to the edge of the building, away from the windows, away from prying eyes. She grew clammy cold as she rode the crest of nausea but through sheer will-power she did not vomit. She felt terribly shaky and the sound of her blood pulsing through her veins seemed to roar in her own ears. Black was closing in.

Inside the inn, Jacques sat for a moment trying to over-come his own anger and the sting to his pride. Thompkins came rushing over.

"Is anything wrong with the food?" he asked softly.

Jacques shook his head and stood. He pulled more than enough coins from his pocket and dropped them into the tavernkeeper's hand. "We are staying at The Oak Horn. Perhaps you would be so good as to wrap up the meal and have one of the boys deliver it. Excuse me."

"Of course," Thompkins said and frowned in concern as he watched Jacques leave. Carefully re-stopping the wine bottle, the older man gathered the meal together on a tray and took it all out to the kitchen where his wife was stirring a sweet sauce for the bread pudding. "Well, that is the strangest..." he muttered.

Mistress Thompkins looked over at her husband. "What happened?" she asked briskly and Thompkins described what he had just witnessed between Jacques and

Marie in considerable detail. His wife watched as he transferred their food into covered clay bowls. "Who had the ale?" she asked.

"She did... that too is strange. I don't believe she's ever ordered ale before."

"Hmmmm," his wife responded tipping her head slightly to the side. "I wouldn't worry, o'er much," she finally commented while tasting the sauce. She grabbed another orange from the crate they had purchased just that morning off a new ship in harbor. Slicing it in half she squeezed the juices into her sauce. "Sounds like she's belly-up and has a touchy stomach right now and maybe a touchy disposition as well. A lovers spat, that's all."

"A lovers …? Belly-up? But, you didn't even see her."

"And how long have they been married now? I should say I'd be more surprised if she wasn't. She's due for a little one, now ain't she? And asking for ale and a dill pickle? That's as good a clue as you can get. Besides, my fine husband, anyone who turns green over *my* food had better be pregnant or have the plague 'cause there ain't any other reason that's forgivable." She stopped her work and caught him with a look and a sly smile. "They'll need some time to patch things up, aye? Then they'll be starvin'. Leave the food to stay warm by the hearth and add two servings of pudding once my sauce is done. Send George round with it in, oh, I should say an hour ought to do it."

Jacques emerged from the inn just in time to see his wife grab the side of the wall to steady herself. Coming up behind her, he grabbed her arm roughly and jerked her toward him. All anger left him when he saw her face. Marie looked bloodless in the fading light of day, beads of perspiration had broken out on her neck and forehead, and she was shaking. But the wrench to her arm had brought her back from a faint.

"What is it? What is wrong?" he demanded more gently, a frown of worry now creasing his brow. "Come," the anger had left his voice and was replaced with an acute stab of panic. Half carrying her, he gently guided her behind the building to the stable where a low bench against the outside wall provided seating. "Sit here," he urged, his voice strained. "You are ill, Marie. You should have told me you were feeling ill. *Mon Dieu.* We must find a doctor."

For a moment she struggled to concentrate on taking deep breaths. The fresh air was a tonic and her stomach calmed but she felt weak and shaken. "Jacques," she said after a few moments. She spoke very softly and was unable to look up at him. "I know I can never be Celimene to you but you must know that I love you more than my own life. I would never betray you."

"Celimene?!!" he echoed in complete surprise. "What on earth brings her to mind?"

"I know how much you love her. And I realize I will never be as beautiful as she... but I had thought... I had hoped... that you might love me just a little any-way."

"Love you? *Might* love you?! You hope I *might* love you *just a little*?! Is it possible that you question how very much I love you?" he said, suddenly feeling angry all over again despite his resolve to control himself. "Have you no idea how much I truly *do* love you?! There is only one woman on the face of this earth that I have ever asked to be my wife and share my name!" he said adamantly as if that said it all.

Marie looked up at him. "Because *she* is not here," she replied weakly, tears glistening in her eyes.

"Is that what you think?" he asked in exasperation.

"It is the truth, Jacques; I accept..."

"Stop this instant!" he commanded in a tone that brooked no refusal but it was more than she could take. His young wife burst into tears. Jacques found himself looking about helplessly. When was the last time he had seen Marie cry? Happy tears of relief at his homecoming perhaps, a few tears of shame but whenever in unhappiness especially with him? He could not remember a time. She was always such a brave little thing, full of courage, full of daring and spirit. No, this was impossible. He really could not bear to see her weeping. He was responsible for this and he was suddenly feeling very contrite and completely undone.

"Marie..." he took her hands in his and kissed them repeatedly."I asked you to be my wife because you are the only woman I would have, and if you want to know the complete truth, I was afraid you would not have me," he countered gently. "Celimene is of another world, a world I have no part in anymore. It was another time and another place. And we had sport. That is all. It was only sport. There was nothing deep between us. It did not break her heart to see me go and it did not break my heart to leave her. We understood these things."

"You did not love her?"

"I had affection for her," he shrugged, "but it was shallow. Love her as I love you? Never!"

"You do not yearn for her?"

"No, of course not," he said without hesitation. "I honestly can say I never have. I am a changed man, *mon amour*. I miss my mother and father, I miss the estates upon which I grew up and by rights should be my inheritance. Sometimes, I even admit, I miss my country... though it made an outlaw of me. But my old mistress?" He laughed softly. "She has no place in this new world or my life anymore. She knew that and I knew that. God has given me all the woman I will ever want or need right here." He squeezed Marie gently, stroking her tear stained cheeks. He bent and kissed her eyelids. "Do you still not know how truly lovely you are?" he sighed. "It takes my breath away just to watch you sleep. You walk into a room and heads turn to follow you but you are so modestly unaware. It happened again just tonight."

"When?"

"In there," he answered tilting his head toward the inn.

Marie looked at him with an expression of disbelief and complete bewilderment.

"You have me acting the jealous lover, thinking the worst of the closest friend I have had since childhood; that is how desperately in love with you I am!"

"You... you were afraid *I* would not have *you*?" she uttered. "How can that be?"

"I have so little to offer..."

"But you are everything... it is I who... am nothing..."

He shook his head and continued to caress her face. "You are the warmest, bravest, most generous, most caring of women. It is so plain to see and everyone adores you for it. You have Richard wrapped around your finger, the savages as well, not to mention the lumbermen... and me? I would walk through flames for you, do you not know this?" His voice was hoarse with emotion.

It was as if she had been blind and now for the first time she truly saw not just desire but the love in his eyes. It moved her so deeply she began to weep again. He was dumbfounded and lapsed into French. This was not the woman he had grown to know who was so stable and clear thinking. What had happened to all her good common sense?

"*Qu'est-ce que c'est*? Now what have I done?" he asked in urgent but gentle frustration. "You are crying because you think I do not love you, then you are crying because I tell you how very much I do love you. Because I tell you how truly beautiful you are? I do not understand. What have I done? You must tell me. What is it I must do?" he demanded softly.

She shook her head. "*Rien. Je ne sais pas.* I am so stupid," was all she could say.

In complete surrender he folded her into his arms and said nothing but held her as she clung to him fiercely.

"Oh, Jacques, I love you so very much. And I thought you were always thinking of her... you never told me," she said in sobs of relief. Finally, she grew quiet as Jacques continued to hold her, kissing her head through her cap repeatedly.

"I have not thought of her since we left France," he replied with finality. "Now, here," he handed her his handkerchief. "Blow your nose."

She obeyed.

"And I do not want you to think of her ever again," he added. "And," he drew a deep breath, "I thought I have amply demonstrated how very much I love you."

"It would not hurt for you to say it every once in a while," she sniffed, wiping her nose again.

"I stand corrected and properly chastised." He bowed his head to her with a sheepish grin. "So," he gave a deep sigh and gently raised her chin with his finger. He forced her to look into his clear gray eyes, eyes which no longer held anything sinister, but only reflected affection for her. "Are you going to tell me what Richard said to you?"

"He said... just that he expected my belly to be big with a little Jacques when he returned," she said flatly.

"Is that all?" he shrugged. "Why did you not tell me this before?"

"Because... I do not want bad luck," she muttered.

"From what I understand, woman, luck is not the essential ingredient," he grinned.

"Jacques!"

Suddenly the realization hit him. "Wait... are you... are we to have ...?" he asked in delight.

"I think so, but I wanted to be very certain before I told you."

Jacques was smiling broadly. "But my darling little wife, this is wonderful! *Fantastique! Merveilleux!* We shall have a doctor look at you first thing tomorrow morning."

"No, Jacques, please, I do not want to go to a doctor."

"All right, no doctor. Whatever you say. So that is what this is all about... the tears, the odd emotions, the illness..." His face was beaming with understanding now as he looked at her tenderly and Marie fought a wave of panic.

"I do not want to disappoint you." Her throat constricted around the words. Jacques was suddenly reminded that Marie had lost her first child. But she had been a mere child herself he told himself and he helped her carefully to her feet in the deepening twilight.

"I think we had better go to the inn before the stable master charges us for lodging here," he joked to cheer her. "And," he added, affectionately kissing her hands again. "I cannot imagine ever being disappointed in anything you do. It is not possible because you put your best heart into everything," he murmured turning her hands over and opening her palms to receive his soft kisses. Marie sighed, caressing Jacques' lips and moustache with her finger tips and stroking his lean faintly whiskered jaw. She felt the muscles work beneath his firm skin and his eyes sparkled with a gleam as he now held her hand in his and urged her in the direction of their lodgings.

"How did Richard know?" he asked as they walked along the lantern lit street, a soft hint of salt sea in the air.

"I do not think he does, it was just by chance that he should say that," she said, then added, "Oh, I know not, perhaps he does know. The man grows more like the Indians every year."

"And, of course, you are right, we do need more room. But what we need is a real house with real floors! I have not done so poorly in this new world that my child cannot be born in a real house with glass windows and wood floors." He stopped in the middle of the quiet street. "Oh, Marie, I feel like such an idiot! I should have built us a house long before this. No wonder you thought I did not care. Keeping you in that peasant's cabin, how thoughtless of me!"

"No, no, Jacques, I never thought anything because of the cabin. I love the cabin. It will always have so many sweet and wonderful memories."

"Memories we will make no matter where we are," he replied and impetuously pulled her into the shadows before pressing her close and reaching for her mouth with his. He kissed her, his tongue flickering over her lips, probing her, tasting her, his hands running over the swelling curves of her body. Through her clothing she could feel his body respond to her. "I do not have the control of a schoolboy around you, woman," he sighed teasingly. "I cannot wait to get you to our room but how do I walk into the inn like this? You see the problem you present me with? You will have to walk in front of me."

"What makes you think I can wait that long?" she countered, a huskiness in her own voice that caused his blood to race. Marie was ready; she reach down to brazenly run her hand over the bulge in his breeches and felt her nipples tingle, wanting his touch.

"Marie... this is madness, we are just off the street," he whispered as her caress inflamed him further.

"Now, Jacques, now! Please..." she begged urgently, feeling extremely wanton and overcome with a fever of desire. She plucked at the laces of her bodice and loosen it just enough to free up her breasts.

"This is too much..." he groaned and pulled her farther back around the edge of a closed shop into the deeper shadows. He caressed one full sensitive breast with his hand and the other with his mouth sending sensual shock waves through her body and she made little sounds in her throat. Quickly glancing first to the left, and then to the right, he saw the back of another stable. "Here, come," he urged and pulled her along.

Just inside the door, they heard horses shift and knicker but it was dark and the honest smells of the animals only served to heighten their primal drives. Marie pulled up her skirts and presented herself like a mare in season. She had found the railing of a stall and grabbed hold to brace herself against it.

In the shadows Jacques could just make out her form and came up behind her; drawn like a stallion to her heat he took hold of her smooth hips. She gasped in pleasure as he thrust into her. She surprised him when she backed fiercely against him taking him in even more deeply.

They were both panting in the darkness, her hair flying out of her cap and about her like a silky mane. She shuttered wantonly in his arms as he continued to move in a slow maddening rhythm, building the tension until at last she could stand it no longer and with a muffled cry she peaked, triggering his own climax. The final wave of satisfaction washed over them together as the horses whinnied and neighed from within their stalls.

She issued a long sigh and he drew her back up against him enjoying the feel of her full warm breasts in his hands. They felt larger, heavier, and as smooth as the finest satin. From behind, he nuzzled her neck, almost biting then kissing her repeatedly. At last he whispered into her ear. "If this is how it is to be for the next six or seven months, I am going to have to stay very close to home, I think."

She grinned shamelessly in the dark, savoring the lingering feel of him and regretting the loss when he finally withdrew. She turned and engaged him in a very long and sensual kiss.

"Do you think you can walk into the inn now, monsieur?"

"Not if you kiss me like that again."

They quickly pulled their clothing together as they walked slowly back through the dark alley way trying to make themselves presentable. Once on the street they looked each other over and exchanged reassuring nods.

"Oh," Marie giggled. She had lost her cap in the dark stable. "Your hair has come undone, we cannot both have our hair in a mess." She pointed to the blond locks hanging into his eyes, loose from the practical leather thong that held it in a club at the nape of his neck. "And what has become of your hat?"

Jacques shrugged as he undid the thong, raked his fingers through his hair, gathered it all together again, and tied it off. "I have the feeling I left it at our table." When he finished, he gave her his arm and they walked toward their lodgings in smiling silence.

Jacques' mind was racing with plans for building and making a home for his growing family. They did not need to build a store, he thought, they needed to build a house, a real house, and Marie could have the whole cabin as her store. They would need at least four bedrooms… no, more like six... and a proper nursery, and a salon, a dining hall, and he should really have an office or a study, perhaps a library as well. And here in the New World with so much building done with lumber, were they not building kitchens separately as a safety precaution? The attic should have space for servants' quarters. Perhaps they should take an extra day and look at some of the newest houses in the area, he thought. Yes, why not? He could not build a chateau but he could provide something a bit more substantial than a simple country cottage for his family. He must find an architect and they must decide on a site.

Marie was feeling more secure and self-assured than she had ever felt before. She stole a glance just to look at Jacques because she enjoyed looking at him, he was so beautiful in a completely masculine way and every expression on his face was endearing to her. He saw her and gave her an affectionate smile. The smile warmed her all over. He loved her! He thought she was beautiful! She was going to have his baby. And he never thought of Celimene. Life was wonderful! Life could not be better! She found herself silently praying that Jacques would never have call to be disappointed in her. She prayed as mothers have done through the ages that their child arrive healthy and perfect and strong. But at the same moment she felt a renewed serge of desire sweep over her, heightening her senses and causing her to wish they were already back in their room. She wanted him all over again, right then, right there, and badly.

Jacques looked at her when he felt her grip on his arm increase. He saw the expression on her face and in her eyes and he felt his own body react. *Thank God we have finally reached the inn,* he thought, *before we get arrested for indecency and thrown into the stocks!*

Chapter 2

His son lie within her. Or his daughter... so small, so tiny, growing day by day inside her warm, protective womb. Sheltered and held safe, nourished and cradled until every finger, toe, hair, and eyelash was complete. That in a few short months a new and untouched life would enter this world was nothing short of a true miracle. It was God's miracle. And from that moment on, he, Jacques-Jean Charte, was charged with the duty of protecting, teaching, and guiding that miracle of life. He would henceforth be a father.

A father! The title gave the young man a feeling of such pride as well as apprehension.

Perhaps because he had known what it was like to grow up a bastard in a fatherless home, Jacques had never been cavalier about starting new life while indulging the youthful pleasures of the flesh. Through a combination of luck and care he had avoided fathering any illegitimate children and now he could only thank God this was so. The concept of fatherhood filled him with a sense of awe and divinely ordained responsibility.

He was twenty-six, no longer a youth. Six years ago he had given up everything, his future title, future inheritance of vast lands and holdings in France, as well as the comforts of living within the love and recognition of his own recently discovered father. All this he had given up in order to remain faithful and true to the Protestant teachings of his Huguenot mother. He had escaped with his life, his freedom, and his best friend Richard Bonchance. In partnership, they gambled on the prospects and refuge offered by the New World.

As Jacques continued to gaze upon his wife who was now twenty, he was reminded of the little serving girl she had been, not even fifteen, who had tenaciously begged to join them in order to find whatever opportunities the New World would allow her. She had been very brave and he had been very blind until one day he realized he was quite hopelessly in love with her.

Now he wanted to clasp her small hand which rested relaxed upon her pillow. He wanted to press his lips against the roughened knuckles, tenderly kiss the calloused palm, but he stopped himself just short of his impulse lest he disturb her peaceful sleep. She worked hard, too hard, and as much as he admonished her to rest there was always another task she wanted to complete. Those two small, strong hands of grace and dignity never were still except in such as these moments of slumber. But on this he would be firm. They should have domestic help and he as head of his household would see to its provision.

He knew she would never think of asking for domestic help for herself. If something had to be done, it was never too tedious, laborious, odious, or undignified for her to do it herself if at all possible. He knew it was a reflection of the peasant world from which she had sprung and it had served her well, served them both well in their beginnings here in this new world. But now? Now, it was time for her to realize she had married a man who prided himself on the standard of living he was able to provide for his family. They were not peasants and he wanted his wife to have soft hands and leisure to spend with her husband and children, friends and acquaintances.

Silently he pressed a kiss to his own forefingers and noiselessly blew it her way. With a last loving look at her face, he sighed. Her face was a face that should have been painted by one of the masters, he thought. What would *da Vinci* have done with her face? Would their child have her face? Jacques smiled and quietly moved away from the bed and soundlessly opened and closed the door to their cabin.

In the pale rosy light of dawn, the well muscled young man silently made his way into the dew dripping forest laced with fingers of mist. He was on the path to the clearing farther up the river which was the site of their new home. He, too, had learned to do "whatever it took" to make honest gains and succeed in this new world. He and Richard had learned to hunt fur bearing animals, lay traps, trade with the Indians, construct a log cabin, and chop wood until his own hands had become blistered and calloused. They had suffered hunger, heat, cold, wet, being almost devoured by insects, almost drowned in a flooded river, almost torn to pieces by thorny underbrush, and being detained as a potential spy. He had been persuaded to bring Marie to the frontier so she could start a trading post. The three had shared the tiny two room log cabin, even after he and Marie were married.

He remembered the day Marie had first looked upon the plans the architect had submitted. He recalled her fascination and how she had so easily assumed the "master bedroom" had meant *their* bedroom, his and hers. She had remarked how they would have more bedrooms than they would need. He had caught himself from correcting her and had said something instead about the wisdom of having extra guest rooms on the frontier.

He had stopped himself short from explaining that the plans had been drawn in keeping with the traditions and practices of the upper classes of Europe. Hatched of arranged marriages where conjugal visits were a contracted duty for producing an heir, separate private rooms for both husband and wife were almost always part of the marriage contract. He had realized at that moment she knew no other way of life for married people than the one they had been living and he was secretly delighted at the thought of her not even conceiving of the possibility of not always sharing his bed.

She had never been to the chateau where his father and his first wife had kept separate bedrooms and sitting rooms as had all the *Pouvoirs* since the very first stones of the ancient structure had been piled one upon another. How would she have known that amidst the aristocracy, a lady raised by prim nannies and nurses was taught that it was not only her right but the expectation that she should establish the privacy of her own boudoir? That marital intimacy was often by appointment only.

Celimene's cottage where Marie had served had been the cottage of Jacques' mistress and the whole point of having a mistress was to sleep with her when one came to visit. In the tiny log cabin here on the frontier the subject had never come up. They lived as the peasants lived, fortunate just to have shelter from the elements and wild beasts. Her early employers in New York Towne, the Van Hootenaugs and the Wingates, all part of this new world egalitarian society, undoubtedly lived no differently than the peasants as well. And so Marie, his unpretentious wife, remained naively unaware. But theirs was a love match and he had no desire to sleep in his home without her in his bed, warm and comforting beside him.

Jacques emerged from the trees and saw the house loom up before him just as the sun broke through the mist. The architecture had an unmistakable French flavor and the sun highlighted the angles of the roof and gables. The roof was finished now and the outside was almost complete leaving only the finishing work within the house to be done. The landscaping he would put in the hands of a competent gardener, if he could find one. It was his plan that they should move in before the baby arrived so that this child and all their succeeding children could be born here. So far, work was progressing better than planned. He was very pleased.

Marie stretched her naked body beneath the thin linen sheet. By the light defusing from the windows she knew the sun was already up. Jacques had failed to wake her. He fussed so about her getting her rest. A smile flickered upon her lips. Could he really imagine that once the work crew took up their hammers that anyone within ten leagues could sleep? Everyday the din of two dozen hammers being wielded with unceasing and relentless vigor created a cacophony of sound that echoed through the entire valley. Last summer it had been the hammering to build the dock and cabins for the workers which had filled the long daylight hours. She feared they would permanently drive away all the cheery little song birds. She would be very glad when peace finally returned to their valley.

Marie knew better than to get up too quickly but she felt the need to empty her bladder. She rolled from the small bed and went first to the cupboard, unwrapped the loaf of bread and tore a chunk to put into her mouth. She sought the chamber pot next. She wasn't up to facing the smell of the privy, not first thing in the morning. Not before she had something solid in her stomach and was grounded for the day. Besides, she would have to dress first. Putting the lid on the pot when she finished, she sought more food.

There was something so luxuriously decadent about walking about the cabin naked. With no Richard, no guests, no children, she could do this. And she was going to enjoy it while she could.

As she ate she felt the baby roll within her and Marie watched the movement below the surface of her flesh. She and Jacques had been married for two and a half years during which he had been gone much of the time but she had prayed many prayers in an earnest desire to become pregnant and give him a son.

Spontaneously, she said another mental prayer.

Thank you, dear Lord, for this child. Please watch over it, keep it safe and healthy, and let it be perfect, Lord, strong and perfect. Help me to be delivered safely and I pray you watch over us all. I ask you humbly in the name of Jesus the Christ. Amen.

Marie put on the large skirt and one of Jacques' old shirts that had become her standard uniform. She wore no undergarments at all, no petticoats, no shift. None fit properly and all the layers were too hot anyway. Next, she put her head through the top of an apron, which was a solid swath of cloth slightly wider than her shoulders and twice the size of her measure from neck to calf with a hole for her head cut out in the middle. Although it was made with little tie tapes along each side, she had stopped trying to actually tie them together weeks ago. Her girth had grown too great. Instead, she secured it from flapping with an odd bit of raw hide tied above her belly. All she needed was a wimple to look like a pregnant nun.

After combing her hair and pinning it into a twisted knot on top of her head, she donned her cap. That was something else she never had to do when they had lived here alone. But society expected respectable women to "dress" their hair which most simply meant a cap. Why? She had no idea. But she had learned that to appear without a cap, hat, bonnet, scarf, hood, arrangement of flowers, feathers, or ribbons… indeed, *something* on one's head was the equivalent of being "undressed." Naked hair, she grinned to herself. It was considered indecent in public and something only a prostitute would do.

Oh, well, everything has its good and its not so good. Like having a baby… the baby is good, the big belly and having to rush to the chamber pot all the time is not so good, she laughed to herself.

She set about the first steps of making fresh bread. As usual, when the weather was fair she took the task outdoors where the light was better and the breezes stirred. She had planks set up and needed only to spread a clean oil cloth to make a generous work surface. As she kneaded the dough, she thought of what she should prepare for the workmen's lunch.

Setting the bread inside the cabin to rise, she was grateful that she would be able to bake it outdoors in her large clay oven, an oven she had designed and constructed herself the first summer she had been alone. Anything to keep from heating up the cabin. She was forever too warm these days. She wondered vaguely if she would ever feel cold again. Of course she would, she laughed at herself, once the babe was born and the winter came, she would know cold well enough. And poor Jacques could come back to his bed.

Out of consideration, he had taken to sleeping on a pallet beside the bed. Poor

Jacques, she had completely lost her appetite for love making, no matter that she was married to a most accomplished lover. She and his baby had kicked him from his own bed. She shrugged; he would survive.

What she really wanted to do was go down and splash naked in the river. But those days were also gone forever she thought a bit sadly. She remembered the summers she had spent alone. Had she really been able to bath outdoors in the sunlight like a savage? She could never do that again. It had all changed when they had brought the first workmen back from New York Towne. And now, she could never be sure but what someone might be coming to her for some goods of one kind or another.

She sighed. Well, was this not what she had wanted? To have a store? To sell goods to people? To have neighbors? Yes, and she should be grateful, she told herself. But still she had a wistful desire for the solitude of that first winter alone with Jacques. Could anything have been more perfect? No interruptions, no distractions. She smiled and as she kneaded the bread for the second time she entertained a treasure trove of wonderful memories. They had been blissful weeks at a time when their good friend Richard was off "checking the far traps" which meant he was visiting some squaw's wigwam on the outskirts of some Indian village.

Marie halted her work, her thoughts turned inward. She wondered what her family would say if they could see her now. Was her father even alive or had he drunk himself into an early grave? And Louis? Her oldest brother would be… thirty now? Somehow she felt he would be happy for her but not Juliette, her older sister, no, she would be jealous and spiteful.

Marie felt the negative sentiment so strongly she shuddered and turned her attention to dividing her dough into loaves. She was making much bigger batches than she used to make and baking almost every day now. As soon as the smell of her fresh baked bread wafted out to her neighbors, the women began arriving until she was sold out.

Poor Juliette. Marie hoped that wherever Juliette was, whatever she was doing that she had found some peace and happiness. And what kind of boy had Baby Shu-Shu grown into? she ruminated. He was the baby brother who had cost their mother her life. She paused for a moment to consider. Shu-Shu would have to be seventeen now. Was that right? Seventeen? Older, by almost three years, than Marie had been when she had first stepped foot upon these shores. Did he ever give a thought for the life it had taken for him to come into this world? Did he try to make that exchange worth what it had cost the rest of them? Had he even lived through his childhood? Marie shook her head and scolded herself. A baby cannot be faulted for how it comes into the world. There is no call for guilt.

Immediately she turned to happier thoughts. "As for having privacy and being uninterrupted… well, I might as well get used to it, right little one?" she spoke aloud to her unborn child. "When you are born Ma-ma and Pa-pa will never be completely alone again," she gave a full throaty chuckle. "But I am certain we will find a way to catch a moment or two for ourselves or you will have no siblings," she concluded and set the bread aside to rise for the last time.

Marie had lunch prepared when the young lad who worked as a helper came to the cabin as he did each day.

"Good morning, Missus," he greeted her in a voice that had a way of snapping out of its manly register for a squeaking syllable or two. He doffed his cap.

"Good morning to you, Kevin," she favored him with a smile.

"Smells real good."

"You are right on time. You must have second sight to know exactly when I have everything ready."

He beamed and immediately took up the large pot of meaty stew she pointed to and carried it out to the wheelbarrow he had brought with him. The wheelbarrow was half full of clean wood shavings kept especially for the task of cushioning the precious cargo of the lunch run. As Kevin settled the stew pot with great care, Marie brought out a basket filled with cornmeal bread which she had learned to make from Sheehoo. It would do for lunch. And finally she produced a huge fresh baked zucchini cobbler which everyone swore was apple and wondered how she could have apples at this time of year.

"Ohhh, cobbler!" the boy exclaimed with an appreciative grin, fairly salivating on the spot. Mistress Charte's cobblers were the talk of the work camp. Although the spices she used in the making were dear and precious, she managed to make at least two such treats each week.

Returning to the cabin once more, Marie carried out a basket of bowls, cups, and spoons along with a cloth which she and Jacques would use for their personal makeshift lunch table.

"Oh, let me take that Missus!" Kevin asserted with a protective masculine air. "That be way too heavy for you to be totin' about." He knew the pretty wife of Master Charte wasn't just plump by nature. He had heard the crew boss say in a most respectful way one evening that they had a deadline to make before the baby came. And although it was not the kind of thing to be bantered about a work camp, he realized without anyone explaining anything more to him that the Missus must be with child.

Kevin settled the last basket into the wheelbarrow and took up the handles to begin the trek over to the construction site.

"Now, you watch your step, Missus," he said in cautious warning. "I'd be pleased for ya t' take my arm t' steady yourself," he added.

Marie smiled a thank you and slipped her hand through the lad's arm while his chest visibly expanded several inches.

"It is such a pretty day, is it not, Kevin?"

He loved to hear her say his name with her soft melodious accent.

"We have been most fortunate to have had such a streak of fair weather," she went on. "I have been praying each day. But now that the roof is complete, I do suppose we could use a good rain."

"It might be nice to have a day of rest," he grinned.

"Ah, yes, a day of rest. God intended for all to have one day of rest in every seven but men who do construction seem to get their days only when the weather is foul." She slowed to step over an especial large root leaving the smoother path for the wheelbarrow.

"It's not so bad. And if we have too long a streak of rain we get too much slack time. The crew gets bored and ya know what they say about idle hands." He was doing his best to sound mature and philosophical.

"No, what do they say?" she asked, pretending ignorance.

"They say the devil finds work for idle hands."

"Ah, yes? I suppose this is true. Well, we must be certain we never allow our hands to remain idle for too long, eh?"

"No, ma'am."

"And I must admit, my gardens all could use a good soaking."

They continued to walk the path through the forest, Marie taking care to not misjudge a tree root and Kevin exuding a protective watch as he pushed along the wheelbarrow. It was so easy to talk to her, the infatuated youth thought to himself, she put a body at ease and she really listened. Kevin had decided some time ago that Mistress Marie was just about the most perfect woman he had ever met.

Chapter 3

The house was complete and ready to receive furniture. It was September and the last of the craftsmen had just completed their tasks. The wood floors were sanded and finished to perfection. The marble hearthstones had been installed and the paint was dry.

Kevin, the plasterer's helper, was leaving with the rest of the carpenters and craftsmen. They were all returning to New York Towne in pursuit of further employment for their special talents. Master Charte was to leave with them and they looked for him as they boarded the packet boat in the harbor.

Jacques was expecting Dufee's ship with a load of elegant furniture for the new house and he had sent word ahead that he wanted to meet it in New York Harbor as he needed to also find some house servants.

"I will be back as quickly as I can," Jacques said holding Marie in his arms, his clear gray eyes looking at her from beneath a frown of concern. "Promise me you will do nothing... nothing, but stay here at the cabin and rest."

She looked up at him and brushed her fingers across the faint worry line that momentarily creased his brow. "Oh, Jacques, I will be fine. Do not worry so."

"Promise?"

"Yes, yes, I promise," she said earnestly and brushed her finger over his silken moustache, trying to coax a smile from him.

"No, I want you to swear... *nothing* until I return. I do not want you trying to go up to the new house or down to the river. I have made arrangements for the animals to be looked after and I want you to do nothing. Swear it."

"I swear although there is still harvesting to be done in my garden…"

"Ah-ah," he shook a finger at her.

"...but... I will be very lazy and do none of it. Please come home to me quickly."

"I will," he stroked her cheek tenderly. "Pray Dufee's ship is not late. And remember if you need anything fire the musket. I have asked the Boots to keep an eye on you. If they hear the musket they will come. I must go now. The packet boat will be ready to sail."

"I wish I could go with you," she said a bit mournfully.

"You do not know how badly I wish that as well. But it is not a risk we should take, *n'est-ce pas?*" He clung to the comfortable French phrase despite their efforts to speak only English in their new homeland.

"I know," she nodded.

Away from prying eyes, he gave her a long kiss and embrace, then, taking up his satchel, he left.

She watched him go and waved from the bluff as he took a small craft down river to the harbor docks. For a long time she sat on the rock which gave her a distant view of the harbor. Looking out over the sparkling waters in the distance, she finally saw the packet ship come into her view. Its sails were full as it headed out to sea. Marie watched until it disappeared beyond the promontory jutting out at the mouth of the harbor. She got up and walked back into the cabin. The baby was not due for another month and if Jacques had to go, this was the better time for it, she told herself. But why couldn't Dufee's ship have just come to their harbor as it had before? She suspected Jacques wanted to do something in New York Towne that he was unwilling to tell her. It must be a surprise, she smiled.

When Jacques arrived in New York harbor, he looked searchingly for the Dufee flag among all the ships lying at anchor both in the harbor and along the dock side of the island point. Denis Dufee, married to Richard's cousin, had been instrumental in spiriting the trio out of the country when the authorities had been in hot pursuit of Jacques. The Dufees, a very prosperous shipping family, were secret Huguenots but had chosen to feign conversion to Catholicism rather than leave everything and risk departure. It was a dangerous game they played and Jacques had learned that using the family assets, Denis habitually risked everything to help a steady stream of Huguenot refugees escape France.

Now Jacques remained a trustworthy contact within the English colonies and the Dufee ships were a direct pipeline to France and the mother and father Jacques had been forced to leave behind.

The childless and gentle *Duc de Pouvoir,* had helped to raise the young boy Jacques, thinking him his younger half-brother, the last bastard son of his father, the old duke. But after years of honoring his arranged and loveless marriage, the Catholic duke was still very much in love with Jacques' Huguenot mother. Upon learning Jacques' true paternity, the young duke had proudly recognized Jacques as his son and heir but the religious climate within France now made that impossible. No one within the aristocracy, the Royal House, or the French Catholic Church would accept the possibility of a Huguenot inheriting ducal lands and powers after 1685. A *lettre de cache* or royal warrant seeking Jacques-Jean Charte's arrest was issued and the young man had been forced to flee. His best friend, Richard, himself an aristocratic bastard without prospects raised by a now dead Huguenot mother, chose to join Jacques in the adventure while Marie, a mere servant, had begged to put herself at risk by tagging along.

Dufee's ship had not yet arrived. Walking briskly to The Pork 'n' Porridge, Jacques sought a room from Thompkins.

"Will you be needing a private room again for yourself and Mistress Marie?" Thompkins asked politely, not seeing Jacques' young wife.

"Marie is at home," Jacques said, "but I would like to try one of your new rooms if you have one."

"You are in luck, sir, I've one left."

Jacques nodded and then rather proudly explained that Marie was in waiting for their first child.

"Congratulations!" Thompkins said and chuckled as he poured Jacques a tankard of ale on the house.

"Thank you," Jacques said as he stood at the counter and the innkeeper saluted him in a toast and then chuckled again as if having a private joke. "What is it that is funny, monsieur?"

"Oh, nothing... just, well, my wife is going to be insufferable for a while." Jacques frowned in puzzlement but said nothing allowing Thompkins to continue at his own speed. "You see, the last time you were here, she said that your wife was belly...ah, with child."

"But we could not even stay here at our last visit, how did she know? I did not even know at first."

"Damned if I know how women do it. So, when is she to be delivered?"

"Not for a month or more but in truth I am not happy to be gone from her."

Thompkins nodded in understanding; it was after all the first child for the young couple.

"Our settlement grows and we have completed a proper house," Jacques continued proudly. "Now I am expecting a ship with my furniture but I came myself to meet it because I also am in search of some good servants."

"Perhaps I can be of assistance there," the innkeeper paused in his task of drying clean tankards. "What kind of service are you seeking?"

"I need house servants... a housekeeper, a cook, a gardener."

Thompkins furrowed his brow in thought. "You know, I recall a husband and wife from the last ship of indentures that just arrived. I was down at the wharf getting supplies. He seemed a decent fellow but lame of leg and no one wanted him. He looked capable enough though. And as they were promised to be sold as a couple, she was left as well. Let me think," he scratched his head. "The *May* something, no... it was the something *May*. You should be able to find it. Seek out the skipper and it would be my guess that their contracts have yet to be taken up."

Jacques drained the last of his ale. "Thank you, my friend," he patted Thompkins on the arm and was about to leave for his room when a family walked in capturing Jacques' attention. A rather anxious looking man with his wife and a number of children looking like stair steps ranging from perhaps two to twelve years in age filled the reception area of the inn.

"I was told you run a clean establishment and might have a room for us," said the father of the group. "We only need one, we will all stay together."

"I am sorry but," Thompkins replied. "I just rented my last private room."

"Oh, my," the wife sighed, looking stressed and tired. "What are we to do now?"

"Are you speaking of my room?" asked Jacques, looking at Thompkins.

He nodded.

"Do you have a reasonable half share?" Jacques asked. "If you can find me an acceptable roommate, I will give them my room."

"Oh, sir, that is most kind," said the harried father, picking up his smallest child who was beginning to whine in a bid to be fed.

Thompkins was scanning the register. "Ah, yes, I have a gentleman in one of the older rooms who requested a half bed... to save money. Looked an amiable fellow. That is awfully good of you, Mister Charte."

"Not at all," Jacques replied easily.

"Yes, indeed, most good!" the weary father echoed. "Thank you so much, so very much. I cannot tell you how much I appreciate this. God bless you, sir." His wife nodded and repeated the sentiment.

The newest guests hurried to claim their private room before coming back to settle into a corner of the dining room with a mission to feed all the hungry mouths.

Meanwhile, Thompkins wondered if he should go back into the kitchen and relay the news regarding Mistress Marie to his good wife or wait until later that night. *Later*, he decided, *closer to bedtime, shorten the time left for her to crow*. He smiled to himself.

Jacques took a seat alone at a small table and looked at the man to whom he had given his room and at his family. That could be him in the future he thought with a smile. He ate leisurely and finally went to find his shared room. As he quietly opened the door, he found there already was a candle burning and light snoring came from the far side of the bed. A wide board resting on edge and slipped length-wise through a slot in the foot board and the headboard, neatly separated the two sides of the bed.

Once retired for the night, neither stranger was much aware of the other. The next morning Jacques rose early to the continued sound of moderate snoring. He dressed, had his breakfast in the dining room, and then strode to Wharf Street and the Harbor Master's offices.

"Good morning, sir, do you have a ship in harbor with 'May' in her name," he asked of the man shuffling papers behind a high-railed separation.

"That be *Shining Maye* out of Liverpool," the man with a voice like a fog horn replied.

"That must be it, and which ship might she be?" Jacques asked.

The harbor master stepped out and pointed up the wharf to a trim ship with very tall masts. "There, the yellow one with the mizzen sail down for repair," and with that he went back inside.

Jacques had no idea what a mizzen sail was but he walked in the direction that was pointed out and there was only one yellow trimmed craft. It had several sails down for work and canvas draped over the rail covered the ship's name. He didn't think it would hurt to ask. As he approached the gangplank he saw a young lad busy on the deck above.

"Ahoy! Is this the *Shining Maye*?" he called out, halting at the foot of the gangplank.

"Yes, sir," the lad looked down at him and wiped his nose.

"Is your captain about?" smiled Jacques.

"Yes, sir," the boy replied with a sideways glance.

"Might I have a word with him?"

"What is it I can help you with?" asked a swarthy cheeked fellow with a head of thick, curly black hair who had just come into view. He wore a gold hoop in one ear and a cutlass in his belt.

"Are you the captain?" Jacques inquired looking up from the pier.

"Aye. Who wants to know?"

"I am Jacques-Jean Charte, monsieur, and I was told you might have a couple of indentures aboard suitable for house service."

"Oh, it's servants ye be looking for?" The seaman immediately became more amiable.

"Yes. May I see them?"

"Come aboard," he gestured.

Jacques walked up the gangplank and stood waiting while the boy was sent below. In a few moments he reappeared, a woman following him and a man with a limp following behind her. Jacques judged them to be in their thirties.

"This here is Mister Donald Sims and his Good Wife Jane Sims," the captain said by way of introduction. "This here is a Master Charte."

"Good day to you." Jacques responded to the introduction. "I am looking for a gardener, a cook and a housekeeper for my home. Do you know how to garden?" he asked the fellow.

"Yes, sir," Sims replied taking his hat from his head to reveal a head of auburn hair.

"What has happened to your leg?" asked Jacques, seeing no sense in beating about the bush.

"I was born this way, sir; it ain't never stopped me from doing a thing."

"Do you fatigue easily?"

"No more than the next man. I can hold my own to a fair day's work."

"Hmm," Jacques consider. "What kind of gardening have you done?"

"I grew up on a farm, sir."

"I see, but what of formal gardens?"

"If you've an idea what you'd like, I'll try my best to make it happen. I figure the relationship between a plant and the earth is the same be it vegetable or flower."

Jacques smiled. He liked the man's calm, straightforward manner even if this was not exactly what Jacques was looking for.

"And you, madam, can you cook?"

"Not what you'd want to eat, sir," her husband said frankly.

Jacques raised his eyebrows high above his aristocratic nose.

"It's true, sir," the woman replied, as she tugged at her cap nervously. "I never been no good at cookin' for my betters but I can keep a house cleaner than a whistle."

"How long have you been married?" Jacques stood relaxed, hoping to put them at ease.

"Goin' on twelve years now," replied Sims.

"And you have no children?"

"No, sir, we ain't been blessed," Sims looked at his wife.

Jacques continued to look them over. "Have you any other skills?"

The couple was silent for a moment as if running an inventory in their minds. Jane smiled. "I pass fair with a needle, sir," she said earnestly.

"Good," Jacques acknowledged and looked at the husband.

"I tinker a mite, always been good at fixin' things... and I can play the spoons."

"The spoons?" Jacques repeated trying to understand the significance of such a talent.

"Yes, sir."

Jacques turned to the captain. "How much are you asking for the pair?"

After Jacques came to agreeable terms to buy the couple's contract, the captain of the *Shining Maye* agreed to allow them to remain on board for another night or two. Jacques hoped that Dufee's ship would arrive by then and with any luck it would have someone on board who might make a passable cook.

The next day Jacques stood again at the wharf looking out to the sea as if willing the ship to appear. He was impatient to get home and now the weather was turning ugly. Looking beyond the harbor he could tell the sea had become very rough as the wind gusted unceasingly. Even within the harbor, the waters were ridged with large white caps. As he stood there, his blond hair whipped about his head having pulled loose from the leather thong that had held it clubbed at the back of his neck. He had not even tried to wear his hat this morning but had left it at the inn. Few people were outdoors except those in the act of taking things inside or securing items from being blown away. Trying to go about the normal tasks and activities of the busy harbor had become impossible.

§

Jacques had been gone for two days when Marie noticed the wind had picked up with considerable force. They were due for another good rain, she thought, and looked toward the skies. She didn't see any clouds but the wind had begun gusting in strong almost vicious blasts off the sea. Her hair was whipping about her face despite her cap and she turned to the cabin and went back inside. She could do no needlework on a day like this. She folded the baby gown she was in the middle of making and placed it in her sewing basket. Setting the basket aside she paused to re-comb her long hair and decided to plait it into braids.

She went to check the windows. Jacques had replaced the oiled skins with a framing of mosquito netting for the warmer seasons which let both air and light in while keeping most of the insects out. Still, an eager and bold squirrel or chipmunk often tore its way through. Every window was tightly covered and she shuttered the one that faced the sea in Richard's old room.

There was never a great deal of light in the small cabin and she so looked forward to all the large glass windows in their new house. Marie prepared some tea and was looking about the cabin for something to do. She was not accustomed to being so restricted or so idle. Surely it would do no harm to go to the barn and look in on the animals. She liked farm animals and enjoyed giving them extra attention when she had the time. Well, she had the time now but still, a promise is a promise and she had sworn to Jacques and would not go back on her word. She lapsed into imagining for the four hundredth time how she would redo the cabin when it ceased to be their home and was to serve only as her store. She must have a proper counter, of course, and shelves built all the way around.

As she sat in contemplation she heard knocking at the cabin door. Rising slowly and going to the door, she unlatched it and was surprised to see Francois Nicholet standing outside bracing himself against the gusts.

"Monsieur Nicholet?" she said in surprise as a gust of wind pushed her backward.

"Madame Charte. Please take care," he warned and came inside shutting the door against the wind.

"Oh, it really is getting quite fierce," laughed Marie then she became aware of a strange look on the man's face and she sobered. "What is it, monsieur? Is there something you need?"

"I am sorry. I have made you uncomfortable," he apologized. "It is only that for a moment... you reminded me of... of someone. Laughing in the face of danger."

"I doubt that we are in any serious danger, monsieur, only a very wicked storm, I fear," Marie said kindly.

"*Oui*, I came only to see if you were well. Is there anything you need, madame, anything at all?" He stood looking somewhat anxious as though he wanted to say something more.

"That is very kind of you, monsieur," Marie responded graciously trying to comprehend what was bothering the man. "I am quite well. There is nothing I need."

"What about water?"

"Water?"she repeated, a bit surprised.

"Drinking water, have you enough?"

"Oh, the stream is very close."

"No-no. Give me your buckets and I will fetch you water. Please, I insist."

Rather than argue, Marie gave Francois both buckets. Again the cabin door let in a gust of wind that set her shelves and dishes to rattling, her hanging pots and kettles to clanging, and some of the herbs hanging from the rafters blew down scattering onto the bearskin spread out in the middle of the room. Holding the door almost shut, she watched the stocky young man go to the stream battling the wind as he walked. She waited and considered that perhaps it was a very good thing she did not try to carry buckets in this wind. She opened the door for his return.

"Stay indoors, madame," Nicholet said soberly while setting the brimming buckets down.

"Thank you very much, monsieur. It was most kind of you to think of me."

"It is my pleasure. But as I say, please, stay indoors until this blows over. It … it may take some time."

"What is it?" Marie asked, sure that the man was holding something back.

He hesitated before he spoke. "I wish not to frighten you, madame, especially in your delicate condition."

"Monsieur Nicholet, it will frighten me even more if you do not tell me."

The man nodded. "I have never seen anything like this before... it is not... what we are used to, eh? But my brother once wrote to me of a storm he had experienced when he was in the West Indies. In the tropics, he said they have them often. The winds reach speeds we can only wonder at and they become so strong they can lift many things into the air, hurling them about like straw... even trees and animals, madame. It is not safe to go out in these storms."

"I understand," Marie responded gravely.

"Would you like me to stay with you?" Nicholet offered gently.

In fact, Marie would have very much liked for him to stay, if only for company, but she thought of what Jacques had told her about the lumbermen, and she saw the loneliness in Nicholet's eyes. She knew she would be using the man unfairly. Not to mention what Jacques might think of the situation or what people might say in gossip. "N..no, I do not think that is necessary," Marie responded with equal gentleness, "although I do appreciate your concern. I will take your advice and not go outdoors. I would ask one more favor of you, however."

His face brightened. "Anything."

"Would you check on the animals, please? Make sure they are all sheltered with enough food and water. My husband made me promise not to go to the barn."

"He was absolutely right to do so. And, of course, I shall be glad to perform that service, madame." With an almost courtly bow, he turned and left, shutting the door securely behind him.

Marie looked at the brimming buckets of water and dippered out a drink. Underneath that merry facade of lightheartedness, there was something very sad about Francois Nicholet, she decided. She found herself wondering how they might attract more unmarried women to the settlement for all these lonely men. Perhaps she would consult with Mistress Wingate in New York Towne. Surely England had its share of young women with little to no prospects who would gamble on a spirited man who was willing to seek his fortune in the New World. And some women, if they wanted to have children, could not afford to indenture themselves for seven years or more, depending on their skills, in order to pay for their passage over. She stretched out on the featherbed. What would Jacques think of his wife becoming a *marieur*, or as the English would say a "matchmaker." She yawned. It was a perfect day for a nap. *I promised Jacques I would do nothing, and so far that is exactly all I have done.*

Listening to the wind whistling over the chimneys, Marie fell asleep.

§

Jacques looked back out to the sea and just at that moment a tall ship with its sails half struck came into view. He watched it tack and maneuver, coming closer and closer. More sails came down but the wind was pushing the vessel along at an amazing speed.

As the French ship approached, Jacques recognized the Dufee private flag, it was the *Dauphine*, the same ship that had picked up the load of lumber from him last year. Jacques was waiting when the captain appeared at the gangplank.

"Captain Trudeux!" Jacques called out in relief. "I am Jacques Charte, if you remember. I believe you are scheduled to go to my harbor next."

"Excuse me, Monsieur Charte," the captain's face looked grim and strained as he gave Jacques a nod of recognition. "I do not mean to appear rude but I must report to the harbor master at once. We have some very nasty weather headed this way."

Jacques fell in beside the man as he hurried to the small office on Wharf Street. The winds gusting dirt into the air made keeping one's mouth closed preferable. But once the report was made, Jacques had every intention of pursuing his own matters.

The captain reported that a hurricane was coming and the town had best take precautions. The harbor master sent word to the authorities and criers were directed to take the news out to the townsfolk. There was little time to prepare.

Jacques caught the captain's sleeve as he hurried from the harbor office. "We must leave immediately for my home," Jacques said urgently. "I have some servants to bring with us and..."

"I am sorry, monsieur, we cannot go back out on the open seas. It would be suicide," the captain shouted above the sound of the wind.

"But I must return," insisted Jacques.

"You cannot go out there now."

"You do not understand," Jacques frowned tensely. "I left my wife alone; she is *enceinte*. If this is going to be bad, I must go back to her immediately."

"I am sorry, monsieur, it is you who does not understand. No one can go out there now," the captain said sternly. "My first concern must be for my ship. Just as soon as I get back on board we are casting off and sailing up river."

"Up the Hudson?"

"Yes, it is the safest thing we can do. You are welcome to join us."

Jacques shook his head. "I will stay here."

"I will return when this blows over and look for you, Monsieur Charte. I am sorry, I have no time to waste. I must leave now."

The young man nodded as the captain re-boarded his ship and began shouting commands. Jacques had never felt so completely frustrated and yet his better wisdom told him the experienced seaman was right. Even if he had his own vessel, it would be fool's play to try to traverse the seas until this weather blew over. He bent his head against the wind and headed off in the direction of the inn.

§

Marie awoke with a start, uncertain why but now she needed to go to the privy. The chamber pot was full but she did not think she could take it with her to be emptied. She went to the door of the cabin and opened it. Once again the force of the wind almost knocked her back inside. It was the strangest weather she had ever seen. She had thought for certain she would have seen rain clouds by now but the skies were still clear. She peered off to the horizon and thought perhaps it was her imagination but there seemed to be very strange formations out there. She turned from the sea and struggled onward around the back of the cabin to the privy.

§

It had begun to rain and the winds drove the needle sharp drops horizontally into the hapless faces of any who were still out of doors trying to tie things up or nail things down. At The Pork 'n' Porridge, an eclectic group of people had gathered in the main dining area. Along with the inn's guests, there were others who, looking a little less savory, a little less likely to frequent the well respected establishment, nonetheless had come seeking shelter by the large fireplace in the sturdy structure. The Thompkins would turn no one away.

All the shutters had been secured, upstairs and down. Now the concern was the large paned window in the front. The window covered a broad expanse of the south wall, it was one of the features of the place that always made it light and cheerful, but on this day the glass and framing seemed to visibly strain against the violent gusts and steady assault. Rain blew so unceasingly upon it, it was as though the sea itself was washing against the panes.

Thompkins, followed by his sons, Hank and George, came into the dining room carrying large wooden planks. He approached Jacques. "I judge you to be one of the strongest and ablest here. Will you come out with me to nail these across the window before it gives way?" he asked holding out hammer and nails.

"Of course," Jacques responded and took the proffered hardware.

No sooner had they opened the door then the rain drove into the room on an unceasing gale of wind causing cries of concern from the crowd taking refuge within and laughter from some of the smaller children. Jacques was drenched to the skin in a matter of seconds. He pushed against the unseen force, hammer and nails in hand. Thompkins held the board, edge to the wind, but as he turned to the outside of the window, the wind seemed to grab and slap the board with a thrust against the boards of the wall, pinching his fingers in the effort.

He yelped and spoke but Jacques could not hear him, the whistle and roar of the wind assailed his ears and muffled the words. He understood when Thompkins was ready for him to nail the plank in place. He raised his arm against the unseen forces trying to flatten him against the wall. With every muscle in his body joined in concentrated effort he pulled the hammer back, aimed at the nail, and guided as much as drove the hammer to its mark. Such was the struggle with every blow until at last the plank became an unmovable part of the structure.

Hank appeared with his plank. The three struggled and at last it was also secured. Young George could not master the forces of nature and fell in his efforts. His father retrieved the heavy plank as it went skidding into the foundation, driven as though of no more weight and body than a piece of tarp. With Jacques' assistance it, too, was nailed in place as Hank helped his brother back indoors. Hank reappeared with yet a final wide board which once in place would complete the cover to the large window. Jacques' arm ached with the efforts of his blows and he felt himself losing control as the final nail was sunk.

The two men and brawny youth allowed themselves to be pushed through the inn doorway and it took their combined strength to re-close the heavy oak door and drop the cross bar into its place against the siren sound of the howling gale.

As they stood dripping, the water ran off them in fast rivulets making large pools upon the wooden floors to add to the sheets of water already driven in. The implacable Mistress Thompkins came forward with an arm full of towels and a mop and bucket. In the now darkened inn, they each sponged and wiped at their faces and hair while she patiently continued to swab up the errant puddles. With the wind put at bay, the crowd joined in cooperative efforts to light a multitude of candles which cast an ironically cozy warmth into the corners.

With the windows all shuttered against the storm, the inn had the atmosphere of evening as Jacques sought his room with the assistance of a pale, fluttering circle of candlelight cast from the taper he carried in its pewter holder. Once inside the room he now shared with five other men, refugees from the storm, he stripped off his soggy clothing and boots. Out of deference to his hosts, he tried to wring the excess water from the dripping fabrics into the wash basin before hanging them by the fireplace to dry. Stepping around the sleep pallets on the floor, he toweled off his naked body as he stood before the fire warming his cold, damp flesh.

He could hear the wind creating harsh whistling sounds as it blew over the chimney opening. What manner of storm was this? He asked himself as he sought dry garments from his travel satchel. Trudeux had said "hurricane" but Jacques was unfamiliar with the word and was not certain what that meant. His heart thudded in his chest as all his thoughts went to Marie. The cabin was strong. As long as she closed the shutters to the windows and stayed indoors, she would be safe, he assured himself. Thank God he had made her swear to stay in the cabin. Once having given her word, he had never known her to make light of it. And she had promised him she would stay at the cabin and the cabin was strong, he told himself again. And it was on high ground, very high ground. She would be safe. This is what he kept telling himself and this was what he had to believe for any other thought would have pushed him to the brink of frustrated madness.

A knock at the door interrupted his thoughts.

"Yes?" he quickly finished lacing his breeches and opened the door. Young George stood in the hall with a pair of wooden clogs in his hand.

"Ma sent me with these," he said pushing the shoes into Jacques' hands. "She says your boots will be a wreck." The lad disappeared and Jacques looked down at the peasant shoes in his hand. His boots were a wreck and stood by the hearth to dry and shrink. He would have to discard them if he could not stretch them out again.

"George?" he called down the hallway.

The lad's head came peeping back up from the stairwell. "Sir?"

"Do you know if by chance, your father has an extra pair of boot stretchers?"

"Oh...I don't know, sir. Ma be usin' three pair for our shoes, Pa's, Hank's and mine. We caught a scoldin' something fierce for not wearing the wood clogs when we went outside."

"To be sure," Jacques nodded. "Well, if there are no boot stretchers available perhaps… do you know if your father has some old newspapers I could use?"

"Oh...I'll ask for ye."

"I would appreciate it. Thank you."

In a few minutes, George returned with a small stack of very outdated newspapers and left Jacques to stuff the toes of his boots in the hopes of keeping them from shrinking so badly they might raise up blisters upon his feet.

Rejoining the collection of stranded guests and strangers huddled together within the main room of the inn, Jacques shivered as he felt the building itself shutter and creak. He felt so completely helpless and impotent, trapped and separated from the one person he most wanted to be near and keep safe.

"I've seen hurricanes as bad and worse," an old salt was expostulating in a roughened voice. "At sea yer only chance is to escape their path. Once they catch you, you join Davy Jones for sure. But being on land is no guarantee of survival," he added gruffly. "I've seen 'em raise a wall o'water as tall as the trees and drive it across an island sweeping every man, woman and child, every structure and piece of vegetation like just so much kindling. Aye, so much kindling, swept away and never to be seen again. Yer only hope is to be lashed up in the top of the tallest palm tree."

"I say," a middle-aged man with a florid face objected. "There's no need for that sort of talk. We have ladies here, and children. Show some discretion, sir."

The father of the family to whom Jacques had given his room nodded his agreement.

The sailor looked up and stared rather insolently at the figure who had spoken but the seaman said nothing more and lapsed into a prolonged silence.

"Here's hot soup for everyone," Mistress Thompkins announced with forced cheerfulness. She had finished the chore of mopping up and emerged from the back, her sons in dry clothing coming up behind her carrying a very heavy cauldron between them. With efficiency born of years of experience, she ladled the soup, and distributed the steamy bowls. When she ran short of bowls she continued by using mugs. Her sons passed around the bread baskets. Master Thompkins appeared in dry clothes, his wet hair combed neatly. He went to his stores and produced a small keg of rum which he judiciously dispensed in limited quantities to any and all as a tonic against the circumstances.

Jacques realized that he had forgotten to comb his own hair, so preoccupied had he been with thoughts of Marie. He ran his fingers through his soggy tresses and drew them back out of his face. *Please keep her safe, dear Lord. Don't let anything happen to her, I beg you.* It was a silent prayer but as if picked up on the ether waves he heard someone clear his throat and speak out. For the first time he noticed Brother Robert sitting within the gathering.

Brother Robert was a Huguenot Pastor who had shared passage on Dufee's ship when Jacques, Richard and Marie had escaped. At the signing of the Edict of Fountainbleau by Louis XIV of France, all Huguenot Pastors had been given just two weeks to dispose of their property, make arrangements and leave France forever or face the hangman's noose. Like so many of the pastors, Brother Robert had stayed with his flock serving them in secrecy until they had melted away. His two week grace period had evaporated and still in France he was in as much danger as Jacques-Jean.

"If we could all pause for a moment," Brother Robert said with authority as he stood on his feet. Although his speech was heavily accented, his English vocabulary had become remarkably good. "Let us take this time to give thanks unto the Almighty." A hush fell over the room and all clatter of utensils ceased. Someone coughed, a child was shushed and then all was quiet except for the howl and roar of the winds outdoors.

"Oh, Great and Glorious Lord and Sovereign, Commander of our souls, and Captain of our lives. We beseech you to forgive our transgressions, our poverty of spirit, our shortsighted concentrations on the things of this world. We ask for your comfort and protection in the storms of life and we thank you for the peace of Salvation through your Son, our Redeemer, Jesus Christ. We ask that you protect us, Lord, from the hazards of this storm as well, and be with our friends, neighbors, and loved ones as they, too, are in your hands. We ask you to bless this food and the hands which prepared it, bless the generosity of the Thompkins and keep their home safe as it shelters so many gathered here. We humbly ask these things in the name of our Lord, your Son, Jesus Christ. Amen."

"Amen," was echoed around the solemn room before the noises of clinking utensils and conversation resumed again. Jacques heard himself say, "Amen" but he had no appetite for food.

It took two days for the hurricane to pass the mid-Atlantic coastline and, without actually touching land, drive itself back out to sea. The people of the coast would never have believed that they had not experienced the very worst that nature had to offer. Only Providence knew it could have been much worse. But their humble prayers had been heard and they had been spared. On the third day, the rain ceased and the townsfolk opened their doors and stumbled out as though sleep walkers arising to survey a dreamscape from their worst nightmare. The solid buildings stood little changed but scoured stark and somehow bleak. The carelessly built, the shanties, the sheds and coops, lean-tos, and poorly anchored structures had all been ripped up, flattened, or carried away, and no longer existed. They were evident only as acres of anonymous broken bits intermixed with the multitude of branches, leaves, feathers, rotten fruit, dead animals and birds, poultry, seashells and eggshells, accented with the occasional doll, wooden toy, torn and ragged fabric, barrel, wheel hoop, broken crockery, and every other conceivable wreckage from the civilized world of 1691.

Following the *Dauphine's* lead, all the ships in harbor had sailed far up the Hudson and weathered through the storm without harm. When they returned, Jacques, with eyes ringed in dark circles, plead a quick end to business and a hasty departure. The Sims were collected from the *Shining Maye* and Jacques bought the rather expensive contract of a French chef he found on board Dufee's ship.

The Huguenot chef had been prized and spoiled by the aristocrat who employed him and kept his secret until a jealous social rival informed on them to the authorities. The chef had barely escaped, leaving everything he possessed behind including his gold, his clothes, and his prized cleaver. He was now a pauper, he sighed, but his contract was for only two and a half years. After that, Monsieur Charte would be looking for another for how could he expect such talent to remain in a little backwater settlement? For now, however, his new employer had the great good fortune to own the talents of Antoine Clarmaunt, a true Parisian chef. The chef sighed again. He missed his cleaver.

The French ship wasted no time sailing out to the south.

Chapter 4

Jacques squinted. He had asked to borrow the captain's spyglass and as he stood peering through it, he saw the cabin. It stood. He knew it! He almost dared to smile. The cabin stood but the storm had wrought many other changes to the harbor and the settlement. Sand bars now stood where none had existed before and they threatened to ground the *Dauphine*. The wharf they had built with such pride was a useless pile of twisted planking. The lower cabins were deep in water with little more than the remnants of the roofs exposed. With concern he wondered if the men who had lived there were safe. The vegetable gardens were a marshy quagmire. Yes, the harbor had been very changed but that was of little importance to Jacques at the moment. He wished Marie would step out and wave to him. He could not wait to tell her they had a housekeeper, a gardener, and a chef! It occurred to him that the smokehouse and chicken coop had disappeared and from his vantage point he could not see to the privy.

The ship dropped anchor at some distance and Jacques was in the first boat to go up river to their landing. The little dock was gone and he leapt from the boat and ran up the old switch-back trail to the top of the bluff. Bursting into the cabin he discovered a ruin.

The split-shingle roof had been ripped away and a very large tree branch almost filled the interior as it lie on their bed and leaned against the inner wall. Everything was a sodden mess. From inside, Jacques could see a large patch of blue sky overhead. Several shelves had been knocked down, jars were broken, food lay about.

Animals, squirrels perhaps, or possums, had been there. And all, even their precious feather bed, was soaked with rainwater and mud. But where was Marie?!

He shouted her name and took off running toward the new house. If the cabin had been damaged and could no longer shelter her, she must have gone to the new house, he reasoned. He saw what looked like pieces of the chicken coop or was it the smokehouse resting out in the field. He saw more boarding caught in the trees. There were broken branches everywhere and several of the trees had been split, another was completely uprooted.

With pounding heart, he made his way through the forest path as fast as he could, unmindful of the mud and wet but managing not to trip and fall. At last he came to their new house. The surrounding yard showed evidence of torrential rains in the eroded ruts and sink holes. Everywhere there were pools of mud but the house itself looked undamaged.

He called out her name repeatedly, went to the door and called inside. He heard nothing. Slogging through the mud around the back, he continued calling. Nothing. Fearful that she might lay unconscious, he heaved off his boots and ran through the new house in his stockings. The house was empty. His wife had disappeared!

Jacques was raw nerves. When he returned to the ship, the captain insisted he calm himself and consider no news to be good news.

Pouring a large glass of brandy and shoving it into Jacques' hand, Trudeux counseled restraint. "You have no evidence or cause to think the worst, monsieur, so assume the best until it be proven otherwise. Where are these other people?" He gestured to the empty cabins. "Have you talked to or even seen anyone who once lived here?"

"No."

"It would seem they saw how the weather was going and all left together. Someone would have been looking after your wife. We must wait and see what time tells us."

Jacques chafed at the very thought. *Wait and see?* Just - wait and see? How could he be expected to simply wait and see? But in fact, what choice did he have at that moment? He drank the brandy.

The captain made the crew of the ship available to assist in cleaning up and putting things in order around the small settlement. The furniture had to be unloaded and moved into the house but first a wooden ramp or two or three were needed to avoid walking through yards of mud. The mill must be brought back into working order to supply the planks. There was plenty to do and work details were formed.

Straggly, muddy chickens looking dazed and disgruntled made an appearance here and there, survivors of the storm. Donald Sims, wearing very high mud boots supplied by his wife, took it upon himself to begin construction to house the homeless poultry while keeping a vigilant eye out for the rooster. "Without the rooster, there won't be any chicks," he muttered to no one in particular.

Jacques chafed to begin a search of the countryside when one of the couples who lived along the harbor shore appeared. They were scratched, ragged, bruised, and weary but they were alive and basically unharmed.

"Have you seen my Marie? Madame Charte?" Jacques demanded while the refugees sat to receive their first hot food in days.

"We had to run to the forest," the mill worker said, his eyes rounded and glassy. "I never seen nothing like it, sir, it was... it was..."

"Yes, I know," Jacques interrupted impatiently. "It was the same in New York Towne. But what has happened to my wife? Did you see what happened to her?"

The fellow shook his head.

"They came and got her," a small thin voice spoke out. It was the mill worker's wife.

"Who came and got her?" Jacques demanded.

"The avenging angels! It's God judgment on us all," she suddenly cried out and broke into hysterical sobbing.

"These people are suffering from shock, exposure, and hunger," the captain said, turning to Jacques. "You cannot expect a straight story from them. They need tending themselves."

"You are right," Jacques replied, ashamed of his behavior. Turning to leave the couple to their food, he saw Jane Sims and waved her over. "I had the tree limb removed from the cabin. See what can be salvaged from inside, and make certain you check out the root cellar in the second room. Then, take those two to the house. They can help you carry what you find. Show them a place to rest. There is no furniture yet, but at least it is shelter."

Jane nodded.

Well, I certainly have my work cut out for me, Jane thought to herself. *Have a couple of mud puppies come into a spanking new house? Not if I have anything to say about it. I need to find a great big bar of soap and a tub for washing. And establish a scrub down area. Those two need to be cleaned up enough to be fit to be sheltered.*

Jacques stood off by himself trying to think. Marie was resourceful. If she had to leave the cabin, where would she go? Why would she not go to the new house? Suddenly, he remembered the Indians and the winter he and Richard had not come back. Perhaps they came and took her, not avenging angels but native Indians. "Start a fire," he cried out a command. "Gather this rubbish and start burning it." Several sailors responded and before long a fire was sending clouds of smoke into the sky.

She has to see it, Jacques told himself, *dear God in Heaven, let her see it and bring her safely home.*

There was more than enough to keep everyone busy. The passengers heading farther south were still on board the *Dauphine.* They saw no reason to remain idle. All volunteered in one capacity or another according to his abilities. The cabins built on higher ground had fared somewhat better than the bachelor quarters built so near the water. All new construction was now to go on higher ground with the exception of the new wharf.

Captain Trudeux introduced Jacques to a doctor by the name of St. Claire who also was a Huguenot making his escape to the New World. His English was thickly accented but he was fluent, a quiet, older man of intelligence and compassion. Jacques told him about the returned mill worker and his wife sheltered at the new house and the doctor immediately sought to look in on them.

William Boot, his wife, and their baby returned wet, filthy, and feverish.

"William, thank God, you are alive," Jacques greeted him with an exuberant handshake.

"Have you found the Missus?" the big Swede asked.

Jacques shook his head. "I had been hoping she was with you. What do you know of her?"

"I went to your cabin, sir," William told Jacques. "I went for the Missus but she was not there. The water, it was coming in at my place and I had to get Britta and the baby out. When we saw she was not there, afraid we were and we run to the woods.

"Did you not see anything of her?" Jacques asked hopefully.

William shook his head sadly.

"Get some food, William... you and your family. Stay in our house where the doctor can watch over you," Jacques offered.

"If Britta and little Thor can stay, grateful I am," the big man responded, "but thinking of the need to clean up our place so they can come home."

"It may be far easier to simply build a new place. If water was flooding in, it is not safe. Find a location up on higher ground," Jacques said as he reached up and placed a hand on the huge man's forehead. "You will see the doctor first, do you hear, and listen to his advice. If you turn sick, you cannot help your family. Do not be foolish, William. Now go," he dismissed the blond giant by pointing him in the direction of the new house.

Seeing smoke brought more mill workers back to the settlement, very hungry and dehydrated but generally in good shape. Doctor St. Claire set up an examination area on the front portico of the new house which was as far as Jane was willing to allow the unwashed to get until they made a visit to the wash tubs at the rear of the house. The thorough doctor diagnosed one badly turned ankle, several ugly gashes from flying debris, a broken arm, and a wickedly pierced hand.

"How did this happen?" St. Claire questioned his patient, whose name he discovered was Clive Tapper. "Did you fall on something sharp?"

"Fall? Naw...put up me arm to protect me 'ead, doc. Better me 'and than me eye, I say. Board 'ad a sixteen-penny nail in it an' could'a split me 'ead plum open. An' there it was flyin' through the air like a bleedin' crow!"

St. Claire was uncertain what exactly the man had said but the hole was big and very ugly. "We must wash the wound thoroughly to remove all this mud."

"Aww, it be all right, doc, just a mite bit sore's all." Tapper grabbed his hand back.

"A cleaning, monsieur," St. Claire countered sternly.

Jane Sims walked up. "Ain't gettin' where there's food less'n you're clean," she scolded. "Now sit still and let the doctor do his job. Doc, you want me to take the scrub brush to 'im?" she asked more as a threat than as a real suggestion although given the nod of approval she would have taken her scrub brush to everyone.

"No, no, not necessary if Monsieur Tapper holds still and allows us to waste some perfectly good cognac on his dressing." With that St. Claire produced his medicinal bottle of French cognac which he poured liberally into the wound.

"Ouch! Jee….hosephat and little angels!!" Tapper yelped as the cognac burned his tender flesh. "What th'… ye be trying to burn me 'and off?"

"No, monsieur," St. Claire looked soberly at the man who had once again snatched back his hand. "I am trying to save your hand. At the Parisian Medical Academy they have learned alcohol cleansing decreases the chances of infection and gangrene. Now we shall put a wrapping on but it is your responsibility to keep it as clean as possible. If you notice any increase in redness, any soreness or swelling...to me you must come immediately, understand?"

The fellow nodded as he watched his hand being dressed, thinking it was a lot of bother over a tiny little hole.

"It may be a small injury but from such as this, you could lose that hand. If you wish to keep it you will keep it clean – understand?" St Claire asked sternly.

Bobbing a nod with appropriate gravity, Tapper walked away genuinely fearful at the idea of losing his hand.

"I want to see you again tomorrow," St. Claire called after him.

The new chef had found his way to the house kitchen which was a brick floored building behind the main house and which he adamantly proclaimed was beyond Jane Sims' established domain.

"*Ceci est mon royaume*, this is my kingdom," he said in clipped French. "Here I am king. I will stay here and you will stay there. Then we shall get along perfectly!"

Jane did not understand a word he said but the tone and the accompanying gestures were clear enough. With gestures of her own and finally a little help from St. Claire, they reached an agreement. She would stay out of *his* kitchen and he would insure a steady supply of hot water for the back porch cleaning stations.

The ship's cook, used to less than idyllic circumstances, made his headquarters at the old Charte cabin. Using Marie's outdoor oven to bake bread and utilizing stores from the *Dauphine*, one decent hot meal was served up to everyone each day.

The mill workers and their families continued to trickle back into the settlement and it was deemed a blessing that no one had suffered more than they did. Confronted with mostly scrapes and scratches, the doctor examined each person with great care seeking to avoid infections. Property could be replaced but people could not.

"Monsieur Charte," Doctor St. Claire approached Jacques on the second day.

"*Monsieur Physicien*," Jacques respectfully acknowledged the older man's proper title.

"I understand your wife is *enceinte* and this is your first child it would seem."

"Yes," Jacques tried to mask his worry with a smile.

"Have you made any arrangements?"

"What? What kind of arrangements? Oh, for the birth, you mean? I had thought to bring a mid-wife from New York Towne but the storm unsettled everything. We have none here nor any doctor. Well, you can see for yourself, this is still a very small settlement."

"Would you like a doctor here?" St. Claire asked a bit hesitantly.

"Would we *like*?" Jacques responded enthusiastically. "But naturally! Every settlement longs to have its own doctor. Might you consider staying?"

"That was precisely what I was considering. I should think in starting over in the New World, one place is as good as another. I am certain New York Towne already has its share of physicians. And one is pleased to know that one is in a place where they are truly needed."

"It is we who would be most pleased to have you settle here, *Monsieur Physicien*. As you can imagine with my wife in her present condition, I could think of nothing more fortuitous. It is like a gift from Heaven."

The older man smiled with pleasure. "Of course, I am not a mid-wife but I will do what I can. And where is your wife, I have not had the pleasure of meeting her?" he asked looking all around.

"That...that is the question. Since the storm, I do not know."

"Oh, well, surely she will return soon, everyone is," St, Claire said kindly and sought to change the subject. "Is there any place for me to live?"

"Look around you, monsieur. There is land aplenty and the governor sells it quite cheaply. All a man needs to do is clear it, build a house and put it to use. But there is time for that. For right now, I would be most pleased to have you stay as a guest in my home. In spring you will have, perhaps, selected a spot you find agreeable and can begin building your own house."

St. Claire nodded. He had found his place in the New World.

Despite Jane Sims' best efforts, everyone continued to be covered in mud and Jacques was no exception. He had gone to the river, removed his boots and jumped in clothes and all but it had done little good as the river was running high with silt. His clothes had become ragged and stained a muted brown and his demeanor had turned just as dark. He had left people in charge with specific instructions to watch over his wife only to find that there was absolutely no one who knew anything about what had happened to her.

"Where is Madame Charte?" a deep voice behind Jacques asked. Jacques spun around and was looking into the dirty face of Francois Nicholet.

"She... I have not found her yet," Jacques replied and was astounded when the stocky Frenchman sank to his knees in the mud and began to cry.

"I should have stayed with her. I should have stayed."

"Pull yourself together, man," Jacques said sharply. "What are you saying... did you see her?"

"I went to the cabin to check on her. I did not want to frighten her. I told her... I told her to stay inside. She promised she would. She promised," Nicholet was blubbering hysterically and Jacques slapped him soundly across the cheek.

"Nicholet! Get hold of yourself, I say!" Jacques growled sternly and pulled the man to his feet. Nicholet stopped short and became quiet. "This is *my* wife we are talking about – Madame Charte. Remember? Now, tell me slowly. When did you see her last?"

"I went to the cabin before it started to rain," he said with more control. "I brought her fresh water and told her to stay inside. I told her it was much too dangerous to go out. The wind was very strong by then. I wanted to stay. I asked to stay but I think I frightened her a little. She told me *no*, said it was not necessary. She asked me to check on the animals. But she promised to stay inside. The cabin is strong. I thought she was safe. Why did she leave?"

"Have you taken a good look at the cabin?" Jacques bit out. Nicholet shook his head, looking toward the structure. "The roof is half gone and the insides are a shambles."

"What?!"

"Thank God she was not inside. A huge tree limb fell through the roof."

"No-no. *Mon Dieu!* She was driven out then."

"I have the feeling she was gone before the limb fell."

"Why is that?"

"The way it fell… there is no way she could have escaped unharmed," Jacques replied grimly.

"We must put together a search party!"

"Wait." Jacques regretted his initial harshness. "Get some hot food for yourself. It is not time yet for worry or blame. As long as people keep returning I have hope."

Nicholet nodded and walked toward the clean water and food.

The more hands that were added to the clean up efforts, the faster the work progressed. The ramps and walkways were well underway. But after three days there was still no clue as to where Marie was and the clean up fires had not brought her back to him. Jacques could stand it no longer. William Boot was back on his feet and supervising the felling of more trees. Nicholet was running the mill to supply the lumber needed to rebuild. Jacques sought out Captain Trudeux and found him back on the ship.

"I cannot just wait any longer," Jacques stated, trying to keep a tight rein on his emotions. "I must look for my wife."

"Where would you begin?" Trudeux reasoned.

"With the Indians. I must. Or it will drive me insane. Please, watch over things in my absence."

"How long?"

"I do not know... I will return, if for no other reason than the possibility that she has come back in my absence."

Trudeux stood dispassionately packing a small pipe with tobacco. "You realize we cannot stay here forever," he said at last. He did not wish to be unsympathetic but he had an itinerary to follow.

"I understand."

"Ah," the captain let out a deep sigh. "You are going to make me say this, are you not?" He fixed Jacques with a stern look as he drew on his pipe.

"Say what?"

"Son, she is either alive or she is dead. If she is alive, she will be back and you should be here waiting for her. And if she is dead," he shrugged sadly, "there is no sense in hunting for her in a huge wilderness."

Jacques knuckles were pure white as he squeezed the table top fighting the urge to lash out at the man physically. "And if she is alive but unable to come back?" He saw Trudeux shrug again.

"But where, remains the question."

"Are you married, Captain?" Jacques asked softly in an eerily calm voice.

"Why yes, for seven... no eight years now."

"How often do you see your wife, sailing as you do?"

"She knew I was a seafaring man when she agreed to marry me. I get home several weeks a year, sometimes a bit more."

"That is all... why did you marry, if I may ask?"

"It is a fair question," Captain Trudeux sat and stretched his legs out in front of him. "It is nice to have a home to go to, is it not? And a few children to care for you if you live long enough."

"So one woman really was about as good as the next?" Jacques asked quietly. "That is as long as she realized and accepted the life you led."

"I have never really thought about it but I suppose you are right."

"*Oui, oui,* of course, but as we are both men and understand these things… being away from home so long, well, you must find comfort in other ports, eh?" Jacques smiled slyly.

"Well, of course," Trudeux smiled back, "it is a sailor's way of life after all."

"Yes, of course. And if anything should happen to Madame Trudeux, I am certain it would not take long to find some other good woman who would do just as well to keep your house for you and rear your children."

"Well, perhaps, but do not misunderstand, I am very fond of Sarah, that is Madame Trudeux."

"I am sure you are," Jacques said as he turned to leave. Stopping at the door he looked back at the captain, a hard edge to his voice. "I am going to search for my wife, *Monsieur Capitaine,* with or without your cooperation because there is *no one* here on earth who could replace her in my life." And he was gone.

Jacques put together a rucksack and wished mightily that Richard was there with him. Richard would be just as anxious to find Marie as he and together they could cover twice the territory. But wishes would not solve the situation. Jacques decided to head out upon the Indian trail, across the ridges in the direction of where he believed the village of the Indians who came often to trade with Marie, was located. At least it was a starting point.

As he trudged along the trail, Jacques looked for any sign, any trace, any clue as to whether Marie had passed by this way. As he went, he found nothing but eventually he became aware of another presence. Something or someone was tracking him. He felt certain. Moving most stealthily, he doubled back and ran smack into Francois Nicholet.

"Nicholet! What is the meaning of this? I left you in charge of the mill!" Jacques barked as he held a two fisted grip on the shorter man's coat front.

"I know. I know. I appointed another...Johnson. He will oversee it. Have no concern."

"Of course I have concern. This is how you follow my orders? What if he decides to appoint yet another?"

"I had to help."

"What is this attachment you have for my wife?" Jacques asked bluntly, suddenly releasing his hold on the other man and pushing him away.

The blood visibly drained from Nicholet's face as he struggled to respond. "I… please, it is not … "

"Did you steal her away?! Do you hope to get rid of me so you can make her *your* wife?"

The blood rushed back into Nicholet's face in a study of tortured embarrassment. "No-no, monsieur, no, never. Forgive me. I mean no disrespect. Madame Charte just reminds me so much of… she could be my own wife's sister. And I was not there to save my wife, I was not able to protect her. I would give anything if only there had been someone to come to my wife's aid. Is it wrong for me to want to help another?"

"No." Jacques thought as he stared the other man in the face. "No, I suppose not. So come. Since you are here let us continue walking," Jacques said gruffly.

After a few silent minutes, he asked, "So, what did happen to your wife, Nicholet?"

There was another silence until at last Nicholet spoke.

"I was selfish and headstrong. Another could have taken the wagon to market but I insisted it be me. I wanted the diversion; I wanted to be the one to gather the latest news."

Jacques grunted as they quickened their pace.

"The Dragonnade came to our village in my absence. They saw her. They found out she was a Huguenot and they took her... they all took her." Nicholet's voice had become tight, almost strangled. Jacques wanted to tell him to stop but he could not. "They dragged her into a tavern and made drunken sport of her all night long. By morning..." he cleared his throat. "She died before I returned... from equal parts shame and injury."

"The shame was not hers!"

"True... but I believe there are degradations one cannot comeback from when they are suffered so publicly. They ripped her flesh, broke her spirit, and killed our son."

"She was pregnant?!" Jacques was shocked.

"No-no, he was three. They said it was an accident but I think they killed him deliberately or perhaps it was just carelessly. And no one came to help. It was more than she could bear."

"Villagers with brooms are no match for muskets and swords," Jacques steeled himself not to show pity. Pity was the last thing Nicholet needed. "We all have our reasons for coming to this new world. I hate what is happening in our old country but I am grateful that you have chosen to help me at this time."

Nicholet nodded and was silent.

The two men continued on mostly in silence. They found the small Indian village and it was deserted. Many of the wigwams had been torn apart or damaged by trees. Broken limbs were scattered everywhere. It was obvious that the tribe had packed off; the shelters held no personal belongings of any value. Jacques had no idea where they might have gone but it made sense to him that if they were running from the storm they would have traveled away from the sea, deeper into the interior.

Jacques and Nicholet split up, each taking a different ridge. For several days they looked for telltale signs of camp fires, smoke traces. They listened for human voices. Dogs barking. Children laughing. There was nothing but the sounds of returning wildlife, bird song and rustling leaves. Neither trek proved productive and finally, exhausted and hungry, they met up again and turned back eastward.

Chapter 5

Son-of-Sky-Hawk spoke no English or French. As his mother's son he became the undisputed leader of this band of *Lenni Lenape* and he was used to unquestioning obedience in most things. In time his chieftainship would pass not to his own son but to the eldest son of his eldest sister, She-Who-Laughs-In-Her-Sleep. It was the accepted way of their people. Her eldest son and daughter had been born of her union with a courageous mate who died bravely in battle with their long time enemy, the Mohawk. And when this eldest son of She-Who-Laughs-In-Her-Sleep passed on to the after life, it would not be his son who would be the next chief but the eldest son of his sister. Thus, tribe and clan leadership passed peacefully through the female line.

A little more than one year into her expected two year widowhood, She-Who-Laughs-In-Her-Sleep caused much talk when she chose to mate with a dark haired *shëwanàkw*. The women of the council gave their permission. The white man lived as one of them. He taught her his language as he learned hers and over time he gave her two more sons. Then, one day he disappeared and was never seen nor heard from again. By this time She-Who-Laughs-In-Her-Sleep had lost several teeth and was not so pleasing to look upon; no one pressed her to mate again. Since that time, she continues to live under her brother's protection and within the shelter of his longhouse where she continues to keep a hearth for her youngest sons who are not yet mated.

Son-of-Sky-Hawk did not understand the white men who had come to their wilderness bringing the white female and leaving her all alone. Being left in solitude was part of the manhood ritual. But that ritual was only for warriors. To abandon a woman was… savage. Worse than savage it was humiliation beyond humanity. Women were the Givers and Nurturers of Life.

The first time Son-of-Sky-Hawk saw the *shëwanàkuxkwe*, he had been very curious and watched her for hours. Like a young fox her hair was of many shades and could float and move easily in the breeze as though it had life of its own. It held streaks of gold that shined like the sun itself while other strands glinted of copper; most was the color of a robin's wing. He had been fascinated and found her pale, naked form very pleasing to look upon as well. She was the first *shëwanàkuxkwe* he had ever seen and she was bathing in the small lake she had created for herself.

One day as she worked outside, he and his sister's sons had finally approached the white woman and she had shown no fear. She did not keep her gaze cast downward but looked him in the eye without hostility and without lasciviousness. But when he had touched her bread dough, she had smacked his hand away like a mother does to a child which caught him by surprise and made him laugh. And so he named her "Woman-Who-Battles-On-Bread" and at that very moment he had felt something he never thought he could feel for a pale female. He had felt a stirring in his loins. He had felt her eyes upon him as she watched him move and observed how he had carefully painted himself. In response, he had stood a little taller and caused his muscles to ripple beneath his tattoos and shell necklaces.

In autumn her men returned only to leave her again in spring. When he discovered that they did not return the next autumn but had left her all alone to suffer the madness of a long cruel solitary winter, he had commanded She-Who-Laughs-In-Her-Sleep to speak for him and offer the white woman his protection as her mate. Her answer was that it could not be because her god allowed only one mate at a time and she was already mated to one of the men. It was the same for women of the *Lenni Lenape*. But if that mate had left for so long as a year, he could expect another to have replaced him at her hearth. Not so with these whites and she had not believed her mate was dead. And so he had commanded his sister to remain as her companion through the rest of the winter. As they later learned, the white woman had been right. Her mate was still alive and he did return.

This woman puzzled him greatly. She was so loyal to this man who left her often and for such long periods of time. He stayed with her now that he had brought others of their kind only to leave her to the elements as she drew close to her time of travail. What kind of person was this man and where was his honor? Once again there was need to rescue her. This time although her mate had left her with others of their kind, none of them could read the signs of the storm. None of them could see the dangers ahead or they would not have built so close along the edge of the great water. Bah! He, Son-of-Sky-Hawk, had no patience for any of them. Only she was worthy of his notice for she had a gentle spirit. And now she was safe with the *Lenni Lenape*, the People, safe with Son-of-Sky-Hawk and he was in no hurry to give her back. And were they not justifiably too busy to return her? And was it not wiser for her to have her child here so his sister could attend? Had She-Who-Laughs-In-Her-Sleep not had to help the other white woman bring forth her child?

Amidst the beehive of activity that comes with establishing a new village, Marie had been set to the task of grinding dried corn into meal. She did not mind the work. It was not physically demanding, at least not once she had set herself up to work in a manner convenient to her big belly. It was a task she could do on her own without needing to speak to anyone. She found the language of the tribe difficult to master and only knew a word or two, and those she knew she spoke poorly. Her tongue could not make the sounds. Her task kept her out of the way of the others but she was tired of wearing the same dirty garments she had left home in and she was beginning to feel more like a captive than a guest.

It had been weeks since the chieftain called Son-of-Sky-Hawk by his people and whom Marie called *Looking Glass,* and his sister She-Who-Laughs-In-Her-Sleep which Marie shortened to *Sheehoo,* had appeared at the cabin insisting on leading her away from the coast. Through the past few years, these natives had come to her often to trade and had proved to be good neighbors who had looked out for her whenever Jacques had been away. She had had no choice but to trust them and in the fury of the storm Looking Glass had literally picked her up and carried her away.

Marie thought anxiously of Jacques. She knew she was safe but he did not. She could only imagine that he was half mad with not knowing what had become of her. She had no idea how their settlement had fared through the strangely violent weather and the sad truth was once the storms stopped she had been afraid to leave on her own, afraid to make the trek without being carried in a litter and no litter was offered to her. She knew she needed to go eastward toward the rising sun but she had no weapons against the animals of the forest, and what if she gave birth on her trek, all alone with no one to help? Or worse still, what if she should die like her mother and there was no one to protect her helpless infant? She shuddered.

As Marie worked at grinding the corn, she thought of the afternoon she had left the cabin at her Indian friends' insistence. She had come out of the privy and saw Looking Glass coming from the forest, walking toward the cabin, Sheehoo behind him.

"Hello," Marie called out, but she felt the word being shredded like a dandelion puff as soon as it left her mouth. She said nothing more but gestured for them to enter her shelter. When they did she shut the door.

"I am very surprised to see you. The weather is turning bad."

"Very bad. We come for you," said the tall brave's sister.

"What? I do not understand."

"Where your man?" Sheehoo asked but it sounded almost like an accusation.

"He had to go to the big village," Marie replied quickly.

"You must come with us," Sheehoo insisted.

Marie was rendered momentarily speechless. This was most unusual behavior even for these people. Why on earth would they assume that she would want to go anywhere in her condition, and certainly not in this weather?

Looking Glass spoke sharply to his sister and she looked anxiously at Marie. "My brother say no more talk. Must come now. Is not safe here."

"What do you mean it is not safe?"

The squaw hesitated and said something in her native tongue. "*Këkhit kshàxën, Këkhit kshàxën* … Not know white man word," she said in frustration. "Big wind brings big water. Even cabin not safe. Must leave now."

"But I cannot. I promised my husband I would stay here. I must stay. It is not safe for me to go out," Marie argued.

"It not safe to stay! Husband no understand this weather. Need go deep into forest," she gestured. "Must come, baby be safe if leave now."

Marie began to panic. She had never known these people to be anything but honest and considerate of her and her well being. They had traveled miles to save her from freezing to death last winter. And now they had once again traveled miles just to tell her for some reason they could not explain that she had to leave. But she had promised Jacques she would stay.

"Why can I not stay here? I know this is going to be a bad storm but this cabin is a strong shelter."

Looking Glass spoke again in agitation. He was impatient to leave and frustrated that he could not explain to the white woman why she must come with them immediately. If only she would just be obedient as his women are, but her independent spirit is what he found most admirable about her. What he could not admire, nor understand, was the behavior of the man she had taken as her mate.

It was a masculine right to strike out into the unknown, to hunt and to fight, but it was also a warrior's responsibility to leave his woman safe with other women and family for company and protection. This man had brought his woman to the wilderness and was always leaving her alone. This was a breech of everything the native considered moral. Only those who were unfit, who had committed some heinous crime against the tribe were punished with the solitary life of an outcast. The other whites had built their shelters far from this woman. Yet, Looking Glass saw nothing to condemn her. She did nothing to dishonor her mate. She worked hard. She had courage. She had a pleasing temperament. It was not justice to leave her alone, he concluded, and his feelings of ire against the other whites were in direct proportion to the feelings of tenderness he held for her.

"Must leave now," the squaw went on with greater agitation. "Take bag, take what need. Leave now. Make safe. Hurry. Hurry. Much wind, too strong, take trees, much water come from sea, nothing here is safe."

Marie was on the verge of hysterical laughter. This was a little too much to comprehend. If she was understanding correctly, Sheehoo was trying to say a storm so huge it could bring the sea up to the cabin was coming. But that was preposterous! Wind was wind, but how strong could a wind blow? Strong enough to lift trees into the air according to Nicholet. But they were far from the harbor and perhaps fifty feet above the level of the water. Suddenly she felt Looking Glass' grip on her arm. She flinched. She could not understand his words but he was speaking to her fiercely and her arm hurt.

"Please, tell your brother he is hurting me," Marie gasped, "tell him to stop."

The squaw who was busy filling a water skin from the buckets spoke to her brother who said something quickly and pulled Marie to the door not releasing his grip but modifying it slightly. Sheehoo grabbed bread and any other food she saw, stuffing it all into an oil bag. She took Marie's fur cloak and hurried after them as they went back outside.

The wind almost knocked Marie over but Looking Glass held on to her and pulled her along. Sure-footed and strong, he kept her from falling as they made their way across the plowed field and into the forest beyond. In the shelter of the trees, the thrust of the wind was weakened but Marie was aware that the tree tops were whipping savagely above them. The clouds were beginning to roll in now and she knew that rain could not be more than minutes away.

Out of breath, Marie cried out above the howling wind. "Please, I must stop! Please! Just a moment."

The brave halted, her words needed no translation. Marie had no thought of trying to escape. Whatever the reason, she was certain these people meant her no harm. They thought she was in danger and they were trying to assist her. But what could they possibly fear? She took several deep breaths. And if there really was danger, what of the others?

"If we are in danger, we should warn the rest of the settlement," she cried above the wind. The squaw said nothing and Looking Glass took hold of Marie again and she had no choice but to continue the march. They pressed on; Looking Glass never relinquishing his grip on Marie's arm and Sheehoo trotting to keep up on Marie's other side.

Rain drops began to fall.

Rain. We need rain, Marie thought, trying to quell the sense of panic rising in her. *It is only a rain storm, is it not?*

As they started up a sharp incline of a hill, Marie felt her legs fail as she almost fell.

"Stop!" she cried out again, panting. "I cannot go any farther. I cannot. I must rest." She held her belly as though it was already a breathing child she wished to draw closer to her. There were tears in her eyes as she kept thinking of her promise to Jacques. She feared for their child. This kind of pace could bring on early labor. *No-no,* she thought with another surge of panic, *I must not lose our baby.*

The brave halted again and released his hold on her. She sank to the ground. The rain was pelting down and the squaw put Marie's cloak about the young woman's shoulders. It felt warm and protective and she wiped the tears from her eyes.

"Please tell your brother, that I understand he wants me to leave but I cannot go any farther for my baby's sake."

The squaw spoke briefly to her brother and suddenly Looking Glass bent and picked up Marie in his arms. Carrying her as gently as possible against his chest which was covered by a kind of loose vest made of shells, he began a steady climb up the ridge. Almost at the crest they were joined by the sons of the squaw. Looking Glass set Marie down and pointed to a litter made of a rawhide seat suspended from a sturdy pole. The two largest of the young men carried the pole between them as they would carry home a fallen deer. After Marie had placed herself into the seat, the group continued on.

From her vantage point within the litter seat, Marie could now look up and about. All around the trees had become as flaying beasts doing a frenzied dance to some pagan god. Marie heard branches snapping, splitting, hitting other branches as they came crashing to the ground below. And now the rain was falling hard.

They traversed downhill and then up again. As they crossed down the other side of the next ridge, the wind was less fearsome and there was no rain but the sky had darkened angrily and it was difficult to see. The young men walked swiftly, easily carrying her between them.

Through the growing dark, she sat sideways and suddenly saw one glittering yellow eye peering out from the black. They were heading straight for it. Marie held her breath momentarily, staring at the evil eye through the gloom. There was something demonic about it, she thought, her mind seeing images that were not there as she tried to see the second eye. Then, with relief and a slight sense of em-barrassment she realized it was no eye at all but a fire.

Sheehoo was older than her brother and the forced march and fast trek up and down the ridges had worn her out. She was falling behind and with the wind screaming in their ears, Marie could not ask her where they were going. She just hung on to the litter ropes and kept silent.

At last she saw the tongues of flame clearly, ringed by a circle of small rocks. And it became evident that this guidance fire was at the mouth of a cave. The braves brought the litter to the entrance just under a shallow overhang of rock and stopped. Marie understood that she was to stand, which she did with difficulty. As she stood, she shook the raindrops from her and walked carefully down, through a small opening and into a narrow passage way. The light from the fire danced about the entrance, reflecting off the rock walls. Beyond this light there was a smaller fire inside the cave and several burning torches wedged in crevices along the walls.

Once within the cavity of the earth, Marie gave her eyes a chance to adapt. She was not well-balanced these days and she did not want to fall. When her vision ad-justed she discovered there was enough general illumination with which to see her surroundings quite clearly. Carefully she picked her way downward finally finding a natural bench. She sat down. Her hair was dripping but her fur kept her warm.

She looked around her. The narrow corridor at the entrance sloped down and curled around to finally open into a sizable cavern and the screaming harsh sounds of the storm had vanished. She realized there were perhaps fifty, maybe sixty peo-ple gathered closely within. Mothers were nursing babies, adults were talking in hushed tones, even the children were subdued as they sat by smaller fires sucking on dried meat.

It must be everyone from Looking Glass' village, she thought. They had all left their homes and come to the shelter of the cave. Why? Surely they did not do this with every storm. Jacques and Richard had spoken of living in an Indian camp in the midst of the winter storms. No, this one was different. In the three years that she had been in the harbor, this was the first time they had come to take her away because of a storm. What kind of a storm was this? Was it as Nicholet's brother had described? Something that would lift trees and blow man and beast like straw in the wind?

In the shadows of the cave, Marie noticed the nearest women looking at her with curiosity. She smiled at them and at the small children who stared openly at her. Later she would learn from Sheehoo that they knew her as *Trading Woman*, the source of the pots, knives, and cloth their men would bring home. That Son-of-Sky-Hawk should make an effort to bring her to safety did not surprise them. Some even gossiped that he had made her his woman and the baby she carried was of his spirit.

She-Who-Laughs-In-Her-Sleep reported to her brother that the *shëwanàkuxkwe* had had some pains in the cave after their arrival, perhaps because of all the fast walking in the storm.

"We do not know much about white women in this matter, my brother. She is small, not like the pale giant who gave birth easily with our help. She has waited long for this child but it is too soon. It would be a great sadness if anything evil should happen."

Son-of-Sky-Hawk listened. He too wished no evil to befall the courageous *shëwanàkuxkwe* and so he decided there was no cause for hurry in taking Woman-Who-Battles-On-Bread back to her cabin. When the storm ceased, he led a scouting party to seek out a suitable site for their next village. They would start fresh as they did periodically, this time leaving six years of their waste, fleas, and ashes behind, and allowing the fields they had been planting to also rest and go fallow. The others would continue to shelter in the caves for several more days hidden from the world until the warriors returned. Woman-Who-Battles-On-Bread could continue to rest.

Marie had rested. Then, when the scouting party returned, Sheehoo told her they were to move on to a new site.

"But I must return home," Marie said, working to maintain her calm. "By now my husband has returned and must wonder what has happened to me. I was not able to tell anyone where I was going."

Sheehoo shook her head. "No one have time now to take you home. All must work to build new dwellings. Make strong and warm against winter to come."

"But…."

"Chief say, must be," Sheehoo said with great finality. "You make ready, leave at dawn."

Everyone packed up their belongings and the next day they left the shelter of the cave at first light. The pace was slow so the youngsters and the very oldest could keep up with the rest. Marie had no trouble keeping up as well but to her dismay each step seemed to take her farther and farther from her home.

For many days since leaving the caves Son-of-Sky-Hawk had avoided being seen by Woman-Who-Battles-On-Bread and now, he thought, even she must realize she is too close to her time to undertake the return trek. She had stopped asking to leave. Perhaps she will find happiness here with his clan. He admitted only to himself that he did not want to see her leave. Let her mate pay for his carelessness.

Let him rise to the challenge to find her… if he can … or lose her forever.

And so Marie sat grinding corn and waiting for her baby to arrive.

Jacques and Francois had passed within a mere stone's throw of the sheltering cave but they never knew it. They heard nothing and saw nothing. The low entrance had been covered over with branches as a camouflage and everyone continued to stay quietly inside while the warriors were away seeking a new settlement site. Evidence of the homing fire that had guided Son-of-Sky-Hawk's rescue party had been washed away.

Upon returning to the coastal settlement Jacques felt compelled to make the rounds and see how everyone was faring. As he looped around the river front he was relieved to see his best friend Richard returning for the season from his trading trip up the Hudson. He had only just arrived and was still mooring his boat to what anchorage was left along the river bank. Jacques shouted a greeting.

"My God, Richard, you are a sight for sore eyes!"

The tall, robust Frenchman turned his dark bushy head and all Jacques could see were his eyes, so thick was the beard and brows on his face, so over-grown was his black hair. Jacques gave him a handshake and a quick embrace. Ordinarily he would chide his friend for his failure to groom or bathe properly before making his way home from town but that was the least of Jacques' concerns this time.

"*Mon ami!*" Richard grinned and suddenly teeth appeared within the beard. "I heard of the storm and decided to head back early. New York Towne is still cleaning up." Richard embraced Jacques briefly and continued to look around. "And I can see you have had your share of ruin as well. The whole harbor has changed. The low cabins are gone. Washed away? Unbelievable! Did you get your new home built? More important, did it survive the storm? And how is our Marie?"

Jacques turned away suddenly to hide the tears that came unbidden to his eyes. He was very tired and hungry and losing control of his emotions.

Richard dashed around to confront Jacques face to face and saw his friend's expression of panicky despair. "*Mon Dieu!* Tell me what has happened!" he demanded.

Jacques talked as they walked up to the new house where Jane Sims had everything under tight control. They removed their boots under her watchful eye and accepted the house slippers she provided. Richard's soiled buckskins and Jacques' bedraggled clothing received critical appraisal in silence, then out of nowhere Jane had sheets to cover the two new chairs they planned to sit in.

It took two servings of cognac for Jacques to get all the way through his story. And Richard found himself in the odd position of being the cooler head. Perhaps it was only that he had become very practiced at hiding his feelings, especially the very tender feelings he should not have for his best friend's wife.

"I would like to interview the woman who said angels came and took her away," Richard said gruffly.

"She was hysterical, a bit...you know," Jacques said dismissively touching his head.

"Of course, undoubtedly she was starving, exhausted, and suffering from exposure but that was then… which was how many days ago?"

"We will go talk to her again."

"Wait, *mon ami,* you look ready to drop in your tracks. Why do you not go upstairs and stretch out on your new bed. Get some sleep. I can find the woman myself. I will talk to her and tomorrow morning we will start fresh, eh?"

"You are right. I cannot think logically anymore," Jacques replied wearily.

"Rest easy… we will find her," Richard said with a believable show of confidence. "I have the feeling she *is* with the Indians and if she is, that big brave… what does she call him… *Looking Glass?* He is not going to allow anything to happen to her."

"Or the baby?" Jacques added quickly.

"That is right, or the baby. Indians prize children and they associate them with the mother, the father does not matter very much."

The significance of this last statement was lost on Jacques as he made his way to the top of the staircase and the master bedroom. He realized that to fall apart and vent his fears would be to acknowledge the possibility of the very worst. He could not do that. He had to believe that his beloved was out there somewhere safe, just waiting for him to come and find her. He fell asleep thinking that it was now too close to her time and she must stay with the Indians... if she was with the Indians. *Of course she is. Richard is right, where else would she be? And until she is delivered of our child she cannot... They would not make her suffer a trip home right now. But to where have the Indians moved? Wherever, Richard and I will find her… we will… she is well…*

Jacques drifted off into a deep sleep.

Richard found himself being waved over to the kitchen building by Jane Sims. Jane had solicited Doctor St. Claire's help in communicating with *Le Chef* and he had agreed to retire to his room for an hour long nap.

"I suggest you bring a clean change of clothes," she said bleakly as she pointed through the doorway to a large steaming cauldron full of hot water at the huge hearth. An over-sized wooden tub sat on the brick floor, and an array of grooming articles including scissors, clippers, straight razor with leather strap, soap, a pumice stone, towels, and mirror graced the heavy utility table.

Richard nodded and fetched his bag. Back in the kitchen, he found himself conveniently alone and he added another log to the blazing hearth fire. He started with the scissors and clipped his bushy unkempt beard as closely as possible in a prelude to shaving. Next he would take five or six inches off his unruly hair and shampoo what remained. And finally he would soap down his entire hairy body, while rigorously but judiciously applying the pumice stone before rinsing off.

As he worked at returning to the civilized world, his mind mulled over the situation at hand. There was no doubt in Richard's mind that the Indian, who was evidently more familiar with what a hurricane was like, had come in and taken Marie away from the coast for safety. It is what he would have done. And with a hurricane, the farther you were from the water, the safer you were. Obviously *le grand chief* had not cared to warn the rest of the settlement, Richard mocked to himself. And although there was no way for Jacques to have known what the weather was going to bring, still there was a tiny disgruntled niggling accusation that pointed a finger and asked how could Jacques have left her side so close to her confinement? Why could he not have waited for the ship to arrive in their harbor? He wanted to find servants, yes. He wanted to surprise her, yes. But in the end was it worth it? He did not think so and that was going on the most optimistic assumption that Marie was indeed perfectly well and watched over by her Indian *amis*. And that the whole escape had not brought on labor too soon or tragically. But Richard had to admit Jacques' presence was no guarantee against the onset of early labor either. The weather alone could have done that.

Jacques said he had found the former village and it was deserted so Richard decided he would go see *Chipsixkwe,* the *Lenape* woman to the north whom he visited often during the long cold winters. Jacques and Marie knew of these visits but did not ask for details and he volunteered none. *Chipsixkwe* was of the same tribe, different clan but she had a relation of some kind in the clan headed by the big brave. Richard was almost certain she could find out where they had moved their village. Surely the warriors within *Chipsixkwe's* clan would know.

Richard began to towel himself off and dress. All might turn out well… but what if, his thoughts continued, what if something terrible… tragic…? No-no, he would not, must not go down that avenue of thought.

Now closely shaved with his hair combed and his person looking squeaky clean in fresh clothing, Richard returned to the main house to encounter the formidable Jane Sims.

"Ah, Mademoiselle Sims," he said gallantly, flashing her his biggest smile full of teeth. With a courtly bow, he bent to kiss her hand, "I thank you most sincerely for the opportunity to scrub the dirt of the wilds away and return to civilization."

"Ohh," she tittered and giggled, "it's *Missus*, I be married to Mister Sims."

"Ah, I appreciate the warning before I find myself haplessly missing my heart," he said very gallantly.

"Aww, go on with you now," she beamed as she turned the rosiest pink of which a human is capable.

"So I shall, if you would be so very kind as to show me to my room. I am… how to say, like a member of this family and I live with my dear friends when I return from my trading treks. But this time they are in an unfamiliar house."

"Oh, of course, of course… just follow me, sir," she invited amiably with a pleasant smile and led the way to one of the guest rooms.

Richard had made a conquest.

When Jacques awoke the morning sun was already well above the horizon. He gave a start and then remembered Richard had returned. Jacques offered up a silent prayer of thanks followed by an earnest supplication on behalf of Marie and their baby. He thought a soft rap had awoken him so he opened the door and found a large pitcher of steamy hot water.

After washing, shaving, and donning fresh clothing, he left the bedroom and was coming down the staircase when Jane came into the main hall.

"Oh, Master Charte, I have a message for you from Mister Bonchance. He said for you to stay here and tend to your business in the settlement. He's gone to seek information from a friend on where the new village is located and he'll be back by nightfall. That's exactly what he said, sir, no more, no less. I hope that makes sense to you."

"Yes, yes, Jane. Thank you. Very good. Might I have some breakfast?"

"Yes, sir. I'll tell Chef Antoine."

Jacques and Richard had been watching the new village discreetly for a full day trying to catch some sight of Marie. Through all the activity of building and putting up food for the coming winter, there had been no sight of a very pregnant white woman.

"Where is she?!" Jacques asked softly but his frustration was evident. "Why can we not just walk in and ask for her?"

"Unless we see her we can not be completely certain she is here," Richard responded. "To ask is to admit we lost her. To assume she is with them if indeed she is not would be an insult and also an admission that we know not where she is."

Jacques felt his heart jump within his chest. "*Mon Dieu!* What if she is not here after all?"

Richard had never heard such panic in his friend's voice before. "Of course she is here..."

"That is why we should ask."

"It is a little like 'finders-keepers' and 'hide'n'seek' with the Indians."

"But they did not *find* her; if we understand correctly, they walked in and *took* her..."

"Or *rescued* her, it is all in your perspective, eh?"

"Whose side are you on?" Jacques asked in irritation.

"Marie's of course, and yours. I am just trying to give you the natives' way of thinking. You did leave your woman alone, big with child and in the middle of a storm." Richard couldn't keep himself from stating the bluntest reality.

"But there was no storm when I left and there was no way to get back once it hit."

"I know, I know. How long has it been now? A month? Do you think perhaps she has had the child?"

Jacques paused to think before he answered, "She may have. *Mon Dieu!* My first child may have been born in an Indian village! It may be right here some-where. I must know."

"Hold on, *mon ami*," Richard said calmly, "I think I may know where they are. You see that smaller hut over there?" he pointed.

"Yes..."

"I have seen only women go in and out of that hut, carrying in food, water, carrying out waste."

"So?"

"It is a bit odd, do you not think? All day and not one male, not one child has come out or gone in?"

"What do you think that means?"

"Some Indians have very strong superstitions about a woman's blood..."

"Blood?" Jacques looked confused.

"You know...their courses."

"Oh."

"Some believe it is very bad medicine for a warrior to come in contact with a woman's monthly blood, a kind of jinx, something to take away their manhood and cause failure in the hunt or weakness in battle… anyway, women must go off to their own hut for those days each month. No warrior wants to even be in a river downstream of a woman who may be bleeding from her monthly, or have her touch any of his food or drink."

"So what does this have to do with Marie?"

"Well," Richard said while keeping a steady eye on the little hut. "Same thing with child birth… you do know there is blood, do you not?" When he heard no reply he turned to look at Jacques.

Jacques looked at Richard with a tinge of embarrassment. "I admit I have never seen a human birth… I have never thought… how would I know such things?" he asked in exasperation.

"By watching the animals," Richard snickered.

"Is there much… blood, I mean?"

"In a normal birth, no, not much but still in clans that believe this way, the women must go to the women's hut to give birth. They must stay there until they stop bleeding. That may be where Marie is right now."

"Well, I do not want her staying there, if she is able I want to take her home!" Jacques proclaimed more loudly.

"Sh-sh… it may be to our advantage that we do not hold to those superstitions any longer. I have picked up a little *Lanape*, come, follow me."

With his musket slung across his back, Richard got up and made his way down the hillside and into the village close to the small hut. Jacques followed him. They both kept their hands open and in sight, obviously devoid of any weapon. Jacques had no idea what Richard was saying but the squaw he encountered sent a youngster running off in another direction. In no time at all a squat little squaw approached and greeted them in English.

"She not finish her cleansing time but she well… have son," Sheehoo said to Jacques with a gaping grin.

"Congratulations!" Richard pounded Jacques on the back. "You have a son!"

"Really? Where are they? Please, I want to see her. Are you certain she is well?"

"She fine. No see yet. Come with me, you sit by fire, eat food, make celebrate," she replied, pushing them toward a communal fire circle.

Jacques took a step, then suddenly turned and bolted toward the small hut. "I must see her!"

The squaw screeched and Richard utter an oath as he threw himself between his friend and the door covering, using every bit of his superior weight to physically restrain Jacques from entering.

"Stop and think about what you are doing, *mon ami*," he growled while holding Jacques back from entering. "Their village, their laws, *n'est-ce pas?* She may not be alone. There may be other women and it is absolutely forbidden."

Jacques stopped struggling. "Marie," he shouted, "Marie, are you well?"

"Jacques? Is that you? Oh, Jacques! Jacques! I am so glad you are here. I knew you would come, I knew it."

"Have you been mistreated?" he asked anxiously.

"No-no, I am well, Jacques, I am fine. I am just very tired," came the voice from within.

"They will not allow me to come in to see you."

"I know. You must listen and do as they say."

"What are you doing?"

"I am feeding our son." He could hear a smile in her voice. "He is so beautiful!" Jacques smiled and sighed softly.

"It is so good to hear your voice, Jacques. I am very sorry, I did not think I would be gone for so long. I did not mean to make you worry."

He heard a catch in her voice and thought perhaps she was crying. "No-no, I am sorry I was not here… oh, *ma chérie*, I just want to hold you in my arms."

"Yes-yes, we are all sorry," Richard said, pushing Jacques toward the fire circle. "Marie, I am taking this love sick puppy away so you can rest," Richard shouted through the door cover. They heard a faint giggling from within.

"Richard? I am so glad you are there as well. Bless you. Take care of Jacques for me."

"You know I will," he grinned toward the doorway.

As they walked to the fire circle, the big warrior Marie called Looking Glass appeared, muttering to his sister.

"I thank you, my friends," Jacques said in obvious relief. "I am in your debt. Is there anything I can do to repay you for your kindness to my wife?"

Sheehoo translated to her brother who simply looked at Jacques expressionlessly with unblinking, enigmatic, black eyes. Jacques would not have wanted to hear what the native was thinking but he certainly understood it was most likely not very flattering.

Jacques sat down feeling the muscles in his body liquefy as he felt genuinely at peace for the first time since he and Marie had parted over a month ago. He called upon all the patience he could muster as he listened to the drums and singing in what constituted a celebratory party welcoming Marie's son into the world. Richard translated. The fact that no one called the baby *his* son was not lost on Jacques either. But that would come when they returned to their own settlement.

Food and drink was surprisingly plentiful and everyone else was having a good time including Richard; Jacques had little appetite. Then, in the midst of it all, as if it was part of a well-known and established ritual, Sheehoo brought out the infant, swaddled up and bound onto a board, Indian fashion. She showed the baby first to the white man with yellow hair.

"You must take hold of the child to indicate that you accept him as your son," Richard said as he sat at Jacques' side. "Then, if you are proud and pleased you turn him up and around to show him off to the others."

Jacques took the bundle, saw big blue eyes and fine hair like golden corn silk and found himself grinning ear to ear. *Sacre Bleu!* No one could say this was not *his* son!

The two young Frenchmen slept at the fire circle with several of the braves who had been too drunk to walk away. It was a short night. Jacques was awake before dawn and chafing to see his wife and take her home. They had a sturdy new house, spotlessly clean thanks to Jane Sims, while Marie and his son were held in an Indian hut built for menstruating squaws and he was sleeping on the hard cold ground. It was insane!

He stood, stretched, and threw more wood onto the fire coals. He went off some distance and relieved himself by a tree. Returning to the warmth of the fire on the chilly October morning, he sat and watched as the rest of the village slowly came awake. A baby cried. He was sure it was his son. The cry did not last long. He nudged Richard.

Richard sat up and vigorously scratched his scalp with both hands causing his thick, dark hair to bush out wildly. He stood, stretched and went off to the trees. When he returned a young girl offered each of them a cup of herbal tea. They drank the hot tea in silence. Their fireside companions were still sleeping. A naked toddler came out of one of the wigwams. He was chewing on something that looked like jerky. He stared at them. They stared back. The toddler squatted in front of them and moved his bowels. Richard gave a short snort of amusement and used a stick to flick the waste into the fire while the child ran back into the wigwam.

"*Mon Dieu,* must they allow their children to act like dogs?" Jacques sighed.

"Good morning to you too," Richard looked at his friend.

"Good morning. I do not mean to be in a foul mood. I just cannot wait for Marie to wake so we can take her home."

Richard smiled. "Would you perhaps allow her some breakfast first?"

"Of course, you know what I mean."

"Perhaps I do not," Richard frowned. "Do you really expect her to walk all the way back to our settlement the day after she has given birth?"

"The day aft … do you mean to say she was giving birth while you were watching the hut, while we were watching the village?" Jacques asked in surprise. "But we heard no cries."

Richard nodded. "Not all women scream their heads off. And that is what I thought I heard someone say, but perhaps it was the day before. Still the question remains the same… do you expect her to walk all the way back *two* days after she has given birth?"

Jacques sat for a moment in silence. "You are right. Where does this creek go? Perhaps we can borrow a canoe to take her home."

"I will ask." Richard was about to stand up again when one of Sheehoo's sons awoke. He was among the group who had passed out at the fireside. Richard spoke haltingly to the youth who responded in kind despite an apparent hang-over. After several minutes, the youth got up and left.

"The creek is no help," Richard told Jacques. "He said it flows northward into a small lake that waters a favorite hunting area but then he said they used a litter to carry Marie to the cave."

"What cave?"

"It does not matter, it is the litter we need. He goes to ask permission to give it to us. It is a seat hanging from a pole. We can carry it and walk her home just like we would carry a deer, only Marie is not nearly so heavy, eh? Marie can hold the baby. Problem solved. We do not really need the one they have, we could make one."

Son-of-Sky-Hawk must have thought the same for he gave a nod of approval to give the litter over to the white men while he kept his distance from the women's hut.

The youth brought the pole and rigging and dropped it on the ground before Jacques who had meandered closer to the small hut. The lad retreated quickly.

Sheehoo came out of the hut, a frown on her face.

"Why you stand here? Men no come so close."

"I want to see my wife," Jacques said trying to keep a pleasant expression. "Please tell her to come out."

"Her time for cleansing not over," the squaw replied, not understanding their attempt to ignore the customs. It was for their own welfare.

"Marie! Can you hear me?" Jacques shouted at the hut.

"Jacques, give me an hour… I will be ready," came the reply.

With a "humph" and a glare, Sheehoo went off to get a bowl of gruel for Marie's breakfast while Jacques turned impatiently to wait out the hour.

An hour later, Marie stepped forth from the hut. All the men in camp except Jacques and Richard were observing at a distance and kept upwind of her. She was wearing a long, leather tunic that fell to her knees. On her legs were pelt leggings tied on with rawhide, fur turned inward. And no one could see the protective soft clout lined with moss between her legs. The leather of the tunic was so soft and pliable, it draped on her body like silk and did little to hide her enlarged breasts emphasized by the criss-crossing of the baby carrier straps. Their son was securely held within the carrier and bound to his board. In her arms Marie held her cloak self-consciously against her chest.

The Indians held no thoughts of modesty regarding the body but with the changing weather most were now wearing tunics themselves for warmth.

Jacques rushed to her and despite their audience gave her a long embrace and many kisses.

"*Mon Dieu!* You are beautiful. You look like a woodland goddess! Oh, my darling! You are well? Really? I have been sick with worry for you. Half mad." He babbled on for some time while Richard patiently waited and Marie murmured affectionate responses. "Come," Richard said at last. "Say your good-byes. I... that is to say *we* are taking you home."

Marie turned to Sheehoo, thanking her again for the gifted clothing and for everything she and her brother had done for her safety. With a good-bye wave to Looking Glass and a "Good morning!" to Richard, she prepared to sit in the leather swing as the men held the pole steady.

"Richard, you lead," Jacques instructed. "I want to look upon my wife and child. Wait, Marie, your cloak, you must put it on against the cold."

"I am not cold, Jacques. It looks to be a beautiful day." She put the cloak in her lap.

And so they began the trek back home. The men easily carrying Marie's weight between them, Richard leading, Jacques in the rear, and Marie swinging gracefully from the leather sling while the infant slept at her back.

As they walked, Marie told them about her experiences with the Indians, the cave they had all sheltered in, how frustrated she had been that she could not walk home and how she had stopped Sheehoo from taking their newly born son to the creek and submerging him in the icy cold waters to wash him clean.

"She told me that is what they do to all their newborns, even in the middle of winter. It makes them strong, she said. I told her 'not mine' and I insisted on warm water to bathe him. I know she thought that this would make him weak which is nonsense of course. I am surprised their babies do not develop pneumonia and die."

"Some do," Richard interjected over his shoulder. "It is like culling the herd. If the infant has not the strength to survive his birthing ritual chances are he will not survive his first challenge in life as a child. It is why you almost never see a sickly young Indian."

"But it seems so heartless! What a shock to go from a warm womb into a freezing cold river." She looked over to Jacques who nodded his agreement.

"But is not life itself often heartless?" Richard asked as he walked steadily forward.

Marie did not reply but she thought of her own mother's death when her baby brother was born.

They went along for some time in silence with only the sound of the crunch of leaves beneath their feet.

"Jacques, I am sorry I had to leave. I know I gave you my word but Looking Glass insisted. They simply would not listen. Do you forgive me?"

"Forgive you?" he replied quickly. "I just thank God you are safe. The cabin is a mess. You might have been very hurt if you had stayed. A huge tree limb crashed down through the roof. Half of it is torn off. We must repair it before you can make the cabin a true trading post."

Marie really didn't want to think about such things at that moment. The baby began to cry and she felt her milk let down.

"We must stop so I can get Baby off my back, he is hungry."

They stopped and Marie rose up with Jacques' help and unstrapped the carrier. The tunic she wore was designed for a nursing mother. It had little ties at each shoulder. She pulled her cloak around her for modesty before she bared her breast for the infant. She knew Jacques would want her to stay covered in front of Richard.

"What shall we name our son?" she asked brightly after she settled back in the sling to suckle her infant and they continued on their way. "We cannot keep saying 'Baby.'"

"Do you have something in mind?" Jacques asked.

She looked down to study the little face nestled against her. "He looks exactly like you, Jacques, I keep thinking of him as *little Jacques*. All he needs is a tiny moustache," she giggled. "I want to name him after you."

Jacques was silent for a moment, flattered but thinking as they walked on.

At last he spoke, "Jacques is a French name, Marie. This is the New World, not France. What would you think of *John?*"

Chapter 6

France - 1700

Huge, fat, perfect snowflakes fell straight to the ground settling one upon another. The gray white of the sky blended into the white gray of the ground behind the thick curtain of moving flakes and it was difficult to be certain of the horizon. Hélène watched from the window of her sitting room on the second floor of the chateau. Tomorrow was the first day of the New Year. How apropos, she thought. Snow did not often come here. But this started a new year and a new century with a new snow making everything fresh and white and clean. At times like this, she did not feel at all like she was fifty-two years old. She wanted to run outdoors, throw snow balls, and make snow angels. Her husband still called her his child bride. She certainly was no longer a bride, having been married for almost eight years. And one would have to be blind to call her a child, she smiled to herself. Her long pale gold hair had turned to pure silver. But still, her face retained a firm appearance while her waistline had grown only a fraction of an inch or so thicker.

Her marriage to the duke had been a quiet, private ceremony so as to attract no real attention although by then, Hélène thought, things in the province were not like they had been when Jacques-Jean had been forced to leave. Out of respect she and Jean-Philippe had waited a full year after the duchess' death to have the simple service. But because it was not a Catholic wedding, it was not considered by anyone save themselves and their household to be of any meaning.

It did not matter to Hélène. Years ago she had reconciled herself to accepting life on its own terms. She enjoyed the company and adoration of her husband, felt blessed in the knowledge that her son was alive and doing well even if he was an ocean away, and she contented herself with tending her private garden and overseeing the domestic management of the chateau. Since Augustine had passed away two years ago, those duties now included maintaining the scrupulous standards of cleanliness which Augustine had worked all her life to establish, and which Hélène had come to appreciate and value.

The general population and peasantry had little means to understand any relationship between disease, pestilence, flies, fleas, and vermin. The fastidious habits required of all occupants on the duke's estates were not understood. It was simply accepted that they must keep animals out of the food preparation areas, keep lids on the wells, and secure the spring houses from filth. They learned to burn or bury all garbage not consumed by the pigs and all animal droppings not plowed into the fields. They learned to relieve themselves in designated latrines only, and if they were household servants, to wash their persons and don clean clothes on a daily basis. There were those who griped and cheated until they were caught, but when the estates consistently escaped any incidence of typhoid, diphtheria, or cholera, and stood untouched in several smallpox epidemics which swept the countryside, everyone began to accept the practices even if they could not understand the reasoning. They thought of it all as a charm.

Whatever the reasoning behind the acceptance of the practices, Hélène was please to continue the beneficial routines the loyal servant had established. And life on the estates continued to be good.

Jacques-Jean had sent a letter to the chateau by return ship as soon as he and Richard had landed safely in the colonies. Then, it had been almost three years before they had heard from him again. That next letter referred to a previous letter. They supposed that it must have been lost. This letter also gave them a permanent location to which they could now send letters. Jacques-Jean had gone on an expedition into the wilderness with Richard, he wrote. He also added that the girl Marie had begun a trading post of her own and was doing well on the frontier. In 1689, they had received the news that Jacques-Jean had married the girl Marie. Hélène had wept. Tears of joy for her son mingled with the sad longing she felt at missing out on it all.

He seemed so in love, so happy. His life was full. Could a mother ask for more? Her son had a good life, she decided, full of challenges and rewards, it was productive and blessed. It was not the life she had thought he would have. It was not the life she would have wished him to have, being banished from his own country so far from everyone who loved him. Well, not everyone, she corrected herself. Richard had been his best friend since childhood and this girl presumably loved him. Who was to say it was not the best life for him. In her mother's heart Hélène came to the acceptance that it was the life God had chosen for her son.

Hélène pulled back from the window casing and walked over to the fireplace, drawn by the warmth. She regretted that she had never even met her son's wife, an irony considering the girl had once worked in domestic service right on the estates. JJ had grown up an extremely attractive man, she considered, trying to be objective and set aside any mother's pride. No, it was a fact; his high forehead, well arched brows, wide gray eyes, patrician nose, blond hair and lean cut jaw line bespoke physical beauty. He also had grace and charm, was well spoken, and was well made of sound body and limb. He had been educated and had developed discriminating tastes. Surely he could have had his pick of half a world of beautiful, refined, and intelligent young women. Somehow Hélène could not quite imagine her son finding any depth of attraction for a domestic servant, no matter how pretty she might be. Beauty, after all, could be most fleeting depending on bone structure.

Hélène felt a pinch of conscience. Had she not been the daughter of a domestic servant? But she had been educated. Her father had been a very high ranking servant held in esteem within the duke's household. And she had never actually been a servant herself. No, she had been a nobleman's mistress which was considered an esteemed position.

In all fairness and reality, Hélène, she told herself, *your son did not really have his pick of matches, did he? He was a hunted man and he has a price upon his head still. He had only two possible futures, the Bastille or exile. No decent woman of France, Catholic or Huguenot, could have accepted ties with him. How could they? Their families would have disowned them! And so he married an orphan.*

A quick rap on Hélène's door broke through her thoughts and she heard Jean-Philippe's voice.

"*Entrée,*" she spoke and watched as he almost spun through the door.

"I have a letter," he cried flourishing the paper in his hand.

"From Jacques?" she equaled his delight.

"From Jacques," he smiled. His hair had thinned and his face had gained a little flesh that was not unattractive, but other than this he looked much the same as he had fifteen years before. "Sit down, sit down and I shall read it to you."

"Wait, I have ordered chocolate, it will be coming soon." Hélène loved hot chocolate on winter afternoons. Chocolate had become quite the rage in Paris where it was ground and served as a very bitter brew processed with water much like coffee and staining the teeth of its devotees an unsavory brown. Within the chateau's kitchens, however, their cook had experimented by preparing it less strongly with milk and adding sugar; it had become an instant favorite.

Jean-Philippe pulled up a chair close to hers but placed it to catch the light from the fire as well as the candles on the mantel. He sat just as a knock on the door announced a maid who entered with a tea cart. She placed a tray at the duchess' disposal. It held a delicately shaped chocolate pot, with tall slender cups and saucers all hand painted in delicate pastels and edged in pure gold. There were several plates of canapés, confections, and sweet pastries as well.

The maid was dismissed and Hélène poured the chocolate as Jean-Philippe put on his reading spectacles and began to read.

Chartes Landing, New Jersey Colony
November 1699
Dear Ma-ma and Pa-pa... or should I say Grand-mère et Grand-père *once again.*

Marie has just given birth to another fine healthy boy and we have named him, James! He now takes his place with his brothers and sisters, John, Phillip, Helen, Louise, and Richard who must now give up his place as the baby of the family. James has no hair as yet, but a very lusty howl and an appetite like a frontiersman. All the children are well, healthy and growing. They send you their love and kisses.

Marie remains ever the best wife and partner any man could wish for in this new land and her sound health is a blessing which has never faltered. She continually delights my heart and has made us all a home of which any man could be well proud. I do not know how she manages it all by herself when the affairs of business take me away for a time, but she does and never complains. She still keeps watch over the little shoppe she established while running this busy household and growing family. She is a most patient mother but is not nearly as inclined to spoil the children as I am. And she has apprenticed several local youngsters to assist her in shop-keeping so they will continue to run things until she is on her feet again. We have asked Dufee to send us another girl to serve out an indenture contract by assisting with the nursery. Our current girl will finish her time of service soon and is to be married.

"It is so strange to me," Jean-Philippe interrupted himself, "how their servants can keep moving on. The servants here would not dare do such a thing."

"*Oui, oui,*" Hélène nodded, "but go on with the letter," she urged.

"Life here continues to be very good to us. The farm produces enough to feed this hungry brood and our apple orchards are doing especially well in this climate. I must admit to my frustration with the vineyard, however. Apple cider is refreshing but no substitute for fine French wine. No matter how I coax and toil, the harvest of the vine is always befouled in some manner and the resulting wine is undrinkable. The English excuse for wine is hardly any better and I would be most grateful if you could arrange a shipment from the old vineyards. It will serve to assure me that my palette has not died and to remind me just how superb a French wine can be. In the meanwhile, I have officially given up on ever having a winery of my own.

"My main business interests remain the lumber mill and the goods trading posts Richard and I established in the Great Lakes Wilderness. We always have some problem or other but that is life. This past summer one of them was burnt to the ground by a renegade Indian war party, but the profits the others took in more than made up for it. Fortunately, the old Frenchman who ran it for us escaped and re-established the site.

"People continue to pour into this land. Every ship brings another load and they push farther into the wilds toward the mountains running north and south to the west of us. This may sound strange to say, but although we live under English law, we do not live in a 'little England.' Whether we first come here as Englishmen or Frenchmen, Swede or German, Pole or Scot, there is a decided feeling here that we are all Americans, another breed altogether.

"Marie has long spoken excellent English and has now picked up a little German since a settlement of them trades at her store. Although our children understandably speak English as their first language, you would be proud at how well they are doing with their French lessons.

"We do not see Richard often these days. He spends much of his time going from outpost to outpost checking on our investments. He seems to enjoy his life of travel and roaming and tells me he has several native women who each keep a hut called a 'wigwam' for him. Thus, he always has a place to stay comfortably wherever he goes. I have long suspected that he has a variety of children along the trail as well, but we have never seen them. He deals with the Indians and our former countrymen and is content for me to remain closer to home within the English colonies. I am very glad to do so as it keeps me near my dear family.

"You would not recognize Richard. He has completely adapted to the savage frontier. Except for rare occasions, he wears only leather trousers and tunics cut in the Indian fashion. Some have most interesting beading on them which his women have done. And the children call him - 'Uncle Bear.'

"The area we settled in has changed dramatically over the years. Marie and I were speaking of it only the other evening. It is nothing like when she first arrived and bravely set up a little trading post on the edge of the wild. There is a proper town now with a main street of cobblestone laid out in an orderly fashion. To add to our church and its school, we now have an official civic building which doubles as a meeting house, a courtroom, and a jail. True civilization!

"The natural destruction of the harbor during the year of the great hurricane will keep us from ever being a port city to rival Boston or Charles Towne or even New York Towne. But keeping the community small and safe is not a bad thing. Each time I must go to New York, I find myself pleased that we are not growing too quickly. The larger communities have an undeniable problem with crime.

"Pa-pa, it is difficult to describe the atmosphere here in the colonies. Ever growing, changing, constantly in motion-this is the best way I can say it. Even in our little community. Marie and I were once in complete solitude in the harbor valley, now there are more than forty families in the area, mostly farming with a few skilled craftsmen in the town and, of course, my lumbermen. We have not had an official census yet but I would estimate an average of five to a family which is no doubt conservative. That would put our population at over 200. And we think in terms of the community here which is the only one our children know. The country of England is far away and has no reality to those here, especially those who are born here.

"The lumber mill remains very profitable. There is no shortage of demand. And much makes its way to England and the Low Countries. But the hillsides do look naked in their plowed little patches. It is sad in a way. The forests, which were so dense and green, are being slowly chopped away.

"Marie has just reminded me to assure you that I am quite well except for having lost a tooth this past year, but it was far to the back and its absence goes unnoticed. People here learn to combine many skills in order to make a living. The fellow who pulled my aching tooth is a perfect example.

In addition to his dental talents, he works as a barber, makes chest plasters for colds and complaints of the lungs, and serves as the local undertaker and coffin maker. Someone said recently that he is also thinking of starting a print shop.

"Americans are truly jacks-of-all-trades.

"Tomorrow this missive goes by packet to New York Towne, there to find it's way aboard whichever ship expects to make it to the shores of France the soonest.

"I know this will not reach you before Christmas but I hope it finds both of you very well and in the best of spirits and good health for the New Year.

With fondest affection, your most obedient son,
Jacques-Jean Charte Power, Jack of all Trades

Jean-Philippe fell silent, staring at the paper as though seeing the image of Jacques himself. Hélène stroked his arm and getting his attention gave him a cup of hot chocolate. He sipped the warm, creamy liquid.

"It is time," she said softly. He looked up at her in puzzlement. "We owe it to ourselves, my love. We should see our grandchildren at least once before we die."

"Do you mean...? To the colonies?"

"We are healthy and we have the means. You know your overseers can handle your affairs here in your absence." She looked at him with a sigh and spoke to what she could read in his eyes. "Oh, Jean-Philippe, I do not care about the hardships of travel, even if I am drowned at sea, it is worth the risk. And you heard what JJ said, it is very civilized now. Might it not be a wonderful adventure? Please... we could leave in early spring and personally deliver JJ the wine he has requested."

This was the first time in their entire lives that Hélène had ever asked anything of him. How could he refuse her? And he could not deny that he, too, wanted to see his son and meet his grandchildren.

"Very well, my love, we will go," he said with a smile of resolve and kissed her hand lovingly. "I will have to obtain the king's permission but, from what I understand, he is very enthusiastic about the growth of New France and the new colony of Louisiana..." Jean-Philippe paused in thought and sipped the hot cocoa. "I will state in my petition that I wish to look over investment opportunities in New France, which should be totally sufficient for approval."

Hélène smiled back at him. What a wonderfully perfect beginning to the New Year and the New Century.

Chapter 7

Chartes Landing - Spring

As the ship keeled to the port side and gracefully turned into the protection of the harbor, Hélène could immediately feel the change in the stability of the vessel. The heavy pitch and roll that had been their steady companion had suddenly ceased and just as quickly her stomach righted itself and regained a sense of composure. For weeks she had been living on the edge of nausea every waking moment of the day. If she had been younger she would have sworn she was pregnant. But she wanted to see her son so badly, she would not complain for all the world.

Jean-Philippe came up from the tween deck to stand beside her. He wore a finely tailored suit of tightly woven, deeply muted iridescent blue-green satin brocade that changed shades in the light like the sea itself. His soft white lace jabot and cuffs ruffled continuously in the breeze, like chains of albino butterflies, while his tricorner hat was wedged firmly upon his neat dark wig to keep from blowing off. The hat's black plumes stretched in the breeze like a cat stretching its tail. The overall effect was very youthful and Hélène looked up at him with a soft smile. French tailors were unsurpassed in making a man look so elegantly handsome.

The *Duc de Pouvoir* had spent the entire trip worrying about his beloved duchess and was delighted that their crossing had come to an end. He thought she was beginning to look overly thin and drawn. He had not seen her eat a decent meal since they had left the port city of *Havre de Grace* on the coast of France and she could not hide the fact that her beautiful gowns were hanging very loosely upon her.

"Is this it?" Hélène cried with excitement. "Have we arrived?"

"This is it," he confirmed, putting his arm protectively about her thin shoulders.

Hélène was suddenly besieged with emotions. Fifteen years ago she had watched her son say good-bye and back quietly out of her bedroom looking so brave, so handsome, and so very young. Could she have stood it if she had known that it would be fifteen long years before she would look upon him again? And that achieved only by crossing an ocean? It was indeed a blessing that the Almighty did not give mortals the ability to see clearly into the future. And it was also a blessing that she would indeed see her son again.

She had missed so much of his life. Now he had a wife and six children, and an entirely new existence carved out for himself in these colonies. A life in which she … they … had had no part. He even had a new name. After she and Jean-Philippe had wed, he had written that he was taking the English name *Power*. His father and mother were the Duke and Duchess of *Pouvoir*, so he, his wife and children would carry that name in the English form. English names, an English colony, a life Hélène had shared only in letters about a land so unlike home. How alien she was beginning to feel and for the first time Hélène questioned if they were doing the right thing in coming here. What if her daughter-in-law did not like her? What if she did not like her daughter-in-law? What if the children were undisciplined, spoiled and insufferable dullards?

Suddenly Hélène grasped her husband's arm and he looked at her with a reassuring smile as if he might have read her mind. She smiled back and tried to set aside her fears. Her stomach, which had been so queasy for so long, was now in a tight knot.

§

"Marie, come along now," Jacques called. "The children are all in the carriage, for what do you look?"

Marie, wearing a new muslin gown of deep gold, which brought out the gold in her eyes and hair, and which was covered in an airy pattern of tiny dark green flowers and vines, was looking at their house as if she were a visitor seeing it for the first time. Everything looked in order, the silver shined, the brass gleamed, the wood had a polished glow; there was no dust, no scattering of toys or papers. The flowers were fresh, the draperies hung evenly, the rugs had been well beaten, the hearths had been scrubbed, the lace curtains were recently laundered and starched, and, she sniffed, it smelled pleasantly fresh, in fact the smell of new wood still lingered.

When her husband had received the letter announcing that his parents were delivering a large stock of wine from the chateau cellars in person, he had immediately commenced upon an addition to the house which included a wine cellar and a bedroom suite complete with side rooms for a valet and a *fille de chambre*. The construction had been a maddening race against time and the clean up of all the ensuing dust and dirt had been an arduous task in itself. But Marie was now completely satisfied that all evidence had been successfully erased thanks in no small part to Jane Sims.

The Sims were still with them. They had worked out their contracts years ago but were content in their lives now as well paid servants to the young couple.

Marie turned, shifting the weight of the baby in her arms, and hurried out the door to Jacques and the awaiting carriage.

"Jacques, will there be enough room for your parents if we take all the children?" she asked as he helped her to her seat.

"We will make room," he replied smiling. "I would not have them miss their grandparents' arrival for want of a little carriage space. We can put them in our laps!" He jumped up into the driver's seat and flicked the rein as a signal to the horses who began pulling the large, open-air carriage with ease.

Marie sat with her back to Jacques on the seat facing the rear. She looked at the faces of her children sitting across from and next to her. John was eight and a half, tall for his age and looked more than ever like a miniature Jacques without the moustache. Phillip was seven and looked very much like his brother except he had very dark brown hair and dark eyes like her father. Helen, their oldest daughter, was six and Marie thought the child reminded her of her sister Juliette in looks, but hopefully she would not develop Juliette's temperament. Louise was almost five and destined to grow into a miniature Marie. Richard would soon be four. He had her lighter brown hair but his features were still so babyish it was impossible to tell who he would favor. And then there was baby James.

All the little faces looking at her were scrubbed pink. All the little heads of hair were combed and wore miniature tricorner hats or festive little bonnets. Only John and Phillip were in little suits and breeches like their father. All the dresses were pressed and clean. All the little boot-shoes, fitted onto dangling feet, were fastened and polished. Marie sighed in relief and could not help from dispensing just one last barrage of last minute instruction.

"Now, please, children, we want your grandparents to know what good children you are and how well you do with your French lessons. So please remember to speak only when you are spoken to, and say *'Oui, monsieur'* and *'Oui, madame.'* Do not forget *'s'il vous plait'* and *'merci beaucoup'*... and remember to curtsy or bow as we practiced."

"Marie," Jacques pulled the horses to a slower pace and turned in his seat. Reaching down he grabbed her hand and pulling it up to his lips, he gave it a kiss. "Relax, *ma chérie,*" he said softly, "they are going to adore you and our children."

She looked up at him, saw the love in his eyes, took a breath and with a smile she gave him a nod of agreement. Still she could not help but readjust her own bonnet self-consciously.

Jacques had timed it perfectly. The carriage arrived at the wharf just as the ship was being eased alongside the wharf. He helped Marie down from the carriage as she held the baby. In turn he assisted each of the children out onto the street to stand around their mother's skirts, the older ones holding the hands of the younger ones. With a parting instruction to wait right there while he went to get their grandparents, he turned and walked to the end of the pier.

Hélène saw her son first. She could not believe her eyes. He looked to her exactly as he had fifteen years ago. She waved from up on deck and saw him waving back enthusiastically.

"Ma-ma!" he cried out as she was assisted down the gangplank and onto the pier. He rushed in, picked her up and swung her around full circle while she laughed and cried. He set her down and soundly kissed both her cheeks.

"JJ...oh, JJ," she hugged him tightly, unable to speak, kissing him repeatedly and weeping.

Jean-Philippe followed up closely behind and joined them, embracing his son with feeling. For a few moments all three stood clinging to each other.

"Pa-pa," Jacques said, kissing his father on both cheeks, a lump in his throat.

"You look well, Jacques, very well," the older man said, his voice heavy with emotion. They parted a little and he kissed his son's cheeks more formally in return.

"And so do you," Jacques grinned with tears in his own eyes. "Welcome to the New World," he added cavalierly, "or at least, to my little corner of it."

Hélène could not stop looking at her son. She drank in the sight of him like the desert drinks a spring rain. All these years with only images in her mind to sustain her, the memories had blurred between Jacques the boy, the youth and the man. And now here he was in the flesh, speaking and breathing. Warm and alive. It was a sterling moment.

As she continued to look, she missed nothing. He was not exactly the same, she corrected herself, but then how could he be? He was thirty-five now, a mature man who wore his years extremely well. He was somehow broader of shoulder and more muscular than the youth of twenty she remembered. He had the appearance of solidity and strength. There was nothing flabby about him she was pleased to note, his belly was flat as a board and there was no paunchy roll around his middle like the dissipated young men of the French aristocracy. And he looked so mature, so wise. She smiled broadly. His face was developing those little character lines that always make men look even more handsome. And his hair had darkened a little perhaps, but was as thick as her father's had always been. Finally able to tear her eyes away, she glanced up at her husband.

"He looks so well," she murmured as if to reassure herself that Jean-Philippe could see Jacques-Jean also, that she was not dreaming up an apparition.

Jean-Philippe nodded and smiled. "Yes, my dear, yes, he does."

Hélène took her son's arm on one side and her husband's on the other. She enjoyed the feeling of solid ground beneath her feet but she savored the feeling of walking arm in arm with the two most precious people in her life. Together they walked to where Marie and the children were patiently waiting.

As they approached, Marie felt her heart leap into her throat and her knees shake just a trifle beneath her layers of petticoats. The richly dressed man and woman before her looked like something out of a fairy tale or off the fashion plates printed in Paris.

"Ma-ma, Pa-pa, may I present my wife, Marie," Jacques said proudly and took the baby from Marie's arms. She immediately dropped a deep curtsy. Hélène went to the younger woman with both arms outstretched, urging her to stand tall. Grasping Marie's hands, Hélène leaned in to kiss each cheek.

"You are lovely, my dear," she said warmly. "I have so wanted to meet you ever since my son wrote of your marriage. I am glad the Lord saw fit to grant me the blessing of finally being able to do so. JJ writes nothing but praises of you and how happy you make him. And I am very happy that he is happy."

Marie blushed, feeling her cheeks turn hot.

Jean-Philippe stepped forth at that moment and kissed each flaming cheek. "I wish we could have been at your wedding," he said, "but better late than never, *n'est-ce pas*? I am pleased that we meet you now. And I can see that my son has his father's appreciative eye for beauty," he added gallantly, kissing his daughter-in-law's hand.

Jacques radiated high spirits.

"And this little one is James," he said proudly holding up his youngest son. There were more kisses and coos as the baby grunted and made unintelligible slobber sounds.

The rest of the children had been quietly watching and listening to the adults speaking in their parents' native tongue. They understood most of what had been said and enough to know when their father began to introduce them. On cue each stepped forward one by one, the boys removing their hats and presenting a leg in their best version of a courtly bow, while each girl dropped a deep curtsy all to the obvious delight and amusement of the older couple.

Jacques finally excused himself to check on the prior arrangements made for a hired rig to pick up and deliver the travel trunks, the shipment of wine, and his parents' personal servants.

"It is an honor to have you come to visit," Marie began nervously. "Was the crossing difficult?"

"We had good weather and I am told we traveled at good speed but I am afraid ocean voyages do not agree with my stomach," Hélène confided in a manner meant to set the younger woman at ease. "To have the solid ground beneath my feet again feels very good even if it does seem to rock a bit."

"It is called 'returning to your land legs.' The sensation will soon go away but I am so sorry to hear of your discomfort. We must take some time to rebuild your appetite," Marie said sympathetically. "I have some herbal teas that may help and you must have a long, long visit to make the tedious journey worthwhile."

"Oh, I can assure you, it is already well worthwhile, is it not, *Grand-père?*" Hélène turned to her husband. "I have noticed those worried looks you have been giving me. But as you can see I have survived the trip in one piece. And is it not beyond wonderful to see our son and his family?"

"Of course, of course," Jean-Philippe agreed, relaxing a little as he observed a little color beginning to return to his wife's delicate face.

"What beautiful children!" Hélène exclaimed clasping her lace gloved hands together under her chin. "I cannot believe these are my very own *grandchildren!*" The endearing lady began setting the children at ease by engaging them in simple conversation with easy questions they could reply to confidently. By the time they had all piled into the carriage, everyone was sufficiently relaxed for the smallest tots to have no hesitation in sitting on their grandparents' laps while John rode up in the driver's seat beside his father.

The ride home was not a long one and Jacques was delighted with the approving looks he saw upon his parents' faces as they entered the neat, curved drive before the three story wood structure he and Marie called home. When everyone had stepped out of the carriage, the smallest children were led away by Sarah, the new nursery maid, while Sims took the horses and conveyance back to the carriage house and stable. Marie and Jacques with sons, John and Phillip, were free to give the duke and duchess a quick tour around their home, most especially the new wine cellar and the grounds.

Finally, they ended up in the back garden. It was neatly kept with defining hedges and mature rose bushes not yet in bloom, while a gay array of spring flowers had burst forth in pastel splendor. The most arresting feature of the back garden, however, was the commanding view of the river valley below on the one side and the harbor town on the other. The duke and duchess were delighted.

"It is hard to believe," Jean-Philippe said shaking his head appraisingly, "and you say none of this was here when you first arrived?"

"Nothing, Pa-pa. This was wilderness, as wild as you can imagine. Nothing but thick forests. The home of wild animals and the natives."

"Oh, yes, you have written about the natives," said Hélène, "what has become of them?"

"Those that are left have gone deeper into the continent," replied Marie. "We have taken their home, replaced their way of life with our own and I do not think they especially thank us for it."

Her in-laws looked at her with curiosity.

"Jacques, we really should bring some chairs out so your parents can sit down. We cannot keep them standing."

"Yes, yes, of course," Jacques sprang into action calling to his older sons to man the doors and the servants to assist in bringing out some comfortable chairs and placing them in the shade where a pleasant breeze was blowing.

"Have you actually met any of them?" Hélène questioned when they were all seated.

"Oh, but of course," replied Marie, "John was born in an Indian village."

"What?" Hélène gasped lightly and turned to her son. "You never told us that."

"There is always so much to write," Jacques shrugged sheepishly.

Jean-Philippe chuckled quietly.

"The red men come in different types," explained Jacques. "Some are quite savage, they live to wage war and with them there will always be trouble and no peace until they are completely conquered. Others are peaceful enough but want little to do with the white man. And still others are quite friendly. Marie's first trading customers here were from a peaceful tribe that lived nearby. She even had one brave who was quite taken with her," he added playfully, "although I had the distinct impression he did not think much of me."

"Really?" Hélène's eyes opened wide.

Marie blushed slightly. She was not going to tell her newly arrived in-laws upon just meeting them that a native had offered to mate with her, although she had told Jacques the story years ago. "His name was Son-of-Sky-Hawk and he brought his sister to live with me through a winter when I was all alone and had become very melancholy. That may have saved my life. I did not realize at the time how dangerous the solitude can be when one is completely alone on the frontier through the winter. A kind of madness sets in."

"You were all alone for an entire winter?" Hélène's eyes were now perfectly round. "*C'est terrible!* It is like being imprisoned without even a jailer, *n'est-ce pas?*"

"Yes, that is very well put," Marie nodded. "But I was not alone for the whole winter, thank the Lord. I had been on my own since the spring and had expected Jacques and Richard to return in the autumn but they never made it. Winter set in and we later learned that Son-of-Sky-Hawk used to watch to see my chimney smoke rise above the trees."

"Oh," Hélène gasped quietly.

"You have no idea how very cold it can get here in the winter. It is a cold that can numb your mind very quickly. Some winters are worse than others, of course, and this was a bad one. My fire went out while I was sleeping. I could have easily frozen in my sleep. Son-of-Sky-Hawk realized what had happened and would not allow me to stay alone after that. The isolation does strange things."

"How extraordinary," Hélène exclaimed softly.

"His sister, She-Who-Laughs-In-Her-Sleep ..."

"What an odd name," Jean-Philippe interjected.

"Well, that is the translation. In their language, it was shorter. I called her 'Sheehoo'; she stayed with me for the rest of the winter. She taught me a great deal about the plants and herbs one can find here."

"And where were you that winter?" Hélène looked to her son.

"That was the year Richard and I were lost in the wilderness and we met up with the Indian Giles who spoke perfect French by the way," Jacques answered.

"*Lost* in the wilderness?" Jean-Philippe repeated.

"Yes," Jacques grinned seeing his father's shocked expression. "Well, it is a long story, Pa-pa. I will tell it after supper. But there is no need to worry, Ma-ma. I do not go into the wilderness anymore you see, I am a perfect homebody."

Marie had risen, graciously gesturing to the men to remain seated, and she slipped her hand along Jacques' shoulder in a look and gesture that eloquently said she was extremely pleased that he was now a homebody. "If you will excuse me, I must check with the cook," she said.

Leaving her husband to visit with his parents, Marie went to the kitchen, now a sturdy brick building to the back of the house. Margot, their indentured cook, was readying a serving cart with tea. As Marie inquired into the preparations for supper, she deftly mixed a separate blend of tea for a second pot and added boiling water.

With the help of Margot's young daughter, Marie conveyed the loaded cart around to the garden. It made a splendid sight laid out beautifully with a variety of treats amid snowy napkins and fresh flower blooms.

"Supper is still several hours away, but Margot has prepared a wonderful tea for us," she announced hospitably, first pouring out a cup of the special blend for her mother-in-law. "Please, may I suggest a cup of this," she said graciously, handing Hélène a small china cup and saucer. "It has among other things a zest of mint and will stimulate your appetite."

Hélène accepted the dainty cup, sniffed and took a taste. "It is quite lively," she said agreeably and sipped more. Marie encouraged the other woman to at least taste something more from the tray but Hélène waved her hand in a sign of polite refusal. "It all looks very appealing, my dear, and very elegant, but my stomach begs for a little more time."

"Of course," Marie replied and served her father-in-law and Jacques.

"May I make you a plate, m'lord," Marie offered as she handed Jean-Philippe his cup of tea. Jacques deferred to his father who nodded at Marie.

"As I recall you love escargot in butter sauce," Jacques said helpfully.

"*Oui...* you have escargot?" Jean-Philippe replied, now sitting up to peer at the tray and cart.

"And goose liver *pâté*," Jacques smiled broadly. "We have a few amenities in our savage wilderness." Marie took the hints and began filling a small plate, first with escargot and then *pâté*. "Do not forget some pressed duck with the raspberry glacé."

While Marie finished arranging a small plate full of food, she relayed the news that the hauling cart had arrived with the travel trunks, wine, and servants.

Jean-Philippe accepted his plate.

"Sims is seeing that the wine goes into the cellar and Jane has shown the ser-vants the way to your parents' rooms. I believe they are unpacking," Marie smiled at her husband, very glad that he had decided to build on for their visitors.

"Oh, but this is quite excellent!" Jean-Philippe exclaimed over the plate of food. "Hélène, my dearest, you must taste... just a little," he coaxed. "Jacques, where on earth did you find your cook?"

"Margot? Why, she is serving out an indenture. I found her on the block in New York Towne. She sold her culinary services for twelve years to bring her son and daughters to the colonies for a better life. The woman is a marvel, *n'est-ce pas?* And now her daughter Cassandra works for my wife and I have employed her son at the mill. Wait until you taste her cream puffs," he lightly kissed his finger tips in a charming gesture. "Divine! If I were not already married, I would have to marry the woman."

"She is not married?" Jean-Philippe asked in disbelief. "A woman who can cook like this?"

"A widow," said Jacques with another typical Gallic shrug.

"This is nothing... mere trifles," Marie joined in, comfortable in the knowledge that Margot was ten years older than Jacques, gray haired and quite plump. "Wait until you enjoy what she is preparing for supper," she added merrily.

"Please, my darling," Jean-Philippe turned again to Hélène. "You love *pâté*, just try a little," he continued to coax and hand fed Hélène a bite.

"It is very delicious," she said trying to sound appreciative. "Really it is, but I am more exhausted by the excitement and the voyage than I realized. If you do not mind terribly, I would like to go to my room and lie down for just a short while."

"Of course, Ma-ma, of course." Jacques sprang to his feet. "Pa-pa, you stay and relax. I will show Ma-ma to your rooms."

"Yes, Jean-Philippe, stay and enjoy yourself. Tonight when I finally get a decent sleep without the rocking of the ship, I am sure I will begin to feel much more like my old self again." Hélène took her son's arm and together they went into the house.

Marie watched them leave and turned back to the duke to see the lines of worry on his face as he, too, watched his son and wife disappear from sight. "Do not worry, m'lord," she said softly. "M'lady is in good hands. She can relax and rest as much as she wants now. The teas will help and I will watch over her."

"She has lost so much weight," Jean-Philippe said quietly.

"Then we will just put some back on her."

Jean-Philippe turned to look solidly at his daughter-in-law appreciating her attempts to uplift his spirits. "Now, what is this *m'lord* and *m'lady*, eh? Does our son call us m'lord and m'lady?"

"No... but..."

"But, nothing. He is our son. And you, my dear, are now our daughter. I speak for both of us, please call us *Ma-ma et Pa-pa*."

"*Oui*," Marie nodded and since he continued to hold her with his keen eyes, she added a soft, "Pa-pa."

And with that Jean-Philippe patted her hand and tried to mask his concerns for his wife.

Hélène slept longer than she intended and when, upon waking, she expressed too great a fatigue to dress and dine with the others, Lotti, her attentive *fille de chambre*, brought a tray to her mistress. After drinking a little broth tea and consuming a few bites of sweetbread, the exhausted lady fell back into a deep slumber. No longer sustained by nervous energy or the remarkable power of her will focused on seeing her son, Hélène's body was finally capitulating to the overwhelming exhaustion created by the rigors of the long ocean voyage without adequate nutrition. Her subconscious had taken over and invoked a self-preserving shut down that demanded rest and nourishment.

Lotti was left to remove the bed tray, tsk-ing in concern for her mistress' state and reporting to an anxious duke that his wife was by all appearances well, without fever, but was once again in a deep sleep. This pattern continued for more than twenty-four hours. Progress was marked by how long Hélène was reported to have been able to stay awake and how much of the nutrient rich food she had been able to eat before beginning another sleep cycle.

Instinctively, Marie felt this was a normal response to the culmination of hardships endured on the long voyage, especially for someone so delicate and of the duchess' age. Did a baby not spend the majority of its time eating and sleeping after its traumatic voyage into the world? As long as the duchess was eating and was lucid, what harm could there be in her finally getting the sleep she so obviously needed? Jacques was reassured by his wife's reasoning and together they convinced the duke that this was not something about which to become overly anxious.

"Give her time, Pa-pa," Jacques spoke encouragingly as he put his hand affectionately on his father's shoulder and the duke nodded, contenting himself with stealing into the bedroom periodically to watch his beloved for a few moments as she slumbered.

Late morning of the third day the odd hibernation came to an end. Hélène awoke and called her maid with the summons of a small bell. The duchess was ravenous and wanted breakfast as soon as possible. Lotti recognized a difference and excitedly returned with a tray heavy with fresh fruits, baked short breads, cheeses, fresh butter, jams, an egg soufflé, slices of cold ham and plenty of Marie's delightful tea.

Attacking her food with a voluptuary's appreciation, Hélène ate as she sat within her bed clothing and instructed her little maid to pull back the draperies, open the windows and allow the sunshine and fresh breezes to bathe the room. In the distance, the sounds of children playing and laughing, rose and fell like a soft wave upon the window sill reminding Hélène that she had family here with which to acquaint herself and she was wasting precious time.

As she ate, Lotti laid out fresh undergarments and was now in the process of shaking out a new day dress, actively inspecting it to assure herself no wrinkles had escaped her notice.

"Ohhhh," Hélène groaned slightly, licking the last pungently flavored bit of jam from the corner of her mouth and waving her hand delicately, "take it away, Lotti. I have eaten like a sow and should be thoroughly ashamed of myself."

"Not at all, Madame," Lotti clucked, shaking her head as she immediately removed the tray, "for weeks you have eaten barely enough to keep a bird alive. It is wonderful to see your appetite return."

"Ah, yes, it is," Hélène stretched luxuriously in the featherbed. "I feel so... rested. Lotti, what time is it? I cannot see the clock from here."

"It is the tenth hour, Madame."

"Mid-morning?" Hélène pondered quietly. "I thought it was much later... but then... Lotti?"

"Yes, Madame."

"What day is this?"

"Day, Madame?"

"Yes. Was it yesterday that we arrived here?"

"Oh, no, Madame, it was the day before yesterday," the maid assured her with a nod and a small smile.

"The day before? I have been sleeping all this time? No wonder I feel rested. Where is *Monsieur le duc?*"

"He has been up for hours, Madame. He forbade me to wake you and went out with Monsieur Jacques-Jean. He said he would be home by midday to check on you."

Hélène stretched again, then sniffed delicately under her arm. "Oh, my," she said softly and suddenly went from languid to intense energy. "Come Lotti, I need hot water, lots of it. I want to refresh myself and we must wash the sea salt out of my hair. I am ready to see this new world we have come to and get to know my grandchildren. You must help me to dress now for I am eager to see everyone."

"Yes, Madame, I will take out the tray and bring your water. Madame Marie will be so happy to hear you are feeling well. She has asked after you frequently."

Two hours later, Hélène emerged from the new wing looking younger and happier to be alive than she had looked for some time. Catching herself almost girlishly bouncing in her steps, she smiled broadly. Life was good.

Marie had just come in from picking a fresh bouquet of flowers for the entry hall and Jacques and his father could be heard walking up the gravel path from the stable yard. Everyone seemed to converge upon the main hall at once.

"Bon jour, bon jour," Hélène called out as she glided through the hall of the wing.

"Bon jour, Ma-ma," Jacques responded as he held the door open for his father and looked very pleased to see his mother.

"Bon jour, Ma-ma," Marie echoed her husband.

"Bon jour, ma chérie," Jean-Philippe smiled broadly. He was slow to speak but his eyes lit up at the sight of his wife and the worry frown rolled off his face and was gone.

"Oh, what a magnificent day and I have slept half of it away! You must forgive me, but there did not seem to be any help for it." Hélène's eyes sparkled and she was exceedingly light on her feet, her skirts swaying as she crossed over to Jean-Philippe first and bestowed a kiss upon his cheek, then went on to her son and to Marie.

"You look wonderful, Ma-ma, have you eaten?" Jacques asked.

"Like a pig, I confess," she laughed lightly.

"Excellent!" Jean-Philippe sighed in relief.

"But I have been sleeping for days I am told. I feel like I have missed everything. Where have you been, what have you seen without me?" she chattered like a girl. "I do not want to miss anything. I want to see everything, too."

"Ah, my darling, so you shall. Jacques and I just went for a ride in the countryside. We shall go again another time and you shall see. But for today, our son had horses that needed the exercise and, you know it has been a good while since I have been in the saddle; I craved a ride. We had a good time canvassing the lay of the land. Jacques was going to show me the mill next. Are you up to coming along?"

"Of course, of course. You could not keep me from coming with you," she said enthusiastically then turned to Marie. "I do not know what you put into your teas but I feel amazingly well. Thank you, so much, my dear."

"You are more than welcome, but what you needed most was the rest."

"No-no-no, there is something quite special about that brew," she said taking her bonnet from Lotti. "I can tell. Come, come. What? Are you not coming with us?" Hélène asked as she adjusted her bonnet on top of her somewhat lavishly coiffed hair. She noticed Marie was not putting on her own hat.

"Jacques will take you to see the mill and perhaps you can come to see the store. I have a few instructions to give Margot regarding supper this evening and then I must go to the store and take care of a few details... if you do not mind?"

"Mind? No-no, of course not. You go do whatever you must," Hélène responded cheerfully. "We will meet you there later."

Jacques took a moment to kiss his wife both hello and good-bye before he left with his parents.

Hélène leaned fondly on Jean-Philippe's arm as they walked out to the carriage house. She looked up at him with her large gray eyes full of mischief and spoke quietly, for his ears only. "Tonight, *mon petit chou*, you must remember that it has also been a long time since *I* have had a ride." She smiled a bit wickedly.

Jean-Philippe returned her smile with a wink and squeezed her hand.

The self-made American proudly guided his parents, who attracted more than a little attention in their rich finery and *haute couture*, around the saw mill and his lumber business. After experiencing the hurricane, William Boot had moved his family farther into the interior and was content to manage a lumber camp far up the river, regularly sending the logs down to the mill. The duke and duchess stood like fashion plates but bemused, wide eyed, and near speechless to see a large delivery of logs floating down the river totally unattended, only to be corralled by the expert lumbermen as the logs reached the mouth of the tributary stream. From the water the roughly pruned tree trunks were lifted and loaded onto transports to be delivered to the mill.

"*Je vous présente Monsieur Francois Nicholet,*" Jacques introduced the man formally in French. "Francois has been with me since I hired the first crew, before we even had a mill. A good man. He also is a Huguenot and is now my mill manager and can get more out of the men with words of encouragement than I have ever seen done with threats and a whip."

Nicholet looked pleased but slightly embarrassed at the praise as Jacques turned to him and introduced his parents.

"I would like you to meet the *Duc et Duchesse du Pouvoir, mon mere et père.*"

Francois bowed deeply to Jean-Philippe and Hélène. "It is an honor and a privilege, *Monsieur le duc*," he said and turned to kiss Hélène's hand. *"Enchanté, Madame la duchesse,"* he said with another bow. It was obvious that he was pleased to have been given the honor of the introduction and equally pleased to be able to speak his native tongue again.

"I do feel compelled to say, lest anyone get the wrong idea... no threats or whips have ever been employed on my estates."

"No-no, Pa-pa, I did not mean you…"

"But the same could not be said for your brother," Hélène offered.

"Your point is well made, Jacques. You have a very efficient operation here," the duke observed. "You must forgive us if we gape a little; to see so much lumber all in one place is a little overwhelming."

"I understand, *Monsieur le duc.* The bounty of the New World can be very overwhelming," Francois said in his affable Gallic manner.

Jean-Philippe nodded.

"And may I ask, *Monsieur le duc*," Francois went on, "how go things in France these days? It has been many years since I left and I have no contacts to keep me personally informed."

"Things are..." Jean-Philippe glanced at Jacques, "not as they used to be but not as bad as they once were since the death of the *Marquis de Louvoir.* And our king is in good health."

"So Louvoir is dead," Nicholet said quietly, not at all interested in the king's health. "The Devil now has a Minister of War. I hope he burns in Hell." The sudden intensity of his emotion took them all by surprise. "Forgive me, Madame," he quickly apologized to Hélène. "I must ask pardon for my indelicacy. Louvoir with his policies was a very personal enemy."

"Monsieur," Hélène addressed the bitterness she saw etched in what had been a very pleasant face without it, "Louvoir had many enemies. Sometimes the best revenge is to step above the injustices and to replace all the unpleasant old memories with more pleasant new ones. No one can stop you from being happy here... except yourself."

Hélène saw a reaction in Nicholet's eyes. Her words had struck a cord for him. Thoughtfully he nodded. These were not platitudes. She spoke with the authority of one who had also suffered. Suddenly, it dawned upon Nicholet exactly what was at hand. This was a Catholic French duke visiting his Huguenot son who lived in an English colony, a son who should by all rights be his heir. His mind filled in the missing details. So, they, too, had reasons to hate Louvoir. He would store away the duchess's words and draw them out later when he was alone and could think on them.

It was apparent that the solitary French expatriate kept the mill going in good order for his employer. The duke observed the respect the other workers showed the man and it was obvious that they liked Nicholet although he retained a reserve and kept a distance from them. Whatever scarring memories he had brought with him to the New World, Jean-Philippe suspected Nicholet kept them to himself.

Having seen the working of the mill, Jacques next took his parents on a slow tour of the little town which had grown up and away from the harbor. From the carriage, he explained how the harbor had been and pointed out what had changed with the hurricane. There were sand bars all over now and the navigable channel was narrow and did not allow for much in the way of traffic. Unable to host a number of ships at one time, growth into a port city of any real size was impossible. Instinctively, people built farther and farther inland as the town became more of a center for the farming community with the sea being the back door instead of the front. Jean-Philippe and Hélène listened in rapped attention at Jacques' vivid description of the storm called a *hurricane*, a word taken from the islands of the West Indies. Having never experienced one they found it somewhat difficult to comprehend. Did they experience that kind of shocking weather often, the duke and duchess inquired? No, their son assured them, they had not seen another storm of its like since. But those that had seen it would never forget it.

The next stop on the tour was Marie's store where they found her.

"But this is not little," was Hélène's first comment as they stepped through the door of the "Chartes Landing General Store." The building itself stood on the corner of two intersecting streets and was a full two stories high. The corner location allowed for large windows on two fronts providing ample room for display to the street. "However do you keep up with all your merchandise?" the tiny woman asked as she looked all around her at the shelves and displays dividing up goods of every sort and nature.

Marie smiled proudly. "Only this floor is merchandise," she explained. "The upstairs is divided between storage and living quarters which I rent out. It has an outdoor stairway for the apartment in the back and someone is always looking for a place to stay until they can get themselves settled."

"Very impressive," Hélène murmured as her eyes slowly wandered over the colors, textures, and shapes of the goods all around her. Then, she looked back at her daughter-in-law. "You are quite a business woman, I think. JJ, my dear, I had no idea. Your letters never described your wife's business properly. You wrote of '*une petite shoppe*,' I always pictured - a small shoppe."

Jacques looked at his mother with a grin reminiscent of his youth and shrugged.

"This is not little at all," Hélène continued looking at Marie, "no wonder you need two clerks to help you."

It was Marie's turn to feel proud as she showed her in-laws around. One section of the store was devoted completely to farm supplies, seed, feed, and tools of all kinds, including ropes, nails, harnesses, and the like. Next to it were housewares, displaying just about everything one might need in setting up housekeeping, including dishes, crockery, pots, kettles, teapots, utensils, tableware, candles and holders, a variety of lamps and lanterns, oils, along with the molds housewives needed to make tapers for themselves. There were also blankets, linens, and small bits of furniture such as stools; most furniture as a rule needed to be ordered and shipped in from New York, Boston, or Charles Towne where furniture makers thrived. There was an abundance of beautiful wood available in the colonies and furniture shipped from Europe was too expensive for the average household. These two sections comprised the majority of the store.

The area immediately around one large marble counter-top was food stocks, everything from flour, salt, spices, and coffee to candies and sweets. In a far corner, Marie had a small display of bonnets and bags, as well as bolts of materials and ribbons in every color imaginable. Yarns, threads, buttons, needles, pins, hooks, tape measures, everything for sewing garments and making linens. An opposite corner catered to the gentlemen with shirts, scarves and handkerchiefs, sturdy linen breeches and stockings, replacement stocks and cuffs, workman's hats, tool aprons and vests, pipes, tobacco, moustache wax, suspenders, and anything else a gentleman might need, short of outer garments. Suits and boots could be commissioned from the local tailor, cobbler, and leather worker. And since few in the settlement ever wore wigs, they needed to be purchased in New York Towne. There was another counter of glossy red cherry wood upon which one found paper-stock, foolscap, parchment, quills and inks, small journals, writing mats, pastes, sealing waxes, and writing salts. A very small area of shelving was devoted to books, mostly primers for children or anyone who wished to learn to read and write English. And another section displayed toiletries of rich but limited assortment. Finely milled French soaps, creamy soothing lotions, delicate scents, assorted mirrors, brushes, combs, cosmetics, powders and talc as well as unguents, ointments and curatives were on display.

"But you have many shoppes all under one roof," exclaimed Hélène.

"I have had to carry everything," Marie explained. "I have been the only store for many years, it is common in the colonies. It is what is called an *emporium* or general store. Now, of course, we have a tailor and a cobbler down the street. And a blacksmith. And the town does have several seamstresses these days but they buy their supplies from me also. I enjoy going to New York Towne and finding new merchandise to bring in. We mostly only see packet boats here but at least they come, the larger ships coming in straight from Europe do not like our harbor. It is too easy to go aground."

"Do you bring everything from New York?" Hélène asked inquisitively.

"We used to but that is changing as well. It is less expensive if I can buy directly off a packet boat. The flour and meal now comes from the local mill but the only customers for it are those who do not already raise the crops themselves. And I do not really do a lot of business in things like soaps and candles because many housewives make their own. It is surprising the way the demand changes. I remember when my best selling items were animal traps. Now, the wild animals are disappearing from the area. Catching rabbits that eat your garden is about all the trapping that is done anymore.

"The biggest demand now is for the manufactured items which we cannot make here… pots, pans, dishes, mirrors, and, of course, farming implements although now that we have a blacksmith, that which is already owned can be fixed or restored. Yard goods are always in demand - good sturdy canvas, linen, cotton calico and Lindsey-Wolsey. You will not see many silks and satins worn in our settlement," Marie chuckled. "And always I must have spices but since they cost dearly, everyone is very frugal with them."

Hélène nodded her head in understanding. "But the ship that brought us came directly here," she said in puzzlement.

"Oh, yes, Dufee, bless him. Thanks to his friendship with Jacques through Richard, Dufee will still send his ship directly here when we have a load of lumber for him. And when it comes, it brings us goods directly from Europe but that is only in harmony with the lumber production."

Hélène looked as though she did not understand and Marie continued.

"I can only order so much merchandise for there is only so much I can sell. The growth of my business is very dependent upon the growth of the town and I am afraid we will never grow very large with the harbor as it now is. It is only expected that Dufee must see to his larger customers first."

Hélène nodded her head and then looked around. "Where have Jean-Philippe and JJ gone?"

"Oh … I think they may be at the bakery next door."

"I thought I smelled something delicious. Is it part of your building? Do they rent from you?"

Marie smiled, "Not exactly."

Ten minutes later Hélène let herself into the bakery shop where she found Jacques and his father having a cup of coffee and a pastry.

"I just heard the most marvelous story," Hélène exclaimed as the men rose to greet her. Jacques assisted his mother in being seated at the small table. "Did you know our daughter-in-law built an oven all by herself when she was alone on the frontier just so she could make good French bread?"

"Where is Marie?" Jacques asked.

"Oh, she will be along shortly... she had to talk to her clerk," Hélène replied dismissively, eager to get back to her story. "From that oven she began selling her bread to the new settlers who could only make something called *cornbread* for themselves, and from that beginning she now has someone still baking each day at the oven and they bring the bread here to sell. Oh, and when the Indians came by they tried to touch her yeast dough and she slapped them away and they gave her an Indian name that meant Woman-Who-Fights-On-Her-Bread or something like that." Hélène was laughing gaily. "Is that not the most marvelous story?"

"You mean she has baked all this?" Jean-Philippe asked sweeping a gesture to include all the bakery goods for sale in the shop. "When does she have time?"

"No-no, Pa-pa," Jacques sought to clarify. "She has taught someone else how to bake the bread at her old oven and truthfully, it has gained quite a reputation but the pastry chef here is our cook's eldest daughter."

"A woman?" Jean-Philippe asked in surprise.

Just then Marie walked in, nodding an acknowledgment to her in-laws. "Excuse me just one moment," she said and went over to the clerk behind the counter. "Hello Prudence, how did we do today?"

"Very good, ma'am. We sold out of the bread by mid-morning and you can see there isn't much else left."

"Good!" Marie looked around. "We can start with all fresh tomorrow. Now, please close out the cash box for me for the day. My husband's parents are visiting us so I will be a little off my usual routines but no matter. Please tell Deborah we cannot sell what we do not have, she needs to make even more bread tomorrow, and baguettes. And tell Cassandra I think we should have some pies this week. Why do you not take these little cakes home for your children, if they sit another day they will be stale.

"Yes, ma'am. Thank you."

Marie came back to the table and sat down.

Jean-Philippe's mouth was open in astonishment. "Those are your employees? This is your bakery?"

Marie nodded modestly. "But Jacques has helped me."

"Not really," he protested. "I only ordered a good iron oven and saw to its installation. Her baker, Cassandra, can now bake the pastries here."

"And you had the men build the shelter over my outdoor oven," Marie reminded him.

"Remarkable," Jean-Philippe said quietly. He was not at all used to seeing women run real businesses.

"Jacques," Marie said quietly as they prepared to leave. "I just heard some terrible news of which I think you should be aware."

"What is that?" he asked looking at her with a concerned frown.

"Mistress Boot is dead."

The duke and duchess tried not to listen but they could not help but hear. "Indians?" exclaimed the duchess with a gasp which immediately set Jacques to wondering if the entire camp had been attacked.

"No-no," replied Marie quickly. "That big healthy girl just died in childbirth."

"*O, mon Dieu! C'est triste!* How sad!" her in-laws voiced almost in unison and the duke made the sign of the cross. They did not know the woman but it was always tragic when childbirth took a mother's life.

Marie turned again to Jacques. "Will you be going up river to William to give him our condolences in person? If so, I will pack food baskets for you to take along. You must find out if there is anything we can do."

"Yes, yes, I should go," Jacques agreed.

"Their oldest was the first child to be born here," Marie explained to her in-laws. "He is a year and a half or so older than John. Oh, this is so very sad," she lamented with a frown.

"Pa-pa, do you feel like taking a small boat ride up river with me tomorrow?" Jacques asked. "If we make an early start we can be back within the day."

Jean-Philippe brightened at the prospect of the adventure and then was reminded of the sober circumstances. "If the situation were not tragic, I would say I am delighted to accept."

Chapter 8

When Jacques and Jean-Philippe landed at the lumber base camp, they found William Boot a broken man dealing with his grief in the only way he knew how – by going about as if nothing had changed. A freshly dug grave, however, was very visible in a grassy spot above the clearing. The children, Thor, Rega, and Ansel, stood abnormally quiet, red-eyed, weepy, and looking disconcertingly apprehensive while the tiny new baby lying in the big Swede's arm appeared half dead.

"William," Jacques called an informal greeting as he approached the giant man. "I came as soon as I heard. I am so sorry. You should have sent me word directly."

"With all respect, it is not your concern, sir. The work gets done. That is all you need to …"

"William, William," Jacques said kindly. "Please, can we sit a moment and talk? Please? Marie sent this for the children," he held up two large baskets of food. "And this is my father who is visiting from France. May I introduce you to…"

Jean-Philippe cut his son short. "Tell him to call me Jean-Philippe," he said quickly, instinctively forestalling any formalities as he held out his hand in the American way. "Tell him how much I regret hearing of his terrible loss."

Jacques translated and added, "Pa-pa does not speak English."

William shook the elder man's hand and accepted the baskets with a nod and pointed to a table set up outside his small cottage. "Pleased to meet you sir, but sorry to say I am ill prepared for visitors."

I am not here in regards to issues of work, William," Jacques continued sympathetically. "I have no concerns in that regard. I suspect work is all that makes any sense to you right now. Nothing can prepare a man for this kind of loss and work can serve us well as a distraction. But you have children and a new baby to think about."

"I know that, sir." William's voice had a very uncustomary hard edge.

"Let us take just a few minutes and think about them," Jacques spoke quietly.

William sat down.

"You have work but they have nothing to distract them from their loss. There are no other women up here and your Thor is what... nine, ten years old? Hardly an age to rear his siblings and care for a new baby while you are with the lumberjacks."

William's eyes were cast downward as he let the words sink in.

"I think you have a couple of choices to consider. We can hope to find a nursemaid willing to come to a lumber camp and pray she arrives before your baby dies. Or, I can take the children with me back to the settlement where they will be looked after most lovingly while you take the time you need to grieve."

Put like that William realized that sensibly those were his choices and the first was hardly wise. A lumber camp is a dangerous place for small children. He'd never had to worry with Britta in charge of their little brood. Now, if he thought about his children, he knew he would think about Britta which was too painful. But if he blocked out all thoughts but work, then no one was thinking of the children.

William let out one unguarded sob, then stiffened and looked to Jacques.

"Take them, sir, take them to safety and I will send you word when I decide what I must do." He got up with the mewling infant and Jacques was about to ask if it was a boy or girl when the soiled swaddling slipped off revealing her gender. Clumsily, William re-wrapped her in a dry blanket stained with urine and poured fresh goat's milk into a small leather glove shoving one of the fingers into the baby's mouth like a teat.

"What have you named her?" Jacques asked softly.

William looked up with an expression that clearly said he had been too unfocused to even think of a name.

"My friend … what would you like to name her?"

"I think… Britta," the sad giant sighed.

Fortunately for Jacques and his father, their trip home traveling with the water current took only half as long and with less effort. Marie was not surprised when they arrived with the three youngsters and a baby in tow. During their absence, she had given it thought and realized it was the likeliest outcome. To that end, she sent out inquiries for a wet nurse and a temporary nursemaid.

The only women currently nursing in their settlement lived a distance away and had other children of their own to watch over. They sent word that they would be happy to wet nurse if the babe was left with them. Meanwhile an older woman who was looking for extra income sent word she would be pleased to be their nursemaid. Now, as Marie took the basket her father-in-law was carrying and looked inside, she immediate sent for Doctor St. Claire.

Marie was aghast at the sight of the infant and wondered how Britta could have birthed such a very small and delicate looking child. She tossed aside the sour glove with which the men had been trying to feed the babe as she hurried to the kitchen behind the main house. There, within the comforting warmth of the building, she gave the tiny girl a quick wash, wrapped her in clean swaddling, and bared her own full breast to the infant. With a little encouragement the babe finally latched on but she suckled very weakly and grew tired very quickly.

While this was going on, Doctor St. Claire arrived and within the main house he turned his attentions to the three other Boot children. His examination disclosed that there was nothing physically wrong with Thor, Rega, or Ansel that a bath, a fresh change of clothing, and a hot meal topped off with Margot's velvety cake would not mend. Joining the company of the Power children would be a healthy tonic he told Jacques before the compassionate doctor went out to the kitchen in search of Marie. Little Britta, he soon discovered, was of much graver concern.

The sound of a crying baby reminded Marie that she was due in the nursery for James' feeding. In response to his lusty howls, her milk began to flow on its own and Britta almost choked.

St. Claire took the infant from Marie just as Sarah walked in carrying the hungry James. Sarah handed off James to his mother for nursing and the difference in the two babies was shockingly pronounced.

The pallor of the infant Britta along with the outline of the tiny bones of her rib cage beneath her pale bluish skin, her feather light weight and minuscule frame all bespoke of an unnaturally early entry into the world. St. Claire had never seen an infant in such condition live more than a few hours, he muttered, at most perhaps a day or two. This one had already survived long enough for her cord to have fallen off. In typical physician style, he knit his brows and grunted several times as he pressed his ear to her tiny chest listening carefully to the beat of her heart and the sound of her lungs. He also checked the healing of her belly.

"Swab her belly with vinegar," he instructed as he gave Britta to Sarah for re-swaddling, then he sat down across from the nursing Marie and shook his head. "It is a miracle she has survived this long. Do not expect her to last much longer. I like not the sound of her heart," he said gravely. "But worse is the sound of her lungs."

Marie gave a small gasp. "What can we do?"

"Everything is upside down when a child comes into the world too soon," St. Claire sighed. "This one needed the shelter of her mother's womb for many more weeks. You know the look of a healthy infant. You see how still this one is? She has no energy to cry. She fights for every breath. And the bluish tinge, it is a very poor sign."

Marie nodded as James, contented in his mother's arms, pulled vigorously on her pap. She could feel the milk flow out of her with ease.

"For now," St. Claire continued, "she must be kept calm and as content as possible and encouraged to eat."

"Surely there must be something more…" Marie prodded.

St. Claire considered. "It hardly seems worth the effort…"

"What?"

"You might fix a small tent over her crib with canvas or sheets and keep a kettle of water boiling nearby with a few drops of oil of eucalyptus in it. The moist air will help her breathe. Watch for a fever. If she congests with pneumonia, it will be over quickly. Time will tell. But the prognosis, madame, is not favorable in any case."

Marie nodded, a tear glistening in her eye. She was remembering her first born, her true first born who had died in France.

"She is destined for a short life in this world," St. Claire continued clinically. "I remember all the other Boot children; they arrived big and healthy, like squalling giants."

"Like their parents," Marie nodded in agreement, a faint smile of remembrance upon her lips.

"I did not know Britta was pregnant again or I would have gone up to see her."

"This is not your fault, *Monsieur Docteur*. There is no blame. I heard Thor say, 'Mama fell.' If she took a bad fall, is it not likely she bled to death? There was nothing you could have done but let us try to give this little one a chance. I am sure she would have been as big and lusty as her siblings if she had arrived later, perhaps that is to her advantage, eh? Perhaps it is why she has survived at all."

St. Claire nodded noncommittally. When he was a young man, no physician would have been concerned with the mundane and messy details of midwifery. Children came regularly amongst the peasants like lambs came to ewes and calves to cows. Most of them lived, some of them died. There was no mystery and it was a side of life that firmly belonged to the realm of women. Every village throughout the countryside had its midwife who usually passed the trade along to her own daughters. Physicians were not tradesmen, and few had taken the time to become very familiar with the eccentricities of the female anatomy.

Neither was a true physician a "sawbones" who cut off gangrenous limbs covered in pus and set broken bones or stitched up torn flesh; a practiced barber could do that adequately enough. The patient either lived or died according to his fate and God's will. There was little to be done about it.

In contrast, being a physician was a learned profession. Acceptable for second sons of the aristocracy and a step up the ladder of esteem for the sons of the bourgeoisie. Why, a physician of middle-class origin might even aspire to marry a lesser daughter of the aristocracy. A physician was revered for his knowledge, his learning, his ability to diagnose and direct his patient along the appropriate course of treatment. Not so long ago only the nobility had physicians attending at their births, like high strung and valuable race horses that required a skilled veterinarian's attention. But all that had changed with the rise of the bourgeoisie, St. Claire realized. He had witnessed the changes in Paris where physicians had found a lucrative niche attending the wives of the wealthy merchant class who could afford to pay the fees. Paying fees was something the aristocracy was notoriously delinquent in doing. And nowhere were the lines blurring faster than here in these colonies. Far from wealthy patronage, setting a broken bone or delivering a baby helped to put food on the physician's table.

With his belly full, James was burped and now fast asleep but Marie knew she still had plenty of milk left. Playing round-robin with the babies, Marie took little Britta back and coaxed her to swallow more milk as it flowed easily from Marie's primed breast while Sarah, heading for the nursery, disappeared with the sleeping James.

Marie looked down at the little face nestled against her. There was no way they could give this child over to another household for wet nursing. She decided at that moment she would have to do it herself and sent for the widow who had agreed to be a temporary nursemaid to the Boot children as an assistant to Sarah.

St. Claire returned every day to check on the tiny girl who clung tenaciously to life. Through the rest of the week, Marie spent hours holding the infant against the warm skin above her breast where tiny Britta lay near the soothingly familiar sound of a heart beat. A schedule was organized ensuring a round-the-clock watch over the babe and a steaming kettle upon a small brazier effused a very mild eucalyptus vapor within the tenting. Even Hélène volunteered for a shift. Marie encouraged the child to nurse every time James nursed and in between as well, her wee stomach could hold so little at a sitting. It was not the schedule Marie would have chosen during her in-laws visit but she could not turn her back on Britta Boot's child.

Against all odds the babe slowly gained a little weight.

Chapter 9

The long summer days provided many opportunities for wandering in the orchards, around the farm estate, and through the little town while the happy sound of children's laughter was never far away.

Jacques took careful notice of his parents' reactions to everything. Hélène and Jean-Philippe marveled at what their son had carved from the wilderness. And as Jacques saw the things he and Marie had built through his parents' eyes, he gained a better perspective on just how much they truly had accomplished together in this new world.

As the days rolled on, there was no end to the number of stories to be told. Jacques and Marie both had many tales to share of their early days and adventures. Most were amusing although some would have horrified Hélène immensely if they were not about a time now considered long passed.

In turn, Jean-Philippe and Hélène updated their son on the changes around the estates in France, which were actually very few. Life generally continued as it had been, at least as it had been since most of the Huguenots had disappeared from France. The Pouvoir estates were peaceful and benevolently managed while outside the duchy there was growing discontent and animosity for the hated aristocrats. But this was nothing new. The aristocracy were all exempt from taxes and many of Jean-Philippe's peers were abusive and led lives of extraordinary extravagance and waste paid for by the sweat of their peasants. And no one set an example of a more wasteful and extravagant life than their sovereign, Louis XIV himself, who was a monarch of absolute power.

The duke also shared gossipy bits on the political events in Europe.

"Of course, you must have heard that we had the former *Roi d'Angleterre* living at our court, did you not? I believe I wrote of it?" asked Jean-Philippe one evening at the dinner table.

"The King of England?!" exclaimed Jacques in disbelief. "No, I had not heard; your letter perhaps was lost. I was aware the kingship had changed, that is all."

"Yes-yes, James the Second of England had to seek asylum with Louis," the older man stated with restrained mirth. "Ah, he is dead now, God rest his soul," Jean-Philippe automatically crossed himself. "Had a stroke last year."

"Seeking asylum in France?" Jacques kept his humor, "Pa-pa if you only knew how ironic that is from my perspective. We have for years had a very difficult time on the frontiers because of the fighting between England and France. And to hear that the English king sought asylum in France? It is more than ironic, it is bizarre."

Jean-Philippe nodded his head and continued, "Well, that is exactly what happened. I am surprised you had not heard."

"When was this?"

"He showed up in France on Christmas Day in '88, a king without a country. The pitiful wretch. What a fine Christmas present for the French Court. What was Louis to do but open his treasury and put him on a stipend? James was, after all, a brother Catholic king but one who had the bad fortune of a son-in-law who drove him from his throne."

"That was only three years after we left," Jacques observed thoughtfully. "I doubt that the Court would be flattered to learn just how unimportant they are here in the colonies," Jacques commented with a grin. "On the frontier we are all of us too busy making our daily bread to care about their courtly intrigues."

That was the Christmas we made vows to each other, Marie thought to herself as she listened, *and I learned just how wonderful it can be between a man and woman.*

"James the Second, was he not the grandson of Mary, Queen of the Scots?" Marie asked putting a finger to the far side of her throat and drawing it across in a quick motion to allude to the woman having been beheaded.

"Mary's grandson's son," Jean-Philippe corrected. "And yes, Elizabeth's pretty but not well advised cousin who was also at one time our queen." Jean-Philippe expressed just a hint of surprise at his daughter-in-law's knowledge of foreign political history. "Still for all her blundering, it is her blood that flows through the English throne today. And it was her great-great granddaughter, also a Mary, eh? Who along with that cold fish husband, William, drove her own father off of his throne and sent him fleeing to France. Of course, Mary is now dead as well, God rest her soul." He crossed himself. "Smallpox, they say. She was still young, only in her early thirties. But somehow it seems a just reward for such a daughter."

Jacques smiled slightly at his father's condemnation. Since James II was Catholic and William and Mary were Protestant this was most likely at the root of the situation. Undoubtedly the Protestant powers did not really want another Catholic king on England's throne. And William who was from the Protestant Netherlands had actually allowed his father-in-law to escape unharmed out of the country. Something his political enemies outside the family might not have been so generously disposed to do. But Jacques did not seek to contradict his father.

"It is difficult for me to imagine that one woman could have allowed another to fall under the blade as Elizabeth did the Scottish Mary," Marie pondered, still thinking of the rather notorious female monarch.

"What was Mary's crime?" asked Hélène, not well versed on English history.

"Treason, intrigue, plotting to take the English throne but her real crime was being younger and prettier than her cousin Elizabeth," answered Jean-Philippe sagely. "They say she was extraordinarily charming and given enough time she could turn any man to her cause. But the woman was silly, completely duplicitous, and incapable of ruling. She should have married a wise, strong man, someone liked and recommended by her nobles and let him rule. Instead, after being widowed in France, she returned to Scotland and selected her own husband, a cowardly sodomite with a pretty face, who was useless to her except to give her a child." He shrugged. "When he was murdered, she married some Scot brigand who headed up her army against the Protestant lords."

"What happened to him?" Marie asked for both the women.

"He had to flee the country and ended up in some Norse prison somewhere." Jean-Philippe looked to Jacques-Jean but he could only shrug in ignorance. "Still, as long as Mary lived she was a rallying point for Catholics and political enemies and Elizabeth knew how to dispense with her enemies."

"But surely she could not have with cold blood sent another woman, another queen, and her own cousin as well, to her death," argued Hélène in disbelief. "I cannot believe even an English queen could be so blood thirsty."

"Why not?" Jean-Philippe replied. "She had no trouble sending her Howard cousin, the powerful Duke of Norfolk to the Tower and eventually the headsman's block."

"Well, in all fairness, Pa-pa, it did take Elizabeth almost twenty years to finally do the deed," Jacques interjected.

"I do not understand why the English allow women to rule," Jean-Philippe sighed.

"What irony," pointed out Marie, "Elizabeth herself when young was suspected of treasonous plotting against her older sister, was she not?"

"One would think she would have been obliged to have some compassion," puzzled Hélène.

"Unless..." Marie paused.

"What?"

"Unless Elizabeth was guilty and therefore knew what guilt looked like," Marie said thoughtfully.

"There are always two ways to look at things," Jacques said pleasantly. "Elizabeth has gone down in history as a good queen. She had a long reign, stopped the Inquisition her sister brought in, and kept England's enemies at bay. And for this the people loved her. So what significance is it, if she had to kill off a cousin or two doing it? Did not her father and grandfather kill off every relative who could lay claim to the throne?" he shrugged sarcastically. "Of course, she had to be torn between wanting to set such a precedent and finding it expedient to her purpose. In the end she had her lackeys do the job for her. Rather like our own King Louis, *n'est-ce pas?* He, too, will undoubtedly go down in history as a good king, even if hundreds of thousands of Huguenots might have a different opinion... but I do not doubt that he continues a pretense of ignorance of the whole matter just as Elizabeth made pretense of not knowing she had signed Mary's death warrant."

The servants had returned and were serving the next course.

"JJ!" his mother exclaimed, looking about in sudden fear for who might have overheard.

Jacques smiled at her. "Do not worry, Ma-ma, he is an ocean away and cannot hear me."

"Still..." she whispered with a gasp, "it is treason. How can you speak so?"

"We are in the English colonies, it is speaking ill of William that might be treason here," he grinned.

"Who knows what history will say of him... Louis, that is," Jean-Philippe interposed before Hélène could take him to task for what he had said earlier of King William. "He cannot seem to come to peace with anyone. It is one battle front to another, constant fighting, and it bleeds the treasury dry."

"And for the purpose of fattening it again, I am sure they will find yet another way to tax the common people," Jacques observed ruefully. "One thing I learned very quickly after arriving here. The monarchs all seem very far away and the people have very strong opinions of their own. Sometimes I feel they only tolerate royalty, rather like pets, and at some point the time may come when the good people on this side of the ocean will no longer have the patience to tolerate them or the taxes they heap upon the common folk."

"Well, I cannot keep up with the English monarchs," Hélène said dismissively, "they seem to be constantly changing."

"English law is very different than French, Ma-ma. English monarchs do not have absolute power. The people have basic rights and there are laws even the king … or queen … must obey."

"Oh," Hélène looked wide-eyed at her son.

"In England there is no *lettre de cachet*. One cannot be thrown into prison to rot just because the king orders it. The English have laws guaranteeing a trial with a jury of one's peers and English law requires a quick process and allows one to speak in their own defense."

It was quiet for a moment as they turned back to their food with greater attention. Everyone was reminded that the lack of these laws in France was what had caused Jacques to be forced to flee. Wine glasses were refilled, dishes cleared and the next course served.

"Still, I think of the Virgin Queen," said Marie quietly, "and I cannot help but feel sorry for her. She lived a life of such political responsibility but she was all alone and never knew what it was to have a loving husband and the blessing of children."

Jacques looked fondly at his wife.

"I doubt seriously that she was really a virgin," he chuckled. Marie blushed. "And she was hardly a woman to evoke pity, do you not agree, Pa-pa?"

"She was extremely clever." Jean-Philippe nodded. "One cannot take that from her. She knew wars cost money and tried to keep England out of them. Would that our Louis could follow her example in that regard."

"Well, it is my opinion that she divested herself of every pleasing feminine virtue, and was every bit as duplicitous as her younger cousin," Jacques voiced.

"And yet," his father pointed out, "politically she used the fact that she was a woman to her country's best advantage. Having others fight her battles for her, come to her rescue as they courted her in hopes of becoming King of England, and engage her enemies while England stayed by the sidelines."

"That is true, but from what I have read she also cultivated the meanest of female conceits." Jacques paused to take more wine. "I do not think she was a very likable person on a personal level, no matter how good a leader for her country. And she was too greedy for power, *ma chérie*," he turned his gaze toward Marie, "to even think of sharing her throne with anyone. Do not waste your sympathy."

"How very tragic," sighed Hélène as she dabbed at her mouth and placed her napkin on her plate as a sign that she was finished.

"Possibly she never knew who she could trust or believe," Marie said softly, "the legacy of having one's own mother beheaded by one's father. How could such a thing not mark a child for life?" The question caused everyone to pause and ponder. "Oh," she gazed about the table quickly, "it is fortunate that the children are not dining with us. This conversation has become far too macabre."

"I agree," smiled Jacques, rescuing his wife. "Let us finish our dessert and enjoy this excellent wine! I thank you again, Pa-pa, for your generous gift." Jacques raised his glass towards his father in appreciation.

After a moment's pause while they nibbled at their dessert, Jacques changed the subject. "Speaking of children... how goes it in the nursery, my darling?"

"Crowded," Marie smiled, "But happy, I think. The Boot children appear to have settled in nicely and our children are delighted with their company."

"Glad to hear it."

"The baby, however," Marie grew more serious, "she does not grow as she should, Jacques. Did William happen to mention how many months pregnant Britta was?"

Jacques shook his head. "No, and at this point I hardly think it matters, *n'est-ce pas?*"

The lively supper was over and they moved on to the drawing room. The men helped themselves to cognac and the women awaited the tea cart. It had become routine for Hélène to accept a special blend of soothing tea before bed.

"These teas have done wonders for me," Hélène commented. "I have added a few pounds and sleep very well."

"I am so glad," Marie smiled with sincere pleasure. "I have been thinking of expanding the herb garden and packaging various blends for the store. Do you think they would sell?"

"But of course. Why not? People are always looking for some curative and one only has to try them to feel the results."

"It is only that they seem so simple. Anyone could grow them."

"But not everyone knows what to grow," Hélène encouraged. "If you have the knowledge why should you not... what is the word... *capitalize* on it, eh? Is that not what the physicians and apothecaries do in France? People pay them for their knowledge, *n'est-ce pas?*"

"There is one I insist the children drink before they go to bed with a head cold. I know they breathe so much better for taking it. I would think every mother would appreciate the relief it gives her child."

"And you learned all this from the Indians?" Hélène questioned.

Marie nodded. "Sheehoo became a very good friend and she was always willing to help me learn. That is why it seems almost a sin to not relay the information freely," Marie said quietly. "I miss her. I cannot help but feel we ran her and her people off of their land. There have been several epidemics of white man's diseases. Smallpox is especially deadly to the Indians as is the measles. My friends decided to leave while they still could. They came to say good-bye shortly after Jamie was born."

"Where did they go?"

"Oh, much farther into the interior, into the mountains. Many days' journey from here. I confess I was very sad at their departure."

Jane knocked on the salon door and entered.

"Excuse me, ma'am, but Sarah says the babies are ready for you."

"Ah, yes, thank you, Jane," Marie nodded and as she rose Jacques and Jean-Philippe rose as well. "Please excuse me," she said. "Unless there is anything else I can do for you, I think I will retire now if you do not mind. I bid you good night." She bent to kiss Hélène's cheek.

"*Bon soir, ma petite*," Hélène murmured.

Marie moved toward Jean-Philippe and kissed his cheek with a "*Bon soir, Papa,*" then she turned toward her husband.

Jacques took her hand and kissed it. "It will not be long before I come up as well," he said.

In the normal daily routine, Marie got up very early each morning to nurse the babies before going to her store, taking care of the books, checking the merchandise, looking over the recent orders, and leaving instructions for her apprentices. Then, she checked in at the bakery with Cassandra and Deborah who began baking long before sunrise. Marie then hurried home to preside over breakfast with the children and attend to her duties in running the house and doing her part in entertaining her in-laws. By evening she was exhausted and it had become her habit to excuse herself shortly after supper to do a final nursing. She was too fatigued to be of much fun or wit, she thought, and it gave her Jacques some time alone with his parents without the children interrupting.

Marie left the room quietly and proceeded to the nursery. The men again took their seats.

"She is a treasure, JJ," Hélène commented after the younger woman had left. The duchess had been observing her son for some days and noted the love with which he always watched his wife depart. "I cannot believe you found her working in domestic service. Where is her family?"

"Somewhere in France she has some remnant left in another province but she was orphaned very early in life," he replied vaguely.

"Ah, I thought as much," nodded Jean-Philippe. "She comes from very good stock, that is obvious. She is so well-educated, so charming and well possessed, so generous in spirit and so... so...."

"Capable?" Jacques supplied the word with a smile.

"*Oui-oui...*capable, *exactement!*" his father agreed. "And I find it quite unusual for a young woman of her age to be so articulate and clear thinking. She certainly knows political history. Undoubtedly misfortune reduced her circumstances and she had to work for a living," the older man said studiously. "It happens."

For a moment Jacques was going to overlook the assumptions his parents had made, but he was struck by the dishonestly of it. In a way it was a slight to Marie. They did not have to know all the personal details of her miserable beginnings but there was no reason for anyone to pretend she was anything but who she was. He was proud of her in every way and certainly her peasant parentage was nothing of which to be ashamed.

"Actually... not," Jacques said quietly looking first at his father and then at his mother. "Marie has made herself into what you see today. She had a very unfortunate and harsh childhood. She was driven out into the world to fend for herself at a very tender age and as a matter of fact she was totally illiterate when we first arrived in the New World. But she had a drive, an ambition... a good ambition: to grow, to improve her lot."

Hélène listened intently and heard beyond the words her son was saying. She would not press him any further on the subject. "Well, she is a lovely person and a most responsible mother," the older woman said approvingly. "Not many women in her position would deign to nurse their own offspring and I know none who would volunteer to wet nurse a …" she was about to say *peasant* but stopped herself, "an employee's child. She makes a warm and hospitable home for you, *mon fils*, and frankly, you two look perfect for each other."

Jacques smiled broadly at his mother and one small golden curl falling over his forehead reminded her of the boy he once had been.

"I will make a confession," she continued. "I wondered some time ago how a simple servant girl could possibly keep your interest. Now that I have come to know her, I can well understand. She is not a simple servant girl and she is most interesting." Hélène smiled. "And on that note I must admit that I have had quite enough happiness for one day. My cup overflows and the pillow beckons loudly to me," she said, rising to her feet. Jacques and Jean-Philippe both began to stand. "Do not disturb yourselves, my darlings," she gestured for them to remain seated. "*Bon soir, mon chéri,*" she bent to kiss her son.

"*Bon soir, Ma-ma.*"

"Jean-Philippe, do not stay up too late. Tomorrow is another day, my love," she said kissing him lightly on the lips.

"I will retire in a bit," he agreed and kissed his wife's hand affectionately.

After Hélène's graceful departure, the two men sat relaxed for a time before the fire, enjoying a quiet communion without having to speak, each sipping the light amber liquid in their glasses. After many minutes, Jacques broke the easy silence.

"I have not yet asked you, Pa-pa, what has become of my scheming uncle?"

"*Du Marshe?*"

"Do we have any other family schemers?" Jacques grinned impishly.

"Ummm, who knows," Jean-Philippe nodded while gathering his thoughts. "But Pierre's story has taken an interesting turn. I believe the peoples of the East have a saying about being very careful what you do because they believe it comes back to you. And our Pierre is not such a happy fellow these days. He is getting back some of the misery he has caused for others."

"Really?"

"*Oui,* I heard he has fallen severely out of favor at court and has been in exile in the country for some time now."

"For Pierre to be forced to live in the country would be like Purgatory, if not Hell itself." Jacques could not help from chuckling. "What happened?"

"I am not privy to all the details," Jean-Philippe spoke in his slow and cautious manner, "but I did hear something about a jealous lover and a duel. Pierre won but the man he wounded was one of the king's mistress' pets. Unfortunately, the wound left him crippled for life and she had a word with Louis and that was it for Pierre. He was told quite plainly to remove himself from court and live quietly in the country. There is even a rumor he has lost his title of *comte*."

"It is amazing the power a little woman has when she holds a man's affections."

Jean-Philippe nodded in agreement. "Especially a man who is all powerful."

"You know, Pa-pa, I actually owe Pierre a debt of gratitude."

The older man looked at his son in surprise. "How is that?"

"One could say he is the author of my happiness."

Jean-Philippe looked intently at his son.

"If you recall, you were in the process of searching for a bride for me. I doubt that you would have picked Marie, and yet, I cannot imagine my life without her except that without her, my life would be so much less. Indeed, I look at William Boot and it frightens me to my core to think of losing Marie."

His father nodded quietly. He was trying to understand. He had lost Hélène for twenty years but he always knew she was there and alive. And he had obeyed the rules of his station out of honor and duty. The New World fostered such a different way of thinking at least in some ways, but human nature remained the same.

"I was reading in one of your newspapers, the Massachusetts Colony passed a law ordering all the Roman Catholic priests to leave under penalty of life imprisonment or execution. Does that not sound familiar?" Jean-Philippe asked his son.

Jacques nodded. "It is what France did to the Huguenot pastors. That was an old paper. The New York Colony has now passed a similar law as well. We were set a very good example of intolerance, were we not? And I must say, you are learning to read English quite well, Pa-pa."

Jean-Philippe grinned. His grandchildren had been schooling him secretly from their primers and helping him interpret the newspaper.

They sat ruminating for a while longer, each lost in his own thoughts. Then, the older man cleared his throat.

"Jacques, I have said nothing before this because I did not want to mention it in front of your mother and, well, the subject has not come up but..."

Jacques looked over at his father.

"With *du Marshe* out of the way and Louvoir dead, there is a possibility I could manage a pardon from the king. I still have friends within court circles. None of this would have ever happened, I am certain, if it had not been for Pierre's instigation," Jean-Philippe kept his composure but the feeling behind his words was obvious. "You were never a criminal, after all. You never did anything against your king. If I were to gain a pardon for you, would you even consider returning to

France now?"

The question caught at Jacques like a wild rose trailer full of thorns; it brought an instant stab of pain and yet simultaneously a familiar heady sweetness. He felt his eyes burn with a very old frustration. Memories of the familiar valleys, vineyards, and river along with the protective comfort of the chateau all kaleidoscoped through his mind's eye. It was easier to deal with his situation if the only possibility remained exile. But if he had a choice? If he could... would he? And the clear simple answer came to him. He liked the life he had built here in America. As much as he loved his mother and father, how could he leave everything he and Marie had built together to simply go back? Return to deal with the old, stale prejudices of the aristocracy, the corruptions of the court and its political intrigues, the fear of a *lettre de cachet* because of an inheritance or a woman or an idea or only a perceived insult... it was now intolerable to even imagine such an existence. And what of the children? France was not his children's home. This was their home and their future was here.

Jean-Philippe could see the answer in his son's eyes and he was sorry he had even mentioned the subject. He and Hélène were coming toward the end of their lives but Jacques-Jean still had so much of his to live.

"Pa-pa, *du Marshe* may have stirred up the authorities against me earlier than they would have naturally come about but I suspect eventually they would have sought my arrest anyway. And I have built a very good life here."

"I understand," Jean-Philippe said hoarsely. "I inherited my estates and I have done my best to manage them well but in reality I am only a caretaker. I have never built from scratch with my own two hands what you have built here. If I had, nothing could make me abandon it."

"The powers-that-be will never allow me to be your heir, you know that."

Jean-Philippe looked at his son and saw the resignation in his face. "You are most probably right," he finally capitulated. "The most we could hope for is royal permission for a limited visit. That is a possibility," he said a bit too hopefully. "If the price on your head is lifted and we gained permission for you to visit, you could come and see us, show the children where you were born... then, you could always return to this place which is now your home."

Jacques nodded more as an appeasement to the older man than anything else. Deep down he knew that a pardon would never be a reality and he would never be allowed to go back to France, not even for a visit. It was not King Louis but Rome and the Church of France that had no pardons for Huguenots unless they formally abjured and renounced their faith. He could never play such a hypocrite.

"Speaking of your new home," Jean-Philippe went on, "this sounds like a silly question but where exactly are we?"

Jacques looked up at his father and then laughed outloud. "You are right, it is most confusing. It is bad enough that ever since we arrived the French and English have been battling it out with each other in territorial disputes, but also within the colonies themselves there has been nothing but quarrels, disagreements, fights, lawsuits, and protests over borders, royal grants, and property lines. I have learned that when the English gained the Dutch lands of New Netherlands, it was split into New York and New Jersey but with a shared governor. Then New Jersey was divided between two governors and who applies to whom for land grants and which shall be honored or where they pay their taxes has been very confused. There is East Jersey and there is West Jersey."

The older man nodded trying to follow what his son was saying. "And you are on which side?"

"A very good question, Pa-pa, and one which I have not yet been able to answer. Logically, one would assume because we are on the ocean we would be East, but not necessarily as there are those who claim in places West Jersey spreads all the way to the ocean. There are many who want the confusion stopped and for it to become just one Jersey. Personally," Jacques lowered his voice in a conspiratorial manner. "I have avoided paying taxes to anyone so I am grateful for the confusion. We are far enough away from the prized harbors that neither side seems to know as yet that we exist."

"But surely that cannot last forever."

"No, I am sure it will not and one day the piper may knock upon my door."

The clock struck half past the hour and both men decided it was time to retire for the evening.

As a nightly routine, Jacques checked in upon his children, kissing sleeping heads and tucking in covers. Then he went into the spacious bedroom he and Marie shared.

Marie had been dozing but opened her eyes briefly when he entered.

"You are still awake?"

"Hmmm," she replied under the heavy drug of sleep.

He bent over the bed and kissed her lightly on the lips and then, pausing, he looked at this woman who had made his life so rich here in this strange and wild land that he now could not imagine any other life at all. He knew his parents and so he knew they would love Marie but seeing her through their amazement and respect for her many facets made him realize how much he had grown accustomed to her. How much about her he took for granted every day. And here she was upon her pillow, her petitely etched face still looking so young in the soft candlelight, so vulnerable with wisps of hair framing her countenance. He felt a sudden rush of desire and gave her full lips a second kiss that was long and probing.

Marie always responded to Jacques' touch. He never failed to stir her no matter the circumstance and now she felt her lassitude slipping away as she parted her lips to receive him. She could taste the mild flavor of the cognac he had just drunk.

"My parents absolutely adore you," he whispered as he nuzzled near her ear. His breath drew the goose flesh up on her and she reached for him, enfolding her arms around his neck, then running her fingers through his thick golden curls. She was aware of the vague smell of wood smoke in his hair and on his clothing. "I knew they would," he continued. "They think I am the luckiest of men and I quite agree," he added, breathing more heavily now as he opened the neckline of her gown and enjoyed the sight of her creamy skin and plump breasts.

As tired as she had been, Marie was now fully awake and rising to her knees on the bed, she sought to help him free of his own clothing. She never tired of his attentions and never had denied him in all their years together. She could not, for to deny him would have been to deny herself and all that he made her feel, and all that he knew how to make her body feel. She kissed him again, his moustache tickling her lip, her tongue teasing his. She kissed his bared skin and inhaled deeply, relishing his clean, male scent. His scent was an aphrodisiac. She breathed in deeply and felt the intoxication rush through her as she pressed closer to him. Her hands moved over him, caressing him, her finger tips and nails tracing lightly over hard muscles causing the hairs to stand erectly on his limbs. She fondled him tenderly as she tugged gently at his lip.

Standing there at the side of the bed, he crushed her to him until she could hardly breathe. He released her and with urgency pulled off her light gown in one swift movement, tossing it aside. He looked at her and let his eyes drink in all the dips and swells and curves that he knew so well. Marie felt his eyes caressing her. His gray eyes had grown soft and tender and his long gaze made her feel beautiful. Never would she understand completely by what miracle of good fortune she had become this man's wife. All she knew was that her heart still pounded under his attention and felt so full she thought it would burst.

Jacques enfolded Marie's soft body within his arms again, very aware of the warmth and delicate fragrance of her skin as it mingled with his own. Her quick little tongue was in his mouth driving him to distraction in their private *pas de deux*. He was also aware of her nipples, turgid and prodding against his chest. He wanted them in his mouth. He pressed her to him, his fingers running down the gentle canal of her spine, spreading to encompass the roundness of her bottom, squeezing gently before he sought her supple thighs. He could feel her tongue circling his ear, her moist breath, hot and vital. He groaned deeply. They both could feel his silken shaft rising between them, begging to be buried within her heat.

They clung together in a music-less dance, giving and receiving, fondling and caressing. Their emotions had expanded beyond thought and words had become too small to have meaning. Suspended together outside of time and the universe with nothing else existing beyond their heart beats, they drifted down into the bed which rose up to receive them. There to scintillate with the intensity of the sun before it slips below the horizon to sleep.

Marie had just finished nursing the babies and found Hélène in the small library off the drawing room. It was early afternoon and the smaller children were taking their naps while the older boys had gone with Jacques and his father.

"Is there anything I can get for you, Ma-ma?" she asked graciously.

"No, nothing. I was just looking at your library, my dear, it is quite large," Hélène replied, looking at the rows of books upon three shelves, most were in English which she could not understand but some were in French: the French philosophers, playwrights, and poets. "The chateau has a library, of course, but its expansion has taken many generations."

"This started with children's primers," Marie explained walking over to where her mother-in-law stood. "Jacques, Richard, and I used them to learn our English. Then, I just kept adding to it."

"And you have read all these?"

"Most of them. Some of them are reference books. They are not meant to read exactly but to look up information when you need it. And Jacques has his own English law books in his study."

"Then you are quite educated, indeed," Hélène concluded with a smile. "And you speak several languages, and run more than one successful business, and keep a beautiful home, and you are raising a lovely, well-mannered family. You have a green thumb for the garden, and my son says you are quite a marks-woman... tell me, my dear, before I become quite jealous, is there anything you cannot do?"

Marie felt the blood rush to her cheeks, momentarily uncertain if Hélène was making fun of her or just teasing. "But of course," she replied meekly. "Many things, I fear. I regret I never had a real education. I know no Latin or Greek and therefore know nothing of what are called the 'Classics.' I also know nothing about art or music, except to sing the psalms at church. I can play no instruments. I cannot swim. I do not like boats very much perhaps because I cannot swim and I have never learned to seat a horse properly."

Hélène clucked her tongue teasingly. "My, my, with such shortcomings, I cannot imagine that you could ever make a suitable wife for my son," she said in mock concern, "but tell me this, do you truly love my JJ?" Hélène was now very serious as she looked unblinkingly at Marie.

"More than any words can express," Marie replied without hesitation.

There was a pause between them as Hélène studied her daughter-in-law. "I believe you," she said at last. She leaned in and gave her daughter-in-law a kiss upon her cheek. "And that is the most important of all for I know he loves you completely and without reserve." She put her arm through Marie's arm and began to walk toward the door to the garden.

"It is a beautiful day. Will you walk with me a little?" she asked, not really expecting a refusal. Outside, Hélène drew a deep breath and savored the sweet smells of the late blooming roses. The birds had begun their migratory gatherings and chirped loudly back and forth through the tree tops, suddenly taking off in formations of flapping wings, practicing for their longer migration to come. Bees lent a soft buzzing to the air as they gathered the season's last nectar offerings. And the leaves rustling in the afternoon breeze were beginning to color in shades of yellow, gold, orange, scarlet, copper, lime, and brown.

At last Hélène spoke again, taking her time.

"I cannot fully express what I am feeling right now, but I will try. The hardest, most difficult experience of my entire life was to see my son driven from his home and turned into an exile in a distant land. I do not know how much you know of me... has JJ told you about his father and me?"

Marie nodded. "A love story with a happy ending."

"*Oui*, but for many years it was not so perfect, I am afraid. Jean-Philippe is an honorable man who was forced into a loveless marriage... in truth, because of *my* stupidity. He honored that marriage and I lived a very lonely existence without him. JJ was all I had in the whole world. All through his childhood we spent our days together as I taught him to read and write and do his sums. And we spent the evenings together, first I read to him but soon he was reading to me. He was quick and bright and full of curiosity about the world and I experienced that wondrous curiosity of childhood again through him." Hélène sighed. "Then when he was twelve he went to live with his father... I felt so alone. My father grew ill and retired so I cared for him... and JJ did not forget us, no-no, he came around often but he was growing into a young man with other interests."

Marie remembered the tavern and how Jacques would meet his friends to drink and talk and play cards. And would it not be naive to think he did not also spend time with women? By the time she knew him he already had a mistress but Marie did not like to remember those days.

"So you can see how losing him was," Hélène was still talking, "... well, without his father returning to my life, I do not think I would have survived it. So, you understand why we have no other children. And I have longed and yearned for some contact, some connection, some way to share in my son's life beyond a letter. To see his children growing, to meet his wife, to have images to put with the words on paper," she sighed. "And now I see. My son has a very good life here, he has done very well for himself and I am so very, very proud. But more important to a mother's heart, I can see that he is extremely happy. And you, my dear, are responsible for that. I can see that you are what makes it all worthwhile for him. You have put the beating heart into his home and into his life."

Marie started to speak but Hélène stopped her with the slightest movement of her finger.

"There was a time when JJ's father quite unexpectedly found himself in possession of everything which JJ has been denied. The ancestral lands, the title, the estate, the grand chateau, the servants, but with it all he was not a happy man. If my son had to be deprived of one or the other," Hélène sighed, "well, he has everything right here that I would want for him, and therefore, in a sense, he has it all.

"And now," she patted Marie's arm gently. "I have a boon to ask of you. The time has flown and if we are to return home this year we should have to leave soon to avoid the winter weather. Marie, the crossing was the second hardest and most difficult experience of my life and I know it was not easy on me. I will not fool myself. This time when I say good-bye to my son I know I will never see him again in this life."

Marie looked at Hélène and felt the tears welling in her own eyes.

"I want to stay here a while longer," Hélène said softly, "but not as a guest to whom you must cater. Not as someone for whom you must rearrange your schedule; I want to be absorbed in as one of the household. I want to enjoy the routines of your day to day activities and challenges; I want to share this portion of time, this slice of your life a little longer. To watch the children grow and learn a little more, and see your seasons change because..." her voice faltered ever so slightly, "because when I leave I know it will be all that I shall ever see of you until we are all reunited together in Paradise.

"But I do not want you to think of me as the nosy mother-in-law who is sticking herself into your business, wearing out her welcome in your home, and of whom you cannot wait to be rid. I would ask to stay until spring but if that is too long, you *must* tell me so. Above all, I would rather keep the harmony between us. And I will understand. I remind myself that I never had a mother-in-law to contend with and this is your home, my dear, you are the mistress here."

Marie could not stay silent any longer but burst into tears throwing her arms around the older woman's neck. "Stop, Ma-ma, stop," she sobbed. "You must stay here as long as you can. Spring will be here before we know it. You must stay at least the full year, longer if it is possible! We have plenty of room and nothing would make Jacques happier."

Hélène was on the verge of tears herself and patted the younger woman gently.

"I thank you, Marie, for your gracious generosity of spirit, but I have been here long enough to see quite clearly that what makes JJ happy is you. So, what would make you happy?"

Marie wiped her eyes and looked at the endearing lady whose delicately boned face held timeless beauty.

"My ma-ma died when I was only a small child, younger than our little Richie is now. What would make me happy is for you to be my mother, not just my mother-in-law."

There was something in the tone of those words that brought a lump to Hélène's throat and she opened her arms to the younger woman. Suddenly, Marie was the daughter Hélène had never had, as though restored to her just as her son had been restored to her after so many years. Tears streamed down Hélène's delicate cheeks as she held her daughter and was held by her.

Chapter 10

1702

Jean-Philippe, dressed only in his breeches and a shirt, stood in the quiet of the early summer dawn watching the sun rise up out of the bay far beyond the garden. His face, still handsomely distinguished, caught the first rose-gold rays of sunlight. He had left his Hélène fast asleep in their bed. He could not sleep and saw no reason to disturb her with his tossing and turning. If he could only reach out across the ocean and pull the two continents closer together! It was an impossible thought but it would have been the perfect solution: to be a river apart, or a channel apart, even a small sea but not a vast ocean apart.

He and Hélène had agreed to stay a full year, then in late summer there were several birthdays which they were coaxed to celebrate once more. Autumn came, more breathtaking than the one before, and beckoning to be enjoyed after which everyone insisted they remain to celebrate his own birthday in November. By then the sailing season was closed so there was another Christmas to enjoy together. It was only the second they would ever share as a family. Spring had been late in coming and so time had flown. In a week, they would mark their second year in America.

It wrenched Jean-Philippe's heart to consider departure. Hélène, the love of his life, was the happiest he had ever seen her. She had gained back her weight and her eyes absolutely sparkled. With a bloom on her cheek, she sat contented with their grandchildren around her, reading to them, telling them stories, going for walks with them or just quietly doing her needlework while they played nearby. Deep down inside himself, the duke knew his wife had no real desire to return home. Everything that was of any real importance to her was right here. But he also knew she would leave it all for him.

And he had to return. He had been absent as long as he was able. There was business only he could attend to. He could no more abandon his family estates than he could have expected Jacques to leave everything he had built in the New World to now return to France, even if that was possible. He had put things off long enough to bask in the ambiance of family but he just could not linger any longer. And he knew he would have to tell Hélène today. Dufee's ship had arrived in New York Towne and sent news via the daily packet boat that it was coming to Chartes Landing at the end of the week, then sailing back to France. They had four days. Just time enough to pack and say their good-byes. And once the decision had been made, the swifter it was implemented the better. There would be too much time for tears as it was.

Perhaps in a few years they could return. Jean-Philippe shook his head. No, in honesty he could not imagine that they would ever return. The crossing had been hard enough on her two years ago. Then, the man was struck by a thought that made him shudder and turn cold. What if she did not survive the passage back? She had been sustained by the thought of finally seeing her son again on their passage over, but what would sustain her on their return? And worse, she would be crossing with a grieving heart. It would be better to leave her here, he thought, his own heart twisting with the pain of the idea. Better to leave her to enjoy this happiness and the remainder of her life than to make her leave it all behind and risk an early grave. She was truly safer staying here... in more ways than one.

Jean-Philippe turned from the fiery orange rising sun and walked back into the house. He had made his decision.

Breakfast was a family affair in the Power home complete with highchairs and cereal bowls to go along with eggs, bacon, ham, toast, muffins, biscuits, griddle cakes, and any number of things that might have been left over from the evening before. Without formality, the children brought cheerful faces, tales of dreams, questions, and the prattling of plans for the day. It was an enjoyable time and Jean-Philippe noted to himself how quiet breakfast would be at the chateau from this time forth, for he would always be comparing it to this. He would miss these pretty little faces so full of the future. And he felt another emotional pain in his heart.

Jacques appeared and joined his family at the breakfast table; he had already spent an hour in his office going through correspondence while Marie saw to the nursery.

"*Bon jour*, JJ," Hélène saw him first.

"*Bon jour*, Pa-pa," the children all sang out almost in unison.

"*Bon jour, mon chér*. Sit down, I will get you a plate," smiled Marie.

"Ahh, *bon jour* everyone!" Jacques drew up his chair and took his seat at the head of the table across the length from his father. "News has arrived via the packet boat, Pa-pa. You asked where we are and now I can tell you. East and West have been joined and we are now one New Jersey under just one governor, who has been announced to be 'the right honorable Edward Hyde, Lord Cornbury' who should be arriving to establish his capital shortly, probably in Trent Towne." Jacques smiled. "And so the piper arrives."

"What piper?" Phillip nudged his brother.

"What piper, Mama?" asked John as his mother floated by.

Marie looked to Jacques, her own question written on her face.

"It is a joke your *grand-père* and I shared," Jacques said easily. "You recall the story of the Pied Piper of Hamlyn? In this case the piper is the tax man, *n'est ce pas?* We knew eventually he would get to our shores."

"I don't understand, Mama," John said as his mother took her seat at the table.

"That is because you are too young to understand and should have no such care.

Please let us talk of happier things than taxes," Marie responded as she urged Britta sitting in the highchair beside her to take another small spoon of porridge liberally laced with molasses. James on Marie's other side needed no such encouragement. He was two and a half and fed himself with great smacks and grins of enjoyment.

Conversation remained light and cheery until breakfast was over and the children were excused to go out and enjoy the day under the watchful eye of Sarah. Tiny Britta stayed in her carriage watching the others play while Sarah kept an eagle eye upon James who tried to keep up with his older siblings. Britta was not yet able to pull herself onto her feet and sat, a habitually bluish tinge to her finger nails. That she was still alive was a miracle.

Jean-Philippe asked his son and daughter-in-law to stay a while before commencing their daily tasks and duties. Their tea cups were refilled and the serving girl left the room while he cleared his throat to address them.

Hélène felt a sense of dread. Jean-Philippe had come back to bed that morning and in the quiet start of the new day, he had made love to her like he had not done in a long time with such passion and intensity and a tinge of... what? Sadness? Desperation? She had known then that he had decided it was time to leave and their lovemaking had been a bitter-sweet experience. Now, she sat quietly listening to her husband speak.

"Our visit has been longer, more rewarding, and more pleasurable than we could have possibly imagined but..." he hesitated, and cleared his throat again. "I have received word from home, there are things which simply cannot be left any longer and I am afraid my king expects my immediate return." In his quiet reserved manner he added, "The ship on which to leave arrives at the end of the week."

Hélène heard herself gasp involuntarily.

"Jacques, you once left asking me to watch over your mother, now I will do the same. There is no reason why she must leave all of you behind just because affairs of the duchy and the king demand my return."

Jacques was stunned. He had been dreading his parents' departure which he realized had to be drawing close. They could not evade the inevitable farewell forever. But never had he considered that his mother might actually decide to stay in America. While he was still trying to grasp the idea, Hélène spoke out.

"Exactly what are you suggesting, Monsieur?" she asked in controlled politeness. "Are you suggesting that I stay here and follow you at a later date?"

"That is a possibility," Jean-Philippe replied rather vaguely.

"*A* possibility? And what other possibilities did you have in mind?" she persisted, still with great politeness.

"I could return in time and..."

"In time?" she repeated, never raising her voice. "I am afraid I do not understand what this *in time* means exactly. Could you explain? Does this mean a year?

Two years? Four years?"

"Hélène," Jean-Philippe looked at her sadly, feeling somehow guilty. "You act as if I am trying to get rid of you. I am doing this for your own good. You are happy here, you have everything you desire. I see you with the children and it puts life into you, a sparkle you did not have in our cold and lonely chateau. Now, Jacques, Marie... can you accept this responsibility? Will you take care of your mother for me?"

"Of course," Marie responded automatically.

Jacques, however, saw something going on within his mother that he knew made his reply completely irrelevant.

"*Everything* I desire? Have you become totally foolish in your advancing years, *Monsieur le duc?*" she asked with surprising strength. "I would never have the courage to cross the ocean on my own. And if I did, when I became ill who would look after me if you were not there? My maid was almost as ill as I was. As for your coming back... it took you fifteen years to get here the first time, I do not think I could wait another fifteen for you to come back for me. No, what I am hearing is that you have decided I must choose between my husband and my son's family, and then you have decided to make the choice for me. There is no choice, Jean-Philippe! I did not come here to die in America. I have a home with you back in France. Or," she said a little irrationally, her voice now trembling and tears coming to her wide gray eyes, "are you so tired of me that you would now try to leave me behind!"

Losing her composure, Hélène got up suddenly from the table hiding her face with her napkin as she ran out of the room. Marie immediately followed to comfort her.

Jean-Philippe looked at his son, despair and misgivings written all over his countenance. His proud, if somewhat stooped, bearing crumbled in defeat. His chivalry had cost him dearly and all it had achieved was the upset of his duchess.

For a moment there was nothing but silence filling the room until the silence became so loud Jacques had to speak.

"Pa-pa, in time she will come to recognize the gesture you have made, and she will appreciate it for what it was but for now, I would go after her quickly if I were you. Tell her how much you do care. Tell her… tell her… ah, I have not the magic words, just be honest and tell her your heart. I understand how you are thinking but we are men and she is a woman. They do not think the same as we, Pa-pa. They never will. Sometimes it amazes me that they understand us as well as they do, all things considered. And most of the time I realize I do not really understand them at all. And so, for our women sometimes we must beg a little for understanding. Right now I would especially beg forgiveness for not letting her know first what you were thinking." He thumped the older man on the shoulder compassionately.

"She is so happy here," the older man sighed deeply. "It is so… pleasant, so comfortable. The life we have at home, Jacques, it is not as you remember. Her church went underground and finally disappeared completely years ago. I was never keen on society but we did accept the occasional invitation and have the occasional visitor, a neighbor, my sisters, and you were there, you and your lively friends, and your mother had her church friends. They are all dead or have disappeared and the neighbors seem almost afraid to associate with us as though some suspicion will rub off on them. I know she is lonely. I only thought to do what is best for her."

"But she knows what it has been like."

"Yes."

"Everything will be well, Pa-pa, but if I were you I do not think I would ever mention leaving Ma-ma behind again."

The older man sighed again. "That is not always in our control."

"Pa-pa?" Jacques looked over at his father, a need for clarification wrinkling his brow.

"Even if I do not say it… that does not mean it could not happen."

Jacques continued to stare questioningly at his father.

"Death! If I die first, your mother is left behind and very, very vulnerable in France today."

"Vulnerable? In what way?"

"You know Henri-Richard will inherit my estates."

"Yes," Jacques nodded, they all knew this.

"I am sorry to say Henri-Richard has grown into a rabid Catholic with a very cruel streak toward Huguenots. I do not understand it. I do not know what he has to gain, unless it is to curry favor with those most close to Louis who are of like mind. I have heard Henri-Richard takes great pleasure in setting the authorities upon hapless Huguenots in hiding or seeking to escape. I have fears I have never expressed to your ma-ma. Fears of what could happen to her if I should die before her."

"You think he would put her out?" Jacques asked in surprise.

"Far worse, Jacques. God forgive me if I misjudge but I believe he would have little hesitation in seeing your ma-ma sent off to prison. He has almost said as much I have been told."

"Prison?!" Jacques looked stunned.

"Your ma-ma has no idea. They have been imprisoning Huguenot women who have been found out or who have lost their protection."

"On what charge?"

"Your mother and I were married by a pastor; that alone is enough to lock her away." He saw the blood drain from his son's face. "Oh, they would give her the opportunity to abjure but as stubborn as you both are about your religion, you can well guess how that would end. No! If I die first, you must bring your mother back here. Even if the trip kills her it would be better than going to prison."

"Ma-ma always has a home here if she wants but Pa-pa, it is most upsetting to speak of such things, thinking of your death… who knows what the future brings or what will happen? God is in control."

"Jacques!" Jean-Philippe's tone was harsh for the first time that Jacques could ever remember. "You said yourself – the Church will never change! The threat is all too real. Even those closest to Christ were not spared persecution in their day. Understand, I pray I do not die first and leave her but if I do, I must have a plan in place to get her out of the country. A plan involving only the most trustworthy, *n'est-ce pas?*"

Jacques nodded solemnly. "You know we will do whatever is needed," he said softly. "Dufee in Paris would gladly help. Now please, go, see to Ma-ma."

At the end of the week, the whole family saw the duke and duchess off on the ship bound for France. Then the Power family made their way home in the carriage amidst a mixture of questions and sadness. The older children understood or at least they had a better grasp at understanding but the younger ones had no concept of how very large the ocean is and why one did not just cross it in a day or return in a week. In the end, they would all miss *Grand-mère* and *Grand-père* but eventually everyone reconciled themselves to never seeing them again.

Arriving home, the tears had dried as the children's minds were distracted by other things and they ran off as young ones do. Adults are not so easily distracted from their personal pain. Marie sought to distract Jacques from his sense of loss and sadness and what better way than with someone else's loss and sadness.

"Jacques, do you realize it has been two full years since Britta Boot died? William has come to see his children only twice in all that time. Someone needs to tell him that our home is not a substitute for a father's love."

Jacques was jarred from his personal thoughts at the tough tone in his wife's voice. "Perhaps you should tell him, my darling, if you think it will be so easy."

"Perhaps I should. You could take me to the camp. It breaks my heart to see the tears his children try to hide from me. Thor is twelve now. He should be working with his pa-pa. And Rega and Ansel are hardly babies any more. They understand loss and they have not only lost their ma-ma but for all intents and purposes, their pa-pa as well."

"Do you really think it is better for those children to be alone at the base camp all day waiting for their exhausted father to return at night? Better do you think than to be here playing with other children, learning their letters in our nursery or going to school?" Jacques looked over at his wife.

She saw the sincerity in his face and thought for a moment before answering.

No, not when you put it that way. But Jacques, he is their father, they need him and they also need a home. And William needs a home. Two years is long enough for a man to wallow in his grief. I think we should try to find William a potential bride. He is a good man. Perhaps someone would agree to be a housekeeper and watch over the children and after a time, perhaps… who knows?" She shrugged in what could only be described as a typically Gallic manner.

"And how would you suggest *we* go about doing that?" Jacques asked with a hint of amusement.

"Perhaps we should ask around."

"And what about little Britta?"

Maria sighed. "Little Britta is a different story. In truth, they are strangers to each other and we are perhaps better equipped to take care of her right here. Every time Doctor St. Claire listens to the child's heart his expression becomes more dour. He does not like to say anything but even the children can see she is not as she should be especially given her parentage."

"Her parentage?"

"Well, yes, just look at her siblings. Thor is almost two heads taller than John. Rega stands at least a head above our girls and Ansel is as tall as Phillip but half his age. Then there is poor Britta. Jamie is six months older and looks six years older." It was a slight exaggeration but her point was well made.

"My darling wife," Jacques said softly, enclosing her in his arms and kissing her lightly on the nose, "I know you would like to solve everyone's problems but you cannot, any more than you can tell a man how long he should grieve. But I am curious, Nicholet has been a widower much longer, why have you not tried to play matchmaker for him?"

"Do you think I should?" she asked brightly.

"No," he laughed. "I just wish to know what you see as the difference."

"To be honest, I thought about it long ago but… well, we have not many single women around. And Francois has no children. Jacques, that makes a big difference."

"Hmmm, well, you are right about one thing. William does have children and he should see them more often. And this I promise I will see to."

Jacques sent word to the base camp summoning William to the settlement. When the big Swede arrived, he was informed that henceforth, he should plan on coming to the settlement every month to give Jacques a report on operations in person and to spend a day with his children.

When William saw his son he was embarrassed. The lad stood close to six feet tall and had no business in a nursery. Thor was on the brink of becoming a man and to the lad's delight William told his son he was to return with his father to the camp.

Rega at nine and Ansel at six were different. They enjoyed the companionship of the nursery and Marie assured William they were more than welcome to stay and continue their schooling.

"They are still so very young, William," Marie said softly. "But please come and see them often. Now let us go to the nursery and see if Britta is awake from her nap."

Chapter 11

1705

Jacques looked at his totally flaccid member resting at the apex of his thighs and smiled broadly. Even completely spent, it was not unimpressive he thought rather proudly. He chided himself for thinking like a schoolboy, for thinking like Richard. He was forty years old and certainly wise enough to know that the true value of a man did not lie between his legs. Then he grinned even broader. This may be true but it certainly seemed to delight his wife.

In amusement he shut his clear gray eyes and gave a deeply satisfied sigh. He and Marie had just shared such erotic passions even he had been amazed. How many men could boast of eliciting such energetic and rapacious responses from their wives after almost seventeen years of marriage? How many indeed? But then, how many wives had the raw sexuality to make their husbands feel as out of control as Marie could still so easily make him feel?

He rolled over and propped himself up on his elbow to watch her. Oblivious to the cold November winds blowing outside the casement window behind the painted screen, she was standing in her private tub, close to the hearth, sensuously sponging herself after their volcanic mingling. Her body, rosy from their lovemaking, was highlighted by the fire in the hearth and after six children, she was more beautiful to him than ever. Her skin was taut, smooth and supple without a hint of sag or wrinkle from her proud breasts to her slender well-shaped legs, and he found the soft slight pucker to her fertile woman's belly very appealing. The firelight, reflected in the rivulets of water running down her body, made her skin sparkle. And she was still so captivatingly unaware of her own *esprit de provocant.*

When she had finished and began patting herself dry, Jacques rose up from the bed and went to a basin to freshen himself. A glimpse in the mirror made him smile again.

A touch of silver was coming into his thick blond hair which he wore more closely cropped these days. Wearing a periwig was not something he enjoyed but he felt it lent a certain stature to his appearance on formal business occasions and it was easier to wear one over short hair. Marie had not wished him to cut his hair too closely, saying she needed something to run her fingers through and he had been happy to comply. His wig hung upon their bedpost most of the time.

"You were a lioness tonight," he commented with a chuckle, spotting the love bites on his neck and on his pectorals along with the small scratches of exuberance on his muscular back. "I do not know, woman," he sighed teasingly while shaking his head. "How do you expect me to keep up the pace? I am not a youngster anymore."

In truth, he did not look more than thirty. His jaw was still trim and firm, and he continued to shave cleanly, leaving only a small thin moustache which was darker than the hair on his head but still turned to burnished gold if he spent enough time outdoors. He sucked in his stomach. The muscles of his abdomen were well defined and as hard as the rest of his body.

Marie smiled, looking very pleased with herself, and picking up her hair brush, she began to run it through her long, thick, gently curling tresses.

"I think perhaps we can expect another addition to our nursery before long," he said casually as he sponged himself off and took up a towel.

"Why would you think that?" she responded casually.

"Because I have seen you like this before, my darling," he said knowingly with a boyish grin.

"Only every time you touch me, monsieur," she countered coyly.

"Yes, but there is a special, shall we say *aggression* that transforms you into an almost predatory creature. Very demanding," he teased, "and most exciting, my love..."

Marie was smiling, hearing only his words but not to where they were leading. She giggled.

"… and it happens every time you are *enceinte*. So, how long has it been since...?"

Marie halted her brush in mid-stroke. She knew the question he was asking. She paused to think. She had been so busy of late, how long had it been since her monthly flow? Could it have been that long ago? It seemed like only a week or two but now that she thought about it, it could have been longer, much longer! She had completely lost track.

"James is almost six, Britta is five; it will be good to have another baby in our midst. What is the matter?" Jacques asked seeing a peculiar expression come into his wife's face.

"Nothing... I just... well... I mean, I cannot imagine that we will have another baby, Jacques. Jamie is our last child."

"How do you know?"

"I have always thought of Jamie as our last child."

"Why is that?" he asked softly, walking up behind her and putting his arms around her. He was looking at her in the mirror in front of them watching his own long sensitive fingers caress her, stroking her hips and belly as they tapered up into her small waist. For many years now his hands had returned to being the soft hands of a gentleman.

"I am too old," she pronounced dismissively. "Besides, your parents came to see *all* their grandchildren. And if we have another child then they would not have seen all of them," she said growing slightly agitated because she knew that did not make a sensible argument. "No, I cannot be pregnant again," she said firmly. "I am old enough to be a grandmother."

Jacques thought that very funny and laughed deeply.

"It is true, Jacques. I am not a girl anymore. Our first born is now fourteen… the age of the boy who," she suddenly lowered her voice to a whisper, "first made me pregnant. And if that baby had lived, he would now be…" she thought for a moment and gasped. "*Mon Dieu*, he would be twenty-two already. Twenty-two! Older than you when you left France!" At that Jacques' expression changed to one of surprise. "Yes, grandparents! We could be. We are old enough. Which leads me to ask, have you had a talk with your oldest sons?"

"A talk?"

"You know, the same talk mothers must have with their daughters… about the birds and bees. John looks exactly like you; each morning when he comes to breakfast I half expect him to be sporting a small moustache. He is by far the most handsome boy in the entire settlement and I have seen the young girls in church flirting outrageously with him. Best he understands about personal virtue and re-sponsibility, *n'est-ce pas?* Before curiosity and youthful urges cause problems."

"Oh, that talk," Jacques grinned. "Fear not, we had that talk some time ago. John matured early."

Marie whipped around to face him. "You do not mean he has already…?

"No-no-no. He understands the virtue of restraint, although I must say I felt a complete hypocrite when talking to him… considering my own youth." Jacques could not help but smile. "But his body has awakened; he is on his way to being a man."

"Where has the time flown?" Marie sighed. "I am sure your parents feel the same way. Your mother had a baby who overnight grew into a young boy who was chased from the country as a dashing youth who greets her at the wharf with six children of his own in tow."

Jacques chuckled at her brief synopsis of his life and then grew more serious. "Speaking of my parents, *mon cœur*, I do not think I ever properly thanked you."

She looked at him in the mirror and met his gaze with a puzzled frown.

"I know they would have never stayed as long as they did if you had not so sin-cerely encouraged them. My mother told me it was only because you made her feel so welcome and comfortable that she had been so happy to extend their stay. It means more to me than I can ever say, Marie," he said softly. "I had two more years with them that I would not have had otherwise."

"Oh, Jacques," she sighed, turning in his arms, reaching up and running her fin-gers lightly across his temple and down the side of his face in a caress. "I love your parents. They are wonderful people, and because of them I have you to love. I wish they could have stayed with us for the rest of their lives but I think it was espe-cially hard on your pa-pa having nothing to really do here while thinking of all there was to be done back in France." She turned back to the mirror and continued to brush her hair. "We women are better able to adapt, I think. Your mother could fill her hours with all the little things and with the children. But your father looked so at a loss to make himself feel useful. He needed to get back to his responsibilities but he would have given her up just to make her happy." She paused again catching his eye in the mirror. "I saw the way your father loves your mother, Jacques, it makes me understand more about you."

"Do not expect me to ever offer to give you up," he said, his voice had grown husky, "I am not as self-sacrificing as my father." Then, he bent and pushing her silky tresses aside, kissed her lingeringly upon the neck. His kiss and his breath just below her ear sent a visible tremor through her entire body. He continued kissing her, enjoying her reaction and watching her dissolve into little shivers and give herself over to wantonly begging for his caresses.

"Jacques, you know what you do to me when you kiss me there," she cried softly, reaching down and drawing his hands from her waist up to her breasts while she pushed her backside into him. "It is not fair for you to do this to me," she said in little gasps leaning her head back against his chest, exposing her sensitive neck further, "after what you just said about keeping up."

"That is not a real concern. Surely you remember that I know many ways to satisfy you, woman," he said at last and salaciously drew her back to their bed where he took complete control over her. It gave him a great deal of pleasure to give her pleasure, to watch her react so intensely to his seductive and erotic caresses and lose herself in the overpowering sensations he could wrench from within her with his touch.

It did not take long before the intense heat of her reaction accompanied by her vocalizations had the unfailing ability to arouse him and bring life anew back to his own loins. Holding himself back while bringing her to repeated peaks of frenzy, they joined in a final release and when finished, were too exhausted to do anything but sleep.

Jacques' suspicions of the cause of his wife's particularly voracious sexual appetite were not misguided. By Christmas, Marie could no longer deny that she was, indeed, pregnant again and she settled into acceptance. But this pregnancy developed into a very nervous one, unlike any of the others. Throughout the winter, she did not feel well much of the time. She felt particularly trapped by the snow and ice, and morose with the sameness of the gloomy days. She was edgy and short tempered with him, with the children, and with the servants. Then, she would fall into fits of remorseful weeping, begging their forgiveness and assuring them that she did not mean to distress them. By the middle of her term she had lost all interest in the physical side of their relationship which Jacques stoically accepted and took in stride. This, while she became obsessed with the time she spent with each of her children, hugging and kissing them tearfully to the limits of their patience until they sought to wriggle free.

Jacques had no way of knowing that in the back recesses of Marie's mind were the memories of a mother who had died giving birth to her seventh child. She did not share this with him, fear that speaking of it would make it an even stronger possibility. What he did know was that this pregnancy appeared to be unique in the strain it was putting on his wife. He lay awake long hours beside her, listening to her breathe. Often he heard the sound of whimpering as she slept and he worried. For the first time in their marriage he began to fear for Marie's health and he prayed for special considerations.

Jacques did not think of himself as a religious man which might have seemed an irony to some, considering his circumstances had derived at least in part from his religious convictions. But he was a man of faith. It was a faith he had learned as a child, a faith in the relationship he had with his Maker, a faith in his Salvation, and a faith in Omnipotent love, guidance, and response to prayer. He had learned these things early at his mother's knee and they had never left him. For years on the frontier there had been no church service to attend but he had an easy acceptance of the will of Providence and never in his darkest hours had he ever really felt abandoned. Likewise, he had a strong faith that when in need his prayers were always heard. As far as Jacques was concerned, God had given him his freedom in this new country, had given him his wife and family, and God would continue to watch over them. And right now, he kept faith that God was watching over Marie.

The lumbermen had come down to work in the mill as they had been doing every winter only this season William and Thor joined them. Jacques was glad to see the big man making an effort to reintegrate himself into the world and insisted they stay at the house in the wing Jacques had built for his parents. After all, he reasoned, thirteen year old Rega and ten year old Ansel were already living there. What would happen in the spring could be decided over the winter but it became clear that Rega and Ansel were less than enthusiastic about any talk of leaving the settlement, the school, and their friends for the vaguely remembered solitude and sad memories of the lumber camp.

The snows had been heavy that season and the melt off of spring was long in coming. One particularly mild day in early March Jacques made his way to the lumber mill office through the streams and standing mud puddles created by the melting snow. His crews were working hard and for a time his arrival went unnoticed. Nicholet came into the office to speak with him.

"Ah, Francois, I was just thinking about you. These production figures are excellent. We shall achieve record numbers this month and of course the governor shall want his bite."

The swarthy mill manager smiled both in pride and at Jacques' little joke.

"I know not what I would do without you," Jacques added and the smile left Francois' face. "What is it?" Jacques asked immediately.

"I have been waiting to speak with you, monsieur... perhaps I should have gone to your home. I kept expecting you to come to the mill and..."

"Good heavens, Francois, what is it? Just speak out, man," Jacques said, seeing the other's unease.

"I have taken a wife."

"Really?" Jacques smiled with genuine pleasure as he rose to shake Francois' hand. "How did you manage that without my hearing about it? But I am happy for you... congratulations! I must admit, I have thought for years that you were a man who might never marry again."

"It was a quiet ceremony at her request."

"Do I know her?"

"I believe not, monsieur. She was the Widow Carver before last week when she became Madame Nicholet."

"A widow?"

"Yes. A young widow who has three children, two boys and a girl. They only arrived in our settlement a year or so ago. The children are bright and we all get along very well. I love them all. I must admit, I am very pleased to have an instant family."

"It sounds to me like you may need a raise in wages to provide for your instant family," Jacques smiled warmly.

"No, monsieur... that is very generous but... Well, the fact is, we are leaving for the frontier to homestead a place of our own. The children are half grown, you see, they will be able to help a great deal and I want to have something to leave behind when I die. I have hopes Penelope and I will have children of our own as well and a farm is the best way to feed a lot of hungry mouths."

"The frontier?" Jacques repeated, struck almost speechless by the shock.

Francois nodded.

"How soon do you plan to leave?"

"As soon as possible. The planting season is coming and we will need to clear land in order to plant."

Jacques sat down hard in his chair.

"I am sorry, monsieur. I realize this is not much of a notice. I can stay a week if you need me, possibly two if you insist but travel is easier if the ground does not become too soft."

"No... no, you are right. Better you get to where you are going while the ground still holds its frost. A week or two will make more difference to you than to me for in the end you will still be gone." Jacques sighed. He was quiet for a moment before uttering another grunt. "Good Heavens, Francois, this is truly a shock. You have been here since the beginning. I have grown used to not having to think about the mill, thanks to you. You have been doing everything. I hope I have always let you know how much you are valued."

"Monsieur, I do not leave because of any dissatisfaction with you or the mill. I have been very happy here. If I had not married I would be more than happy to stay forever. But now I have a family, you see. I must do more than just work for another man. Land prices have become expensive in our settlement. I cannot afford to buy cleared acreage for a farm but I have the heart to carve it out of the wilderness much as you did."

Jacques nodded. He understood completely. He pulled a bottle of cognac from his desk along with two glasses.

"So," he fought to gather his wits, "we must toast to your future." He held his glass up to the other and took a generous swig. "And now, who would you recommend as your replacement here at the mill?"

Francois was quiet for a time, obviously mulling over his answer. "I regret that may be a difficult choice. You have two foremen who are perhaps your best candidates but they have developed a rivalry between them with men loyal to each. No matter which one you promote to manager, the other and his followers will resent it."

Jacques sighed again. "Nothing is easy, is it?"

Francois smiled sadly. "I regret to leave you with this dilemma."

"Francois, give me the rest of this week. And I insist on a party in your honor. Saturday night, after the mill shuts down, we will have a dance in my barn. The entire town will be invited. You and your bride shall be the guests of honor. No, do not object. I insist on this. You have been my right hand and I am going to miss you sorely. I mean to honor you, my friend, whether you like it or not," Jacques said sincerely. "After that, you are free to do as you like."

As soon as Jacques returned home, he sent for William to come to his study.

"Have a seat," Jacques offered and poured them each a small cognac. He remembered their first meeting with William standing uncomfortably stooped under the low ceiling of the tavern but with an ingratiating smile broad upon his face. He was now able to stand tall in the Power home where the ceilings were comfortably high but the smile had been replaced with a world-weary sternness. "William, I have had some news and wish to discuss it with you."

William sat silently giving Jacques his attention.

"As you can see, our little settlement has grown to a comfortable size. We have decent people living here and in all these years we have never had another storm like the one that drove you to take your family up river into the wilderness. The wilderness can be a harsh and lonely place for a man alone and for his children. How intent are you on returning there in spring or could I persuade you to stay here?"

"You mean move my household back here?" the big man asked, thinking of Britta's lonely grave upon the hill.

"Exactly. You have done an admirable job running the crews of lumberjacks, now I would like you to think about running the mill itself."

"But Nicholet...?" he responded in puzzlement.

"Yes, Nicholet. He has been my right hand here in the settlement, you have been my left hand up in the wild… but I find I am about to lose him. He has married a widow with children and they are determined to set out for the frontier and homestead a farm of their own."

"I did not know."

"No, as yet few people do. The point is, I am at a loss for a mill manager and I would very much like it if you would consent to do the job. I think your children would be very happy to stay here. It seems they have become fast friends with mine in our nursery and they enjoy going to the school. We will find you a house or build one quickly with help from the mill. What do you say?"

William sat quietly, obviously in deep thought. "I do not know what to say, sir… think on this I must."

"Of course and while you are thinking, give some thought to which of your men you would recommend to take your place at the lumber camp. But do not think too long. I am giving a party in the old barn this Saturday for Nicholet. We must celebrate his marriage and wish him good luck in his new venture, eh? The whole town is invited. I would like you to be there and I would like to announce that you are replacing him… if you agree."

The big man rose from his chair. "Much I have to think about, sir," he said and took his leave.

Marie was retaining water and suffering the ensuing discomforts. Her ankles were swollen, and her legs, feet, and back ached excessively. This was all a new and miserable experience for her and Doctor St. Clair was concerned. He had restricted her from all salt which included the meats and fish preserved through the winter with salt. In the kitchen Margot fussed to find something worth serving to her mistress. A party was the last thing Marie was interested in.

"My advice is that you stay home in bed," St. Claire told her.

"I cannot do that," Marie responded a trifle petulantly. "Monsieur Nicholet has been a valued employee and has been at the settlement since before you, *Monsieur Docteur*. I cannot insult him by failing to make an appearance."

"I doubt that anyone would be insulted! You are under my care, although heaven knows you do not seem inclined to be under my orders," the doctor grumbled peevishly.

His strange relationship with Madame Power had begun with the birth of her second son. When he would have restricted her to confinement, she insisted on continuing with all her daily tasks both at home and at her trading post. Then the Indian squaw showed up and he was out-numbered. When labor began and conventional wisdom recommended the patient retire to the birthing bed, madame had insisted on remaining upright and walking and the squaw had encouraged her. When madame's water broke and he ordered her to occupy the birthing chair he had commissioned to be made for the occasion, she had growled much like an angry dog and gone down to the floor on all fours. It had been most startling to see a white woman grunting out a baby just like one of the savages.

"I will only make an appearance," Marie offered as a compromise to St. Claire. "I promise to be no more than fifteen minutes, twenty at the most."

"Do as you will, madame, you will anyway," huffed St. Claire as he left the house but he promised to see her at the party.

The old barn had been cleared out, cleaned, and decorated festively. Almost the entire town turned out. After the harsh winter, most were ready for a party. Jacques was aware that his mill men expected an announcement that night naming Nicholet's replacement and Jacques was much relieved when Boot officially accepted the job.

Marie forced herself to don a new dress made especially to fit her awkward silhouette. Jane assisted Marie in arranging her hair since the effort of holding her arms up fatigued her quickly. By the time she was prepared, she felt exhausted but she was determined to make an appearance. She wanted to be gracious. She, too, liked and appreciated Monsieur Nicholet and all that he had been to the settlement and Jacques' mill. It was difficult to believe he was not going to be in the midst of their small community any longer.

Jacques escorted Marie to the barn and she smiled and held his arm as she said all the right things to the new bride and groom and their surrounding company. They were delighted to see her as were so many others present. They had not seen much of Mistress Power for many months. Then, after barely ten minutes, debilitating pains began shooting down Marie's leg. They were so severe she could scarcely control herself.

"Jacques," she breathed into her husband's ear with urgency, a catch in her voice, "take me home, now, please." A fine sweat had broken out on her forehead and he instantly scooped her up into his arms while her face fell into his neck and she bit her lip to keep from crying out.

"Tell the doctor to come," he called out before he carried his wife back to their house and up the stairs to their room. Marie could barely stand. He assisted her out of her clothing and she was getting into their bed just as St. Claire arrived.

"Go back to the party, Jacques, you must go back," she urged him. "It is important. You are the host."

Jacques saw the agony written in his wife's eyes although she held a small smile on her face. He did not want to leave.

"Go, go," St. Claire pushed him to the door; closed it and turned to Marie. "Tell me where it hurts."

With Jacques gone, Marie dropped all pretense and cringed. "My leg! Ohhh, *mon Dieu!* It feels like someone put a knife in my thigh and is twisting it around." She groaned again.

"A muscle spasm," St. Claire pronounced as he tried to elevate her feet which made the matter worse; pain like a lightning flash streak into her buttock.

Marie stiffened with a gasp. "No, not a spasm. It is not the muscle. It is something else. Inside." She stuffed the coverlet into her mouth to stifle her cries and rolled to her side, knocking the pillows to the floor as she writhed upon the bed.

Jane was hovering, helplessly wringing her hands wondering what she could do.

St. Claire ordered up warm bricks from the kitchen and a hot water bag while they waited, which sent Jane on her way. He mixed a tincture of opium in a diluted glass of cognac and made Marie drink it.

She made a face and shuddered. "This tastes horrible! Is it safe for the child?" she asked truculently, barely sipping it.

"Such stress for the mother cannot be good for the child," he shot back. "Drink it, it will not hurt. You would drink anything that Indian woman gave you but for me you are stubborn as a mule."

Marie looked at the old man and gave him a fond smile despite her clenched teeth. "*Monsieur Docteur*, please do not be angry with me. Please. I meant no offense. She was a wise woman and here long before you. It was habit."

Barely mollified, St. Claire grunted just as Sarah knocked at the door. The warmth of the hot water bag she brought eased some of Marie's discomfort.

"Better?" St. Claire asked.

Marie grunted, groaned, and then nodded, her teeth clenched. "Somewhat. I do not understand," she whimpered, trying to keep the tears at bay. "I feel like I am falling apart. What is this new complaint? I have never had such pain before, pregnant or not."

St. Claire gave a Gallic shrug and muttered. "Life changes us. Things change. Nothing is ever the same. You have had six very healthy pregnancies, Madame Power. You have never miscarried. You have buried no children. Do you realize how very rare this is? Sooner or later, one must expect something." Marie found his response discouraging and frightening. "Now, if I may… allow me to examine your belly," he said gruffly.

From beneath her covers, Marie obediently lifted her lawn shift above her protruding abdomen and drew the covers modestly down to her hips. St. Claire gently sought out the form of the child within her womb. "Hmmm," he said as she continued to press the warmth of the hot water bag against her thigh. "Oh, there…ha, I see a tiny foot, *n'est-ce pas?* I press a little and he reacts – good, good." He smiled and covered her belly again. "So, nothing seems wrong with your baby."

It was reassuring to hear but she had never thought it was the baby. "But what is wrong with the mother? What is the reason for this pain, *Monsieur Docteur?* So sudden, so intense, and out of nowhere without warning."

St. Claire said nothing but with his ear pressed against her chest he listened to Marie's heart, measured her pulse, and finally modestly pulled aside the bed cover to observe the suspect thigh and buttock. They looked completely normal, healthy, no sores, no wound, no discoloration, no bruising. The feeling she described was a complaint he had heard before and it had more to do with the spine and the nerves perhaps than the muscle. And that was a land of complete mystery. But a muscle spasm could be most painful. And he had heard such complaints most often from men but men were smart enough to drown the pain in a good brandy if they could afford it.

Unwilling to allow to go to waste the small glass of cognac he had prepared for Marie, he downed its remains knowing his arthritis would soon be soothed. He settled into the bedside chair.

"If you were not pregnant I would recommend putting you into a brace or stretching you on a table, but this we cannot do. So…from now on you must be more careful."

"I have been careful, very careful."

He scowled at her interruption. "From now on I want you to stay in bed, surround yourself with pillows, do you understand?"

Marie nodded as Jane arrived with two warmed bricks fresh from the kitchen hearth and wrapped in clean flannel. St. Claire handed Jane the hot water bag and placed the bricks on the bed in contact with Marie's pained thigh.

"And now, how does that feel?"

"Manageable."

"Good." St. Claire turned to Jane. "Tell the cook to have several bricks warming at all times – not burning hot – but warming at the hearth in case Madame Power has future need."

"Yes, sir."

He turned back to Marie. "If the pain returns apply the heat again and take a teaspoon of this." He withdrew a bottle of laudanum from his bag. "Also, as of this moment, you are going to stop lifting your children, even Britta."

"But…"

"And do not allow them in your lap."

Marie snorted. "I have no lap anymore."

"Be that as it may, you have my instructions. I am going to tell Monsieur Power all this and advise him to keep a very close eye on you," the doctor continued with a finger raised in her direction. "He has been far too lenient and you are far too independent, madame," he shook his finger at her. "Now you are reaping the suffering for it. It is time you listened to the wisdom of your elders. Bed rest is what you need and a proper confinement."

"Do not set my husband upon me like the *gen d'armes*," she called after St. Claire as he left the room. "Do you hear me, *Monsieur Docteur?*" she raised her voice. "And tell Margot I have a taste for tea and cream puffs! Please?"

Alone after St. Claire's departure, Marie lay propped up within the bed stroking her belly, grateful that the warmth of the bricks had taken away the sharpness of her pain and left her with only a tolerable ache. This was nonsense, she told herself. She had a store to manage, a home to oversee, the children… *And if you were dead?* A voice within her asked.

Marie sighed with the realization that it could all go on without her. Felicity had been her apprentice for six years already. She knew what she was doing; Marie had taught the girl well and she was completely trustworthy. Lyndyn Peterson had joined them over a year ago. Cassandra, Margot's daughter, who made all the pastries in the bakery had already spoken to Marie of buying that business and paying Marie rent for the space. She, too, knew what she was doing.

Marie's thoughts next went to Sheehoo. How she missed the Indian woman's sturdy reassurance and wished desperately she were here now. Was it just good fortune that Marie had never miscarried? Was it luck that all six of her deliveries had been relatively easy, her babies healthy and strong? Had it been her youth or had all the little things the squaw kept sending to Marie been partly responsible? Vaguely Marie recalled having dreamt of the woman but she could not remember anything specific. Where were they now, Marie wondered? Had the native and her brother escaped the sickness? Were they well and still alive?

As she continued to stroke her belly, Marie realized it bothered her greatly that the woman who had been there for every one of Marie's healthy deliveries would not be present for this one. It also bothered her that while she had been in her twenties for all those births, she was now almost half way through her thirties. Was not Ma-ma about this age when she died?

Marie's heart thudded in her chest. She did not want to leave her children as Ma-ma had left. In some small icy part of her stomach her fears grew. Jane arrived with her tea and pastries.

"Jane, since the doctor has restricted me to bed, I will have need of a supply of paper, quills, and ink. Oh, and Monsieur Power's portable writing desk. I am going to write instructions for Margot while I am thinking of them now. There are teas, Jane, that I have always taken after birth which guard against infection and childbed fever. The doctor will not be inclined to agree but once I have this baby, please make certain I get the teas daily.

"Of course, ma'am. Don't you worry none; we'll take good care of you."

"Thank you, Jane, but I confess… this time for the first time, I do worry."

Chapter 12

When he was a boy his mother had taken him to the Market Day Fair in the village and he had seen a juggler. Jacques remembered clearly watching the man keep first three, then four, then five, and finally six balls all in the air at once. Jacques had been fascinated, awed, and mesmerized. Later, no matter how hard he practiced he was never able to master the trick. He never understood how the man did it. He felt a little like that juggler now.

True to his word, Doctor St. Claire told Jacques about the restrictions he had given Marie and he charged Jacques with the responsibility of enforcing them. Jacques had to be firm with his frustrated wife. With love, he appealed to Marie's reason, her sense of honor, and her loyalty to him. She had vowed to love, honor, and *obey*, he reminded her, and this was the part about obeying. He had been lenient and indulgent because she had always been in such very good health… but now? Now, they must listen to the doctor. She was to stay in bed. Just to be certain, he also met with the house staff and informed them of those same restrictions. They were to keep an eye out for Madame's compliance. She was given a silver bell and they were to be at her immediate beckoning but she was to stay in the bedroom and off the staircase. She could send messages to her store and to this end their sons were to make themselves available.

Nicholet and his new family were gone, grateful for the monetary parting gift Jacques had bestowed.

Boot, after talking with his children, had accepted the new position asking only that he be allowed to go back and pack up what few belongings he had at the camp and tend to Britta's grave. It was agreed and William recommended another hulking big man by the name of Sven Olafson to replace him.

Jacques promoted Olafson without reservation and the lumberjacks left for the season. William was just about to leave himself when an infestation of pests was discovered threatening to ruin the apple crop and possibly kill off the entire orchard. Jacques was desperate. He asked William to delay his departure for a short time while Jacques made a speedy trip up the coast to beg advice from other orchard owners closer to New York Towne. Upon his return, he asked William to delay once again in order to join Sims, the oldest boys, and himself in the orchard. They worked around the clock to save the fruit trees using the suggested formulas for home remedies of repellents and washes. What harvest they would have this year remained to be seen, but the trees had been saved.

Exhausted, dirty, hungry, and feeling every one of his forty-one years, Jacques was finally able to come home to eat, to bathe, and to sleep, not necessarily in that order. Once home, he found Marie obediently in bed and being entertained by their daughters but miserably uncomfortable. He was too worried about her to sleep, which was just as well for no sooner had he sponged himself down and put on fresh clothing, when a messenger from the mill arrived bidding his speedy attendance. Jacques grabbed some leftovers from the kitchen and was on his way again. There was trouble and he was needed.

Now he sat in the mill office. He had just settled a dispute between several of the men, a dispute that had almost come to blows. This was getting ridiculous, he thought, and once Boot got some well-deserved sleep he would be leaving during which time Jacques had other things to occupy him than the childish rivalries of the mill workers.

As Jacques sat in a state of numb fatigue, seeing the juggler in his mind, there was a knock at the outside door. "Come," he snapped, wondering what the devil was wrong on the mill floor now. It had not even registered that being the *outside* door, it was unlikely a mill man knocking.

"Good afternoon, Mister Power," said a familiar voice. It was the settlement's preacher, Reverend McCullen, a scholarly looking Scot of sparse build, lean and bald under his stiff white wig.

Jacques rose immediately. "Ah, good afternoon, Pastor, please come in and have a seat. Forgive me," he added, brushing away the crumbs of his food. "I was not expecting... I mean I thought you were one of the mill crew. What brings you here?" Jacques returned to his own chair.

"I regret having t' interrupt yer day, sir..." a slight burr accented McCullen's speech.

Jacques waved the apology aside. "Actually, I am pleased to see you, it is preferred to the alternative," he added.

Reverend McCullen looked at him, clearly puzzled but noted the dark shadows under Jacques' eyes and the drawn look about his mouth.

Jacques chuckled, "I should explain… I was afraid at first you were yet another of the mill workers coming to complain about yet another of his co-workers. Never mind. What can I do for you, monsieur?"

"I came to remind ye of yer promise to go to New York Towne 'n seek another teacher for the school. With school's end for the year coming fast upon us, we canna wait if we are t' geet a qualified person for the coming year."

Jacques gave a sharp intake of breath. He had completely forgotten. The schoolmaster had tendered in his resignation in order to move on to a wealthier post and Jacques had promised the people of the settlement that he would seek out a replacement.

"Good lord," he exclaimed. "I forgot!" Jacques raked his hands through his hair. "Forgive me, Pastor, I have had too much on my mind. My wife... is not doing well in her confinement. I lost my mill manager, as you know, and my orchard was attacked by pests... I am sorry. It completely slipped my mind."

"I've taken the liberty t' line up several candidates who are all available in New York Towne at this time. They are each eager for the position, sir. Perhaps, ye could find the time t' take a few days t' go t'....."

Jacques was shaking his head. "That is not possible," he stated emphatically. "My wife's time is coming near and I simply cannot leave. She has been so ill. It is unthinkable that I should be away this close to the baby's arrival. I hope you understand. Surely someone else can go and do the interviewing?"

"As the founder of the community," Reverend McCullen replied a bit stiffly, "ye were the preferred choice."

"What of yourself? Can you not interview and make a selection?"

"Ye were the preferred choice, Mister Power. I really dinna want the responsibility."

"But you are active in the school. You have to work with the candidate; surely you can select someone you feel can do the job. Someone that you feel you can work with and who is a compliment to your shortcomings and vice versa."

The thought of having shortcomings obviously did not set well with the little man as he went rigid and red rose up from his neck to encompass his entire head.

"I mean to say, you would naturally be looking for someone who was stronger in subjects that you might be a bit weaker in and who does not necessarily have to be strong in the subjects you are best versed in," explained Jacques with more than a hint of impatience in his voice.

The other man seemed mollified and nodded. "If that be yer wish, Mister Power, I shall endeavor t' do me best."

"Excellent! I am certain you shall do just fine," Jacques said encouragingly and ended the interview by putting on his own coat and hat in preparation to go back home and check on Marie.

Sacre Bleu! *If Nicholet was going to leave, why could he not have done so while Pa-pa was still here?* Jacques thought wildly as he strode to his horse. *Now that is totally irrational!* It was more than three years since his parents had left and three years ago Marie was not pregnant and there had been no infestation on the fruit trees.

Not that Jacques would have expected his father to take over running the mill, but being a presence on hand would have forestalled childish squabbles. And being a source to tap for advice certainly would have given the duke something to do. *If Marie is right about Pa-pa needing to feel useful then involving him in the business was exactly what might have convinced him to stay a while longer.* Now Jacques could not even write his father for advice for by the time the letters went back and forth across the ocean, the problems would undoubtedly be resolved one way or the other and it would only cause his parents to worry. That was why he had not written to them about Marie. How could he? How could they help from across an ocean when he could not help and he was right here?

He was just feeling overwhelmed, he told himself. Everything always has to happen at once. And where was Richard? Again winter had come and gone with no word. Jacques tried to bring nothing negative home with him from his business concerns so he did not discuss any of his current problems. This was not easy for him. He had grown used to sharing things with Marie. Often she helped him to see things in a completely different light and he valued her opinions and counted on her viewpoint more than he realized. But for now, the only thing he could do was not to add to Marie's stresses and worries by adding his own problems to her concerns. Jacques lived alone with his burdens and as summer unfolded he found himself turning often to earnest prayer.

It was almost three months since Nicholet's send off and Marie was still unable to walk without assistance. She stayed in bed as the doctor insisted, only getting up to use the chamber pot, or sit by the fire while her bedding was changed, or sit by the window as Jane brushed her hair. She did nothing she was ordered by the doctor not to do, yet the pains in her back and leg were often more excruciating and debilitating than ever. And when they came, the only relief to be found was from the laudanum and that made her want to sleep.

In late June, labor began with a nightmare that had Marie crying and calling out. Jacques woke her to comfort her but when she realized her contractions had begun she gave him a look that chilled the blood in his veins. It was a look reminiscent of the look upon his mother's face when his parents had departed at the pier. It was the look of love in a final farewell.

Jacques sent for Doctor St. Claire who seemed far too relaxed when he arrived, gruffly reminding Jacques that this was nothing new to any of them. But it was new, Jacques protested. Never had they faced such chronic misery before. The old doctor said nothing but pushed Jacques from the room and shut the door in his face. Jacques stood at the closed portal listening, hearing Marie's pitiful groans from within.

He continued to pace outside the closed door, miserable in his impotence to do anything more and unable to set aside the huge knot of raw fear within his stomach. Back and forth, up and down the hall he strode, pausing every time he passed the door behind which his wife lie. Sometimes he heard her, sometimes he heard the doctor, and sometimes he heard nothing. The times he heard her were a mixed blessing. He knew she was still part of this world, still alive but often the sounds she uttered were so unnerving. It had never been like this before.

He recalled John's birth shortly after the hurricane. The Indians had taken care of her and the first time he saw her she was walking about happy and smiling. With Phillip's birth he had been nervous, of course, but Marie had been smiling when he was pushed out of the room. The Indian woman had been with her. And Richard had been there with him, and he had taken Jacques out of the house and distracted him with inconsequential things around the grounds, with the animals and the sheds and the new barn under construction. Richard had distracted him many times and things had always gone well and he had become comfortable with the whole process. But not this time. This time things had been so different from almost the very beginning and this time Richard was not there to distract him. And where was Richard? They thought for sure they would see him last fall. Then they expected him in spring. It had been too long.

"Papa?" It was his son, John, calling to him. "Is everything all right?" the youth asked hesitantly. "Is Mama going to be well?"

Jacques looked toward his son's voice and suddenly realized all the children had settled themselves along the staircase and they were watching him, looking up to him, studying the situation and seeking reassurance amidst the vibrations of foreboding he was emanating in his wild pacing back and forth. How long had they been there? The whole household was awake. Hours had passed. It was midday already.

Jacques willed himself to relax and smile.

"Of course, of course, soon you will have a new brother... or perhaps a sister... who knows, eh?" he walked toward them, moved down the staircase and ruffled the hair on each precious head as he went. "What do you think, John, shall we let the girls have another so they are not so badly out-numbered?" He patted John on the shoulder in a manly gesture and put an arm around ten year old Richie. Jacques picked up spindly James who was stretching out in a growth spurt and he reached out for Louise who at eleven was the dainty miniature image of his beloved Marie. Momentarily, he sheltered her under his arm. He stroked Helen's tender twelve year old cheek and accepted Phillip's awkward embrace with a one armed embrace of his own. Britta, tiny and quiet, was in Sarah's lap flanked by Rega and Ansel who were reliving the vague tortured memories of their own mother's death.

Slowly Jacques led all the children down the staircase and into the library where he began to read to them, favorite stories from books Marie had collected. Jane brought lunch in a basket, like a picnic and spread blankets on the floor. Time passed. It was time for dinner but no one felt like eating. Jacques' voice was growing hoarse from his steady narrations.

The clock struck bedtime for the children but Jacques motioned Sarah to leave them be as the youngest had already nodded off around him, successfully escaping the adult world of cares. Thor, having eaten his dinner after his day at the mill, silently joined them. He said nothing but one could read in his face that he believed Mistress Marie was following in his own mother's footsteps. It was just what happened sooner or later.

They heard the door upstairs open and the doctor called out a demand for hot water. Helen went quickly to the kitchen with the message and hot water was brought to St. Claire in good speed by Margot who was pulled inside to assist. Jane was already within.

The sun had just begun dipping into the trees on the hillside when they heard her. It wasn't a scream but a cry so sharp, so filled with misery and over so quickly that everyone froze for a moment. Tears sprang to Jacques' eyes. He gave the sleeping Britta to Sarah and bounded up the stairway two steps at a time. He had never invaded the sanctity of the birth room before. He had always waited with patience and respect to be invited in but not this time.

This time he grabbed the knob and flung open the door just as a bloody matter streaked baby was laid upon Marie's belly. The doctor looked up, startled and unhappy about this sudden invasion, and told Jacques he had no business being there, and to leave immediately but Jacques did not hear him. He was looking at his wife lying on the bed, pale, drenched in sweat, still, quiet, motionless, all apparent life wrung from her and seeing the birthing chair with its catch bucket filled with what appeared to be blood, all the blood, blood and rags and shapeless tissue everywhere and the room began to spin uncontrollably as suddenly the floor flew toward him and hit him on the head.

Jacques had fainted and crumpled down.

"It serves him right," muttered St. Claire gruffly, barely looking at the man sprawled out near their feet. "Leave him there," he told the women assisting him, "but shut that blasted door!"

Sarah had left Britta in Thor's lap and followed Master Power in an effort to detain him. St. Claire was glad to see her. "Shut the door!" he barked again. "And come here."

The doctor worked to clear mucus from the infant's throat and nose, seeking to hear that first re-assuring squall. It came. He finished severing the umbilical cord and picked the infant up off Marie's deflated belly and handed the babe off to Jane who set about washing her. The Powers had another healthy daughter.

"Blame fool. I have my hands full with three patients in this family, a fourth I do not need," the old man grumbled. "Let us proceed to clean up." He finished delivering the afterbirth and deposited it into a basin, throwing a towel over it.

"I never saw so much birth water," he said upon observing the catch bucket. "One might think the woman had swallowed an ocean. You take this basin out and dispose of it, either burn it or bury it deep. Take that oil cloth too and scrub it down," he instructed Margot who left quickly. "How does the baby? Is she wrapped up nice and warm?" he asked Jane. He stepped over one of Jacques' legs to reach a stand where he washed his own blood streaked hands and arms clean. "Here let me see this little one." He reached out to take the baby from Jane. "You can clean up mother now and change the sheets."

As Jacques regained consciousness, he was first aware of a sound that he next recognized as the vibration of feet walking on the floor upon which he was lying.

"He is coming around. Help him up," St. Claire instructed, the baby still in his arms.

The words came from a far off place but Jacques was aware of hands pulling at him and as he struggled to gain back control of his legs and get up, two sets of hands helped and steadied him.

"*Pour l'amour des grands Tout-Puissant!* For the love of the Great Almighty! I have a mother and child for which to care, I do not need a father to nursemaid in the bargain. *Monsieur Pouvoir, quel est le problème avec vous?* You know better than to come in before you are invited. One would think you were new at this and needed a keeper," the doctor had lapsed into French, partly because of his own upset, partly in a conscious desire not to belittle the man in front of his own staff.

Jacques was not listening. "Marie!" he cried out.

"Marie is fine," the doctor said less harshly as he came closer to the staggering husband. St. Claire looked at Jacques more carefully with some concern. He gestured with his head in the direction of a chair beside the bed and the two women led Jacques to it.

"Now sit down before you fall down again!" St. Claire commanded. "Get him some cognac." St. Clare was aware that this pregnancy had not been easy on

Jacques either.

"Is she well?"

"She is fine. And so is your little daughter," the doctor, now smiling, held the babe up and nestled her into her mother's arm. "And if you can keep from falling on top of them, I will let you get up and take a look," he said with a gruff and not completely unwarranted concern.

Jacques stood carefully, peered for several long minutes at his wife and the baby lying, eyes closed, in her arm.

"She sleeps?" he asked softly for reassurance.

"Hmmm," St. Claire nodded. "She is exhausted; it has been a very long day and she has worked very, very hard."

"But she is… well?"

"Yes-yes," the old man poured himself a small glass of cognac from the tray on the bureau and tossed it down.

Gratefully, Jacques sat down again. He sat beside the bed, not moving, silently giving thanks. The women had cleaned up everything and St. Claire gathered his things. After one more scrutinizing glance around the room ending upon the mother and child asleep together, St. Claire patted Jacques upon the back.

"Congratulations, Pa-pa," he said and left, heading toward the kitchen. He was hungry and the brandy was going straight to his head. He needed food.

Fifteen minutes went by while Jacques watched the steady rise and fall of his wife's breathing. Then, their baby began to cry and Marie stirred. As her eyes opened she saw Jacques hovering over her but she did not smile. Instead her free arm went out and wound around his neck; she pulled him to her in an almost desperate embrace. She said nothing but began weeping uncontrollably.

Jacques tried to comfort Marie but her sobs grew stronger as she clung to him with her one free arm. The baby's cries also increased.

"Marie, the doctor says you are fine. All is well. You are well," he repeated over and over trying to reassure her, stroking her, petting her. "The baby is well. The doctor says everything is well. Do not cry. Please, do not cry. Oh, please, do not cry, my darling, my love, my life, my heart." He kissed her cheeks and eyes repeatedly, tasting the salt of her tears as he tried to sooth her. Still not really understanding what had happened this time but relieved to have it over, all he wanted was to see his beloved smile once again.

The continued cries of her new infant finally registered and she adjusted the baby to insert a nipple into the tiny mouth. As the babe grabbed hold and began to suckle, Marie sighed deeply. She was convinced she had just cheated death.

The next day Jacques was at his wife's bedside as they discussed names. Jacques wanted to name their new daughter Marie. Marie suggested Jeanne-Marie. Jacques kissed his wife tenderly but shook his head.

"Every one of my grandfather's children had to be Jean or Jeanne something. I do not wish that name for my child."

"Britta's daughter is Britta … and Britta died." Marie said quietly.

Jacques was startled by the comparison. "But the mother was already dead when William named the child." As soon as the words fell from his lips he regretted them.

She looked up at him but said nothing.

"Marie!" he gasped softly. "That is not going to happen. You must not think like that. I cannot bear the thought."

She saw the hurt in his eyes. "My poor Jacques. I am so sorry. I have been… a terror."

"Sh-sh-sh.." Jacques kissed her hands tenderly.

"No, it is true. I know it. An absolute terror. How did you put up with me? But I have been so frightened. I thought I was going to leave you and the children like my mother left us." Marie knew she must tell Jacques of her fears to have any more children and prayed he would not resent her for it. "Oh, Jacques…" she sighed softly, "I really do not think I should have any more children…"

At that same moment St. Claire walked in followed by Jane who was faithfully carrying Marie's special tea to her. "So what do we call this latest addition to the Power household?" the doctor asked.

"I never knew my grandfather's mother but I always thought she had a lovely name," Jacques looked to his wife. "She was Isabeau...what do you think of *Isabelle* in her honor?"

"Isabelle," Marie whispered and looked to her new infant. "It is a beautiful name."

When the doctor told the story of Jacques' faint with more dramatic flair than anyone might have guessed him to have, Marie had to laugh. It was the first real laugh of complete amusement and abandonment that Jacques had seen her have since last Christmas. It was worth his loss of dignity to see her laugh like that again, he thought, and he laughed with her, and thanked the Lord again for sparing her.

They brought her a cane and she wept. There was something about it that said she had stepped over a line and her youth and vitality were forever gone. Where was the young girl who had chopped her own firewood to keep herself through the winter? Where had gone the girl who pushed wheelbarrow after wheelbarrow full of rocks up the hill? Where was she who had tilled and tended a huge vegetable garden all on her own? Where indeed? She was now old and a cripple, the cane said, and unable to carry on in the fullness of life.

It did not help one bit that as Marie once again brushed her own long, thick hair she discovered not the stray single gray hair easily plucked but an actual patch of gray, at least a dozen or more hairs in all, springing from her scalp in an obvious streak. It all said she was becoming an old woman, she told herself. And she looked at the cane with a resentful eye.

But... if she was ever going to go downstairs again, if she was ever going to eat at the dining table with her family or walk in the sunshine of the gardens, visit the animals, and see for herself what was happening in her own store – if she was ever going to do these things without landing on her face in the dirt because her leg suddenly failed to support her, then, Marie had to admit, she needed a cane.

Both her legs had grown weak from lack of use during her months restricted to bed rest by the well-meaning doctor. But her right leg in particular could no longer support her in leading up a step or down a staircase. It threatened to collapse at any moment just in crossing a room. And sometimes if it were not for the cane, she could not walk at all.

And then there was the pain. St. Claire could offer no explanation or cure for it. He counseled patience, tolerance and, finally, acceptance while prescribing laudanum to make Marie more comfortable.

It was almost three months since Isabelle arrived. Doctor St. Claire was out in his small carriage on a gloomy overcast late summer day and he decided, on a whim, to turn up the road to the Powers' home to check on his youngest patient. Feeling every bit his age in the chilled damp air, he reined the horse to a stop, climbed down carefully, and tethered the animal to the hitching post. Then, he automatically took his bag from under the seat and walked up to the impressively large front door.

It was almost time for an afternoon refreshment. Jane opened the door. She greeted St. Claire casting her eyes down to the boot wipe by the door to make it obvious she expected him to use it before being admitted. He did and she led him into the drawing room where Marie was playing with her new baby before a warming fire. Candles and lamps were lit throughout the room giving it a cheery, hospitable glow despite the dismal day.

"Oh, good day, *Monsieur Docteur*," Marie smiled weakly as Jane showed him in. "Jane, would you bring tea now, please?"

"Yes, Missus Power," Jane said. "Do you want me to call Sarah to fetch the baby?"

"Not yet, Izzy is being very good and I think the doctor would like to visit with her."

Jane nodded and left.

"Please have a seat," Marie said graciously, she was wearing a simple linen over-shift and skirt with a shawl much like the peasant women of France wore and the elderly doctor observed that it made her look unpretentiously charming and young until one noticed the cane set off near her side or saw her try to walk.

"I happened to be nearby and thought I would stop in." St. Claire put his bag down and bent over to pick up baby Isabelle. He hefted the child, judging her weight gain, laid her down flat on the couch to press his ear to her chest. Then he set her upon his lap and let her play with his buttons. "Well, this one looks like she is doing just fine. And how is mother?"

"Mother is always so tired," Marie responded with a lethargic sigh. "But I have done nothing for which to be tired. I just do not seem to be able to get my energy back, *Monsieur Docteur*. It is so very frustrating. I remember after John was born I tied him on my back Indian style and was off bartering at the cabin and helping to clean up lingering wreckage from the storm - within days. I cannot imagine doing that now and it is already three months. Now, all I want to do is sleep."

St. Claire put the baby in her cradle and turned to Marie. "Let me give a listen," he said and sitting beside her he bent to put his liver-spotted ear against her chest.

"You have a strong heartbeat," he said in typical fashion. "Sleeping well?"

"All the time. The medicine you gave me sees to that and the baby is not disturbing me. Sarah brings her to me, takes her from me. I hardly need do anything but nurse the little thing. But I never really feel rested."

"Your milk appears to be good, the child continues to grow." He smiled encouragingly. He knew better than to suggest a wet nurse. Madame Power was adamant about nursing and he supposed it was something she could do to feel needed. St. Claire's bristly gray hair and wild eyebrows gave a gruff appearance, but his eyes were very kind as he observed and took her pulse. "How old is John now?" he asked after a moment.

"John? Why, he will turn fifteen very soon," Marie replied softly.

"I remember the year he was born," the doctor chuckled, "the year I arrived here after that horrendous hurricane. We are fortunate not to have seen anymore storms like that. But I can tell you, I certainly do not feel like I used to back then. That has been fifteen years ago. I tell myself, I am fifteen years older and I cannot expect to feel like I did then, not anymore."

Jane came with the tea and while she served, St. Claire looked around the drawing room.

"You know, I have always liked the way you have done this room. The light colors all make it look so bright and airy. Any room that can be cheerful on a sunless, dour day like today has something special to commend it."

"*Monsieur Docteur*, I had no idea you had an eye for interior decorating," Marie responded with a faint smile of amusement. "Please... try the little cakes. Margot does a wonderful job with them. Thank you, Jane. That will be all."

He took his tea and chose a cake. Jane left the room. When the door closed, Marie spoke again.

"And so, in your transparent but diplomatic way you are telling me that I am fifteen years older and cannot expect to bounce back onto my feet as quickly as I used to," she looked at him calmly but her subdued impatience was building.

"You are a very perceptive lady."

Marie sipped her tea and said nothing for the moment.

"Not only are we all fifteen years older, but you have had seven babies, my dear. Each time it takes a mother just a little longer to get back on her feet, there is really nothing terribly unusual about that."

"I can accept that, *Monsieur Docteur*, but not all women turn into invalids as they approach thirty-five," she added sadly. "It is one thing to expect to take longer to recuperate but another to fear you will never recuperate at all."

"Is the medicine managing the pain?" He had been skirting the question, hoping for a positive answer. He was a physician, after all, sworn to help, pledged to heal but he had no idea what to do for Madame Power's chronic condition other than to prescribe a pain killer.

Marie's countenance darkened. "I suppose, but I find I can go nowhere without assistance. I cannot trust my leg not to buckle. I dare not carry my own baby across a small room so afraid am I that I will be pitched to the floor without notice. I manage the stairs only by always leading with my good leg and holding on to the banister for dear life. How long must I live like this, *Monsieur Docteur?*" Marie's voice trembled as she fought back tears.

"Are the pains still so severe?" he asked clinically.

She shook her head. "Not most of the time. I would go insane if it never eased…but then sometimes it is like something catches and it is un-endurable and I must call for the bricks and take a good dose of the medicine. Am I doomed to live like this for the rest of my life, so unable to do all the normal things I used to do?"

"Your family understands."

"I am the one that does not understand," she retorted in frustration. "Jacques and the children are extremely solicitous. I feel like I am waited on hand and foot. But while it makes me feel very loved and pampered, Doctor St. Claire, it does nothing to make me feel any less like a completely useless invalid. Jacques even brought in another girl to serve in the nursery. He cannot do enough for me while I feel completely worthless. My body has betrayed me." In an uncharacteristic show of frustration Marie's fist slammed down on her weak leg.

"You have a family who loves you," St Claire reasoned. "You must learn to relax and let them love you. Your husband has the means to pamper you, let him pamper you. You do not always have to be doing for others you know, this is your time to do a little *taking* for a change. It does not make you an invalid just because you need some extra time to recuperate. You do not always have to be orchestrating a half dozen campaigns. Good heavens, most of us do well to wage one major campaign in a lifetime."

"I have no military background, Doctor St. Claire," Marie shook her head with a frown, "but I would translate that to mean, you think I have tried to do too much." She set her tea down and checked Isabelle, who was now sleeping. She judged the child to be a little too warm and reached to pull her farther from the heat of the hearth. St. Claire saw a tell-tale grimace flash across Marie's face.

"Well, let us consider," he said amiably. "Through the years I have heard your name bantered about in connection with several ladies' committees. You have been the driving force in the woman's auxiliary at the church. You volunteer for the school, you run a business, you run a home, you are an attentive mother and wife, and you have been known to wet nurse other people's children, how much do you expect of yourself?" He was now looking at her sternly with an expression that was more accusation than admiration.

"But Jacques works very hard as well."

"He is the man. Do you try to put him to shame?"

"No, of course not," she gasped and said nothing more for a moment. "I do not understand," she said at last in almost a whisper. "Shame him, how?"

"Let him be the man and take care of you."

Marie was stunned at the thought of shaming Jacques in a way she had never conceived. "Am I really as bad as that?"

Doctor St. Claire continued to look at her.

"I remember my mother-in-law saying something…" Marie half muttered. "I assure you, *Monsieur Docteur*, I seek no recognition. I do not wish to appear prideful…"

"No one thinks that, that is nonsense. You are the most selfless and giving person I know but perhaps you give too much, eh?"

"It is just that I feel so blessed," Marie said softly. "My life is more than I could have ever dreamed. Often I wonder *why me?* What did I ever do to deserve all these blessings? But now I have become frightened that it will all disappear. And for all I may have been doing in the past, Doctor St. Claire, at present I can do almost nothing." A tear rolled down her cheek. "I want to give back and do for others. I do not want God to think I do not appreciate how He has blessed me. Does that sound childish?"

St. Claire listened. He drank the last of his tea and set down his cup and saucer. He wished he had an answer for her physical limitations.

"I do not pretend to have any idea what God thinks, madame. But I can say, I do not think He thinks as we think. Now, in my professional opinion, you are enjoying a normal recuperation for a healthy older mother of seven children who has strained her back. By spring you are going to feel much like your old self again, I have no doubt. But I prescribe a reduced schedule of involvements from this time on so you can live a long life and enjoy doing the most important task at hand, raising this little girl and her brothers and sisters.

"In the meanwhile, when the pain is bad, continue to take a spoonful of laudanum. Here I will leave you with a fresh bottle. I will be traveling the circuit to the outlying farms… at least one baby is due soon. When I will return I do not know." He opened his bag and took out a full bottle. "You owe it to all the people who depend upon you to take care of yourself. A small spoonful remember, use it sparingly," he nodded to her. "And I expect you to follow my advice."

"Yes, *Monsieur Docteur*," Marie said soberly.

"Do you continue eating calf liver at least twice a week, hmmm?"

She nodded.

"Good. It builds the blood. And please, relax and stop worrying. Now, before I go, I should look in on Britta." He grasped Marie's hand with a friendly bow and said, "You stay right there with your baby daughter, I can show myself to the nursery."

Marie nodded. "Good day, *Monsieur Docteur*, and thank you for stopping by."

After St. Claire left, Marie poured herself another cup of tea but found she had no appetite to drink it. She thought again of Sheehoo and wished she could talk to her. Marie pondered what herbal medicines she might start taking to restore her energy. Perhaps something she had given to her mother-in-law? She must consult the notes she took. And what might the Indian woman have suggested for her back?"

It had been so sad the last time she had seen Looking Glass, his sister, and her sons. They had come to say good-bye in early spring after James was born. More and more farms were cutting into their hunting grounds but more than that were the outbreaks of diseases. Sheehoo told her they were moving deeper into the mountains to the west, deeper into the Indian forest and away from the white settlers. They had not said it with animosity or accusation. It had been a simple statement of fact. Marie had felt a pang of guilt, not so much for herself and Jacques but for the rest of the whites who were becoming so populous that they crowded the Indian from his world and struck him down with disease. She had felt their loss then and she felt it now, such a longing to see those wise old friends who had disappeared deep into the wilderness.

Most likely that would never be but she prayed they were safe and healthy. She reminded herself she had quite a family of her own now. Seven little blessings, one for every day of the week, all healthy, all bright, four boys and three girls, surely that was enough! She had given birth to seven... no, *eight* children actually! She had forgotten to count the poor little thing she birthed when she was barely thirteen. Eight was one more than her mother. *No,* Marie suddenly remembered, *Mama had a child die also... and a miscarriage. It was actually the ninth pregnancy that killed her.* A sudden panic swept over Marie. She was now into her thirty-sixth year. Was her mother not thirty-six when she had died? Marie did not know for sure. But she was more certain than ever that it was definitely time for her to stop having babies.

The energy Marie had summoned up to appear normal in her conversation with St. Claire was gone and she was left drained. All she desired was to return to her bed and forget everything. The medicine would help her do just that.

Marie called for Sarah to take Isabelle.

Chapter 13

When Renée Séraphin arrived at the Power household after Isabelle's birth there was no sign upon her that said "Poison." There was no warning in her papers that she was dangerous and should not be left unguarded to mingle with the rest of the world. Quite the opposite, she had arrived on Dufee's ship looking totally defenseless and harmless. The new assistant nursery maid was a waif-ish creature with thin, almost bony limbs, a slender build, and almost boyish in her lack of hips or breasts. Her raven black hair was her only commendable feature but even that seemed to overwhelm her pale thin little face, a face that could never be thought of as beautiful or even pretty. And yet, when she chose to, Renée could become animated and so energized that she had an attraction difficult to define. Physically, her cheeks pinked up with the increased flow of blood, her eyes which often seemed dull brown would appear black and twice their size and her whole body gained vitality. Her apparent youth was certainly on her side. One learned soul had likened her to a portrait of Ann Boleyn, the woman who had bewitched an English king.

The first mate of the *Dauphine* knew well how attractive Renée could be. During a card game at a local tavern in their French port, she had surreptitiously crawled under the crowded table and performed *fellatio* on him with such expertise he had been captivated indeed. Never showing herself to him or the company he was with at the time, slipping away before he could come to his senses, he had gone in search of her. It had not been difficult to find her again. She had wanted to be found. And when he saw her appearance, almost as much a young boy as a girl and seeming sinfully young as well, it had only served to stimulate his lusts further. He was driven to spend the rest of his leave with her and while he was totally besotted, she wheedled an agreement from him to vouch for her character, to draw up papers of minimal indenture, and to give her passage on his ship to the New World. The papers said she was a sixteen year old orphan. To the first mate's meager credit, this was one lie of which he was totally unaware. She looked hardly four and ten but, in truth, she was far beyond four and twenty.

Through the long journey across the Atlantic, she had continued to give him service in any way he wished and in his mind it was the shortest voyage of record.

She spoke no English and was sent to work in the Power nursery where she was smaller than the oldest boys and where it was perfectly permissible for her to speak French since the children were expected to be fluent in that language as well. Marie empathized with the girl, not seeing her as she really was. Marie herself had struggled those first weeks in the New World trying to make herself understood and trying to understand a strange new language. Marie never forgot these things and had the tendency to think others as genuine as herself.

"Sarah is in charge of the nursery," Marie explained in French from her chair in the bedroom, a rather languid pace to her speech and now prone toward repeating herself. "You are to always follow her direction. She takes care of the new baby and oversees the rest. Our oldest boys have outgrown the nursery, of course. The other children know the rules. They are well behaved. Your responsibility is to stay with little Britta.

"Britta is fragile. She is six but she looks much younger. She has not grown as she should but she is a very good child. Her heart, it is not strong. The doctor says excitement is not good for her. Do you understand what that means?"

"I do not know, m'lady," Renée replied slyly.

"She should not get overly excited. Britta is fragile. She cannot keep up with the other children. She tires easily and she should not be startled."

Renée nodded.

"We try to keep her life as calm and serene as possible. She is a good child. Very sweet tempered. I think she realizes she is different. She is fragile. You will find watching over her very easy. Your responsibility is to stay with her all the time."

"That is so sad, m'lady."

"Sad? But she is happy and we love her. Do not say sad things to her. Never make her feel that she is different. Just watch over her with care. From the time she awakes to the time she retires for the evening, you are not to leave her side except when she is napping; she takes long naps twice a day."

"Of course, m'lady." Renée gave Marie a little curtsy.

From the very start, it was obvious to Renée that the child was different from other children. She was small perhaps and fragile, but she was very blonde as the monsieur was blond yet she did not look at all like any of the other Power children or like the madame. For this reason Renée immediately assumed Britta was monsieur's love child brought home to be raised with his other children. And for this reason and because they shared a similar physique, Renée warmed to Britta and watched over her diligently.

Renée had a way with the children, seeming to be little more than a child herself. She was not rigid in enforcing their rules; she joined in little conspiracies against Sarah and played their games with seemingly as much pleasure as they when Britta was napping. Of course, Marie and Jacques never saw this side of their new servant. In their presence she seemed always to be trying to keep the children in order and struggling against their getting the best of her while being most solicitous of Britta. That is exactly how she wished to appear to her employers. She had given herself the advantage. She was not lacking in mental skills and had more than two dozen years to draw upon whereas they saw her as an ignorant, naive, and innocent child who nonetheless fulfilled her primary duty quite well.

The Power household had long been a place of on-going domestic harmony and gentle temperaments. Mistress Power's unexpectedly difficult pregnancy was a true exception both excused and forgotten. Those who had worked elsewhere before coming to the Power home instantly recognized and appreciated the difference in the atmosphere. Those who had not, still realized the blessing of the tranquility and appreciated the benevolence of their employers for, sooner or later, they all had friends or acquaintances who lived and worked in far different circumstances and complained about them. And so, when Renée joined them, none were ready to carry tales on the girl or express their personal misgivings. But they saw better than any other a clearer picture of her true character and the way she looked at the master when the mistress was not present.

"I tell you she reminds me of a snake staring down a mouse just before it leaps out and swallows it whole," Jane told her husband Donald in the privacy of their room one night. It was his habit to borrow the most current newspapers, once Jacques was finished with them, and relax in the evening by reading. He was trying to read now.

"Hmm," was all he uttered.

"With those great black eyes. Mark my words, there's something rotten in that one."

"Hmm" was his only response.

Not long after this, on a quiet Sunday afternoon, Donald Sims chanced to hear some unusual noises when he went into the barn looking for a fresh bag of chicken feed. He paused and quietly sought to investigate. Later that evening he shared his discovery with his wife.

"Wife, you'll never guess what I came across today," Donald said pulling his shoes off before retiring for the night.

"What might that be, husband?"

"Thor and that new gal, rutting like heathens in the hayloft."

Jane gasped. "I told ya she's no good. And him just out of the nursery."

Donald snorted. "He's been out of the nursery a long time. The lad's going on seventeen and from what I could see he's every inch a man who knows a thing or two about the process."

"Donald!" she exclaimed in indignation. "So ... what did ya do?"

"Well, I thought about throwin' a pail of water on 'em but it ain't none of our business," he said as he dropped his own breeches to the floor and crawled into their bed.

"Still..."

"The lad needs to sow his wild oats somewhere. Might as well be with the likes of her rather than a decent girl."

"And what if she ends up with a bun in the oven? Trappin' him into marriage, the poor boy," Jane said in sympathetic disgust.

"Like I say, not our business."

"But surely the mistress should be told. I'd not want someone like that 'round my children."

"Keep your peace, woman," Donald warned and rolled over to sleep.

Renée could smell masculine sexual frustration. It was as easily recognized as the smell of apple blossoms in the spring or lilac in the summer, she thought. Yet, it was not really a smell but an instinctive discernment that spoke to some primal part of her brain. Sexually frustrated men, whether they be lords or peasants, were the easiest pawns in the world to manipulate.

Monsieur Power was incredibly handsome and effused an easy sensual charm that made soft and pliant putty of all the women in the household and yet, by all accounts, he was totally in love with his wife and had eyes for no one else. Renée had heard that before. She had not laid waste to an outstandingly handsome man in a long, long time. It amused her at how quick were the servants who spoke a bit of French to tell her he was a truly faithful husband who worshiped his wife and never strayed from their marital bed. Stupid servants! Did they not realize it was like waving a red flag of challenge before her? She giggled to herself, as she mindlessly played games in the nursery. And what's more, who did they think was Britta's pa-pa?

One day she chanced to overhear Helen and Louise speak in French of Britta's pa-pa. Renée drew them out in casual conversation and learned the truth of Britta's parentage. She also learned that Thor and his brother, Ansel, and his other sister, Rega, were Britta's brothers and sister and had lived there before their father completed his new house. So that was why Thor knew rudimentary French, *at least enough*, she smiled to herself slyly.

So Britta was not a love child. And monsieur and madame had been married for how long? And he had never strayed? If that was true, it was in the past and held no bearing on the future. He was, in fact, ripe for felling, like a sturdy oak that cannot defend against the slender blade of the saw. But even more significantly, she could smell his frustration and she had seen the bottle of laudanum beside the bed near madame. Renée was very familiar with what laudanum could do and she saw the evidence of it in madame's behavior.

After Isabelle's birth, Jacques turned his attentions back to his business affairs which had been left somewhat neglected. Boot had the mill production back on track. They had loaded the *Dauphine* with as much cut lumber as her hold could carry on her last visit.

The apple crop had come in more bountiful than Jacques expected but the harvest was ugly and unattractive. No good for selling in the open markets of New York Towne or within the old Swedish settlements along the Delaware. What better time to experiment with fermenting apple juice? Hard cider and vinegar were both highly marketable by-products of the fruit. Now that Boot's house was finished, Jacques needed to set a crew to building a large shed and a press for processing the apples.

At his father's suggestion, Jacques had also started a small dairy herd. The English Parliament had passed the Wool Act to protect their own wool industry by limiting wool production in Ireland and completely forbidding any export of wool from the American colonies. There was no benefit in raising any more sheep than they could utilize themselves but beef and dairy were a different story. They had long had a few cows for their personal needs but raising cattle for meat and cheese had become a growing necessity. Game in the area was rapidly disappearing. But for the milk cows to continue producing through the winter, they needed a warm barn. The herd had outgrown the barn it shared with the rest of the animals. It was another project he had pushed aside for too long and it was imperative that a new dairy barn be completed before the winter set in.

As Jacques went about checking on all the various projects and activities, Richard came to mind from time to time. It had been a very long time since they had seen him. If Jacques had had the time to give it more thought, he might have considered the possibility of ill fortune. Instead, he was lulled by the distractions of life into not realizing just how much time had passed. Would not his old friend be surprised to see them with yet another baby? But, then, why should he be surprised? He had off-spring all along the path into the Great Lakes and back. Yes, but with how many different women, Jacques thought almost prudishly?

He supposed someone would have to tell Richard the story of Jacques' faint. He ought to get a great laugh out of that. And he would probably not stop making jokes about it for weeks...or months. Jacques sighed. No, undoubtedly, it would be for years. Well, Richard could laugh all he wanted. Jacques doubted that Richard felt about any of his squaws the way Jacques felt about Marie. In fact, Jacques did not doubt that perhaps Richard cared more for Marie himself than for all of his Indian women put together. Who knows what he would have done if he had been in Jacques' shoes, walking in and seeing Marie as she had been, looking more dead than alive, after crying out in that most terrifying way. Jacques trembled inwardly a little, reliving it again.

Whatever would he do if he ever lost her, he wondered? He could not imagine the emptiness of life without her. Somehow everything but the children would lose meaning and the children were meant to have lives of their own. It was impossible for them to be to him what she was. Without warning his stomach drew up into a knot and he tried to shake it off, refusing to dwell upon it. Life without Marie would simply not be life anymore; it would be like trying to live with half a body, half a heart, half a brain, half a soul. She filled every corner of his being with warmth and contentment and affection. And as he thought of his beautiful, warm, and capable wife, he felt very familiar stirrings and desires. It had been a long time.

Isabelle was three months old already, he considered. Three months was generally the time they waited after a baby was born. It seemed a decent and sufficient time for Marie to recuperate before they resumed their intimacies. At least it always had been. But this time? As much as he missed that part of their life and longed to make love to his wife again, Jacques decided he would not suggest it yet. He would watch for some sign from her. She still seemed somehow not back to her normal self.

In fact, when he came home at night and was filled with a desire to share his day with her, she frequently seemed so unfocused of late. Often he felt sure she barely heard him; she was not interested and she hardly ever made much of a response. To make love to her when she was in such a state, lacking energy and passion, was not what he needed or desired.

Renée bided her time. Planning and anticipating the devastation of a victim was as deliciously enjoyable to her as the actual execution and achievement. Often times it was the most enjoyable part although she had to allow that in this case, she looked forward to the dalliance itself with growing tremors of excitement. In guarded moments, she had begun mentally stripping the master of his clothes and imagining what she would do to the magnificent male body beneath. No fat doughy dilettante was he. No pasty-faced, flatulent, pot belly with habitually bad breath. No, this one she would enjoy and she had begun living for the day when she would hear him beg for her favors. She would use him and expose him and let reality lay waste to this fairy-tale marriage of his.

The numbers and ages of the children in the nursery around her attested to his attentions to his wife. Renée also knew they shared the same bed each night. That was no household secret. But something was not quite as it appeared, she was certain of it. It was normal to smell the frustration in a new father the first month or two after a birth. But the latest little addition to the Power family fairy tale nursery was well over three months old now. And Renée could sense the frustration growing stronger.

Night after night she lie awake going over the possible ploys she could orchestrate. What worked on one man would not necessarily work on another. She played through various scenarios, discarding this one and that. This was not one with which she could overtly flirt; instinctively she decided that would not work with him. And she knew she was not and never would be a beauty who could strike a man dumb with one smoldering glance. Indeed, his own wife was a very attractive woman; he had beauty at his fingertips. No, it was not beauty that was important. Inhibition? From what she had gleaned from the staff, the mistress was no blue-blood and somehow Renée felt that inhibition was also part of madam's charm. Variety? Perhaps. If he had truly been a faithful husband for all these years it was obvious constant variety was not one of his obsessions but which man walking the surface of the earth does not want some variety in his life? It was human nature. Hence, the world held a multitude of colors, shapes, forms, tastes, smells, and... women. At some point in every marriage there must come that time when one or the other or both of the partners has some small craving for something different.

She smiled and decided this was one point to work with. She must always be as different from madame as possible which certainly was not too difficult. Her boyishly wiry build was certainly different. And she would promote a less assured, more inept persona lacking in confidence and education. That would certainly be a difference. Is there any man who does not like to feel superior to a female? And just how superior could this one feel to his wife who was reported to possess all kinds of skills and talents? But he could be made to feel very superior to poor little Renée.

One always needed to keep in mind the basic character of one's victim, Renée considered. This one prided himself on honor, on chivalry. He was a self-believed champion of the down trodden, a lord who came to the colonies and gave up his lordship to rub shoulders with the common man and serve him with his own innate superior intelligence. *What a prince!* The girl almost snorted aloud in the quiet of the night. They always thought they knew best, she thought bitterly. They always justified themselves and rested on their self-satisfied beliefs that they, in fact, were the nobles obligated to set things right, set up things right, do things right, determine what was right… and what was *right* was always of their definition.

Renée had begun operating within the framework of her basic plan. She cultivated a certain attitude of befuddlement and tongue-tied awe. She went out of her way to be in his path, to tremor blushed greetings, and to act outrageously grateful for his every attention. On the pretense of speaking for his youngest children she barely whispered exorbitant flatteries. And Jacques was only human. He began to notice the girl. There was something about her that reminded him of Marie as she had been many years ago and yet at the same time Renée was really nothing like Marie.

One might call it luck or devilish providence that Renée had stumbled into a facade that was not totally unlike the young girl with whom Jacques had first fallen in love. She had no idea what Marie had been like at fifteen, sixteen years old. She saw only the accomplished, intelligent woman who was also so lacking in energy and in a tediously dragged out state of childbirth recuperation. Perhaps there, too, was something with which Renée could work.

In the quiet dark of the nursery, while everyone else slept, Renée lay awake thinking. If only he slept alone, as most lords do, she could easily slip into his bed in the quiet of night. It would be so easy now, he was ready, he was needy, and in the blindness of passion, he could be brought low. She could toy with him then. Like a cat with a mouse. She had confidence in her sexual prowess and he would want her again and again. She would go to his bed often. She would pleasure him and excite him with what men liked to call "whore's tricks." After a time, she might feign pregnancy... that would set him upside down. What would his precious wife think of Renée having his little bastard? Of course, that could not last long. She could only feign fear of pregnancy, for she could never have a child, not anymore. But sooner or later, after she had tired of him and tired of making him sweat and suffer, she would let madame know and there would go the pretty fantasy of a faithful husband. Being such an honorable man, he could hardly deny the truth of his own infidelity.

And how might she play that scene? The poor little waif, so badly used and taken advantage of by the household master who could not control his base carnal lusts? Oh, to be sure. It was such a common bit of melodrama it was almost laughable. She could imagine the look of horror, of hurt, of irreconcilable betrayal on madame's face. The fairy tale would exist no more. The thoughts of rendering the marriage irreparably broken and ravaged had an almost unbearable sexually exciting effect on Renée and in the darkness she strained against her own touch for release.

But Master Power did not sleep alone and Renée was becoming increasingly frustrated with that fact. He had to be caught off guard, she realized. He was not one to ever come to her. Others had, but not him. No, she must take the first step when he was aroused and needy and unsuspecting. It must happen before he even realized it was happening. Only then would he be willing to make it happen again. After all, once, thrice or thirty times, what difference did it make? Betrayal was betrayal. And finding release from his frustration would help him to justify their continuing liaisons. But how was she to catch him off guard the first time?

Renée was aware of everything. Over the past few months, John had grown to a full hand's width over the top of her head. She noticed the beginnings of a moustache on his smooth upper lip and the deepening of his voice. She smiled to herself, John was very pretty, indeed, with his soft curly hair and large gray eyes heavily rimmed in long dark lashes, a smooth, untouched youth who looked so like his father that Renée could easily imagine they were one in the same.

Britta was napping and they were playing hide and seek. John had tried to beg off and Phillip would not agree to play if John did not. They were too old, they said, but Renée had smiled at them sweetly and asked them to play as a favor to her because the younger children wanted them to play so badly. John could not refuse.

The ground rules were that they were to restrict themselves to the main house since the weather outside was not pleasant and no one wanted to be bothered with putting on wraps and taking them off, and putting them on and then again off, searching both indoors and out. But John was feeling more man than child and chafed to get away from the nursery banter. He broke the rules and headed for the new barn. He had agreed to play their silly game but he had not agreed to stay in the house. He climbed the ladder to the loft and threw himself back into the soft, spongy pile of new hay. The new barn was warm and smelled of clean wood and sweet hay. It was a pleasant place and he would rather be alone here to try and sort through all his changing feelings and the moods that seemed to swirl within him.

Renée had seen John leave and waited until she, too, could slip out undetected.

She sprinted to the barn, checking first to ensure no one saw her. The children could go on indefinitely in the house trying to find everyone, trying to find her, trying to find John. There would be sufficient time before they would have to go back.

The youth was startled but tried not to show it when Renée appeared out of nowhere and threw herself beside him in the hay.

"You are breaking the rules," she admonished in French with a giggle.

"So are you," he replied in kind, a note of assertion in his voice.

"*Oui,* I know," she murmured and rolled up to kiss him full on his young sweet un-expecting mouth.

John felt Renée's warm wet tongue in his mouth and lost all ability to reason. He only knew that his body was reacting in powerful ways, and feelings… sensations… desires... were bursting out of every pore. He felt her hands tugging at his clothing. He had no desire to stop her. Instead of feeling embarrassed, he felt empowered to let his own hands do some exploring of their own. He was vaguely aware of her urging him on, encouraging him. Then, he was very aware of her naked body over him and sliding on top of his swollen, erect member.

Animal instinct took over and John grasped her hips with his hands and pulled her fiercely onto him again and again as he arched up into her. His senses exploded in thousands of white hot little sparkles like the showering embers of a rocket. He rode a wave of feeling that wiped out every other thought and emotion, as well as every other awareness. It was incredible, like nothing his young body had ever experienced but it was over all too quickly.

The youth inhaled deeply and was aware of Renée's warm body covering his as she lay almost weightless upon his smooth, hairless chest.

"Are... are you all right?" he ventured hesitantly.

She lifted her face to him and smiled broadly, her eyes huge and black. "I could only wish that it had lasted longer... but do not worry, the first time is often very short, in time you will learn to sustain your pleasure by pacing yourself."

He did not know what to think. Her casual reference to his first time, and thereby his virginity, made him begin to blush, then, her implied promise of a next time made his blood race, then, the realization that they were both lying naked in the hay of his father's barn and had no business being there together and could easily be discovered made his heart thud.

Renée felt his heart beat beneath her.

"You are a very handsome man, John," she cooed, as she bent to kiss him again, her long black hair sweeping across his chest like a silken net dragging over his flesh. She had emphasized the word "man." He was hesitant at first and she knew he was thinking too much. Her tongue dipped into him as though to drive away his thoughts. She felt him respond and return her kiss, his own tongue now demanding entrance into her mouth. She let him taste and feel and explore while her hands moved sensually over his young, healthy body.

He felt her break contact with his mouth although he did not want to let her go. But she began to kiss him all over, her lips like a searingly hot coal that left no pain on his neck, his chest, his nipples, down across his belly, and farther and...*oh, God, what is she doing now?*

John was beyond thinking again.

It had been at least a half hour, perhaps more, and Renée was aware, even if John was not, of the need to reappear in the house before anyone became suspicious.

"Do not go, not yet," he held her thigh possessively as they lay side by side, panting. "In a few more minutes I am sure I can do it yet again."

"I must go. I shall be missed and we do not want anyone to discover our little secret," she smiled conspiratorially. She pulled on her clothes rapidly and left him as quickly as she had appeared.

That had been too easy, she thought as she walked to the house, but it had done something to alleviate her own frustrations.

Renée was aware of how much medicine madame took and the effects of its abuse. One day while madame went out to the kitchen and Britta was down for her nap and everyone else was occupied, Renée took a small empty bottle from the pantry and stole into the master bedroom. There sat the bottle of laudanum. She filled the small bottle in her possession and tucked it into her pocket. She would look for opportunities.

Renée's goals had changed. Why should she be content to just destroy a marriage and move on? The Power farm was a pleasant enough place. Monsieur Power was a successful man of stature within the community able to provide an enviable lifestyle to those under his protection. And Madame Power was fast becoming a weak fool on the road to self-destruction!

Madame hardly ate anymore and once Renée began lacing madame's teas with extra doses, she had begun demanding more of the laudanum on her own. She had wheedled an extra bottle from the old doctor who was himself a fool. Could he not see that his pretty patient was turning into a useless withering opium addict? Day after day, Renée watched monsieur's frustrations mounting as his wife drifted in and out of opium laced daydreams, not listening, not caring, sitting in a stupor and sleeping as much as little Britta.

How easy would it be to walk in one afternoon and place a pillow over her face? Would it not appear as though the drug had taken her? Perhaps the drug would take her if Renée could get her to take a large enough dose all at one time. But for that she would need another bottle. The next time the old doctor came to the house Renée would steal one.

Once madame was gone, Renée smiled to herself, who better to console monsieur than she? She had great confidence in her powers.

Marie sat before the fire, the dancing flames were mesmerizing. *I should... I should... What...? Oh, yes, the store, the store. I should check on the store. It has been... too long... should go. How? Cannot walk. Cannot make the distance... call for carriage... maybe... too much trouble... it can wait.*

She vaguely remembered making arrangements with Jacques' father to ship a small but steady supply of wine from his vineyard for her store. *I wonder... has it arrived... will it sell?* In their small and rustic community, no one could predict how much she could really sell to uneducated pallets. *No, it is winter*, she thought hazily. *No ship from France in winter. But the herbs...*

Their little community did not yet have an apothecary, and the simple medicinal teas she offered had become extremely popular. *Popular, yes... should check... should check... check what?* She watched the flames dance. *...something.*

Jane found Marie dozing by the fire and shushed the children to keep them from disturbing her. It had become a common occurrence.

Jacques had made the rounds to the children making sure they were tucked in for the night. The older boys had long shared their own bedroom. The older girls shared one as well. Entering the bedroom he and Marie shared, he found her propped up on her pillows nursing Isabelle. Quietly watching with affection, he leisurely removed his clothing and crawled completely naked into the bed beside her. Marie did not seem to notice.

"What a lovely sight you are together," he said tenderly pulling the covers over himself and kissing his little daughter upon her curly head. She was asleep. Then, he kissed and nuzzled his wife's shoulder.

A tap at the door brought Sarah.

"If the mistress is finished nursing I'll put the babe to bed," she said discreetly, keeping her eyes averted. She took the child as Marie released her. "Good night, ma'am ...sir." And Sarah was gone, shutting the door in her wake.

At last, they were alone and Marie was still awake. It was a rarity and Jacques ached for her touch. It had been almost eight very long months since she had lost all interest in his caresses. It was the longest abstinence from her since that miserable winter with the Eric.

Jacques' hand repeatedly caressed the smooth, soft skin of Marie's arm and elbow. He inhaled deeply, her scent maddening his senses. He ached for her and longed to demonstrate once again how very much he desired her. His lips zeroed in to the sensitive spot on her neck just below her ear but this time there was no trembling, no passionate sighs, no response of any kind.

Marie felt the heaviness coming upon her and her only interest was for escape. She remembered vaguely that she wanted to talk to Jacques about something but she could not remember what. It could not have been that important. It would wait, she sighed deeply, drifting in a hazy fog. Everything could wait.

His hand moved beneath the sheet to her hip, stroking the length of her thigh.

He ran his hand along her body and she pulled away to the very edge of the bed.

"Jacques," she muttered in a sigh, "not tonight."

"But why my darling? I have missed you so…"

"My monthly flow." It was the easiest thing to say.

With great self-control Jacques blew out the candle and tried to make sense of it. He felt her rejection like a blade cutting across his heart and a wave of hurt washed over him stinging in the wound as alcohol might. He felt anger growing hot in defense. He had an overwhelming urge to reach over and rip her gown away, exposing her lie for what it was, he knew she wore no clout. In all the years they had been married, he had never known her to lie to him - until now. What had changed? He wanted to shake some reasoning out of her, some logic, some feeling... no, he wanted to shake *truth* out of her. But he feared where direct confrontation might lead. What if Marie demanded her right to a room of her own? A man could be master of his house but no man was master of a woman's heart unless she allowed it. And it was not in him to force any woman to share his bed or receive his body against her will. He had noticed the way she had avoided looking at him. There had been a time when she had taken pleasure in looking at his naked body, when she had warmed him with her eyes. Had he now become something loathsome to her? Did she blame him because she had suffered so while carrying Isabelle?

What had happened? Why was he losing her? Why had she become a string of excuses? She was tired, she had a headache, she was indisposed, she was feeling ill, she was in pain. She avoided him, stiffened, and pulled away whenever he touched her, every overture he had made since the baby was born had been solidly rebuffed and yet, when they were around the children, around other people, when he could not in all decency reach out to make love to her, he saw something of love in her eyes when she looked at him. Or at least he thought he did. Or was he crazy? Was he just imagining it because that is what he wanted? What was this torturous game she was playing with him? It was madness. If only she would tell him the truth. The truth! What does a man do when the woman he loves stops telling him the truth?

In the darkness, Jacques reached over and pulled Marie to him in one swift, angry, powerful grasp of his arm about her waist. Before she could struggle or speak he leaned into her ear.

"I am your husband!" he said in a harsh whisper. "If I cannot make love to you the least you can do is allow me to hold you!" And he held her tightly, torturing himself with the feel of her warm, pliant body next to his.

She said nothing, only moaned softly; she was completely relaxed and he could hear her breathing, the deep breathing of sleep. She had not even heard him.

Chapter 14

" Jacques-Jean!!" A familiar voice boomed out and Jacques spun around in the mill office to see a large fur and hair covered figure filling the doorway and blocking the light.

"Richard? Richard, you old bear!" he shouted back with a joyful grin of recognition and strode across the room only to stop himself short before making contact. "Oh, *Mon Dieu!* Richard, what is that stench? Skunk?" Jacques' eyes were beginning to water and he backed up several steps.

"Ah, sorry, I forgot," Richard replied and quickly doffed his outer garment to leave it outside on the cold, hard ground. "A very, very small drop, from the stink gland of the creature," he replied, adding proudly, "I shot him cleanly through the eye before he had the opportunity to spray."

Jacques was wiping his eyes with his handkerchief and holding his nose. "So why would you pollute yourself like this?"

"It works better than an armed guard to keep the thieves away," Richard laughed and proceeded to embrace his friend.

"Ohhh, Richard … you still smell like something died in your pockets," Jacques gasped.

To that Richard only laughed while Jacques went to his desk drawer and pulled out a bottle of spirits. He poured each of them a drink "To your return, *mon ami.* Sit. Sit. We have been expecting you for months! We thought for sure you would arrive for Christmas last year… but …" he shrugged and gestured saying without words that an explanation would be appreciated.

Richard nodded, ignoring the proffered chair. "Yes, yes, I know. I regret not sending you word. I apologize. I would have been back long before this but… I had a little accident."

"What happened?!" Jacques asked with genuine concern and Richard looked a trifle sheepish.

"I caught my foot in a damn bear trap. It was mid-autumn, leaves were deep all over. I got careless. I stepped back into the thing and POW! To tell the truth, for a time I thought I would end up losing the leg or at least my foot. I was miles from my hut and had to hobble back. I think I would have lost the foot for certain if my woman had not nursed me so well. She stitched me and made dozens of healing poultices. It was a struggle and painful beyond belief but finally I was able to put weight on it again. From there I had to learn to walk again in order to return and now – *voila!* Here I am! So, how is everything in civilization?"

"Everything is... civilized," Jacques said rather flatly still looking down at Richard's feet. "Which one?" he asked pointing from one foot to the other. They looked the same covered in calf high moccasin boots, scuffed, stained, and caked in mud.

Richard lifted his left foot and flexed it with pride. "And Marie is also good?" he asked with a smile.

Jacques didn't smile back but shrugged. "Things are always changing," he replied watching the movement in Richard's foot, then looking up under Richard's sharp scrutiny he added with more enthusiasm. "We have a new daughter. She is already four months old. We named her Isabelle, after my *grand-père's mère*."

"Congratulations, you ol' stallion!" Richard reached out and clapped him on the back with a broad grin. "Still good to stud, *n'est-ce pas?*"

It was just Richard being Richard but for some reason Jacques found his harmless comment very irritating and he worked hard not to show it. "The pregnancy was a challenge this time."

"A challenge?" Richard frowned. "To whom?"

"To both of us… but it is over. And I am certain Marie and the children will be just as glad to see you as I. But I strongly recommend a hot bath and a barber before you come near the house. Madame Sims would have your liver for lunch as you are now and bringing the smell of skunk near the house as well." He laughed mirthlessly. "For the love of Heaven - burn those clothes! *Dieu, mon ami,* you reek beyond toleration!"

At that Richard laughed again deeply. Even he realized his buckskins had become too stiff with soil and sweat to wear another day. "That is only because you bathe too much! If you did not you would not know the difference."

"I remember the winter with the Erie. Neither of us bathed and I still could smell your stink as well as my own."

They laughed together.

"So, what news of the posts?" Jacques asked, pouring them each another drink.

"They thrive. The trappers must now travel far into the interior for decent pelts. There is no time for them to come all the way back to the coast to sell them and buy supplies. Our posts give them a fair price for their skins and we charge fairly for supplies. Because we are much closer to their camps, it costs them far less travel time. That gives them more time with their traps."

"But ours are not the only trading posts," Jacques added thoughtfully.

"No, of course not, and more appear every day. The French have now established a fort at the far northwest shores of the great lake of the Erie, a place they call *Detroit* and trading has been established for decades at *La Baie Verte*, on Lake Michigan, tapping deeply into the interior but we give some of the fairest prices and there is still plenty for everyone to make a profit. And speaking of profits..." The big man reached inside his clothing and pulled several bags filled with gold out from each side of his tunic. He plunked them down on the desk with a jingling thud. "This is why I chose the perfume of the skunk. Put this into that fancy safe of yours. It is your share, *mon ami*."

"So you sold the skins already?"

"No-no, that is just the gold we took in selling merchandise and supplies."

"From the trappers?" Jacques asked in astonishment. He could not imagine that the trappers were now paying for supplies with gold.

"No-no, from the forts! The skins are still on the boat and *they* come from the trappers as always. I did not stop in New York Towne to sell them. I could not wait to get here," he stopped to scratch violently at his crotch, "and to rid myself of some unwanted stowaways. But I see there is no ocean ship in our harbor, did I miss it or do you expect one yet before winter closes in?"

Jacques shook his head. "A packet boat will come but Dufee is not sending another ship until spring," he responded automatically, still looking at the four heavy purses and grappling with their reality. "Do the forts not receive their own supply ships?"

"Of course, but there is always something they did not get or the ship is late, or it has been lost altogether; so it goes and so they come to our posts for emergency goods. One cannot allow a garrison of men to starve," Richard grinned again. "In some cases we are selling one week to the French and the next week to the English. Do you want the skins here, or can we still store them for the winter in the old cabin?" Richard asked pouring himself another larger drink.

"Richard..." Jacques looked at his friend with a frown, "it just does not seem right anymore."

"What?"

"This," he gestured to the gold. "I did not earn this. You are the one who travels the rivers, watches over the posts and transports the goods. You do all the work, my friend. I have not been to even our closest posts in years. This by rights all belongs to you."

"We are partners!" Richard said roughly. "I already have my share buried at the bottom of my chest. Jacques, we started this together, and at first we put labor into it fifty-fifty, it is true. But it was your gold that got the trading posts going. Without it, I would still be trading one on one with the Indians, one canoe load at a time. Besides what would I do with it all? I have everything I need," he gulped down the last of his drink and wiped his mouth with the back of his hand. "I take that back," he said, scratching his crotch again. "I have almost everything I need. But right now I do need de-lousing, a bath, a barber, and a tailor if I am going to see your pretty wife and pretty children and claim my room and supper at your house tonight." He laughed and started to turn. "So, where do you want the skins?"

"The cabin is fine. I believe the key is at the bakery. But do not go there in that state, you will frighten the shop girl to death."

"I will have them brought here for now," Richard grinned and walked out. "See you later."

Jacques sent word to the house that Richard had returned. Jane was to make up his old room. And in honor of his return, they were to hold off on the children's supper so they could eat with the adults tonight. Perhaps, he thought to himself grimly, having Richard back would put some spark into Marie.

When Renée heard the news she saw her opportunity. The children would all be downstairs attending supper; everyone would be occupied for some time. She had managed to dose Madame Power liberally; the woman was in no condition to leave her bed. Every twenty or thirty minutes Renée returned and prompted Marie to take another spoonful as if it were the very first time. She was so confused and addled she did not know the difference. While everyone was downstairs, Renée knew she could administer the final doses and by the time monsieur retired for the evening, madame would have breathed her last.

When Jane Sims answered the door in the late afternoon, Richard stood outside smelling of Bay Rum and looking vastly improved with a fresh shave and haircut and a new suit of clothes. He twitched only a little at his unaccustomed restrictions and habitually tugged a finger in his cravat as though somehow it kept getting tighter around his neck.

The life he led kept Richard trim and powerful although he had gained a few extra pounds through his long restrictive recuperation. This added to his mass. His heavy head of dark hair was now liberally mixed with shocks of rough gray which had an unruly look even after being freshly cut. He had never owned a wig and would never consider wearing one, preferring to wear braids when his hair again became long enough. His eyebrows had grown bushier with kinky gray hairs but the barber had managed to trim those as well. With his full beard removed, the skin beneath was several shades paler and more youthful than the brown leather of his forehead.

He gave Jane a broad grin. "How are you, Janey?" he asked with a wink that made the older woman blush profusely.

"Why Master Richard, aren't you a welcome sight! Now, mind you wipe your feet." The big man obediently used the boot wipe. "Come on in," she flung open the door approvingly.

"Every time I come back you are looking younger and prettier. Is this a new frock? Very fetching! That husband of yours had better treat you right or I will steal you away from him!"

"Oh, shush, Master Richard, how you do go on," the bony housekeeper glowed with pleasure at his flirty attention.

Richard set a large bundle of gifts down as he heard multiple footsteps rapidly coming nearer.

"Uncle Richard!" "Uncle Richard!" The older children ran up and hung on him while the youngest one looked on shyly. Only John held back, now considering himself too old for such a juvenile greeting.

"John, you are becoming a man!" Richard said quite loudly as he reached for the youth and pulled him into a bear hug. Then, he stood back with his hands on the lad's shoulders and looked at him intently. "What is this I see? A moustache like your pa-pa? When did this happen, eh? I remember the day you were born! How did you become grown up so quickly?"

John's smooth cheeks turned pink as he stood proudly.

"So," Richard threw a mock punch at him, "do you think you can get the best of me now by yourself?" He encouraged the lad and soon they were wrestling. "Or do you need your brothers to help?"

That was Phillip's cue to join in and soon Richard was down on the floor of the foyer being overrun by all of them. The youngest children were on top of the others which is how Sarah found them when she walked in.

"Children, children, enough! Your father will be home soon and we shall eat."

Richard got up in good humor, looking around for Marie. "Jane? Where is Madame Power?" He saw a cloud pass over her face and Sarah ducked out of the room quickly. "Janey? What is it?"

"She rarely gets out of bed these days," Jane said and to his surprise he saw her break a sob into her apron.

Richard said no more. He bolted from the foyer and took the long, sweeping staircase two steps at a time, never pausing despite the pain it inflicted on his recently injured foot. The door of the master bedroom was not completely closed so he knocked and swung it open simultaneously and caught Renée in the act of force feeding laudanum down Marie's throat with the aid of a large spoon.

"*Sacre Bleu!!*" he roared. "What is it you think you are doing?!!" he shouted at the girl.

Startled, Renée dropped the large spoon, spilling the liquid on the coverlet. True fear made her heart race within her chest, not just at having been caught in the act but at the menacing size of the man standing over her with the fiercest look she had ever seen. It was as if he looked straight through her, knew her for what she was and was ready to pound her into dust for it.

"I… she…"

Richard snatched up the bottle, reading the label. "How much?" he barked at her. "How much did you give her?" he thundered and with one large hand he grabbed Renée by the throat as if to choke the answer from her.

"Only a… spoonful… monsieur..."

"Ach!" Richard snarled and tossed her aside. He spread open Marie's eye lids and looked at her pupils. "God curse you for a liar!" he yelled at Renée who had fallen against the wall.

Jane had followed the big man and appeared in the doorway. "Get me wet towels," he cried out to her as he grabbed the basin from the washstand and a feather quill from off the side table. Richard began shoving the feather down Marie's throat to gag her, forcing her to vomit. He bellowed for the kitchen to prepare a clean mix of thick grease, raw eggs and charcoal.

Renée's mind was racing as she backed away. Her instinct was to run but running was an admission of guilt. The only way to salvage this was to play stupid, she told herself. And she had been stupid not to secure the door! Who was this man who breached the portal of madame's bedroom with such easy familiarity… her brother, a cousin? Why had she not heard of him before? If she had had only ten more seconds, just ten seconds more… no one would have ever known. Madame would have slipped into unconsciousness on her own. The family would have been occupied for the evening. And it would have been over.

Richard continued using the feather, until the purge arrived. He forced it down Marie's throat until she wretched again and again. Moaning and crying, she begged him to stop. He washed her face and neck, looked again at her eyes and insisted she get out of bed and onto her feet. When she did not move fast enough he lifted her out and onto the floor where with Jane's help they began to walk her about the room. "Her dressing gown, sir," Jane said and grabbed the warm wrap. Jane had just finished fastening it modestly about Marie when Jacques arrived home and was struck dumb by what he found.

Sarah had the children downstairs but they all spoke at once telling him Uncle Richard had run up to Mama and had been shouting. Jacques himself bolted up the stairs to find Renée cowering against the wall while Richard and Jane walked a barely conscious Marie around the bedroom, vomit was in the wash basin and all over the bed linens.

"What is going on?" Jacques asked in bewilderment.

"A good question, *mon ami*," Richard replied in French. "one that I could ask you. I found your wife half dead and this one trying to finish the job with this poison." He swooped as they passed close to the bed stand and grabbed the bottle of laudanum, tossing it to Jacques. "I suggest you call for your doctor and keep that little viper under lock and key until we can get to the bottom of all this."

"She speaks French, Richard," Jacques replied in English. He could not help but feel sorry for the young girl he saw quaking in the corner. She looked ready to die of fright on the spot.

"Good, then there is no mistaking what I think of her. Waste not your sympathy."

Jacques stepped in to relieve Jane of the burden of half dragging Marie around the room. "Tell Sims I need to see him," he said, "and send John on horseback to fetch the doctor. Tell Sarah the children are not to wait, let them have their supper. And could you see to changing the bed linens?"

"Yes, sir, right away," Jane nodded briskly and turned to leave the room in haste.

"And Jane," Richard called after her, "ask cook to make a very, very, very strong pot of coffee.

Just then Marie threw up again.

Sims appeared and Jacques gave him instructions to confine Renée under lock and key until they could question her. Sims carried out the chore gladly without any sympathy for his charge.

Jane brought fresh linens and proceeded to change the bed, then she helped Jacques change Marie's bed gown while Richard turned his back. When the coffee arrived they poured it out into a shallow bowl to cool so they could pour it into Marie without scalding her.

Finally Jane left the room taking the dirty laundry with her and when alone with just Jacques and Marie, Richard spoke again.

"If you do not mind my observation, you seem to be taking this with exceeding calm," Richard said darkly, puzzled bewilderment obvious in his voice.

In reality Jacques was barely holding his emotions in check. Through clenched teeth he responded, "What would you have me do, Richard, rent my clothes and heap ashes upon my head? You arrived here remembering a Marie that has not existed for almost a year. You have no idea what it has been like, this is… just another episode. And my best friend now looks at me as though this is all my fault. I am certain that we will find there was no evil intent… an accident, a mistake, that is all." Jacques' voice had become so strangled that for a moment he could not speak. "Marie has required much care these last months," he said at last when he could steady his voice.

"Is that when the little witch, arrived?"

"No-no," Jacques shook his head dismissively. "Renée only arrived after Isabelle was born but Marie has been troubled ever since this last pregnancy began. Two-thirds through her term she was crippled by severe pains in her leg… her leg, her back, it is hard to know which and the doctor gave her… that is when she first began to take laudanum."

"You are right. I do not know what has happened here over the last two years but I know what I saw, my friend. That little witch was forcing the drug down Marie's throat and Marie was trying to push her off but she had not the strength. Judging from her state I am all but certain she would have been dead before morning. Do you not still sleep in the same bed with her?"

Jacques resented the question but decided under the circumstances to answer honestly rather than tell Richard it was none of his business. "We did, we always have until just recently."

"A fight?"

"No, nothing so shallow, Richard. Truthfully, if you must know my shame…" Jacques looked at his life-long friend with tragic sadness upon his countenance. "Marie has shown no interest in me for months. It finally became unbearable to be so close and not be allowed to…" he did not finish.

Richard glanced over at his friend and felt a surge of pity. Is this what the Olympians had felt when their worshipers turned away in disinterest. Man was not meant to be adored as a god. "Well, it is no wonder, *mon ami*," he said kindly, "drink enough of that poison and no matter who you are you will care about absolutely nothing, not even your next breath."

The two men continued to walk a half-conscious Marie in circles as Jacques relayed everything he knew and could remember from the time Marie first realized she was pregnant with Isabelle. When he finished Richard spoke.

"Your fine doctor has allowed your wife to become an opium addict."

"No," Jacques responded in disbelief. "It is not possible!"

"Yes, and since I doubt that this was his intent, I must conclude that the little witch has pushed it along."

"No-no, Richard. What reason could she possibly have to do that? This was just an unfortunate accident, an over-dosage."

"Ah, my dear Jacques. You are a successful gentleman of the upper-class in the colonies, a most happily and satisfied… until just recently… married man who has had no call or reason to ever visit the underbelly dens of iniquity where you might have come in contact with opium addicts and see just what it does to them. Unchecked it does not take long to steal a life away."

"And when did you become an expert?" Jacques half scoffed in retaliation.

"Many years ago when in my early teens, in Paris, yes, I gained a modest education."

Jacques looked at his friend.

"A cousin," Richard said without elaboration. "But what shocks me is how the doctor could keep handing over the opiate to your wife in such quantities as to wield this damage so quickly without suspecting mis-use."

"Perhaps he did not remember how much he had given her," Jacques offered, refusing to believe deliberate neglect on the part of St. Claire. "He has grown quite old."

"Well, he had better remember how to help her through what is next to come. It is called *le sevrage*, the weaning, as the level of drug decreases in the body and the body begins to turn on itself. It is not a pretty thing to witness, my friend. Her body will burn and ache for the drug, she will sweat and shake with chills at the same time. She will cry and perhaps curse and beg for it until you will want to give it to her just to ease her suffering – but you must not. If you love her, you cannot. You must be the stronger if you want her to overcome this and survive or, Jacques, eventually it will kill her."

Richard looked over at his friend and saw tears coursing down Jacques' cheeks.

"How could I let this happen, Richard? Right under my nose. What kind of protector am I?"

Marie groaned and grabbed for the basin as she wretched again.

Doctor St. Claire was horrified when he arrived at the Power home and was told the situation.

"I told her only a small teaspoon, just one small spoon when she got those sharp pains in her back," he said in his own defense and looked at the large spoon taken from Renée.

"We think she had help learning to want much more," thundered Richard. "Did the number of bottles she was going through not seem suspicious?"

"I…" St. Claire thought hard. His mind was not as clear as it used to be, his memory not so sharp. He recalled noticing a bottle or two missing but he thought he had just misplaced them. "I thought I had miscounted," he said in shame.

"*Monsieur Docteur*, what do we do now?" Jacques asked anxiously.

St. Claire looked around. "Your children should not be exposed to this."

"The women will keep them occupied," responded Jacques.

"Monsieur Power, you misunderstand my meaning. Every patient is different, but this will take days, even weeks depending on her and how much and how long she has been affected."

"You were giving her this when she was pregnant." There was accusation in Jacques' tone.

"I know, I know, but just the mildest dose… no, it is more important to know when she began to take so much more."

"I believe you should estimate from shortly after the baby was born," Richard spoke. "Is that not when the little witch came? Perhaps for three or four months now."

Jacques said nothing and St. Claire paused thoughtfully, "Three perhaps four …" he half muttered to himself. "Within a week or two we should have her purged. But do you wish to keep her here close to your nursery and the other bed-rooms or should we not go farther from the rest of the house. Your new wing, perhaps?"

"Boot and his children have moved out," Jacques nodded. "We have rooms to spare."

"Good. Have your servants remove everything except a bed and a couple chairs. Have them bring blankets, water, an empty pail and a large chamber pot, changes of clothing… for her. And of course we will need a fire," the old man added, rubbing his limbs against the cold chill that was his constant companion of late.

"Is that really necessary, *Monsieur Docteur?*" Jacques grimaced. "I mean… to make the surroundings so stark?"

"It is for her own good, to keep her from harming herself. She could turn violent," replied St. Claire. "And the less there is around, the less that can be damaged or soiled."

Jacques carried his wife down to the room that had been made up for Richard but he did not ask for anything to be removed. There was nothing she could damage or soil that he cared about. He cared only for her and he would not put Marie in a room as bleak as a prison cell. He closed off the wing and a roaring fire was soon going in the bedroom hearth, driving out the chill. One could keep vigil while the other two could sleep in the maid or valet's room or refresh themselves or bring in more wood or food from the kitchen. Everything was assembled and all they could do was wait.

Marie was quiet, sleeping somewhat restlessly but quietly. St. Claire warned that this was the calm before the storm and urged them to eat and sleep while they could. He would watch her.

Jacques saw to the rest of the household, explaining to the children that their mother had taken ill and since they were not sure if it was contagious, she had been removed to *Grand-père's* wing and they were not to try and see her. Richard ate with them and sought to mollify their fears, joking and telling them stories.

The night passed.

Jacques was awake by dawn and as he lie in the narrow bed originally set up for his mother's attending maid, he wondered if they had over-reacted. He could hear St. Claire snoring in his chair and Marie still slept quietly. Had Richard stirred them all up over nothing? Forcing Marie to swallow old bacon grease mixed with raw eggs and charcoal would make anyone throw up. It was disgusting to even think about.

He heard the rooster crowing from the chicken coop. All was peaceful. He dozed off again and woke an hour later when he heard Marie begin to moan.

He found her doubled up in the bed clutching her belly. St. Claire awoke, checked her pulse and her eyes and told Jacques this was the beginning. She was being seized by belly cramps. As she curled up writhing in agony she began to beg for the medicine. Just a little she pleaded to stop the unbearable pain. St. Claire told her she had had seven children and she knew how to handle pain. Jacques had to turn away.

For the next five days they attended her in shifts as she was plagued by nausea and vomiting until she had nothing left in her to vomit. She could not tolerate food. The mere mention of it made her heave but the doctor insisted she drink water. They must guard against dehydration he warned and she tried to be an obedient patient. She drank the water he pushed at her and within minutes she was throwing it up. Her stomach cramping came back and as she moaned in pain, Jacques and Richard each wished it was him in her place.

St. Claire ordered them out when diarrhea hit and she soiled her bed. He cleaned her up, changed the linens and got her to the chamber pot the next time. She grew restless, unable to sleep, tossing and turning until on the fifth day the chills and sweats began.

By turns Marie wept and pleaded. She shook so violently she could not bring a cup to her mouth without spilling most of the contents all over herself before it ever reached her lips. Jacques held her cup, steadying her head and tried to get water into her. She was perspiring profusely and begged for relief, just the smallest drop of the medicine to ease her pain, to settle her nerves, to stop her quaking. It was enough to wrench pity from a stone but for the two men who both loved Marie, it was an excruciating trial of endurance and resolve.

Jacques' response was to hold her as tightly as he dared without inflicting injury, hold her against the quakes that shook her body until his own arms began to cramp, hold her through the sweats that drained her as he willed his love to somehow transfer into her and give her strength. He held her to give her a sense of protection and something to push against when the pains running throughout her body gripped her violently. How could this have happened? He kept asking himself the question over and over and the guilt building inside him was crushing his soul. And he prayed.

Richard's response was to hold his tongue for the first time in his life. He told himself he must keep from uttering a torrent of words born out of rage and anger, frustration and unacknowledged love, words of accusation and condemnation that would have served no purpose but to heap more guilt upon the two men sharing this ordeal with him who already were drowning in their own horrendous sense of guilty culpability.

St. Claire, stretched out for a nap in the room next to them, was feeling his blame as sharply as his age and recognized that it was his neglect that had created this tragedy. He was no longer what he had been, he could see that now. He could no longer trust his own faculties. He had outlived his usefulness, he sighed bitterly, and he had become a worthless old man.

Dawn streaked across the horizon of yet another day.

"The Indians put great store in sweat lodges," Richard was saying quietly. "They believe the body can sweat out evil." He wrung water from a towel and handed it to Jacques. Jacques took it and gently mopped Marie's face and neck, moving on to her arms and the soft skin above her breast.

"What evil? She has never had an evil thought in her life," Jacques murmured.

"You are right," Richard nodded in agreement. "In this case the evil was put into her." He stood up and tended the fire in the hearth. The room was comfortable and did not warrant all the perspiring Marie was doing.

"Did I ever tell you they think we are mad to allow our medicine men to drain away our blood? Blood is considered the most powerful manifestation of the life force. I am glad you did not allow him to bleed her, Jacques. She needs every bit of her strength right now."

Jacques thought of Augustine, the wise woman who cared for all the maladies at his father's chateau. "Gussy never believed in the practice." He mopped Marie's forehead again and sighed. "St. Claire has done his best to care for our settlement but I realize… he is becoming very aged."

"You may have to advertise for a replacement," Richard suggested in subdued tones. "Do you know Boston now has a population of over seven thousand? I believe that includes slaves."

"Seven thousand?!" Jacques echoed softly allowing the thought to register and deflect his thoughts from Marie's condition. "It is even larger than New York Towne which I read is now over five thousand."

"Boston is said to be the largest city on this continent," Richard added.

"You see… how can we compete? I am certain they have no problems attracting doctors and teachers. But what can our little settlement offer besides farmland and lumber work?"

"It is not like you to sound melancholy and defeated, *mon ami*. This settlement has a very attractive bucolic pace." Richard looked long at his friend in the quiet of the dawning light but Jacques said nothing for a long time.

"The trembling has subsided, at least for now," Jacques said hoarsely loosening the blanket around Marie as she lay in his arms. "Will you see if Jane is about, if so, please ask her to give you more fresh shifts. This one is soaked in sweat."

Richard grunted with a nod and left the room.

"Jacques…?" Marie said weakly, stirring and limply trying to shuck aside the confines of the blanket. "Jacques, what is wrong with me? Am I dying…?"

"No-no, my love, my darling, not at all, everything will be better soon, soon you will again be well."

"I think I am dying," she murmured gravely. "Just like Ma-ma."

"No, Marie," he felt panic, "you must not say this. You are not dying, you are not, it only feels that way perhaps but you will get better, believe me, you will."

"I am so sorry… I do not want to leave you. I knew I must not… must not have another baby..." she whispered.

"What? What must you not? I did not hear," Jacques asked but Marie had lost consciousness again.

Richard returned carrying a stack of delicate muslin shifts and sturdy cotton flannel nightgowns.

"Jane said perhaps you might use the flannel. It will keep Marie warmer and also soak up sweat better."

Jacques took a flannel gown. "She is right."

Richard turned to leave but stopped. "And what about the witch?" he asked.

"Who? Oh, Renée? I had forgotten all about her. It has been days. Is she still under lock and key?"

Richard nodded.

"I cannot believe there was any sinister intent. The girl knew no better and you saw how Marie begged us for it. How could you expect the child to refuse her?"

The look on Richard's face clearly said he did not agree.

"Now if you would give us our privacy, I am going to bed-bathe my wife and get her into the fresh flannel. I will continue to stay with her, and perhaps sleep just a little. If you are not satisfied, Richard, you may interrogate Renée. Personally, I am too exhausted. I have no desire to try to blame the girl. This is *my* fault, my responsibility; I should have seen what was happening before my very eyes."

It maddened Richard that Jacques should acquiesce to such guilt but he knew his friend well enough to know argument at this point would achieve nothing. And, Richard admitted to himself, Jacques was to blame. Indeed, this had happened right before his eyes. But what exactly had happened? His gut told him Renée had a purposeful hand in it, a personal motivation, and his gut was rarely wrong.

Richard sought out Renée for questioning. Hoping to trip her up in a lie or wring a confession from her, all he got for his efforts were tears and repeated pleas for forgiveness and a confession to ignorance and stupidity. His instincts told him he was not wrong but in the end he was forced to release her and let her resume her duties. He took the precaution to search her room. If she had more laudanum, he could not find it.

"Watch her," he instructed Jane, "in future do not let her near Madame Power or her food or drink. I am going to the kitchen to tell Margot the same."

Jane nodded her agreement. "I ain't never liked that one," she clucked. "and the way she looks at the master when no one else is watching is down right shameful."

At that Richard raised a bushy eyebrow, pausing in contemplation.

"Master Richard? How is the mistress doing?" Jane asked, a sincere frown of worry on her brow.

"God willing, she will be well, Janey," he said encouragingly and strode out to the kitchen behind the house to find Margot.

Jacques dozed as he sat with his back against the headrest of the bed with Marie in his arms. Suddenly she kicked out with a gasp as her legs were seized with cramping muscles. He awoke to see the muscles in her legs standing out as rigid as wood. Her toes were being drawn back as if trying to touch her knee. She continued to kick as she panted and moaned in stifled screams. He tried to help her straighten her legs.

"I must stand. I must stand," she whimpered and rolled off the bed to the floor. She would have fallen if he had not been there to catch her.

Standing to bear her own weight forced her muscles to stretch out again but they were not relaxed and continued to pain her mightily. Weak from her ordeal, still she tried to walk and she clutched Jacques' arm for support.

"We will get you warm blankets, my love," he said, "and the bricks to warm your legs. Please get back into bed."

"Not yet, not yet… I must walk, I must stand against the pain," she moaned and continued on until the warm blankets and bricks arrived.

When Richard returned to the guest wing he brought a tray carefully prepared by Margot with everything she could think of to temp the mistress. Margo had piled on enough for all of Marie's guardians as well.

As he entered the guest bed chamber by way of the valet's room, Richard found Jacques messaging Marie's legs as she begged the doctor for something to ease her horrendous cramps.

"You must drink more water," St. Claire told her gruffly. "You are cramping because you need water. Jacques, let me bleed her to relieve the humor."

"If she needs more liquid," asked Richard, "how does bleeding her of liquid help?"

St. Claire could not answer.

"Marie, my dearest one, drink, please, drink. It will ease you," Jacques coaxed as he held a glass to her lips and she drank a few swallows before bursting into more weeping."Oh, please… my whole body aches. I cannot endure it any longer. Make it go away. Jacques," she grabbed his arm, "if you love me, make it go away."

"Some food will help," Jacques said softly, seeing himself as a cruel ogre to deny her a small spoonful of laudanum. To avoid her eyes he tucked the warm blankets and heated bricks around her legs.

"Yes, look at what Margot has sent," Richard displayed the tray before setting it upon a small table.

She looked completely disinterested.

"You must eat something, my darling," Jacques cajoled. "Food will give you the strength you need to see this to the end. The end is coming, is it not doctor?"

"Yes-yes," St. Claire nodded quickly. "The end is coming. I see the cook has made a fine chicken soup, it smells most delicious. I want you to take a spoonful."

He handed the small bowl and spoon to Jacques who proceeded to feed Marie, one small spoonful at a time. It was warm and Marie knew Margot's soup was delicious but she only opened her mouth and swallowed because Jacques wanted her to do so. She had no appetite. And the smell of it made her feel ill.

"Please, Jacques," she whispered after several spoonfuls, "no more." He saw the sweat beads popping out upon her forehead again as she began to shake violently.

It had been two weeks and the worst was over. Marie was back in the master bedroom convalescing, the children were allowed to see her and little by little she was gaining back her strength and her appetite. Jacques, as much to assuage his own guilt as to appease Richard, made certain Marie was never left alone. If Jacques himself was not with her, then it was Richard or Jane or eldest son John who kept her company and watched over her without trying to appear a nursemaid or a prison guard.

Marie, ashamed of what she had put everyone through, accepted her convalescence and made no complaint. She felt weaker than she had ever felt in her life. Childbirth had never made her feel this debilitated. She made every effort to eat but each bite was a challenge. She did not completely understand what had happened to her but she was aware of the strong and undeniable hunger she still had for the "medicine." She acknowledged it and confessed to it. It was a hunger that seemed to cry out from every part of her body but she also had the intellect to understand once Doctor St. Claire explained just how harmful taking the drug again would be. Marie had an amazingly strong will for survival and she set that will against her cravings and not against those who were trying to help her.

She did not remember much of those last days just before Richard's arrival. They were a blurred fog of fantasies, dreams, and memories and she was not certain what had been reality. Nor was she able to confirm any ill intent on the part of anyone, including Renée but even now she could hear a voice from the past telling her she must never give up hope.

What she did share in conversation with an extremely gentle and solicitous Richard was the genuine pain she felt now that she took no laudanum to counter it. He could see it in her eyes, pain from her back that she accepted without complaint but which hobbled her into a ghost of the woman he had known, the woman the others had lost almost a year ago.

Jacques tried to return to their bed. He chided himself for what he now saw as childish and selfish behavior, knowing something of the demons his wife had faced while he had only thought of his carnal desires. He made no demands upon her, only cherished the nearness of her until it became apparent that his weight within the bed often brought her more pain and discomfort. And so he stoically had a second narrower bed set up in their room.

Renée hid herself within the workings of the nursery and licked her wounds. Anger and frustration bubbled within her. She had tried and she had failed to eliminate madame and now madame was watched over, guarded, and cared for like a queen. Renée snarled viciously within herself. There would never be another opportunity so simple and so devoid of consequence. It had come and it was gone and she had failed thanks to that big bear of a man who continued to look at her with suspicion and condemnation every time he saw her, convinced of her guilt. Renée had no desire to hang upon a gibbet and thus the plan to murder Madame Power was dead but one could not be hanged for the murder of a marriage. Renée turned back to her original plan.

Little Britta could be a lively child verbally but of late the lightest activity reduced her to panting and wheezing. She had never tried to run and jump as the other children did but within this past year she had almost ceased to move around at all. She sat in her bed or in a chair or on the floor, playing with dolls or looking at books or just watching the others around her play. She took colds easily; it was one of the banes and threats to the well-being of her under-developed little body.

Renée watched over her as attentively as possible and tried to protect her from the drafts of winter but she recognized the signs when Britta caught another cold. It started with a sneeze that ignited into a fever by nightfall. Congestion followed and slipped into the chest accompanied by a dry unproductive cough.

Renée sought out Jacques. It was still early evening although already pitch black outside with the shortness of the daylight hours. He was in his study, surrounded by candlelight. She scratched at the door.

"*Entrée!*" Jacques called out.

Renée peeped in. It was the first time she had allowed herself to be seen by him since that night a month ago. Renée suddenly ran to him, throwing herself at his feet, hugging his ankles, kissing his boots, and begging a tearful almost incoherent forgiveness for all that had happened with madame.

Jacques was overwhelmed with both his own discomfort and a sense of pity for the girl. She reminded him of the serfs in France who often threw aside their personal dignity to grovel in the dirt and beg forgiveness or favors from their lords.

"Come, child, come," he said reaching out and lifting her up off the floor. "You are no longer a peasant. This is America. Stand tall, please. Please… you must not kiss my boots. Stand up."

"Oh, dear kind monsieur, forgive me. Forgive me, I beg you. I only did as the madame wished. I did not know it was so wrong…"

"Hush, hush." Her cap had fallen from her head and he stroked her glossy hair. "No one blames you. Please do not cry. Here, my handkerchief, now wipe your eyes."

Sobbing prettily, she took the handkerchief and dried her large dark eyes. "There is nothing I would not do to make it all up to you, monsieur … and to the madame."

"I understand. But there is nothing for you to do. Madame is mending, she will be well soon," Jacques said with as much hope as he could muster. "Now, what brings you to my study this night?"

"Monsieur, I fear for the little girl, Britta. Madame told me I have charge of her and I watch her very carefully but she has taken another cold and her chest… it sounds very bad but I did not want to disturb madame."

"No-no, you were right to come to me. Let us go to the nursery."

Jacques followed Renée up the stairs where he observed Britta and placed his own ear to her chest to listen to her breathing. Next, he consulted Sarah who agreed that Britta's condition was fast becoming most alarming. John was sent to the Boot home with a message to come quickly. St. Claire was called for again but Jacques did not want to disturb Marie.

Marie, who was reading within the warmth of her bed, sensed a disturbance within the home. Jane was with her working on her mending. With Jane's assistance, Marie put on her slippers, a heavy dressing wrap, and a shawl. She left the bedroom with the aid of her cane and Jane, and went in search of what was going on. The two made their way together to the nursery.

St. Claire arrived and lost no time in setting up his instruments to bleed the child as William Boot watched.

"No, Jacques, no," Marie whispered, pulling on Jacques arm, "better we get a chest plaster. Do not allow…"

"William is her father," Jacques said sternly, "it is his decision."

Marie took his words as a rebuke that hit her like a blow and she dropped her head. She was a bad mother, she told herself. For months she had been very inattentive to the children and to this little one. For months she had thought only of herself and escape through the laudanum. If she had paid more attention, perhaps Britta would not have fallen ill. Marie moved away and took a chair by the bedside commencing a prayerful vigil.

The little girl lay quietly on her bed. Her baby face pale and laced with a bluish tinge, her lips and tiny fingers growing ever bluer, her soft blonde hair circling her little head. Marie watched her tiny face, noting the serenity and peace with which she slept and imagined Christ coming down a long staircase to finally take the little girl up into His arms.

The next day in the fifth hour of the morning, little Britta's heart gave its last feeble beat. St. Claire pronounced her dead.

"No one could have predicted when she was born that she would actually live beyond the week, much less six happy years and I think we all know it was due to the extraordinary love and tender kindness of Madame Power," St. Claire said and Renée silently seethed.

William nodded his head, took Marie's hand and kissed it with a bow of gratitude. Tears began to flow down Marie's cheeks and would not stop. She made her way to her bedroom and began to cry as if her heart had broken in two. She did not understand why. They all knew Britta was living on borrowed time; they had always known any day might be her last. The doctor had been warning them for years, warning them ever since she arrived. And yet Marie cried and cried until she fell into an exhausted sleep.

Chapter 15

St. Claire and Jacques both agreed that it might be therapeutic for Marie to spend some time with her store and Renée noticed. And if it was at night, she also noticed Madame Power was staying later and later. She was leaving her husband at home alone. Once the children were in bed and asleep, the servants retired. Monsieur Power spent his time in his study awaiting his wife's return. And most evenings he had to fetch her home himself because she stayed so late. The stupid woman seemed oblivious to the opportunities this presented.

Renée had overheard madame tell her husband that she would be late this night and he said he would come for her; he did not want her out on the streets alone. They agreed he would fetch her at eleven. Renée understood more English than she admitted to and her heartbeat increased. She would help Sarah get the children to bed on time, by nine the household would be fast asleep and she would have two full hours in which to finally see her plan reach fruition. She was wet in anticipation.

John could not sleep. He had been listening to his brother's breathing for an hour. It had been weeks since his encounter with Renée in the hay loft and he was more confused than before. She had opened a door and taught him about things to which he used to have only a vague knowledge and now she ignored him. They had locked her up while his mother was ill. He did not understand this either. Now she was out again and he had tried often to catch her eye but she looked at him as she looked at all the others and there was no special connection, no glimmer of recognition that said she remembered their time together. He was more frustrated than ever, if that was possible. But it *was* possible for now he knew what he was wanting. He also knew that such behavior outside of marriage was frowned upon. Did he want to marry Renée? He did not think so. He just wanted to spend more time in the hay loft with her because she knew how to scratch the itch that had become his constant companion. He needed to talk with someone, someone who could help him sort out what he was feeling. Phillip was too young to understand. Unfortunately, Uncle Richard had taken a trip back to New York Towne or John knew he could talk to him. This was not something one talked about to one's mother. But then, Papa was not impossible to talk with, he was actually quite easy to talk with and suddenly John felt he would feel much better if he talked with his father.

It was nine when Renée silently stole down from the attic to the pantry and heated the hot chocolate, an exotic and sensual drink only now becoming popular in the colonies. Earlier she had readied and set aside everything she would need. Now, the pot of chocolate was ready. Should she bring only one cup? No, she would bring two, feigning expectation that madame would be there. With what could only be described as a malicious smile, Renée picked up the tray and began to carry it to Jacques' study.

The tap on the door startled Jacques. He was reading one of the new books his parents had sent to them from France. He was attempting to distract himself from what was always on his mind these days but he was having little success and the bawdy adventures of the novel's hero were not helping. He missed his wife when she was gone and he missed her when she was there.

"*Entrée!*" he invited.

The door opened almost hesitantly and there stood Renée trying to steady a tray almost as big as she. This was totally unexpected but instinctively Jacques stood and went to assist the girl who looked on the verge of falling.

"What is this?" he asked not unkindly.

"Chocolate, monsieur," she replied very softly.

"Chocolate?" Jacques repeated. The girl did not give up the tray but allowed him to carry most of the weight of it and guide it to his desk.

"Do you know chocolate, monsieur?" she asked with just a trace of nervous tremor in her voice.

It was a drink that Jacques was vaguely aware had begun to come into fashion in Paris about the time he had left the country. It had never been a concern of his to go out of his way to find it or taste it here in the colonies.

"I know about chocolate," he replied pleasantly, "but I confess I have never tried it."

"It is very delicious, monsieur," she looked at him shyly. "I thought you and madame would like some."

"Madame is not yet home."

"Oh." The girl look chest fallen in disappointment.

"But I must thank you for the thought," Jacques smiled at her, feeling somewhat chagrined at what they had put her through over Marie.

"It will get cold. Please... let me pour you a cup, if you have never had it before, I do so want to know what you think of it," she was very animated now and her eyes sparkled attractively.

"Then, you must join me," he offered and Renée's heart raced.

Things were going better than she had hoped. Jacques signed for her to take a seat and poured them each a cup of the dusky beverage. As she took the cup he handed her, she allowed her finger tips to barely brush his hand.

"Excuse me," she said quickly.

Jacques smiled; there was nothing for which to be excused. He took his cup and was aware of the girl watching him intently, awaiting his reaction to chocolate, no doubt. He smiled again and took a seat in the chair opposite her. He took a sip. He had been told chocolate was a very, very bitter brew that stained the teeth of its devotees but this was sweet and creamy.

"But this is very good," he exclaimed in surprise and was rewarded with a bright smile from Renée. "It is not bitter at all."

"At first they tried to drink it only as a ground bean brew, like coffee, but someone thought to dilute it with scalded milk and add sugar. I think it is very delicious," she said brightly and added, "It seems to wrap itself around the tongue before it slides down the throat." The image she created in the way she said it was somehow erotic.

Jacques continued to sip. It really was a pleasant drink, totally unlike what he had thought it would be, and it did feel somewhat sensuous on the pallet.

"So, how are your English lessons coming along?" he asked conversationally.

"Oh, monsieur," the young girl seemed to blush. "*Anglaise* is a very difficult language and I am not doing very well. I am afraid I shall never learn it."

"Nonsense, we all felt that way at the beginning."

"Even you, monsieur?" she looked at him with her dark eyes wide in incredulity.

"Even I," he assured her.

"I cannot imagine anything being difficult for you," she said softly, her lips very moist.

"Life presents many difficulties; I must overcome my challenges like any other," he said with a touch of introspection.

"But sometimes the challenge is more than a man can be expected to overcome," she replied softly. Jacques said nothing but drained his cup. This was Renée's cue. She rose to set her cup aside and made as if to take his cup.

"You have chocolate on your mouth, monsieur," she said and was about to straddle his lap and lick chocolate from his lips with her tongue when another voice was heard.

"Papa? Oh… I didn't know anyone…" John stood at the door seeing Renée bent toward his father looking as though they were sharing a kiss.

Self-consciously Jacques dabbed at his mouth to remove the chocolate, "John? Come in. I have just been introduced to chocolate. Have you ever tried it? Would you like to try some?"

"Perhaps another time." John felt he had interrupted something between his father and Renée, something he was not meant to see. It was awkward and it made him angry – jealous for himself and indignant for his mother.

"Oh, the time!" Jacques exclaimed as he looked at the clock on the mantel. "I must leave to fetch your ma-ma. Renée, please remove the tray," he added dismissively and left.

"What are you doing?" John asked when they were alone.

"I am clearing away the tray," Renée replied smoothly, covering her seething rage at having been interrupted in the middle of her ploy.

"That is not what I meant. What were you doing with my father?" John followed her to the pantry.

She set the tray down and turned to the boy. "Are you jealous?" She smiled wantonly, teasing him and fanning his jealous passion.

"Come with me," he said softly, grabbing her arm and pulling her toward the outside door.

"Where?"

"To the hay loft."

She stopped with surprising strength in her resistance and laughed. "Are you mad? Why would I want to go out into the cold to a cold barn with cold hay?"

"It is not so cold tonight. Renée, I want you, I want to be inside you… like before," he pulled her to him and was kissing her wildly. She pulled back and stared at him, a quiet salacious smile upon her lips and he saw her eyes travel from his eyes downward.

"I can see that," she cooed. "This house has many bedrooms, much warmer than the barn," she led him to the stairs. "What about your room?"

"No, Phillip is there."

"What about the room across the hall, the one next to your parents?"

"My father sometimes uses that one… come, this way to *Grand-père's* rooms. Richard is not here."

He easily pulled her down the hall. Renée allowed him to lead her and she proceeded to do whatever he wished as her mind fastened upon this newest tidbit of information. So, monsieur no longer slept with his wife! This she would have to investigate.

Richard returned from his trip to New York Towne with two very interesting companions in tow: a tall, svelte Viking of a woman who spoke no English but could match him stride for stride and a short Chinese fellow who spoke English no one could understand and had to take two steps to each of their one to keep a pace. She had a thick silver-blonde braid coiled upon her head like a crown and he had a long black pigtail flowing out from the middle of his shaved head. Richard made introductions when they arrived at the Power home.

"Meet Ingrid. Do not concern yourself with her last name; I cannot pronounce it. And this is Master Wang Long Sun."

The Chinaman bowed low before Jacques while the striking blonde female just smiled, displaying a large, wide mouth full of beautiful teeth.

"I think you should send for that fellow you have working at the mill… Boot, is it not? He will be helpful in speaking with Ingrid. Meanwhile, Master Wang can help Marie."

"Help her how?" Jacques asked in puzzlement.

"Ah, have I neglected to mention? These two are both experienced in the healing arts."

Just then Marie hobbled into the room leaning on her cane. She was willing to try anything and did not need to be convinced. The conventional medicine of their day had not been able to help her so why should she not look to heathen cultures for something else? Had she not already found some of the native Indian ways to be better than their own?

Wang was assigned the valet's room connected to Richard's room in *Grandpère's* wing while Ingrid was made comfortable in the upstairs guest room.

Jacques insisted on staying to oversee what was happening as the dining room was closed off for privacy. Marie, clad only in her thin muslin shift and a sheet, was pushed as much as told to lie stomach down upon the table which had been covered with layers of blankets for padding. Master Wang produced a bamboo container filled with hair thin needles of pure gold and proceeded to insert them through her shift and into her flesh at specific points.

Jacques gasped when he watched the first needles glide into position but Marie assured him as she lay quietly that she felt almost nothing at all beyond perhaps a tickle.

The Chinaman worked with amazing efficiency, poking, prodding, testing reflexes and inserting the thin gold needles. He placed some in her feet, at points on the back of her legs, into her derrière, along her spine, at points in her arms and even in her scalp. When he finished he covered her with a very light weight sheet and indicated as much as verbalized that she should relax, sleep if she like but remain there for an hour. He retired to the kitchen where Margot had been told to feed him and she discovered he could eat enough for three grown men.

Meanwhile, William Boot arrived and Richard introduced him to Ingrid. As they waited for Jacques, William and Ingrid enjoyed a lively conversation all in Swedish and none of which was understood by anyone else. When Master Wang left for the kitchen, Jacques joined them and through William he learned that Ingrid was a childless widow who had developed a talent for therapeutic massages, especially for problems of the back and legs and her large, strong hands were the tools by which she made a living. She was a very animated and exotically attractive lady with the regal bearing of a princess and her large hands were not man-ish but graceful and in keeping with her overall statuesque size. She had mesmerizing eyes that slanted upward like a jungle cat and were underscored by the highest cheekbones any of them had ever seen. From the moment they met, William's gaze seldom left her.

With a generous amount of gold, Richard had bought from each one of this strange pair the promise of a month's attendance upon Marie at Chartes Landing. After that it was up to them if they chose to stay but if they helped Madame Power return to her former good health, their reputations in the settlement would be made. Everyone knew the good lady and how she had been stricken the night of Nicholet's good-bye party almost a year ago and how she had not been the same ever since.

William conveyed all this to Ingrid and in return he translated Ingrid's request for a narrow table to be made to stand at an unusual height. She was very specific about the dimensions. In the small trunk she had brought with her, she explained, there was a leather covered pad as thick as her fist which would be placed on top of the table. Upon this she would give her massages.

Jacques instructed William to work with the woman and make whatever she needed. He excused himself and went back to the dining room to find Master Wang plucking needles out of his wife yet drawing not one single drop of blood.

"How do you feel?" Jacques asked as he watched Marie sit up, modestly keeping herself covered.

"Strange… but good," she answered obediently.

Jacques nodded. "I must confess," he added softly, "seeing you lying like that before another man's eyes with his hands all over you was more than a little unsettling."

"I do not think of him as a man," she replied quickly. "I must dress."

"I will help you."

"Jane will help me. I have sent for her. Thank you."

"As you wish," he said quietly. "I have been told the woman called Ingrid is an expert at massaging the muscles for therapeutic benefits. She will start giving you daily treatments beginning tomorrow when a table is completed for her. Master Wang shall also see you each day."

"We must come up with some better arrangement then this if I am to get these treatments every day. I cannot keep doing this…" she gestured to her unseemly surroundings.

"I agree. Perhaps a table in our bedroom?"

Marie nodded. "Thank you."

"I can take no credit. Richard found them and brought them, as you know."

"I just meant… it is kind of you to care so much."

"Of course I care," he said gripping her shoulders and looking with sad eyes into hers. "I desperately want you to feel better, Marie. I want you back the way…"

Jane came into the room carrying Marie's dressing gown and house wrap.

"Well, I shall leave you to dress," Jacques said stiffly and left.

Just before lunch the next day William and his son Thor brought Ingrid's table to the Power home. They installed it in the master bedroom where Jacques' narrow bed used to stand. That second bed had disappeared.

"Does Thor speak Swedish well enough to be an interpreter?" asked Jacques of William.

"Yah, Mister Power, for sure," the giant man nodded.

"Good, you can return to your duties at the mill if you will leave him here with us."

"Of course." William seemed a little disappointed to leave.

Jane was on hand setting up a screen for Thor to sit behind under her watchful eye. The Scandinavian folk were rather notorious. Rumors of their naked frolics in the snow and sauna baths of mixed company were common knowledge up and down the Delaware River. Nobody in the house really knew what to expect from this "massage woman" but Jane would make sure young Thor kept his eyeballs to himself.

He's a brawny lad, I must say. Tall as his da now, ain't he? And just look at him gaping around. Looking for that little hussy, are you? No sportin' in the hayloft for you, my great brawny lad, not today. Master has that one locked up, neat as you please. Don't know what she done this time but she done something wicked bad for the master to keep her locked up again.

Thor sat dutifully behind the screen and spoke for Ingrid who told Marie to remove her clothing and get under the sheet. Jane noticed the lad blush as he translated the words. *Maybe there is still hope for you, after all,* Jane noted with approval.

Marie, who had never been overly modest, had no hesitation in complying but getting up onto the table presented a painful challenge accomplished only with Ingrid's assistance.

The leather pad was covered with a clean sheet and Marie stretched out, face down while Ingrid drew another sheet over her. Section by section, Ingrid's powerful hands and a touch of therapeutic oil commenced to work kinks and aches out of Marie's long abused muscles; aches she had not realized existed. Ingrid found sore spots and applied pressure, giving Marie a momentary jolt of pain until under the pressure the soreness began to dissipate and disappear. She heard bones moving along her spine with astonishing clarity as Ingrid leveraged Marie's own body weight in the task. Finally, she had Marie turn over onto her side and drawing Marie's leg up so her knee almost touched her chest, Ingrid applied pressure with her hand to the small of Marie's lower back. Marie felt and heard a crackling and all the pain in her lower back was suddenly gone. When the session was over, Marie hopped off the table like a spring lamb and Jane was there with her dressing gown.

Next, Ingrid began a critique of Marie's bed and suddenly it became much more difficult for young Thor to keep up with the flow of words.

Ingrid was incensed with the sag of the bed and parts went flying as she pulled it apart.

"This is what you sleep upon?" Thor translated faithfully. "Look at that, it bows like the hull of a long ship. This is why you have a back like an ancient one. This may work for small children but you are a grown adult. You must put down boards for a firm solid base and the boards need many holes bored into them for the air to flow; you add a good solid mattress of cotton ticking. Only then, if you want, you can have your feather bed with new goose down, for sure it is warm but gives the back no support, yah? This must you do, mistress, and you keep the back young, healthy, like Ingrid's," translated Thor.

Ingrid was making gestures of flexibility and ended with a demonstration. Right there in the bedroom she bent backwards until her hands touched the floor and her legs came gracefully over her head and she was back on her two feet with a smile.

"I see you tomorrow, mistress, yah?" And Ingrid capped up her oil and made to leave.

"Thor," Marie called over to the screen, "Ask her a question for me, please. Ask her age. Tell her I wish to know."

Thor did as Marie requested and Ingrid's face broke into a huge smile that almost closed those exotic slanted eyes as she replied.

"What did she say?" Marie asked quickly.

"She says she will be forty-six on her next name day," Thor replied.

Forty-six! Ingrid amply demonstrated that being almost forty-six was certainly not old. And if forty-six was not old, how could thirty-five be old? Marie could hardly consider her life to be over. How foolish she had been. As long as she had good health, the years did not matter. Good health was the key but keeping her health was dependent upon having no more babies, of this Marie was certain. Even St. Claire had said every baby takes something out of the mother, so how much more could be taken out of her before she had nothing left?

Jacques was advised of Ingrid's recommendations. He saw to it that sweet smelling, fresh cut boards were brought to the house to make the bed base. Into the boards multiple holes no bigger than a wine bottle neck had been bored. But a cotton stuffed mattress was a challenge. That would necessitate a trip to New York and until then Marie would have to use an ordinary pallet.

That evening Jacques invited Richard into his study. As soon as they were alone, Richard said sharply, "I understand the little witch is again under lock and key. Did she try to hurt Marie again?"

"Not precisely, but I have a favor to ask of you," Jacques replied and poured them each a drink.

"Anything, you know that."

"I must get her out of the settlement," Jacques said and handed Richard a glass of cognac.

"Yes, and what has she done this time?"

"It is not important. What is important is that she be removed as far from us as possible."

"I noticed the bed you had moved in so you could watch over Marie has been taken out again. Does this mean you are back where you belong?" Richard asked hopefully.

Jacques failed to respond.

"I guess if the girl is locked up, she can pose no threat to Marie but why would you move away from her?"

"It is difficult to explain, Richard."

Richard shrugged. "One word at a time can explain anything. *Mon Dieu*, Jacques, what is happening to you two? There is no one on earth I love better than I love the two of you, yet of late every time I go away, I come back and things seem worse between you. But instead of yelling and screaming and throwing pots and pans at each other so you can kiss and make up, you are both so very polite you make my teeth ache."

"Ohhh, Richard," Jacques groaned, slumping in defeat into a chair, raking his hands through his hair. "I do not know when I started to lose her. I do not know why. I only know that every day I feel her slipping farther away from me and it seems there is nothing I can do to get her back."

"Can you two not talk about it?"

"We used to talk. We used to share everything and we had no secrets from each other. We used to be so exceptionally happy."

"And so you should be again." He saw Jacques slowly shake his head. "We have freed her from the laudanum. She is getting the help she needs from the healers. So… why did you move from the room?"

"She threw me out," Jacques finally answered softly.

"That does not sound like Marie," Richard raised his bushy brow and set down his glass. "What did you do? And what has this to do with the witch?" Richard's gut suddenly began to ache as he considered the worst possibility. "My God, man," he stood up facing Jacques, "you had sex with that whore! Tell me I am wrong!"

"She crept into my bed…" Jacques stood to face his friend.

"In the same room?! In a bed right next to Marie?! No wonder she threw you out!" Richard was speechless for a moment before he roared. "I ought to flay the skin right off your pale behind. What has happened to your sense of honor? What would your father say if he knew, huh? A man so honorable he *never* let his wife know about your mother and here his son is humping a whore in the same room with his wife!" Richard's anger exploded through his arm as his fist shot out and knocked Jacques across the room.

Jacques went flying against his chair and fell to the floor upsetting the small table beside the chair and sending a candle, candlestick, pewter goblet, and small book all sailing through the air.

"Get up! Get up you… you… get up and take what you have coming!" Richard stood over his friend and bellowed.

Jacques lay sprawled upon the floor, his lip bleeding where it had been smashed into his teeth. "I will not fight you," he said as he pulled himself to his feet.

"So now you are also a coward?!" Richard lashed out again and back-handed Jacques hard enough to raise an instant welt under his eye and send him reeling to the floor again. Richard leaned down and grabbed Jacques up by his shirt front, making a fist to hit him again. Instead, he let Jacques' head drop back to the floor. "Achhh," Richard groaned in an utterance of disgust. "If I scar your pretty face it will only sadden her by reminding her of your deed every time she looks at you."

Pulling himself to his hands and knees, dizzy and still seeing stars in front of his eyes, Jacques turned to sit down heavily upon the floor. He actually wanted the beating and wished Richard would continue. Staggering, Jacques pulled himself to his feet again, gesturing, "Again, *mon frère*, hit me again. Please. I deserve it."

"With pleasure, *mon frère*." Richard made a fist and hit Jacques hard, catching him in the solar plexus, knocking all the air out of him and leaving him strangled for breath like a fish out of water gasping upon the ground.

Richard sat down in his chair. In truth, it did not give him pleasure. His rage was now vented and his anger was being diluted with incredible sorrow. Tears filled his eyes and spilled down his cheeks. There were some things in life which once done, could never be undone, once tainted could never again be made pure. The tears continued to flow.

With a loud gasp, Jacques finally drew breath and lie just breathing for several minutes before he finally voiced words. "Richard, I swear… I swear on the lives of my children… I thought she was Marie. It has been so long and I thought finally she had come to me, finally she wanted me again. I was in ecstasy at the very thought. I love her still that much."

"And you could not see a difference between that skinny witch and Marie?" Richard spoke harshly in disbelief as Jacques sat upright.

"The room was pitch black. The hearth had gone cold, there was no moon… it was like being deep within a cave."

"And you could not *feel* a difference between that flat chest and bony butt and Marie?" stormed Richard.

"In truth… her body was not the first thing I felt."

"What then?"

"Her tongue. Her mouth. I was dreaming… of Marie, my dreams became mixed with reality. I awoke and I thought it was Marie I felt… I had no control… she was sucking me dry…"

Richard knew something about erotic dreams. "So you never humped her?" he asked for clarity.

"No! It is more accurate to say she raped me."

Richard uttered a low rumble that almost passed for a laugh. "Do not try to sell that to an English judge and jury. Tell me first you did not enjoy it."

"Of course I did, at the moment… until I cried out Marie's name and heard her answer from across the room. Can you imagine my shock, my confusion? I grabbed the girl's arms and pulled her up and off of me. Marie lit a candle and only then did I see who…"

"The succubus," Richard muttered

"Do not call her that, please," Jacques said softly fingering his lip which was swelling and making it harder for him to speak clearly. "Still in all, she is but a child who somehow thought that was what I wanted of her. Is the entire household aware of my frustration? It is my fault."

"Oh, stop martyring yourself," Richard growled and laughed at the same time. "That infant is pushing thirty years of age."

"What?!" Jacques looked up at his friend with his good eye, the other now half swollen shut.

"In my search through New York Towne this trip, I met several very interesting fellows. One was a friend of the *Dauphine's* first mate. He relayed a very fascinating story. Renée gained her passage over here in exchange for being the first mate's whore, her idea not his. He thought she was fifteen, perhaps younger, until he happened to meet a fellow from her old village right there in New York Towne. I talked to this man myself. He remembers Renée to be sure and he swears she is at least twenty-eight if she is a day. She had quite a reputation by the time she left her village. They say she is a home wrecker and determined to destroy any marriage she can."

It was quiet for a moment while Jacques digested this news.

"I do not know if that makes me feel better or worse," he said at last.

"I told you she was trying to kill Marie," Richard said.

"But why…?"

"To make you a lonely widower, of course, so she could become the next Madame Power," Richard replied as if it was obvious. "Then, when she tired of you, she could slip you the poison, eh?"

Jacques shuddered. "Thank God in Heaven she did not succeed… but has she succeeded in destroying my marriage?" he asked in abject misery.

"That, *mon ami*, is up to Marie," Richard replied softly and extended an arm to help his friend back up and onto his feet. "Leave Renée to me. I know a place she should go. Give me her letter of indenture and I will find a new mattress in the bargain. While you must heal things with Marie."

"Richard Bonchance, *mon fils!* It has been too long since you have visited us. It is good to see you looking so… so well." The sturdy French nun smiled approvingly at Richard's appearance as he walked across the courtyard of the home of the Sisters of the Eternal Heart, an obscure order tracing their beginnings to the Clares, the female counterpart to the Franciscans.

"*Supérieure*," Richard bowed respectfully to the Mother Superior, then leaned down to plant a kiss on each of her robust pink cheeks. "I am surprised you can recognize me in my civilized disguise," he laughed, stroked his shaved chin and held close his wool cloth coat against a sudden gust of wind.

"Oh," she chuckled and held on to her wimple. "One does not forget a son who has been so generous and kind. I pray for you every night, Richard Bonchance, and both God and I love you. Come, come, inside *rapidement!*" She led him out of the cold wind and through the door into her office. "Sit," she gestured gracefully to a functional straight-backed chair. Aside from a small plain desk and chair placed upon a very worn rug, a crucifix hanging on the stark wall, and a simple *prie-dieu* in the corner, it was the only other piece of furniture in the room except for the brazier glowing with warmth. "Is that your boat I saw from our bell tower?"

"*Oui*." Richard nodded as he waited for her to sit, "this river branch is the only smooth road to your door."

"And what brings you to us at this time of year, Richard? The boy does very well but winter closes in upon us quickly and you do not look outfitted for your trade."

Richard had become acquainted with the secluded order cloistered away in the far north woods when one year he was caught by an unexpectedly early snowstorm. The Sisters thawed him out, fed him hot food and sheltered him until it became safe to continue on his way. Their order was dedicated to prayer, poverty, and assisting any who came to their door seeking aid be they French or English, Christian or heathen, Catholic or Protestant, white man or red. Raids and battles had been bubbling around them for years but the Sisters were respected by all and left alone in peace to grow their vegetables and herbs, and tend to, without judgment, any hungry, sick, or injured soul who happened to stumble upon their doorstep in need of sanctuary.

Ever since their hospitality had saved his life, Richard had either sent or delivered a yearly gift in gratitude, keeping in touch and confident that if he ever needed help with the French authorities or a safe harbor, here was a friend he could rely upon. And he was correct, they continued to do him a most important service.

"I will see him later but right now I have a problem, Mother," Richard began gravely, "and I think you are uniquely situated to provide the solution."

"*Oui?* Let us have some tea while you tell me all about this problem."

The next day Richard departed to sail back to the New Jersey colony and

Chartes Landing. He had left behind two things: twice his usual gift in gold and Renée Séraphin. And he took with him the assurance that Renée would never be allowed contact with "the boy."

Upon his return to Chartes Landing, Richard sought out Jacques first and found him in his office at the mill. His lip was healing and the swelling of his eye was much reduced.

"Do I want to know what has happened to her?" Jacques asked from behind his desk. He had visions of Richard tossing the girl overboard in the middle of the ocean.

Richard shrugged gravely. "She is alive… well tended in mercy… but not free anymore to spread her poison through an unsuspecting world."

"Where…?"

"She is housed in a nunnery where she has opportunity for redemption. May God's will be done."

Jacques nodded. "Thank you."

"How goes it here?" Richard asked hopefully.

"Nothing has changed," Jacques said glumly, "except Wang and Ingrid are working wonders with Marie."

"Yes? Well, for now that is the most important thing, *n'est-ce pas?*"

Richard left Jacques to his ledgers and made his way to the main house where the children accosted him playfully. The noise of their shouts and laughter brought Marie.

"Richard! Welcome back! Children, children, enough! Leave your Uncle Richard be," Marie said smiling and the children scattered.

She knew Richard had left on some mysterious trip taking Renée with him and she never wanted to speak of the girl again. Day after day, Marie cursed her action in lighting the new candle that fateful night. Burned into her mind's eye was the sight of a naked Renée throwing off the blankets, exposing Jacques' naked body beneath her as she turned to stare at Marie with his essence running from her mouth. It had been the most malignant, hateful look Marie had ever seen on another human being and she could not forget it. Oddly, she remembered very little else of that night, only quiet unceasing tears and the strongest desire she had had since her "cure" to renew her acquaintance with laudanum and seek its escape. Fortunately, she could find none.

"Hello, Marie," Richard said getting up from the floor and brushing himself off, he took her hands and eyed her appraisingly. "You look… wonderful!" he proclaimed and gave her a hug and a kiss on the cheek. "And I cannot help but notice – you carry no cane!"

"Yes," she said and found herself blushing. "It feels like a miracle. Ingrid and Master Wang have made a new woman of me. I go up and down the stairs like a normal person again. Richard, I can touch my toes! I can lift my legs! How can I ever thank you?" She looked into his face with all sincerity.

Her smile was the only thanks he needed.

"Come, Richard, sit and relax." She led him into the drawing room and took a seat herself.

"And what about… the craving?" he asked hesitantly.

She smiled at his caution. "I never think about it - except when someone brings it to mind."

"Oh, forgive me," he flustered.

"I am only teasing you, Richard. In truth, it is behind me. I would not wish to be tempted by it so keep it out of my house, if you please. But it has no hold on my thoughts."

"That too is good news."

"Would you like some tea?"

"Tea?!! Marie, you should know better," he grinned. "Where is Jacques' good cognac?"

She laughed. "Where it has always been, help yourself from the cabinet."

He rose to pour himself a small drink. "So, I had a mission. I was to bring back a new mattress stuffed not with pine needles or horsehair or feathers but with fine cotton fibers, *n'est-ce pas?* And my mission has been accomplished."

"Oh, Richard," Marie bounced up off the settee. "Where is it? Ingrid has been fussing about it."

"On your porch," he replied. "Sims is putting the wagon away and he will come to assist me in getting it up to your room. Ah, here he is now."

The two men carried the new mattress up the staircase and Jane was not far behind with fresh linens.

"So, have Ingrid and Master Wang said anything about staying here at Chartes Landing?" Richard asked when he saw the massage table standing to the side.

"I would be very surprised if Master Wang stayed once his month is up," Marie replied. "There are no other Chinese here and I am certain he is lonely… but Ingrid? Well, perhaps. She and William have been seeing much of each other." Marie had a mischievous look in her eye. "I will be very surprised if she does not stay and I will be most happy if she does. She keeps my back feeling like I am twenty again."

The mattress was in place and Sims left taking the old bed pallet away with him. Jane put down a mattress pad, a new featherbed, snapped a sheet and began to make up the bed; Marie, going to the opposite side, helped her.

"She is a lively woman," Richard said as he stood against the door frame watching and admiring the efficiency with which the women worked together, "and he is a good man who has been alone for too long."

"Yes."

"A good match. I never like to see people alone if there is a better possibility, eh?

"And what about you, Richard?" She paused in smoothing the coverlet and fixed him with a studied look.

"What about me?"

"Are you still so happy out in the wilds?"

"It is a good life… the best one I can have since Janey's husband will not let her run off with me," he blustered and made as if to grab Jane as she hurried her pace and scoot through the doorway and down the hall giggling like a school girl as she went.

Marie chuckled as she also left the bedroom and turned toward the nursery. He stopped her with a hand to her arm and watched Jane Sims disappear from the hall below.

Making certain they were quite alone, he asked softly, "So now that you have a nice new firm bed, can you not forgive him and let him back into it?" He saw the expression on her face suddenly freeze as her eyes went dead; it was as if he looked upon a statue's face.

"I do not know what you are talking about," she replied so evenly that it raised the hairs on the back of his neck.

"Marie?"

"It is me you should have beaten, Richard," she said and quickly walked away leaving him speechless.

Chapter 16

Every year Jacques gave the mill workers and lumberjacks their Christmas bonuses and wanted to give them twelve days off so the family men could spend time with their wives and children in celebration of Christ's birth. It seemed the decent, generous, and Christian thing to do. But every year he faced the same opposition. William Boot and his foremen always advised against it saying it was too much time for the unmarried men to be idle and inevitably they would end up in quarrels, fights, and trouble born out of too much drinking, card playing, gambling, and whoring. So Jacques always compromised. He shut the mill for one week only and everyone got paid for those days as long as they showed up for the Christmas church service.

The last day of work Jacques went to the mill to hand out the Christmas bonuses. Marie had done the same with the clerks in her store and she and Jacques both saw to the household staff. All the giving, reminded Richard that he had completely forgotten the bundle of gifts he had brought with him for the children at the time of his initial return. With Marie being almost over-dosed to death, it had been a reasonable oversight he told himself.

"I brought something for you," he said to the children as he came from the guest wing before the dinner guests were due to arrive. He carried a large package and they gathered around him with excited curiosity. He opened the bundle and withdrew a pair of well-made and beautifully decorated moccasins for each of the youngsters and he had two Indian dolls, one for Helen and one for Louise. But the most popular gift was the bow and arrow set he produced for each of the boys.

"Oh, Richard, weapons? That does not seem like a very safe toy," Marie said in concern as she walked in upon the scene.

"That is because they are not toys, but safe enough," he replied slowly losing his train of thought as he looked at her. She was beautiful but he saw the sadness beneath the pleasant and hospitable face she wore. "The boys just need to be taught how to use them," he said seeking to reassure her. "Young Indian boys have bows from the time they are barely able to walk. They do not hurt each other with them. Your sons are almost young men," he said, winking at the four, then he stopped to look at John. "This one *is* a man!" he exclaimed and John smiled, pleased to be distinguished from the other children. John had turned fifteen and Richard sensed that he had had his first experiences with a woman, although which woman he did not know and did not ask. Phillip was still thirteen, Richie was now ten, and Jamie had just turned seven.

"I tell you what, boys. For now, you can put your bows aside up here on the mantle. Then, tomorrow I will take you out and teach you how to shoot... that is, if it is acceptable to your ma-ma," he added, looking back at Marie.

"Is it? Is it, Mama? Is it?" Their expectant faces all looking to her at once.

Marie looked at the hopeful faces and then at Richard.

"Very well, but you must promise to listen closely to Uncle Richard's instructions and be very careful," she warned, wishing he had not put her in such an impossible position. She could hardly say no; after all, it was Christmas. "And you, John and Phillip, you must watch out for your younger brothers."

"We will," replied John with dignity.

"We promise," added Phillip.

"Oh, yes." "Thank you!" "Thank you!" clamored the other two.

Within minutes Jacques came in from seeing to things outside the house and he was immediately shown the gifts before he retired to dress for dinner. Marie took the opportunity to slip away herself. The children chattered in pride over their moccasins which continued when the Boot children arrived and joined them.

As Marie sat at her dressing table quietly contemplating the small calendar on the wall, she saw the year 1706 was rapidly coming to an end. A year ago by this date she had finally accepted that she was once again pregnant and now Isabelle was already six months old. The time flew by so quickly.

The coming of Christmas never failed to bring the Wingates to Marie's mind. The last time Marie had seen them, Master Wingate had suffered a mild stroke and was relying upon Samuel Cooper more and more to run the business. Had it really been twenty years ago that she had worn a beautiful dress for the very first time in her life at the Wingates' Christmas dinner? She had wanted so badly for Jacques to love her and she had been so very much in love with him. And they had talked of a trading post, and she had dreamed of having her own store, and a grand house, and a carriage and servants. And she had all of that now and it was… of little importance.

She was most proud of her children and she had never even given much thought to having children back then. Yet she now considered them her most important accomplishment and they were growing into fine young people but it was her desperation to have no more that was now destroying her marriage. It was all so confusing. She had lost Jacques because she had pushed him away. And yet she was still so in love with him. She always would be, but without his love in return she found the world tasted like ashes. She had never been worthy but he had loved her once… "once upon a time" as the children's tales began.

Once upon a time, she would have accepted being just his mistress, but he had made her his wife. If she had been his mistress would it have hurt so much? Would she not have expected to share him then? Had being his wife left her unprepared for how very much sharing him would hurt? But it was losing his love that hurt the worse of all. A hurt far different than the physical pain she had suffered, a hurt that ate at her soul but it was her own fault.

Twenty years. Marie looked to her mirror. She saw a familiar reflection: a wife, a mother, a maturing creature who had as yet no real sign of age except for a dramatic streak of white growing off-center at the edge of her forehead. Her smooth skin, perhaps a bit pale, had returned to a healthy tone without the daily dosing of laudanum.

But the laudanum had kept all the pain at bay.

Come spring, she must insist on a trip to New York to visit the Wingates. They were very aged now and who could know how much longer…? A tear slipped down her cheek. She was feeling extraordinarily melancholy but... she had a Christmas dinner to preside over.

The table would be full. All the Boots would be joining them, Richard was here, Ingrid and Master Wang were invited as was Doctor St. Claire and all the children, except for baby Isabelle, were old enough to be on their good behavior dining with the adults. The Sims and Sarah were like family and if it had been up to Marie, Margot and her children would have been seated with them as well, but Margot preferred to stay out in the kitchen which was her domain where she hosted the lesser servants and her grown children were happy to join her there. And Felicity and Lyndyn from the store had families of their own in the settlement, so they always respectfully declined Marie's invitations.

Marie had commissioned a new dress from one of the seamstresses in Chartes Landing. Copied from fashion plates received directly from Paris, it had a much narrower silhouette, mimicking the close fit look gaining popularity in masculine fashion.

The narrow over-skirt was cut away to expose the formal petticoat which was also more narrowly cut. The fashion plate had shown it ending in a small train but Marie saw that only as a "dust mop" and told the seamstress to leave it off.

The ensemble looked suitably mature yet feminine with multiple layers of sheer filmy ruffles added to the chemise and meant to peek out at the neckline and cuffs giving a lovely soft touch. Marie had selected rich dark green velvet for the dress with a lime green satin brocade for cuffs and bodice while the petticoat was of heavy cream satin with touches of scarlet embroidery. Christmas colors.

In the process of its construction during the past week, Marie's dress had been seen by every female over the age of twelve within the settlement. It was so radical and sophisticated, a departure from the billowing skirts which had dominated high fashion for ladies for as long as anyone could remember. And in future with a few minor modifications, it was a style Marie thought she would find easier to wear behind the counters of her store while presenting a more serious business look than the standard country-ish garb she had been wearing for ease of movement.

She pressed a powder puff to her nose and sighed. Her guests awaited.

Ingrid took the opportunity to show off some unusual finery of her own. She came down to dinner wearing a heavily beaded and embroidered tunic replete with Scandinavian designs. It was a compliment to her tall and slender figure yet so tastefully simple. Each wide and draping sleeve was held together by a row of finely carved bone buttons placed a hand's width apart along the top length of the sleeve and allowing her gracefully muscled arms to peek through. But most alluring was her matching headdress with its long fringe of gold links, lapis lazuli beads, and pearls cascading down from a narrow band fit about her head. The strands swayed gently with every movement like a metallic wig having bangs across the forehead and straight tresses on each side which fell beyond her shoulders to her breasts. It said quite clearly that she was not from humble origins. No one could wear that much gold and be considered among the struggling who lived from hand to mouth. And if one would have asked her what had prompted her coming to the New World, she would have candidly responded – a sense of adventure and a need for change.

Jacques was determined to be a good host. He had dressed his part in an impeccably tailored new suit of dark claret brocade with a dark green waistcoat, white silk stockings and thin black suede shoes. He kept the cider glasses and wine goblets filled. But for him the day lacked the sense of joy he had always been accustomed to sharing with Marie and he had to work at not appearing withdrawn and morose.

He had gone to their bedroom before dinner, knocked on the door and waited to be invited in. He had found her sitting at her dressing table.

"I want to give you your Christmas gift," he said, holding out a slender box. It was a token of his love and something he had been months in procuring. He would not have it spoiled by the unfortunate incident with Renée.

She turned to face him. "Considering the circumstances, I can hardly accept," she said softly with downcast eyes. She had no gift for him and she felt like such a hypocrite.

He felt his face go hot with anger at what he took for a rebuff. He opened the box himself and yanked out a necklace, dropping the box still containing matching earrings down on the dressing table. Roughly he placed the necklace around her neck and fastened it.

"You are my wife and you will look the part," he said and left the room before she could turn to the mirror and see.

When Jacques left, Marie looked at her reflection. Around her neck lay a beautifully wrought necklace of gold set with seven perfectly matched emeralds. Seven – for their seven children, perhaps? She took up the earrings, two more emeralds each hanging from a diamond solitaire setting. Were these meant to be him and her or were they symbolized by the diamonds while the emeralds were in expectation of two more children?

The emeralds matched her dress. To not wear them would be churlish. She fastened the earrings to her ears and wiped away a tear. The set was beautiful. It must have cost Jacques a small fortune, she thought. She would wear them because that was what her husband wanted.

The dinner party all sat around the elaborate holiday table. Richard always had tales to tell of his adventures in the wild and he enjoyed telling them while keeping everyone entertained. He was coaxed into re-telling the story of how his foot was caught in one of the traps and how he had suffered, not completely certain he would not lose it. The story had gained added embellishments Jacques had not heard the first time and he found himself looking at his wife. Alternately, frowns of concern and smiles of amusement played across her face with her attentions completely focused on Richard.

Jacques decided to take the opportunity to relay the story his grandfather used to tell of how his family was massacred and his *Grand-père* alone, being a student away from home, had survived to start a life within the protection of a Catholic duke. Jacques skipped over the more gruesome details but it was important his children understand and remember their heritage. Inevitably this next led to the tale of his escape along with his best friend and a very young girl who would one day become his wife.

It was difficult for Marie to hear Jacques' last tale, it was so filled with pride and admiration for her that it made her ashamed of herself. So she sought to change the subject as quickly as possible by asking Ingrid and William about the stories she had heard of Swedish saunas. William assisted in the translation as they laughed and described them.

"The Finnish brought the practice to Sweden hundreds of years ago," Ingrid replied with William's help, "and a commonly accepted part of life it is, especially in Northern Sweden. In the beginning they were always with the smoke... one made a big fire within the cabin to make it very hot and then let out the smoke before the people went in to sweat."

"That sounds like what the Indians do," Marie murmured.

"I have a *badstuga... bastu*," William said for himself. "Yah, what you call bathhouse or sauna. Once a week I have Rega to start the fire to heat the stones. When I come home from the mill, together we all take sweat bath. It keeps us clean and healthy."

"You heat stones?" Marie asked.

"Yah, much better to heat stones. Not so much wood used and the smoke, it stays outside. We bring the stones inside and pour water on them to make the steam. Much easier to breath than smoke, yah? When too warm we become, we pour water over us or jump in river... if winter, we can roll in the snow. Also important is branches, beat the back, legs, arms, back side, beat, beat... is very good for circulation, raise blood to surface of skin, yah."

Ingrid spoke and William added, "In Northern Sweden many women give birth in *badstuga* and many more go to ahhh... how you say, pure... ah, make pure..."

"Purify?" Marie offered, "for purification?"

"Yah, yah, for purification after the childbirth."

"That is fascinating. So you believe you are sweating away impurities from the body just like the Indians. And you are all without clothing? Together?"

"Oh, sure... everyone must be naked to get good cleansing. In old country, invite neighbors to share, no sense to waste good hot cabin. Every one come over... not much clothes, sit naked in *badstuga* and after finish when body cool down put on clean clothes, feel very good."

William said something directly to Ingrid and Marie got the distinct impression he was inviting her to join him in his *badstuga*. And Ingrid smiled and nodded in the affirmative.

How extraordinary, Marie thought, *and Thor would be there no doubt with this beautiful woman and his pa-pa, and Ansel and Rega, all naked but with no embarrassment. They were so open about their bodies. Like the Indians had been.*

"Enjoy it while you can," Richard said philosophically, noticing the expressions on the faces of the Sims.

Margot had once again outdone herself preparing the holiday feast and the dishes kept rolling out from the kitchen. At last the hour struck late. Jacques sent John and Phillip to start fires in the bedroom hearths. William and his children thanked their hosts and departed for home. Sarah ushered the children to bed, but not before they kissed both Papa and Mama good night. The Sims helped to clear the table before they too retired. Master Wang announced he would be leaving on a mid-day packet boat to return to New York Towne while the weather remained mild. After William left, Ingrid retired to her room and soon only Jacques, Marie, Richard, and Doctor St. Claire remained.

"Madame Power," St. Claire spoke to Marie as she walked him toward the front door. "I have not had a chance to ask how you are doing."

"Well enough," she responded flatly.

"Hmm…you seem a little despondent; how are you sleeping?"

"Not as well as I used to," she admitted.

"*Oui-oui.* Any sense of restlessness, bouts of anxiety?" he queried.

"What would I have to be anxious about?" She forced a smile.

"I just want you and your husband to know, those are all typical symptoms of the final stage of your healing."

"*Merci, Monsieur Physicien.* I will keep that in mind," she said graciously and helped him with his outer coat.

"Good night, madame."

"Good night."

Marie went into the drawing room to join Jacques and Richard who had not as yet taken a seat.

"I think the dinner went well," she said as she and Richard both sat. "Everyone seemed to enjoy themselves."

"It was outstanding," Richard offered, patting the sides of his abdomen. "I could not eat another bite, indeed I do not feel the need to eat for days."

"Thank you."

From his position at the head of the table, Marie did not know if Jacques had heard William talk of the *badstuga.* She wanted to mention what she had learned but she feared it would sound too provocative. She was painfully aware that Jacques had not spoken to her all evening and had made no comment at all on her new dress, if he had noticed it. Perhaps he did not like the style, and thought it better to say nothing than offer her false flattery. And he was angry about her reaction to his gift. How was she to have known it was expensive jewels? Jewels she did not feel she deserved.

"I heard Master Wang is leaving as you predicted, but it looks like Ingrid has a reason to stay," Richard added.

"What?" she asked, as if a bit distracted. "Oh, yes, I am so very glad."

"Would you like to join us for a little brandy?" Jacques spoke at last as he poured out snifters for Richard and himself before he took a seat.

"Oh, no, but thank you. It has been a long day and I am a little tired. If I may I would like to retire."

"I heard the doctor say something about 'you and your husband should know'… what exactly should I know?" Jacques asked mildly.

"It was nothing. He was asking how I was sleeping. It seems not sleeping well is one of the symptoms of the last stage of the cure. But I am fine." As she rose she motioned for them to remain seated. "I will see you in the morning." Marie stopped to press a kiss to Jacques' forehead. "Merry Christmas, Jacques, and thank you. You are much too generous." She fingered the necklace at her throat and they both knew to what she referred.

"Merry Christmas," he replied but he did not kiss her hand as he always used to.

"Merry Christmas, Richard," she said bending to kiss his cheek.

Richard rose out of his chair instead, grabbed her into a bear hug and kissed her soundly just off center of her mouth. "Merry Christmas, Marie! And if I forgot to tell you so earlier, I have been thinking it all night… you look extraordinarily beautiful, like *une Parisian duchesse, n'est-ce pas?*"

Marie gave him a crooked smile and left the room before he could see the tears coming into her eyes.

Richard watched her go and turned to Jacques and slowly shook his head.

"What?" Jacques asked a bit peevishly.

"Since when does she need to ask your permission before retiring for the night?"

"She does not," Jacques replied defensively.

"Do you know what she said to me the other day?"

"I am afraid I have no idea what my wife says to you." There was an edge to Jacques' voice.

"I will tell you. She got an expression on her face that I cannot begin to describe but it raised the hairs on the back of my neck, then she told me I should have beaten *her!*"

Jacques' head snapped up to look at Richard.

"Yes. I ask you - why does this woman think she deserves a beating? From what I have witnessed and what I have been told, this year has been the worst year of her life... in every way." He tossed down the rest of his brandy and set the glass on the side table in disgust. "Good night, *mon ami*. Right now I think I prefer my own company."

Chapter 17

Shortly after breakfast the following morning, Richard gathered the boys around him and with bows and arrows tucked under his arm, he walked them out to the meadow. It was unseasonably pleasant for the end of December and Richard was glad to make use of it.

First, he demonstrated how to string a bow. It was a feat requiring strength and coordination. Each boy had a bow matching his strength and age. It took practice and effort but one by one each learned to brace one bow end against the inside of his foot at the arch and bend the other end within reach to slip the loop of the raw hide string over and into the notch on the end. Little Jamie was only able to string his because the bow was quite small and very weak. It was only intended to teach him the principles and give him the opportunity to develop good habits.

Richard established a target deer with an old pillow case stuffed with straw. He drew a circle at the spot for the heart. Then, he marched off the paces, set up the target line and gave each one instruction.

Each took his first shot then together they walked to the target and retrieved their singular arrows. All had gone far afield and Jamie's had not come close to the target. He was excited all the same.

Richie never expected to beat his older brothers but John and Phillip developed a rivalry when Phillip decided he was going to do as well and even better than his older brother. When, at last, they had all at least hit the target, Richard told them it was enough for the day.

Not to be outdone by his older brother who had hit his last shot very near the circle, Phillip, fuming at his failed attempt, grabbed his arrow and pulled back the bowstring for one last shot before leaving.

Simultaneously, little Jamie, upon hearing Richard say they were finished, ran out without warning to retrieve the target pillow.

The arrow had already left the bow when, out of the corner of his eye, Phillip caught sight of Jamie. He yelled for his younger brother to stop but it was of no use. John and Richard turned just in time to see the arrow hit the small boy's leg. It pierced the surface and held there.

Richard saw the child look down in startled surprise, too stunned to move or cry. Phillip's face blanched white, his fear and panic dissolving into remorse and sorrow.

"You imbecile!" screamed John at his younger brother. "You could have killed him!" Tears broke over Phillip's lower lids.

"I didn't mean it," Phillip rushed up to the smaller child, a sob in his voice. "I'm sorry, Jamie. I didn't mean to hit you, I swear."

It was then that Jamie decided perhaps he should be crying as well.

"Now, now," Richard said trying to keep things calm. "Everyone relax and take a deep breath. Phillip, we know you did not mean it. Hey... Jamie, you are a brave little Indian and Indians never cry. John, collect up the bows and arrows, I am going to carry Jamie. Come now; let us get you off your leg. That is it," he said swooping the small boy up into his arms gently. Taking off in long strides across the field, the other boys had to trot to keep up with Richard.

"Never walk in front of anyone aiming a bow," he warned too late. "You must always stay behind the person with the bow. Never walk in front of anyone aiming a bow!" he repeated. "Did everybody hear that?"

As the big man strode back to the house holding the child as lightly as a feather, his heart pounded with the fear of facing Marie. Every sane man alive knew better than to confront a mother lion or bear or wolf with her cubs. And here he was bringing back a cub to its mother - wounded. At that moment he would have traded a year of his life to be able to go back in time and not be the bearer of any bow and arrow gifts.

How had this happened, he asked himself? It had happened so fast! One must watch every second. Thank God and all the saints, even if he did not believe the saints could do anything, the child was not hurt badly! It was only a shallow wound. It could have been so much worse. Richard's heart pounded to think how much worse.

Marie glanced out the window and saw Richard moving toward the house with her youngest son in his arms and her other three sons running behind. Her heart raced madly as she tore out the door, not daring to speculate. As they covered the ground between them, she saw the arrow in Jamie's leg and actually felt relief.

"He will be fine," Richard stammered, breathing hard. Marie nodded and tried to smile for her young son's sake.

"John. Go, see if you can find Master Wang. He leaves on the packet boat but it may not have left yet. If not, then Doctor St. Claire, and get your father," she said.

John thrust the bows and remaining arrows into Phillip's hands and took off to get a horse from the stable.

"Richard, how did this happen?" Marie demanded.

"It should not have happened, Marie, I blame myself," he said before Phillip could speak.

"Indeed," Marie's eyes flashed, "I told you weapons are not suitable toys! Bring him into the house. To the dining table!" Then, seeing the bows and arrows in Phillip's hands she grabbed them in a fury and carried them with her. When they entered the house, she slapped them up onto the mantel. "No one touches!" she announced to her sons.

Richard deposited the boy on the cleared table and went to beg cranberries from the kitchen. He had seen the Indians use the dark red berry with its bitter astringent qualities to treat arrow wounds.

Master Wang arrived with Jacques. Marie had managed to get Jamie to drink two cups of willow bark tea by liberally lacing it with honey and he was distracted from his pain. The arrowhead was simple and smaller than most, a rather neat little triangle without barbed sides. Master Wang took out his gold needles and placed several in various locations before he removed the arrow. It came out quite easily but the removal made the leg bleed profusely for a few minutes and the youngster cried.

"Why you cry?" Master Wang demanded. "You no hurt and bleeding stop once leg go up." He took some of Jacques' favorite cognac from the sideboard and doused the wound.

Jacques and Richard both flinched imagining the sting but Jamie just watched. In fact, he thought it was funny that Papa's favorite cognac should get poured out on his leg.

"Now, I bandage. Give glass milk with this," he gestured to the cognac. "After drink put to bed with leg up, up on pillow." When he had finished tying off the bandage he removed the gold needles and ran them through the spilled cognac on the table before packing them away. The Chinaman sighed. He would have to stay one more night at the Power home and catch the next packet boat.

When Jamie was finally asleep, Marie rejoined Jacques and Richard in the dining room. Richard had explained to Jacques what had happened, blaming himself for the incident. Jacques, however, saw that Phillip's temper had been involved and was equally disturbed by this aspect.

"I need to have a talk with him," Jacques was saying referring to Phillip, when Marie came in.

Richard got up. "Is he well?"

"He is asleep," she said flatly. "Richard, I want those weapons out of the house. Take them back, burn them, I do not care what you do with them, just get them out of here!" she snapped.

"Marie, I cannot tell you how sorr...."

"I know you are sorry, I know, but please get rid of them."

Richard nodded and took the bows and arrows from the mantel and was about to toss them into the fire below.

"No!" commanded Jacques. "Wait. There is no need to destroy those. The boys will learn..."

"Learn what?!" Marie gasped. "When I think of what could have happened!" Marie was now shaking, her nerves finally succumbing to the traumatic drama. "When I think..." she looked at Jacques explosively. "It could have been his eyes! He could be blind now, or his heart... he could be dead!" Suddenly she was shaking violently and sweat broke out upon her forehead. It reminded all of them of what she had been through with the cure and that it was not yet over. Jacques jumped up and grabbed her into his arms to hold her until she ceased shaking. He felt her struggling against him, filled with frustration and anger but mostly fear and he kept her pinned to calm her.

"I do not want them in this house, Jacques! I do not want them! They are not toys!" She was crying now but the shaking had stopped. "He could have been killed! Do you not care that he could have been killed?"

"You can ask me if I care about the life of my own son?" Jacques retorted forcefully, breaking through her growing hysteria. He held her from him but firmly by the arms. "Of course I care, I care more than for my own life. But I will not have my sons raised like little girls! I blame myself that I have not seen to their education as I should. I am reminded that both John and Phillip should already be receiving fencing lessons. And they should know how to shoot."

She stared at him and gasped.

"You once said to live each day in fear is not living," Jacques continued, his expression was one of dark determination. "You were right. My sons are living in a world filled with peril. They have to learn to survive. You cannot protect them in your skirts all of their lives. They must learn to be men! They must learn to protect themselves and their families. This has been a lesson, a valuable lesson. And we can thank God the price paid for it was not high. Do you think Jamie will ever forget? And what of Phillip? In a temper fit he took a shot in poor judgment - is this not a good lesson for him as well? And John and Richie? You cannot witness such an accident without learning something of value. No! I will talk to my sons and they will learn lessons from this. And they will learn to treat weapons with respect and without anger. But their best protection in this world is to develop skill and sound judgment. That cannot happen if you constantly protect them by clearing all the hazards from their path. The day will come, Marie, when you and I will no longer be here to protect them."

Marie stood dumbly, her eyes wide, her hands twisted into her apron. Suddenly she felt like a wayward child who had been soundly scolded. Her face turned red and she felt a different kind of anger. *His* sons? *His* sons? They were her sons, too! Her temples began to throb. Marie turned on her heels and left the room without a word. Blind with tears, she ran up the staircase escaping to the sick room where they had put Jamie. After assuring herself he was well, she stretched out next to him on the bed and cried herself into an exhausted sleep.

Richard was suddenly aware that he was holding his breath and he exhaled before turning to the sideboard. He poured himself a cognac. He was certain it was possible to feel worse than he did at that moment but he was not sure how. He had never witnessed Jacques and Marie exchanging words like this before and it burned through his insides like a fire brand while at the same time leaving him with a sinking feeling in the pit of his stomach. And he had unwittingly set the whole scene in motion.

"Would you like one?" he asked referring to the drink.

"I think I had better," Jacques replied. Suddenly, he slammed his fist down on the table hard and the sound echoed through the room. "Oh, God, what have I done?!" he cried out in a muffled groan.

Richard had poured a small glass for Jacques and was replacing the decanter but at this he took back the decanter and filled the glass with twice as much, then, set the drink down before his friend.

"What is it that you think you have done?" Richard asked slowly.

Jacques grabbed up the drink, and emptied the glass in one breath before sinking to his chair. "Bring the bottle here," was all he said.

Richard started to speak and then said nothing but he brought the decanter to the table. Jane knocked and poked her head through the open door.

"Dinner is about ready, Master Power," she said in a restrained voice. "Would you like me to have it served in here or would you rather we feed the children in the breakfast room?"

"Feed the children where you like, Jane. Thank you," Jacques said dully. "And help Sarah see them to bed at the appropriate time. My friend and I are going to my study where we will most likely get very drunk and we do not wish to be disturbed."

Marie awoke to see daylight and for a moment she thought it was still the same day. Then, she realized that the light was wrong, it was coming from the east. She had slept the entire night with Jamie and she had barely moved a muscle. She was stiff. She checked her son. He still slept soundly. She peeked beneath the covers at his leg. It looked well enough. No bleeding. No discernible swelling. No hot red of infection.

As she rose she realized someone had put a quilt over her. Had it been Jacques? Why had he not awakened her? Was he still angry with her? She had been so angry with him yesterday. Why had she been so angry? Most of what he had said was true but she did not think she was trying to make sissies of their sons. She had just been so frightened. Did he not understand that? She longed for him to hold her like he used to and tell her he still loved her. That he was not angry with her anymore. She would go to him, she thought, she would put her arms around him and everything would be right again.

But when Marie went into Jacques' bedroom she discovered he was already gone, the bed neatly made. She was disappointed. She went to her room, took out fresh clothing and rang for Jane to bring her hot water.

"The master said to tell you the doctor is coming soon and will be looking in on little Master Jamie," Jane said as she brought in two buckets of hot water. "After eating enough for six the Chinaman left again."

"Thank you, Jane," Marie replied with more dignity than she felt. "I will be ready in a few minutes. Tell Monsieur Power I will be down shortly."

"Master Power hasn't been to bed all night," Jane disclosed, "I just thought you'd like to know. He and Master Richard stayed up... drinking."

So that was why the bed looked untouched. Marie nodded. "Thank you, Jane, that will be all," she added, dismissing the woman.

In minutes Marie had bathed herself. Freshly groomed and in clean clothes, she went down the staircase looking for the others. They were in the breakfast room.

"There is your ma-ma," she heard her husband say and the children all went to her giving her morning kisses and hugs.

"Good morning. Good morning," she hugged and kissed them all back then she turned to the men. They looked amazingly well for having never gone to bed, amazingly sober for having been drinking all night. Perhaps Jane was wrong, Marie thought fleetingly until she noticed the blood shot eyes the two men had in common.

"Jacques. Richard." She nodded to them. "Good morning. I must have been very exhausted. I did not plan to sleep straight through the evening."

"It is understandable," Jacques said crisply. "You had an upsetting day. The children and I have had a good talk. I think we have all learned much from yesterday's events."

"Yes," she replied softly, hurt by the coolness in his tone. "Jamie will be waking soon. I should be there. I am going back."

"Sit down. You had no dinner; you need some breakfast," Jacques said calmly. "Jane, will you please watch over Jamie until he wakes so Madame Power can have her breakfast?"

"Yes, sir," Jane replied and left to go back upstairs.

"Children, you can go outside and wait for your Uncle Richard," Jacques instructed and they left the room without a word of protest. They were sensitive to a growing tension in the home, subtle changes from the way things used to be. And now this accident had created much upset between their mother and father. They were glad to escape with John taking a mature lead in shepherding his siblings outdoors.

Marie poured herself coffee from the sideboard and put an apple muffin and a slice of ham on a small plate. She set these down at the table and sat down herself. She took up the muffin, then set it down again. Her stomach was tight and she had no appetite.

"I was very upset yesterday, Richard. I hope you can forgive me," she looked at the burly man. "I do not really blame you. I know you love the children like your own."

He nodded and looked relieved.

"Jacques," Marie couldn't bring herself to look at her husband. She felt extremely uncomfortable and that made her feel defensive. She remembered his stinging words of the day before. "I did not realize you thought I was turning *your* sons," she emphasized the word stiffly, "into sissies. I think I have a normal mother's concern. I think your mother would agree with me. We are, after all, the ones who face death just to give them life." She looked at him and saw her words had hit their mark. "But much of what you said is true. The world is full of dangers. They must learn to defend and protect themselves, just as I learned to shoot a musket."

"I am glad to hear we are in agreement on this. Which is why I have asked Richard to take them out every morning and continue to teach them to handle the bows safely," Jacques stated, smarting from her verbal lance. "I have also decided that the two eldest shall begin fencing lessons immediately even if I must instruct them myself. And we shall have musket lessons, as well. There is nothing that I do day upon day that is of more importance than teaching my sons how to defend themselves. I am ashamed that I somehow forgot this."

She nodded silently. She knew Jacques was right and did not disagree but she felt the chasm between them growing wider. She felt powerless to change it. Powerless was a terrible feeling. How could she have forgotten it? She had spent the first fifteen years of her life feeling powerless. Escaping to the New World had given her the very first taste of choosing her own destiny, her first sense of having some control over the tides of life that were knocking her about. Then, later it was love; Jacques' love had made her feel real empowerment. But that love was obviously gone now and she did not know how to get it back.

"Marie, you must eat. You have not a spare ounce of flesh since your ordeal," Jacques said more softly.

"I know, you are right," she nodded and slowly cut the ham into tiny pieces putting one in her mouth and chewing very slowly, willing her stomach to accept it..

St. Claire arrived and Jacques excused himself from the breakfast table to greet him. As they walked to the sick room where Jamie slept, Jacques paused.

"*Monsieur Docteur*, the evening of our Christmas dinner you spoke to my wife just before you left. I believe you said she should share your thoughts with me but she seems to have forgotten."

St. Claire looked off in the distance, "Ahh, yes-yes, the last phase of withdrawal. I was warning her of what to expect as you should also be aware. Restlessness, anxiety, melancholia, problems sleeping. These should be expected. I had noticed she seemed very melancholy. She admitted she is not sleeping well. I expect she is also experiencing bouts of anxiety which may bring on a change in temper and perhaps a certain restlessness."

"What must we do?"

"Just be patient, monsieur, just be patient. That is all we can do… and keep her from upsets and any more laudanum."

Jacques had spoken with each of his sons separately and there was to be no punishment for the accident. He knew the sight of their youngest brother in his bandages was punishment enough. They would learn to respect the weapons and behave appropriately. They had returned to good spirits, if only he could say the same for his wife. The feeling that she was shutting him out persisted. A door had closed and he didn't know how to reopen it.

At the end of the day Jacques and Richard sat comfortably in wing-backed chairs before the hearth in Jacques' study. The sound of the children's voices disappeared down the hall with their mother. It was their bedtime and Jacques knew they would not see Marie again that evening. The house grew quiet, almost too quiet with only the sounds of the fire crackling near them. The temperature was dropping and the heat felt good.

"More brandy?" Jacques asked of his friend.

Richard nodded and Jacques refreshed their glasses.

"You have an enviable family," Richard said in this rare moment of quiet contemplation.

Jacques nodded but said nothing.

"John reminds me of you when we were boys," Richard offered, breaking another prolonged quiet.

Jacques smiled slightly and nodded. "I see his mother in him as well," he said softly.

"He is your spitting image, Jacques! People so often say that of children but in this case it is true. John looks just as you did when we were boys. In truth, I look at him and I feel like I should be fifteen again or I could almost believe I am fifteen again. It is uncanny. Now Phillip… I do see some of Marie in him."

"Perhaps it is not John's appearance but his personality. Sometimes he sounds exactly like his mother… or at least the way his mother used to..." Jacques didn't finish his thought. "I agree he does favor me in appearance."

"More than just favor," Richard nodded. "Now Phillip, he only *favors* you."

"Yes, perhaps. Marie says he has his grandfather's coloring."

Richard nodded.

"Phillip has quite a temper," Jacques confessed. "Something else he may have inherited from his grandfather. The boy gives me great concern. I have been trying to teach him to control his short fuse."

"He is young yet."

"Not too young. He is old enough to do damage, and he is old enough to take responsibility for his behavior."

Richard nodded silently.

"We were not much older than John when we first began to sport, remember?" Richard asked with a devilish twinkle in his eye.

"Were we really that young?" Jacques sighed introspectively. He had the gut feeling John was no longer a virgin himself and thought to tell Richard but decided against it. It was John's secret.

"Almost, but of course we had no idea how young we really were."

"We were very ignorant."

"But very eager," chuckled Richard.

"Too eager," Jacques smiled, "and pitifully clumsy."

"Fortunately, there are always those who love to teach. I remember many a woman who was very patient with me. Ahhh, but the one I always dreamed of… oh, I have not thought of her in years! Do you remember the Widow Millet-Dubois?"

"I remember."

"I cannot begin to tell you how many wet dreams for which that woman was responsible. I used to lie awake at night fantasizing about the body beneath those black silks, the breasts behind that black lace. A widow at… what would you guess? Twenty-five, perhaps? Twenty-six? When you are young it is so hard to judge age." Richard lifted his glass and took a swallow. "She was one woman God never meant to be alone! Eyes like violet pools. I caught her eye once in the village and I swear there was an unspoken invitation there. It took me years to forgive myself for not having had the courage to act upon that invitation. She was a firm and juicy peach, rosy ripe for the eating if ever there was one. I could only imagine what she might have taught me," Richard sighed. "It broke my fifteen year old heart that she moved to Paris before I had the courage to find out."

"Twenty-three."

"What?"

"She was twenty-three," Jacques said calmly.

"How do you know she was twenty-three?" Richard's brows shot up in surprise.

"It came up rather casually in conversation," he replied, a smile twitching beneath his moustache.

"What conversation? Are you trying to tell me you actually had a conversation with her?"

"Several."

Richard snorted. "I do not believe you."

Jacques shrugged.

"And the proof of your tall tale is easy, no woman over the age of sixteen simply tells someone her age."

"She did not just tell me her age. We were talking about things and..."

"What kind of things?" Richard interrupted..

"Things. Nothing in particular. Well, actually, she was talking about when she was married. She had mentioned how long she had been married. And later she mentioned how old she had been when she married. It was simple mathematics."

Richard said nothing for a moment and, then, replied with a note of acceptance. "Very well. So she was twenty-three. What difference does it make?"

"Absolutely none."

Richard grunted.

"Except you were right, for one so young she had a tremendous amount to teach." Jacques burst into laughter at the look on his friend's face.

"No..." Richard growled, "do not try to claim...." he shook his head in disbelief. "I do not believe it! The Widow Millet-Dubois? You would have told me!"

"Some things a man keeps to himself," smirked Jacques.

"We were only fifteen!"

"I was almost sixteen."

"You and the Widow Millet-Dubois?" Richard continued to question in disbelief. Jacques simply nodded his head. Richard stared and shook his head. "Naw, this is going too far. You are trying to... how do the English say it — pull my leg."

Jacques just continued to look at him pleasantly, the cares and tensions of the past months finally lifting from his face.

"You are joking, are you not? Oh, come now. The widow? You really expect me to believe you had the widow?!" Richard asked in disbelief.

"More like the widow had me," Jacques replied and they both began to laugh.

"I knew she was not meant to be alone!" Richard gasped and as the laughter subsided he said almost pouting, "I cannot believe you never told me!"

Jacques also grew more sober. "I knew how you looked at her; you told me you dreamt of her," he said quietly. "I was afraid if you found out it would end our friendship."

Richard looked at his friend a long time. "I think by now we know our friendship will survive much more than that." It was quiet for a moment and his face broke into a grin.

"At least one of us was smart enough to accept that invitation before she left for Paris. Why did she move to Paris, do you know?"

"To find another husband perhaps, or..."

"Or what?"

"I do not know. Now that I am older and have had children with Marie… I remember certain things about the widow and her body the last times I saw her and I wonder if perhaps, she was *enceinte*. In Paris she could have easily passed a baby off as her late husband's child."

"Do you think it was your child?"

"If there was a child, there is no way of knowing," Jacques shrugged. "I hope not. The widow had a very active social life and I had no exclusive claim."

Richard nodded and it grew quiet again.

"So who will your sons learn from?" Richard asked at last.

"This is a different time and a different place," Jacques replied soberly. "I hope to teach my sons a more prudent path."

"Just do not turn them into prudes."

"Of course not! But this is not the countryside of France, Richard, and they are not the offspring of an aristocrat. There are no plump little peasant girls who would consider themselves privileged to be gotten with noble bastards. In this world a bastard is just that, a bastard. A child born out of wedlock and without a father's name."

Jacques rose to poke at the fire, stirring it and adding another log. A knot of sap flared and he backed away, satisfied.

Richard watched the flames dance about the logs. It was hypnotic. He realized he had become much more comfortable with the Indian way of viewing children. A child belonged to his mother and his father was the brave who chose to claim him, to teach and guide him on his path to manhood. There was no such thing as a bastard amongst the Indians, the very concept was alien and incomprehensible to them.

"My name's sake looks much like Marie," Richard said at last.

"Louise is her exact copy," Jacques sounded almost wistful as he sat down again.

"It is amazing to see all the little traits, likenesses, and peculiarities we can pass along to our children," Richard observed. Jacques agreed. But he was aware that Richard was not speaking of only Jacques' offspring. Richard never spoke directly of his own children but it was obvious that he was thinking of them all the same.

Chapter 18

As agreed, Richard took all the boys out for an hour or two every morning, reinforcing his bow instructions. There was no rough-housing, wrestling, or uncontrolled behavior during this teaching time.

John and Phillip began to ponder how they could obtain more arrows. What if an arrow should break, they asked, what would they do? Richard smiled and told them that when they mastered their skill and demonstrated their adherence to safety, he would see to it that they had more arrows. He knew he had more to give them before he departed but for now, one arrow each was enough of which to keep track.

Musket lessons came next and Jacques was drawn back in time to when he and Marie spent her Sundays on the outskirts of Harlem as he taught her how to shoot. They had accomplished a great deal since that time, they had been so blessed. They once had so much. A perfect partnership. He sighed. Could he learn to live with her like a loving brother if that was what she now wanted? He felt hollow and bereft at the very thought.

The weather remained mild and Jacques was determined to make the most of it by getting out with the boys every day and they took to their new lessons with gusto. Within a day or two a routine was established. Richard took the boys in the morning after breakfast. After lunch Jacques set aside his business concerns and taught the rudiments of fencing and musketry to John and Phillip.

"When can I learn, Papa?" asked Richie.

"When you are twelve we shall start your lessons," Jacques replied with a smile. "The musket is heavy and the foil requires balance. I do not expect you boys to really develop your skill with a foil until you have finished growing, but we can make a start, *n'est-ce pas?*" He ruffled his second youngest son's hair and was reminded of Marie's, the color was the very same, light brown with golden streaks.

Helen and Louise were sitting on the fence rail watching. They had the fence post between them to secure their balance.

"I'm twelve, Papa," Helen called over to her father. She wore a proper little cap upon her head and considered herself quite grown up.

Jacques looked over at his daughters. "Yes, you are," he conceded to the eldest.

"Can I not learn too?"

"You want to learn the foil?"

"No, Papa, that's silly but I want to learn the musket just like Mama did."

Jacques stopped still and saw Richard standing back with a huge grin on his face.

"She has you there, *mon ami,* and it was you who taught Marie."

"Your mother was going to the wilds of the frontier where bears and wolves roamed. Are you going to the frontier?" Jacques resisted the thought of his sweet, gentle daughters firing weapons.

"I don't know, Papa. You and Mama always say we don't know what the future may bring? Perhaps some day I shall go there with my husband just like Mister Nicholet took his family to the frontier."

Richard was pleased to see that Jacques still had his sense of humor. He had just been bested in a logical argument by a twelve year old girl and he had the grace to smile about it.

"You are right my little Helen. It is a skill that may come in handy some day, why should you not learn, eh? You may join your brothers after their fencing lessons and Louise, next year you shall join them as well."

The girls jumped down from the fence and ran to hug their father. "Thank you, Papa." "Thank you." They cried out together as he hugged them back and bestowed a kiss on each of their heads. The girls returned to the fence rail and were content to watch their older brothers hop about with sticks meant to resemble rapiers and the sisters giggled at them.

Richard went back into the house where he found Marie sitting in the bright sunshine mending a small shift that doubtless belonged to one of the girls. He thought she looked incredibly sad.

"I do not know how much longer we can expect to keep this wondrous weather," Richard said conversationally. She nodded. "Marie," he pressed again, "I left something with the pelts at the cabin, I need to get it."

"Oh, of course, let me give you the key," she replied pleasantly, setting her needle aside. When she returned and held out the key to him, he avoided taking it.

"Come, walk with me, Marie," he coaxed, "it is a beautiful day, who knows how many we have left before the snows come, and I would like your company."

She hesitated.

"Come, a walk will be good for you."

At that she nodded and took a light coat from the hooks on the wall by the back door.

"Jacques," she called once they were outside, "Richard needs something from the old cabin. We are going to walk over, the exercise will do me good."

He nodded that he had heard and watched them walk away, Marie somber, head bent.

"Thank you for spending so much time with the boys. I know Jacques often wishes he had more time to spend with them," her voice became almost sad. "He has much to be responsible for in taking care of all of us."

"They have already learned to use their bows very well. With continued practice they shall become excellent bowmen. I am certain John and Phillip will continue to be very careful and they will help the younger ones to remember as well."

Marie said nothing.

They strolled along the forest path that led to the old cabin. The day was especially fine with a mild refreshing breeze and just a hint of chill. Marie inhaled the astringent smells of the evergreens and suddenly felt extremely melancholy and desperately lonely. When they reached the cabin, she found herself overwhelmed by its memories. She was shaking but tried to hide it as she unlocked the door.

"You go ahead, Richard, get what you need. I am going to sit down for a moment," she said.

He had seen her shaking and frowned with concern. She went over to the cliff's edge and sat on a rock overlooking the river to enjoy the view and gather her composure. It was the same rock she had sat on when she was pregnant with John watching the ship take Jacques away before the hurricane. Had not life been much simpler back then?

"So, how is everything, Marie?" Richard asked, coming back out of the cabin after only a few moments.

"Everything? Everything is a very broad subject, Richard. I cannot begin to catalog *everything,* much less judge its status," she joked ruefully.

"That is not what I meant," he said, plopping down beside her.

"Then, what did you mean?" she asked looking at him. "You are not still concerned about my upset about Jamie, are you? Richard, believe me," she placed her hand on his arm. "I know it was an accident not negligence."

"Good," his big hand covered hers, "but that is not what I meant either. I mean... so, how is everything with you, *truthfully?*"

"I have told you, Richard, everything is fine. And I thank you again for bringing Master Wang and Ingrid to help me."

"I seek no thanks for that," he said softly and continued to look at her until she felt tears welling up in her eyes. She withdrew her hand and had to look away.

"Stop staring at me, please. It is not polite, you know."

"Marie, this is me, when have you ever known me to be concerned with what is considered polite?"

"Well, maybe it is time you grew up and learned some manners."

"Perhaps you are right but I doubt seriously that it is my manners that are causing your upset."

"I really do not know what you mean," she said and began to rise. Richard reached out a strong hand and held her there.

"I can see something is wrong!" he exclaimed with sudden intensity. "*Sacre Bleu!* A blind man could see something is wrong and both of you are miserable. What has happened to you two?"

Mutely Marie looked to the river.

"Two and a half years ago I left two people who still acted like young lovers who could not get enough of each other. Today I see two people who are, for the most part, just so very polite it makes my skin itch! Something has happened in between, and I think I am right to say whatever it is has made monks of both of you."

He stopped and stared at her relentlessly until she finally spoke.

"It is very personal."

"Perhaps you remember that I am the one who heard you two shake the walls every night in this very cabin years ago... or have you forgotten?"

Marie's face turned a deep crimson. "You were supposed to be sleeping," she replied weakly.

"And so I was," he winked when he caught her eye. "But we have shared much together, nonetheless. Now tell me, what is it?" he asked more gently. "Has Jacques done something of which I am not aware? Tell me. If he has, I will beat him within an inch of his life this time."

"No-no," she gasped and shook her head in protest.

"You do know that he was actually innocent... I mean, the witch pretended to be you in the dark. You do know that, eh?"

"He said as much but I was unprepared for how much it hurt just the same."

"She is a devil. I saw that from the very first."

"Please, Richard, do not speak of her. It makes me see her as I saw her that night. I do not want to think about what happened."

"But you must forgive him."

"No-no, Richard, you do not understand. There is nothing to forgive. Jacques has done nothing wrong. It is me! If he did find another woman, I could not blame him. It would kill me but I could not blame him. I am driving him away," she cried out hoarsely, with a sudden gasp. "I am going to lose him, if I have not lost him already and I do not know how to stop it." Marie broke down into deep racking sobs as he drew her against his big chest and held her. He waited patiently giving her time to cry herself out.

Marie cried into Richard's shirt for several minutes while being held in his big arms. It felt so good to be held. Marie felt protected and safe without need to worry that the possessor of those arms would want to push the embrace further into intimacy. Finally, her sobs began to subside.

"I am sorry," he said at last, "I am not a gentleman and I do not carry those fancy white hankies to offer a lady so she can blow her nose."

Marie could not help but laugh. She wiped her eyes with the backs of her hands. And then, with her nose stopped up and running, she impulsively reached for the hem of her under petticoat and blew her nose.

"That is what I have always admired about you," he nodded with an approving smile, "you are, above all, a practical French girl. Feel better now?"

Marie shook her head dejectedly from side to side.

"I remember one time when we slept upon the ground and I awoke to find a snake in my shirt. That is how I see her, a snake who crawled into the bedding and slithered up..."

Marie put out her hand to stay him, "Richard, please, stop! If there was anything to forgive, I forgave him long ago. It is my fault he is so... vulnerable."

Richard frowned. "This is not just about the witch, is it?"

Marie shook her head again, feeling some satisfaction to hear Renée called that. "It all started after you had the baby, did it not?"

She said nothing but tucked the soiled hem back under her skirts.

"I gather you did not have an easy time with this one... is that it? Did something change in you and you do not have any feeling anymore?" he asked softly.

"Oh, no," she cried in anguish, "not at all. Jacques has only to touch me and my bones turn to water... except with the drug, with the drug I truly cared for nothing," she said sadly. "But I will confess I pretended to have more pain to keep him away and I took more of the drug so I would not feel and now I use her as an excuse..."

"But why? Marie, you will have to excuse me if I am a little dense but what exactly is the problem?"

She still said nothing.

"Marie, I have not seen my friend this frustrated since that first winter in the cabin. But now it is worse because you are husband and wife and you are not youngsters. Every day a new hurt is piled upon the old and he knows not what to do. Whatever the cause, I can see that it is affecting both of you. It is ripping at the very core of your marriage. What is it, Marie?! What is going on?!"

"Oh, Richard," her face dissolved into anguish and her speech became erratic. "You have no idea how much I feared that I would never conceive. Those first two years I kept wondering what was wrong with me. My biggest worry was not being able to give Jacques the children he wanted, the sons I had prom..." she broke off and looked at him. "I am not making any sense to you, am I?"

Richard shook his head slightly.

"I thought Jamie was our last; he was supposed to be our last and when I discover I was pregnant again... you see, I had thought, oh, I know not what I had thought... but those first years we made no child and it was all I could think about. It was like a force of will. I begged the Almighty and willed children to come and they finally came. Then, when I decided it should be over, I guess I just thought it was supposed to be over because that was also what I willed."

Richard was going to say something but decided to just let her talk.

"I am too old now; I cannot keep having babies, Richard. It is going to kill me. If not this baby, then the next... or the one after that. I truly thought Isabelle would be the end of me. She was not but if I have another, I think I will die just like my mother. She died after having her eighth child! It just wore her out. I do not want to leave my babies orphans like she left us." Tears were running down her cheeks. "I do not want to leave Jacques. I do not want to die, although lately, I have begun to wonder if it might not be the best solution for hhh..."

He grabbed her by the shoulders and shook her. "No! Do not ever think that way, do you hear me? No! I will listen to anything you have to say but not that! You are never to think that way again, do you understand? None of us wishes to live in a world without you in it!"

The fierceness in his voice startled her and for a moment she stared wide-eyed into his eyes. Slowly she nodded and he released her.

"What am I going to do? I miss him so much but I must not get pregnant again! And I cannot bear to live if I have lost his love."

She looked up at Richard again through her tears and was stunned to see him smiling albeit sympathetically and shaking his head.

"Marie," he said fondly reaching out with his forefinger to tap the end of her straight slender nose. "It is hard to imagine such innocence in such a passionate woman and mother of seven."

She looked at him in speechless puzzlement.

"First, you must remember that your husband is a man of the world, an educated man not a peasant. You need to talk to him about these fears. A man can do many things to not plant seeds in the field. Jacques knows these things. Right now, he is beside himself with worry and frustration and hurt all because of you. Yes, yes, you have hurt him and very badly. But he has never stopped loving you. How could you even think that? Ah, ah, now do not start crying again or your eyes will be so impossibly puffed up and red, your children are going to know something has happened. I will be accused of beating you."

She gave a little laugh and smiled despite herself.

"That is better. Jacques is, after all, a big boy. He has not been hurt so badly he cannot mend. Now, come with me," he said taking her hand.

Richard led Marie into the forest. She followed him blindly at first and eventually realized he was looking for something.

"What is it, Richard, what are you looking for?"

"I will show you when I find it."

They continued walking, wandering this way and that and finally, Richard pointed to a plant.

"Here! Here it is, see it? Look. It is rather distinctive and it has this substantial little root." He dug the plant out of the ground with a stick. "This is one of the plants the Indians use," he said handing it to her and assessing the area he added, "This is a very good patch here, remember where it is. Never dig it all up though; always leave some behind to continue growing."

"What is it?" Marie asked, mystified by what this plant had to do with anything.

"I do not know what we might call it or if it has an English name. I only know the Indian name."

"What is it for?"

"When you have enjoyed each other, you make a pot of tea with these roots the next day; you drink this and you will not conceive."

"What?!!" Marie looked at him in stark disbelief.

"It is true. The Indian women use it. Indians generally do not have more than two young ones at a time, one they can strap on their back and one they can take in their arms to move quickly, eh? In times of danger or when there is a need for speed. They wait until those grow able to travel well on their own before they have another infant. But you do not think they just stop having pleasure, do you?"

Marie thought back to when she had stayed in the cave during the hurricane. It was true; she could not remember any of the women having more than two small children with them although some with babies had older children.

"I cannot believe this!" She looked at the plant with wonder. "This plant can stop me from conceiving?!!"

"Just do not forget," he smiled. "Now, let us gather a bunch of these and go home. As the natives say, harvest one, leave four. In spring I will show you another whose seeds you can chew. And Marie... have pity on your poor husband and talk to him," he counseled wisely.

"Oh, Richard," she moaned, "I have been so stupid. But I thought I had said something and he just ignored me. I know not why I did not insist on discussion. Somehow I felt it was my problem to solve," she said. "Who could I talk to? The one person I might have talked to is around no more. But you might know the Indians would know of something."

Suddenly she gave Richard a spontaneous hug. "Thank you," she said with a lump in her throat. "I thank God for you, Richard. Now, if Jacques will only forgive me. He must forgive me, Richard," she said almost desperately, her eyes brimming again with tears.

Richard smiled. He was more than pleased to think that he had helped her, that he might have been able to help both of his dear friends. But he was also very aware of the soft fragrance of her female scent and forced his arms to stay at his side this time not trusting himself to embrace her at that particular moment alone in this quiet green bower of tall evergreens.

The children were finished with their lessons for the day and Jacques looked in the direction of the cabin wondering what was keeping Marie and Richard. He thought of asking Richard if he would like to go for a ride through the cultivated countryside, like old times in France. Jacques wandered back and forth, debating whether to go to the old cabin himself when he saw the two of them walking arm in arm, coming out of the trees but not from the direction of the cabin. Her skirts were lifted! She was smiling and laughing like he had not seen her do in months! And Richard was looking exceedingly pleased with himself!

Marie felt like a stone had been removed from her heart. She could not wait to talk to Jacques; she could not wait until they were alone again. What a relief to know there was something they could do to resolve her fears. She felt absolutely lightheaded and was smiling with gladness and only half listening to Richard as he talked on. She looked up and saw Jacques and the smile froze on her lips.

His face held a look of complete betrayal. Beyond hatred or anger, she saw the tormented hurt and her heart skipped a beat in her chest. Suddenly she saw herself and Richard as Jacques saw them and it made her feel guilty, doubly so because she knew how she had been rejecting her husband, lying to him, making up excuses to push him away. In a reflex re-action, she pulled her arm from Richard. She was still carrying the load of roots in her skirt; she looked down and realized her petticoats and even parts of her legs were clearly exposed.

"Jacques!" Richard called out, trying to greet his friend lightly, but he, too, felt guilty. He had been in love with his best friend's wife for years. And suddenly his guilt showed in his face. It was the confirmation Jacques needed to believe the worst.

"Jacques, are you well?" Marie asked. She blanched at the hatred she saw welling up in her husband's face as he looked at his best friend.

"Go into the house, Marie!" he ordered in a tone he had never used with her before and she shrank away and backed toward the house in obedience.

Jacques had no gloves with him, and so, as he stepped up closer to Richard, he slapped him across the face with his bare hand in a ritual demand for satisfaction on a field of honor.

"This is the one thing our friendship cannot survive! Since it is I who challenge you, you may choose the weapons," he said fiercely, his eyes had become like circles of ice, his nostrils flaring and his lips stretched tightly beneath his moustache.

Richard accepted the blow without flinching. There was no anger in him. And he would not raise his hand to his lifelong friend, not this time, not now, not like this.

"Jacques, I am guilty of loving her. This is nothing you have not known for years but I swear on the grave of my mother, I have never touched her and she has given you no cause for shame."

Jacques looked at the larger man standing in misery before him and the anger began to drain away. He wanted to believe without feeling he was a fool. He had known Richard his entire life. They were closer than most brothers. Richard had been friend enough to share Jacques' destiny in his flight to the New World. He did not want to fight him but just the thought of being made a cuckold by Richard had made him abandon reason. And Richard was right. Jacques had long known Richard was in love with Marie, it just had never been said; he could not be faulted for love.

"Jacques," Marie said softly coming up beside her husband, her skirt spread out to reveal its contents. "They are plants, Jacques. Richard showed me plants. We were gathering plants to make a tea... for me... they were in the forest... he showed me something to help me... to help *us*."

He turned slowly and looked at her. He looked into the face of his wife and he believed her. From that open, guileless face without pretense he knew it was the truth but the pain even this caused him was excruciating.

"How is it, madame, that Richard has been taken into your confidence while I, your husband, through all these long months have not?" His voice was so low it was almost a whisper.

Tears began streaming down Marie's cheeks as Jacques turned from her and walked away. She looked after him and then at Richard. He saw such grief and despair in her expression that he felt as though a cold hand was squeezing his heart within his chest.

"Go inside," he encouraged her. "Take care of those, they need to be washed and dried so they do not mold. Everything will be all right," he reassured her.

Richard took off after Jacques and followed him into the barn. It was better that they should talk alone. It was easier to hear difficult words if there was no one else to witness.

"Jacques," he said walking into the barn. "Look, my friend, before you start wallowing in mountains of self-pity and wasting more precious time…"

Jacques reeled around to face him. "Stand away from me, Richard!"

"I will not! Not until you face a few things. You are angry with me now because I know something you do not, something about your own wife. It hurts your pride, maybe? Well, this is not about your pride, my friend; it is about the woman you say you love."

"Do not dare to question my love for her!"

"I do not question that you love her! I also have a good understanding of how very, very much she loves you! Great God Almighty, if she had not always been so much in love with you, so blind to anything but you. It was you and always you from the very start." The two men stood face to face, motionless. Jacques was mute. "But now I know what fears she has been living with," Richard continued. "I know what has brought a terrifying panic into her life and I told her she should have talked to you. Somehow she thought she had and you refused to hear her. Perhaps that was the opium. But why do I know this now, Jacques, eh?" His expression was one of accusation and he held it through several silent moments before he answered his own question. "Because I asked her, because I would not let her refuse to talk about it, because I insisted she explain herself and would not let her hide it. Did you do that?"

Jacques' expression changed to a deep frown.

"That woman has worshiped at your altar since the early days in France," Richard went on, "there is nothing she could ever deny you if you insisted. Why did you not insist?"

"I will never force her." Jacques retorted angrily.

"Not sex! I am speaking of words, words of explanation, of insisting on knowing her reasons for withdrawing, insisting on knowing her fears!"

"I..." Jacques was at a loss. Why hadn't he insisted she open up to him, share her thoughts, her fears? Fears? What fears? Perhaps he had had some fears of his own. But what had she to be afraid of? He still did not know what this was all about. "*Je nais se pas!*" he shouted. "I know not! What in the name of all that is holy is going on?"

"What do you know of Marie's family?"

"Not very much! She has never said much about them. I always assumed it was not a very happy subject and it was unpleasantness better left buried. Her mother died, she was raised by an older sister who also died; she ran away from a drunkard father with a foul temper," Jacques shrugged, indicating that was all he really knew.

"Do you know how her mother died?" Richard asked accusingly.

"No!" Jacques replied defiantly.

"She died in childbirth, Jacques! Marie said she died after having her *eighth* child. Isabelle is your seventh!! Marie is petrified of becoming pregnant again and certain it will kill her!"

Marie hung the precious plants up off the rafters in the snug brick kitchen so they could dry. She was glad that Margot was absent. When finished, Marie hurried into the main house and to their bedroom to wash her tear stained face. Thankfully she came upon no one; the youngest children were taking their naps and the others were off amusing themselves or doing chores. She took off her soiled skirt and petticoats and put on others. She ran a comb through her hair and tried to make herself look presentable.

Richard was right, she thought, she should have talked it out with Jacques. Why had she not talked to him, she asked herself? All these months of avoidance and excuses, lies, deceits, and pretenses. Why? Had she not trusted him enough? She felt so... she could not think of anything low enough to describe how she felt. Jacques was her love and her life and she had betrayed his confidence and his trust in her. She was a disappointment to him and she had hurt him. How could she hope to ever gain back the trust she had lost? How could she expect for things to ever be the same again? If only they could close the gaping chasm between them and wipe the slate clean.

Jacques opened the door to their bedroom and seeing her, came in and locked it behind him. Before he could speak she burst forth. "Forgive me, Jacques! Please forgive me! If you do not forgive me, I shall die of a broken heart."

She saw him shake his head. "You are made of far stronger stuff than that, Marie." He stood looking at her and she could not read the expression on his face.

It was her turn to shake her head. "I do not think so."

"And I do not understand. You were ready to sacrifice our... intimacies. Does that part of our marriage truly mean so little to you that you would sacrifice it rather than *talk* to me?"

He saw her shake her head again this time very slowly with confusion and bewilderment registering on her face.

"I... it... but I..." Drug-laced memories ran through her mind, memories in which she was sure she had said something to him, memories of short conversations... could they have been dreams? "Did I not say I must not have more children?" she asked weakly. "I thought you were ignoring my wishes." She looked to him and he was shaking his head.

"When have I ever ignored your wishes?"

"I was so frightened… was it a dream?" The tears spilled out and ran silently down her cheeks. "I was sure… you wanted more sons and… oh, please Jacques, forgive me," she begged and broke into sobs. It was enough to break his own heart. He crossed the room and took her into his arms.

"Sh...sh...sh.." he shushed her as he held her, fighting back his own tears. "You did not tell me," he said, his voice growing hoarse. "*Mon Dieu*, I had no idea." He buried his face in her hair, it smelled of sunshine and fresh air. "I cannot bear the thought of anything ever happening to you. I know not what I would do," he said, his voice choked with emotion. "I need you as much as I need air to breathe. You are not your mother, Marie; there is no reason to think you must share her fate. But if you do not wish to carry any more children, we will not make any more, I promise. I promise. If I do not have *you*, nothing else matters," he said holding her tightly, protectively.

She had heard the choke in his voice and she began kissing his neck, his cheek, his jaw, his eyes, his nose and tasting the salt of her own tears as she rubbed her cheek against him. "Jacques, you understand it is not that I do not want your children? It is what each pregnancy takes out of me."

"But you have given me a treasure house of healthy children. I ask for no more. Do you have any idea the torturous thoughts I have been thinking?" he asked while pulling back to look her in the face again, venting all his hurts of the past months. "Do you know what you have put me through? The dark fears I have been living with? That you no longer wanted me? That you no longer loved me?"

"Oh, Jacques… I…" she stopped herself. To say she was sorry was simply not enough. Her eyelashes were heavy with moisture as she looked into his eyes, darkened with emotion. "Beat me," she said softly but with gathering strength. "You must beat me."

"What are you saying!?" He recoiled in shock.

"It was my fault but Richard beat you. Now… you must beat *me*."

"Marie, no! Absolutely not!"

"Here," she pulled away, frantically ripping at her bodice and tearing her shift in an effort to expose her back. "No one will know. No one will see. Take your belt now, and beat me, Jacques, beat me to take away the pain that is in my heart for what I have done to you, please." She slumped to the floor, doubled over the dressing table settee, making her back vulnerable and presenting it to him.

"Marie," he said softly with a touch of horror still in his voice. Reaching down he lifted her back to her feet with no more effort than one would lift a child. "I could never raise a violent hand to a woman, any woman... much less you, the very loved mother of my children, the woman for whom I would die. What kind of monster… barbarian... must you think me to be?"

"No-no, not barbarous but very correct. You must, Jacques, you must; it is my *just* punishment. The punishment will pay for all I have done and wipe my conscience clean. If you do not, I will hate myself for the rest of my life!"

"Marie… please..." he continued to shake his head slowly.

"You must," she demanded. "A hickory stick perhaps. The school children, I hear, get no less."

Jacques was reminded of how he had allowed Richard to punish him; he had wanted the beating to purge the guilt. Marie was seeking the same. How could he deny her that? But he would not take a whip to her and he would not make a fist.

"Very well," he said gravely and taking her arm he walked her to the bed. Sitting down upon the edge, he took hold of her and settled her face-down across his knees. Tossing her petticoats up toward her head, he exposed her naked bottom, as smooth and firm as an apple. He had no heart to strike her. He wanted instead to do so many other much more enjoyable things to her. "How many strokes must I give you?" he asked hoarsely.

"Twelve," came the muffled reply.

Jacques raised his hand and brought it down upon her pale bottom.

"Harder," she demanded without a flinch.

He sucked in his breath and struck her again leaving his hand print clearly visible, flushed out pink upon her white flesh.

"Harder!" she cried again.

Jacques clenched his teeth and put the full strength of his arm behind the next strokes, twelve in all. When he finished, her derrière was aflame, as red as a ripe tomato, and her thighs were trembling; his own open palm stung fiercely. He could not wait to tip her back onto her feet and when he did and her head emerged, the unbidden tears in her eyes were accompanied by a smile.

"Now," she hiccuped, "you truly must forgive me."

"Of course I forgive you," he said with a sharp release of breath, reaching out and pulling her close and giving her an angry shake. "I had already forgiven you without any such… such... punishment. I love you too much not to forgive you. It was you who insisted on this, who needed this, not I, *n'est-ce pas?* And now the slate is wiped clean! But you must make me a promise, Marie; if there is ever anything in the future, no matter what - no matter how hateful or fearful or strange - you must never, never, ever shut me out again. Marie, I am your husband! You must always share your troubles and your fears with me in a true conversation. I cannot read your mind!"

"Yes-yes," her head bopped in agreement.

"Swear before God," he said fiercely, grabbing her Bible from the side table and thrusting it before her.

"I swear, Jacques, I swear," she said solemnly with her hand upon the book. "With God as my sacred witness."

He replaced the Bible and for a long moment they stood looking at each other. As if by unheard cue they both began frantically disrobing. Within seconds they were naked and in each other's arms.

She was gasping breathlessly, her bottom burning like a scorching fire and she wanted him with an intensity to match it. This coupling must overwhelm it, overpower it, and drowned it out along with all the horrible memories of the past year.

He was of no mind for gentleness or patience. Not this time. This time she had made him do something he had been completely loathed to do. That and the memories of all the hurts and all the rejections were making demands of their own – demands to conquer, to dominate, to possess, to subdue in a primal savage coupling unlike any before; only then would those demands be satisfied.

She was his and only his. He was hers and only hers. They were one flesh to be nipped and gripped and grabbed and scratched and bit and pinched and pummeled and pounded and pulled and yanked until they were utterly exhausted and completely satiated: survivors of a marriage re-birthed.

Chapter 19

1710

Jamie unconsciously cringed as he heard the sound of the shears snipping loudly by his ear.

"Hold your head up now," his mother scolded softly, "straight. Keep your head straight. If you want not to lose an ear, quit pulling your neck in like an old turtle!"

A rap on the shoulders with the broad side of the comb served to remind the young boy to relax his shoulders and allow them to drop down exposing his neckline more easily for the hair cutting.

"That is better," Marie sighed and continued with the chore she did not like anymore than her son did. "I will soon be finished and you will be done for another season. Will it not be nice to have a fresh haircut for your birthday? Eleven years old already, my goodness, it is hard to believe. Soon you will be a man," she added jokingly, never for a moment believing that this slightly built child was anywhere close to becoming a man.

Not a man for some time, Marie thought to herself, but her babies were definitely growing up. Jamie was now eleven and Izzy was already four and a half. Marie thought back to the year Isabelle was born. It had been the very worst year of her marriage, even worse than the year she had struggled through not knowing if Jacques was alive or dead. But that was now a long time ago. The small wound on Jamie's leg had healed cleanly and the small scar was barely visible. And there had been no real wounds to her marriage, only wounded feelings which had quickly been forgotten upon reconciliation. She and Jacques had bonded closer and stronger than ever.

She smiled to herself when she thought of the spanking. She had been very careful sitting down for several days after that but it had done its job. She had paid a price for all the hurts she had caused her Jacques, all the deceits and lies, and she felt her slate had been wiped clean with her conscience satisfied. They both had been freed to start fresh like newly weds and Jacques, now understanding, had introduced her to a number of ways to avoid getting pregnant. One of the surest was something called a *skin*, made of animal intestine and found in Paris. Most ladies did not know of their existence. He told her they were sold to men chiefly as a protection against the diseases of whores and could be found in Parisian pubs, barbershops, chemist shops, and could even be asked for at open air booths on the streets of the city. They were expensive but Jacques had the means to afford them and he ordered a supply, through Dufee, to be used whenever Marie could not make her special tea.

There was no way she could ever thank Richard Bonchance enough for his intercession during that period, but it was a subject not to be spoken of again. Richard's confession that he loved her had made things awkward among them until he went away and stayed away for two more years. When he returned, his admission had been rendered down to simply a sincere acknowledgment of brotherly affection and admiration. Everyone went on as though nothing had happened, but in fact, could Marie ever forget each time she drank her special tea? She loved Richard dearly, just like a burly brother, a nursery mate whom she could confide in and that was how she tried to convince herself he really thought of her. But deep down, she was no longer that naive. There was a nuance of formality in her attitude toward him from that time on and she was mindful of keeping a certain distance between them physically. Something, she chided herself, she should have been more mindful of before. She had been too relaxed and too familiar with him, she told herself.

Jacques and Richard still thoroughly enjoyed each other's company; they were life long friends who had shared too much for that to ever change. Marie wished Richard would take a wife and settle down to raise his own family but despite growing complaints of arthritic pains for which she brewed him willow bark tea with mint and honey when he came to visit, he would not give up his life as a wanderer in the wilds.

Ingrid was now Mistress Boot and she continued to offer therapeutic massages within the community. Marie had a standing appointment each week and her back continued to feel like she was still twenty. Jacques and Marie had both been invited to visit the Boot's *badstuga*. Jacques had declined but Marie had expressed an interest to try the experience if they would restrict the participants to only women for her visit. Marie knew that at first the Boots thought this rather Puritanical but they had graciously agreed. Then, William built a new *badstuga* with a changing room entry and began to advertise "Men's Night" and "Ladies' Night" while charging a modest fee; by all accounts it had become very popular, especially in cold weather and had fast become the favorite way for the community to deal with the common head cold.

As Jamie waited out the last minutes of his physical restriction, he fiddled absentmindedly with the heavy gold ring he wore on a chain around his neck. It was a copy of the one his father wore and each of his brothers had one as well. John, who had just turned nineteen, wore his ring on his little finger just like Papa, but John was considered a man who was expected to take a wife of his own soon. Phillip was seventeen and wore his ring on his ring finger like John used to wear it. Richie, who was fourteen, had tried to wear his ring on his finger and had almost lost it. Mama had insisted he put it back on the chain until he grew older.

Jamie was old enough to have heard the story several times of what had happened to his great-great-grandfather's family when France began persecuting the Huguenots and he felt he understood why many within the colonies did not want Catholics around. But the story that delighted him the most was the tale of his parents' escape from France and how his father had narrowly missed capture by hiding beneath the skirts of a lady friend. That part always made Jamie laugh.

Jamie slipped the ring on and off, on and off, on and off his largest middle finger. It fell off much too easily for him to wear on his hand, but someday he would. He and his brothers had received their rings from *Grand-père* when he and *Grand-mère*-his-beloved-duchess, had come to visit. Of course, Jamie did not remember it personally. He had been only a baby. But he had heard the stories often from his siblings.

§

"Grand-père is a real duke who lives far away in a castle just like in the fairy tales," Jamie's older sisters told him. "One day he and *Grand-mère*-his-beloved-duchess, took a ship from far across the ocean and came to see us."

When Jamie was five, he had asked Louise why *Grand-père* and *Grand-mère*-his-beloved-duchess, did not come back to visit again now that he could remember it and she had told him it was because they were much too old.

"Were they old when they came to visit us before?" he had asked at the time in his babyish five year old voice.

"They were old but not so very," Louise had replied to him with the more worldly wisdom of nine.

"How could you tell they were old?" Jamie asked looking intensely serious.

"Because *Grand-père's* hair came off at night and *Grand-mère*-his-beloved-duchess had hair that was all gray."

"Ohhh," Jamie had nodded, appropriately impressed by her deductions.

"Besides they are Papa's parents, so they have to be old."

"Oh." Five year old Jamie had followed the logic perfectly. "But Papa has hair," he had stated emphatically.

His sister had giggled.

"Papa has beautiful, curly hair that hangs on the bedpost," his sister said astutely.

"Does that mean he's old?"

Louise had only been teasing but Papa did have a wig hanging from the bedpost. That made her stop for a moment and consider. Papa never seemed old so she gave a little shrug in imitation of what she had often seen her parents and Uncle Richard do. After a moment she added, "Mama says in the cities lots of men wear wigs and take them off at home."

"Why?" Jamie had asked

"I don't know, just because they do, that's all." Louise had become bored with the conversation and with that had run off abruptly to play dolls with her sister.

§

"Will I have to wear a wig when I grow up?" Jamie asked suddenly as his mother snipped across his dark blond bangs.

"A wig? Why? Only if you want to, I suppose," Marie answered.

"Will it make me old?"

"No, of course not. Wigs are for fashion, nothing more," Marie shook her head wondering where children came up with their ideas.

"Does a wig make you lose your hair?"

"Of course not."

"Maybe it does."

"Whatever would make you think that?" Marie set the scissors aside and began to gingerly untie the linen from about Jamie's neck, trying very hard not to spill hair clippings all over the floor. Usually she did all the hair cutting outdoors but today the November wind was blowing stiffly and she wanted the job done before tomorrow.

"Louise says *Grand-père* wears a wig and he lost his hair, but Papa almost never wears a wig and he still has his hair and Uncle Richard never wears a wig and he has great, great bunches of hair," Jamie observed.

Marie chuckled. "Well, that is true but it is because your Uncle Richard is half bear." She glanced up to see her son looking at her very seriously. "I am only joking, goose," she smiled. "Richard is not really half bear, but he is not your blood uncle, either."

She took the cloth to the door. As she stepped outside, the wind whipped it fiercely and sent the hair clippings flying. Closing the door quickly she continued speaking.

"You see, these things just happen in families. Your pa-pa's hair is quite thick although at times he wears a wig; his ma-ma told me your pa-pa's hair is like *her* pa-pa's. It is not nearly as thin as his pa-pa's hair and according to what I have heard, he often did not wear a wig as well. You and your brothers will very likely always have thick hair like your pa-pa or like my pa-pa's which was also very thick and heavy."

"Did your papa wear a wig?"

Marie found the idea very funny. "No," she laughed, "my pa-pa never wore a wig but that makes no difference."

"Why didn't he wear a wig?" Jamie persisted, thinking this disclosure only added to his argument.

Marie had often made casual references to her family through the years but had never told her children about the pain of her early life. "He did not wear a wig because he was not a man of fashion. Simple country people, rich and poor alike, are much less likely to wear wigs than the dandies of the court."

"Is Papa a *dandy*?"

"No-no, not at all, but people of higher station are also more inclined to wear a wig on more formal occasions. Your pa-pa wears a wig only when the affairs of work and his status within the community require it, but his hair has changed little except that it is cut shorter."

Marie did not have to explain to the young boy that his father was an important figure in their community. Jamie could sense respect in the way people treated his father, the way men deferred to his opinions, and listened when he was speaking. He knew his father was much admired by the people around them and many were in his employ.

Jamie also was beginning to realize other things as well. It had struck him recently that among all the houses in the town and around the valley, he saw none nearly as large as theirs. John used to talk about how he had helped Papa add on to the house when they heard that *Grand-père* and *Grand-mère*-his-beloved-duchess were coming to visit.

Jamie had memories of hammers whack-whack-whacking away, day after day, when they built onto the house again several years ago. When the hammering stopped they had a special room for Mama to keep a large tub in. The servants filled the tub for their baths and when finished they only had to pull a plug and the water would drain down a hole and through a pipe into the garden below. Mostly, Jamie remembered the smell of the newly cut wood, and playing amidst the curly shavings strewn about the ground.

He clearly remembered when John and Phillip had been given the room which had been built for *Grand-père* and *Grand-mère*-his-beloved-duchess. It was large and very airy with two separate dressing rooms and was situated over the wine cellar. John and Phillip were the eldest and it had seemed fitting that they should have it. Jamie and Richie had been equally happy to now have "the boys' bedroom" to themselves. Helen and Louise shared "the girls' bedroom" while Isabelle still slept in the nursery with Sarah. Mama and Papa had their own room, of course. The smallest bedroom was called "the sick room" because that's where you went if you were sick, Uncle Richard had a room, and one room was always kept as a guest bedroom. The cook had a room off the kitchen, and the rest of the servants had rooms above the carriage house and in the attic. Helen complained once of not having her very own room and Mama had scolded her and told her to be grateful they did not have to live in a one or two room cabin and she did not have to sleep with all her brothers and sisters in a loft as did most all the other children in the world. Upon overhearing, Jamie had thought of the loft full of hay in the barn and had considered that sleeping out there might actually be fun at least when the weather was pleasant and had suggested it the very next time Uncle Richard had come to stay. To his surprise, John and Phillip had jumped at the idea to give up their room instead. Mama fussed when the weather turned colder but they only laughed and told her all the cows and the hay kept the barn pleasantly warm even if the smells were somewhat "earthy."

In addition to the old barn and the dairy barn they had a large coop for their chickens, a shed for all the tools, the apple press house, the smoke house, the spring house and, of course, the carriage house and stables. Once, before Jamie was born, the family said the kitchen had burnt down and had to be rebuilt which was why it stood no closer to the house than it did and it was now completely brick. The worst thing about building houses of wood, Papa often said, was that they made too good a fire. Every year at least one of the houses in town burnt down.

Papa had huge marble hearth stones shipped from all the way across the ocean to put into their house, his brothers told him. It was to protect from fire and Jamie was certain no one had any finer.

Jamie's haircut was finished and he was feeling quite grown-up and looking forward to his birthday celebration as his mother excused him. His papa had promised tomorrow Jamie would get his first lesson with a musket, a year sooner than any of his brothers and he considered that it was just in time. To the south in a place called Northern Carolina, the dirty Indians had massacred a settlement and it had started another Indian war. If any of those heathen redskins tried to massacre them at Chartes Landing, he and his brothers and sisters would all be able to fight them even if Mama wouldn't. Mama knew how to shoot but she told stories about a time before Izzy was born when the Indians were her friends and she would not allow any in the household to say *dirty Indian,* not within her hearing.

Jamie looked around quickly to make sure his mother was not looking at him. She had an uncanny ability she called "mother's ears" to hear what he was thinking even when he didn't say anything out loud.

Business at the store was brisk and Marie found it necessary to spend more time there to make up for the illness of her newest apprentice who seemed to have developed a malady rendering her quite miserable. Marie was concerned.

Caroline Weaver, the daughter of one of Jacques' mill workers, had come to

Marie after her fifteenth birthday and begged for an opportunity to learn the retail trade. Marie liked the girl. She was bright, was able to read and write, and had such an earnest desire to learn. Her ciphering also was excellent and after almost a year of training Marie did not like to think of losing the girl. Felicity had served out her apprenticeship, married, and moved to the Pennsylvania Colony where farmland was abundant so Marie was in need of the help.

Caroline was a pretty little thing, with long, shiny, copper colored hair and skin so clear and pale it looked like milk. Her huge, dark blue eyes held a serious look that gave her an air of maturity. But of late, Caroline's willowy figure had grown gaunt as she suffered a digestive upset of some kind. Marie was baffled as she tried to think of something to assist the girl in her recovery. The young apprentice refused to see the new doctor who had taken over St. Claire's practice. She did not have a fever but circles had taken hold under those huge blue eyes. Today she had begged another day off.

The afternoon shadows were lengthening upon the street and Marie was pleasantly surprised to see Jacques when she looked up in reaction to the jingle of the bell over the door of the store. He often stopped by to say hello or walk her home when he knew she was there.

"Marie," he called as he looked around the store and saw that it was empty.

She came toward him and gave him a kiss. Then, she stepped back. She knew those worry lines upon his brow meant something was disturbing him. "What is it, Jacques?"

"Can you close the store? We need to talk."

"There is no one here, we can talk. Must I close the store?"

"We have a problem," he said sternly.

"Yes? What is that?" she looked at him calmly.

He had begun pacing back and forth as if trying to find the words. Just then, old Mister Freeman came in seeking rope and nails for his farm. As Marie patiently waited for the indecisive farmer to make his final selection, two young brothers appeared with a list from their mother. By the time she had filled their order a half hour had passed. She went to the door, put up the "CLOSED" sign and pulled down the shade.

"I am sorry, Jacques," she said turning to her husband, "it happens every time. You have no one for hours and then..."

"Marie," his voice demanded her attention.

"What is it?" She looked at him.

"It is Phillip."

Marie blanched. "Is something wrong?" she asked quickly. "He is not hurt?!"

Jacques quickly shook his head. "No-no, he is not hurt."

She relaxed again. "What about Phillip now?" If he was not hurt, what could possibly be so upsetting she wondered, and thought perhaps Jacques was getting a trifle melodramatic in his advancing fatherhood. Phillip was always causing some upset. He was too prone to leap before he looked.

Her husband's expression remained unusually serious. "Silas Weaver came to me today. I must give the man credit; it took a great deal of courage. After all, I am his employer. Did you know Phillip was keeping company with your apprentice?"

"Keeping company? With Caroline? Why no, I had no idea." She looked surprised. "When could he be seeing her? You mean he has been coming to the store when I am not here?"

"I do not know but Weaver tells me Caroline is now expecting Phillip's baby."

Marie gasped. "*Mon Dieu,*" she lapsed into the old language.

"Weaver blames it all on the idea of allowing a young girl to be left unchaperoned. He claims the only time she is out of their sight is when she is here and so it must have happened here. He feels we are responsible for the loss of his daughter's virtue."

Marie looked at her husband, ever the chivalrous gentleman. He had nothing to do with the store, never had, but said "we" to share any possible blame although if there was culpability it really lay on her alone.

"Jacques," this time her brow held the frown. "I am trying to recall any time when I would have left her here alone. She is still learning and very young. I cannot think of a time for longer than it takes to visit the privy. Either myself or Lyndyn are always with her."

Jacques' eyebrow shot up sharply.

"No, I would trust Lyndyn with my life... besides he has never seemed especially interested in the girls."

Jacques nodded. "Weaver is distraught and very angry. I cannot say that I blame him. If it were Helen or Louise or Izzy, I cannot think what I might do. We live in a very small community and once word of this leaks out, his daughter's reputation will be in ruins."

"Have you talked to Phillip?"she asked softly.

"Not yet."

"Jacques, please, let us talk to our son before we jump to any hasty conclusions. It is only right and fair. Does Caroline say Phillip is the father?"

"Of course, she says it is him. Why else would Weaver have named him?" Jacques almost snapped and was immediately sorry. His second son had always been a trial, it was just his nature. It was not Marie's fault. If anything, Jacques blamed himself. It had been his responsibility to raise his sons to be honorable men. And he had somehow failed. "Forgive me, I mean not to take it out on you."

"Jacques," Marie reached out to him and stroked his cheek. "Caroline is a sweet girl, and very comely. We both know what hot blood is prone to do. Let us not be hasty in judging. We must talk to Phillip and learn his intentions before we think further. We will talk to him together, yes? And *I* want to know exactly where their romantic rendezvous took place."

Jacques looked down at his wife and saw the compassion in her eyes. She was not faulting him and he felt a sense of relief. Through her eyes he was beginning to see the situation as being something they could work through rather than an indictment of his failure as a father.

"He is very young to marry," Jacques said quietly.

"Yes," Marie nodded, "but not too young. I was in the New World fending for myself when I was much younger than he and I had no family to lean on. Our Phillip has family. He also has the capacity for love and for responsibility. And Caroline is a capable girl."

Of all the words Marie might have chosen to describe her young apprentice, it was the one word that struck a reassuring note with Jacques.

Dinner that night was a rather normal affair for the sake of all the other children. But when it was over, Jacques asked Phillip to come to his study and Marie gave instructions to Sarah and Jane to see to the clean up and the children while she also went to Jacques' study. Jane Sims raised her eyebrows. Something was afoot, she thought as she saw the heavy door close. Young Master Phillip was in some kind of trouble… again; that seemed for certain.

Jacques thought of the times he had gone to his father's study in the chateau. Of course, when he had been Phillip's age, Jean-Philippe and he had both thought they were half-brothers but still he recalled the dignity with which the older man had always treated him. He would try to maintain the same attitude toward this, his own flesh and blood.

After Marie entered the study, Jacques closed the door. Marie took a seat; Jacques sat and motioned for his son to be seated.

"I think you know already what this is about," he said calmly.

Phillip sat in one of the high-backed chairs and looked nervously from one parent to the other. As Marie looked at her son she realized that over the past year his shoulders had broadened and his stature filled out in a darker copy of his father. With his handsome face, dark brooding eyes and thick curly brown hair, she could understand how Caroline had found Phillip irresistible.

"I'm not certain I know what you mean, sir," Phillip replied evasively.

Jacques absentmindedly stroked his moustache. He thought of Jean-Philippe and chose his words carefully. "Silas Weaver came to me today…"

The young man tensed.

"Do you have feelings for his daughter Caroline that we should know about?" Jacques asked without accusation.

"Feelings? I really don't know her that well," the boy replied.

Jacques was about to say his son surely knew her well enough it would seem but held his tongue. "But you do know her?" Jacques asked with reserve.

"Yes, I've seen her around," Phillip's dark eyes avoided his father's.

"Phillip, she is a very bright girl," Marie spoke up. "I have been very pleased with her work at the store. She has a good head on her shoulders. But did you know that she has become quite ill?"

Phillip visibly reacted. "Ill? What's wrong? Will she be all right?" he cried out.

"So you do have feelings for her," his mother replied quietly, "you *care* for her well being, yes?"

Phillip flushed red.

"I do not believe her illness is anything too serious," his mother went on, "but the cause of it is. She is going to have a baby and that little baby should have a papa."

The word "baby" stuck in Phillip's throat as he stared at his mother.

"That often is the result of sporting," his father said firmly.

"Not sporting," Phillip rose to their defense, "it wasn't sport, sir. I love her. I love her and I want her to be my wife!"

"Well… at least we now understand what *feelings* are involved," Jacques said dryly. "So, you do love this girl and I presume she loves you?"

Phillip nodded his head dumbly.

"You are very young, son, but you are not too young. I would have advised waiting a few more years but this baby is not going to wait. It would seem a wedding is in order."

Phillip looked at his father and tears smarted in his smoldering eyes. For an instant he had expected to be berated, castigated, lectured, and possibly disowned. To his amazed bewilderment, his parents seemed to understand. He knew his behavior had been undisciplined and against God's teachings. He and Caroline had given in to their lusts. He could not even blame Caroline as he had so pressed her, playing upon her tender emotions until she had finally given in to his demanding passion. It was all his fault and he had not been surprised to find her a virgin. It had been wrong but his parents were willing to stand by him. It touched his young heart more than he would show.

"Jacques?" Marie again spoke. "We could move John into the guest room or we could move him back in with Richie and Jamie, then Phillip could bring Caroline home to live here until he can build a home of his own." She looked at her son, "It would give you a chance to get on your feet and position yourself to support a family," she counseled. "We must speak with your brother, but I cannot imagine that he will object. You will need the larger room when the baby arrives."

"Or we could build on to the house again," Jacques suggested.

"I would think the young couple would rather have a home of their own," she said softly, "remember when we were first married?"

Remember? It seemed like only yesterday or a short year or two ago, and now, his second son was going to make a grandfather of him, Jacques thought. And Marie, with her lively eyes and youthful beauty, was going to be a grandmother… not just hypothetically from some ill-fated babe she had borne when she herself was only a child but for real. How was it possible? Where was time fleeing? This pale brooding youth sitting here had been but a baby himself just a short time ago. How was it possible that he had already sired a child of his own? And now he would be seeking to establish his own home. and be head of his own table. Jacques nodded and found himself going to the sideboard and pouring each of them a small cognac.

"What about the rooms over the store?" Phillip suggested. "Perhaps we could rent those from you and Caroline would be right there at the store."

"Mmmm," Marie thought. "Do you not think it might be easier if Caroline is here with Sarah to help her in the nursery? And you must admit our home is much nicer than the rooms over the store."

Phillip considered. "Could we have them until the baby is born? For our… honeymoon, so to speak? When the child is born, perhaps we could move in here for a time."

Marie looked at Jacques and he knew what she was thinking. The little cabin and the intimacy they shared alone when Richard was away. How could they deny their own son the same opportunity for memories and romance?

"To the happy couple," he said in a toast with a nod, and his son looked at him with such gratitude that Jacques could not be unhappy.

"I have just one question," Marie said as she put her glass down. "Since Monsieur Weaver claims the only time Caroline is out of his sight is when she is at my store, exactly where did you two manage to... ?"

Phillip flushed beet red with embarrassment at his mother's question. "After her parents went to sleep," he muttered, "I would bring their dog a treat and climb up to her window." He avoided his parents' eyes.

Marie fought to keep her face expressionless. "I am glad you did not break your neck."

Jacques and Marie were proud of their first born's reaction when they took him aside and explained the situation. John was prepared to give up his half of the large suite and move into the smaller extra guest room. With a gallant attitude reflective of his father, he told himself it would not be for long. Phillip would soon move out into a home of his own or John himself would find a pretty maiden who took his fancy and build his own home.

The wedding was quick and quiet and the Weavers considered their daughter's honor to have been rescued. They were now extended family. Caroline and Phillip moved into the rooms over the store and created their own little haven while Marie insisted on charging no rent so that they could save their money toward furnishing their own home. Jacques' mill would supply all the lumber needed to build a house come spring and Phillip was now employed full-time at the mill.

Jacques' next shock came shortly after Phillip's wedding; Thor Boot came to Jacques' office and asked permission to court Helen. Jacques blinked at the tall, brawny lad who was almost twenty-two and stood a full head taller than he. What could he say? His eldest daughter would soon be eighteen and she was a beauty who could shoot a musket as handily as her brothers and dance with elegance and grace.

"You may call upon her," Jacques replied after a failed attempt to stare the good-looking young man down. "But your hands you will keep to yourself," he almost growled as he arched a patrician brow. "And do not even try to invite her to your family *badstuga;* do we understand each other?"

Thor nodded and shook Jacques' hand. Once again they began to see a lot of Thor Boot at the Power home and Helen did not seem at all displeased.

Chapter 20

Early Spring 1711

The girl stumbled into the Emporium looking more dead than alive. She wore patched breeches and an old coat at least two sizes too small over which was tied a tattered blanket riding across one shoulder. Her long brown hair, caught in tangles with burrs and brambles, had mostly come loose from a single braid and straggled limp and greasy from under a shapeless brimmed hat. Mud spattered and dirty, she struggled to walk in heavy, broken down work boots too large for her feet.

"Hello?" Caroline looked up from the counter she was dusting. It was mid-afternoon in early spring, not an especially busy time of day and her hair, like molten copper, spilled out from under a pert little linen cap. "Can I help you?" she asked as she moved away from the counter and toward the stranger.

"Missus Power… looking for...Missus Power," the younger girl croaked through dry, chapped lips.

"I'm Missus *Phillip* Power," replied Caroline, still a bride but showing a bulging tummy and very proud of her new name. "What can I help you with?"

The girl peered at Caroline, confusion registering in her bloodshot eyes. "You from France?" she slurred, at which point her eyes rolled back into her head and she crumpled to the floor.

"Mother Power!" Caroline cried out as she kneeled on the floor beside the girl and removed her hat. She was hardly more than a child, Caroline discovered. "Mother Power, come quick!" she screeched as she began chafing the girl's wrists.

"What is it?" called Marie from the back office. She hurried out afraid something had happened to her pregnant daughter-in-law. Neatly coiffed with a shock of white hair streaking out from under the dainty lace topper that served to "dress" her thick brown and gold locks twisted up in a neat chignon. She was sveltely attired in a tailored dress of navy blue surge that vaguely resembled a man's suit with its closely hung skirt. "What… oh *mon Dieu!*" she gasped as she came upon the body spread out on the floor. "Who is this?"

"I'm not sure, Mother Power. She came in asking for… well, apparently *you.* Do you recognize her?"

Marie began to shake her head and stopped. Something about the child did look vaguely familiar. She reached behind the counter for a bottle of smelling salts. "Caroline, would you fetch a cup of water, please? I have a pitcher on my desk."

The smelling salts revived the girl and she recoiled from the potent odor with a gasp and a cough. "I need to find Missus Power," she said again, struggling to sit upright. "Pa said."

"I am Madame Power," Marie replied kindly.

"From France?"

Caroline arrived with the cup of water and Marie helped the young girl drink the entire contents, slowly.

"Yes," Marie said calmly, "long ago I came here from France." She had to smile. She now spoke excellent English but her accent was quite unmistakable except perhaps to a child.

The girl looked visibly relieved. "Good," she gasped after swallowing the last of the water. "Pa said you'd know what to do."

Do about what? "Let us start with your name, hm? Who are you?"

"Martha Carver," the youngster replied and suddenly huge tears were rolling down her dirt streaked cheeks. "Pa said they was fixin' to come back for another attack… 'Go Martha,' he said, 'go to our secret place and hide and no matter what you see or hear, you are not to come back.' He made me swear, gave me a sack of food and his canteen full of water and told me I must stay there for a night and a day and another night and then I was to start running fast as I could toward the rising sun and when I got back here I was to find Missus Power who come from France. He told me you would know what to do."

The name meant nothing to Marie who was still trying to place the child. So many people had come through her store on their way to the frontier. "And who is your pa-pa, Martha?" she asked gently.

"My real pa died of an injun arrow but then Ma married Mister Nicholet and he said we was to call him 'Pa'… and now he's dead too… and Ma… and Ezra and Michael." Martha was now wailing with the sorrowful admission that her entire family was dead and she was all alone in a bewildering world.

"Nicholet?" Marie gasped. "Francois Nicholet?" In a flash Marie remembered the light-hearted young Huguenot who had known such tragedy when his first wife and son had been murdered by the Dragonnade of France; those soldiers who thought nothing of tormenting, torturing, and raping Huguenots. Francois had run Jacques' mill until he married a young widow with three children… that was it, the Widow *Carver!* This was one of her children. He had been so happy to finally have a family again and wanted to homestead a farm on the frontier. And so they had left the security of Chartes Landing and now… were they indeed all dead?

Martha bobbed her head as she continued to cry. Marie forced herself not to cry as she gathered the child into her arms and rocked her gently. After several minutes she asked, "And did you walk all the way back here? How long... ?"

"No... " A sob broke her speech. "I found Ol'Lil in the far pasture and I rode her pretty hard. We barely stopped."

"And where is Ol'Lil now?" Marie asked.

"Out front."

"Oh." Marie considered the poor animal and looked up at Caroline. "Lyndyn is still up in the stockroom. Would you ask him to come down here, please."

"Yes ma'am." The younger woman immediately moved toward the staircase and called up the stairwell.

Lyndyn had become Marie's "right arm" in the store. Lean and agile if slightly built, the bespectacled young man had served out his apprenticeship and stayed on as a trusted employee. Somewhat timid in nature, he had no desire to strike out on his own, risking everything in his own storefront. He adored Marie, as a beloved mentor, and was very happy with the status quo. He took care of his mother and younger siblings since his father passed and felt no pressing need for any other relationship.

"Ah, there you are," Marie said as soon as she saw him approaching. "Please take the animal outside to our stable. It has been ridden in from the frontier and undoubtedly needs to be rubbed down, fed, and watered. Tell Monsieur Sims to treat it with loving care." She smiled. "And you might want to wipe that dust smudge from your face."

"Yes, ma'am," he said and looked to the mirror on the counter. He grimaced at what he saw and fastidiously employed his handkerchief as he left.

"Caroline, would you and Phillip plan on coming to supper tonight? I think everyone should be together when I relay this news."

Caroline bobbed her head. She and Phillip were living temporarily in the apartment above the back of the building. It had been very convenient through the winter and continued so while she worked at the store but she had agreed that taking advantage of the Power's hospitality once the baby arrived made sense.

"I am taking Martha home with me. When Lyndyn returns, lock up the store for the day. I will see you at supper."

Marie gathered up her things and led Martha out through the back where the buggy was waiting. In a short time they were pulling into the circular graveled drive of the Power family home. Lyndyn had already given Ol' Lil over to Donald Sims and was starting his walk back to the store.

"Lyndyn," Marie called to her young clerk as she rolled up to him, "jump in! You can take the buggy back with you so it is there for Caroline and Phillip to use."

He easily hopped aboard the rear of the buggy, riding with them to where she reigned them to a stop.

"Donald," Marie addressed a man in his fifties who appeared from within the stable, "would you please tell your wife to ask Sarah to find a set of clothing from my daughters' old things that will fit this little one and bring them to us in the kitchen? Thank you."

Donald Sims tipped his hat and nodded his understanding before going off to find his wife Jane. He was generally a man of few words.

In a scene reminiscent of Marie's own childhood she led Martha to their brick kitchen behind the main house and had her strip out of her rags which Margot, the cook, promptly began burning. There was always plenty of hot water in the large iron cauldron which hung in the huge fireplace. Marie slipped out of her jacketed top and donned an apron. In no time she had filled a tub with pleasantly warm water and was vigorously scrubbing the girl.

Marie was a little surprised to learn that Martha was thirteen. She had been eight, she said, when they had left Chartes Landing. Five years! And from what Marie could gather, they had not been easy years. Despite having the two older boys to help, clearing the land had been very difficult and harvests had been scant mostly because of the treachery of the local Indians. During her own early years on the frontier, Marie had been blessed to have friendly Indians as neighbors, the Nicholet family had not. To the contrary, apparently the natives had been thieving, malicious, and destructive until the hostility escalated to all out violence. Marie shuddered. Francois had not been a man prone to aggression or violence.

"The first year we didn't see no injuns," the girl talked as Marie soaped her up. "but the harvest weren't good neither. Pa said we still had too much shade. Then, the next year, we had more cleared but our harvest kept disappearin'. We thought the animals was takin' it. The next year we finally figured out it were injuns stealin' it. And Pa and Ezra couldn't hardly get nothin' done 'cause they was always chasin' em away from our field and Ma lost her baby. The next year they was stealin' right out of our storage. Last year they burned the whole harvest. Ma cried a lot and said she didn't know how we was gunna make it through the winter but Pa and Ezra hunted us food. But the injuns they just wouldn't let us be."

After a shampoo, rinse, and towel down, Martha stood at last dressed from the skin out in fresh, clean garments, and she had calmed enough to eat the food Margot set before her.

"I am so very sorry for what has happened to your family. I did not know your ma-ma very well, but I did know your Pa-pa Nicholet for many years. He was a very good man and he worked very hard."

The girl lapsed into silence as she ate and Marie decided to wait until she was finished before she combed out her hair. At last Martha pushed her empty plate aside.

"Would you like more?" Marie asked.

"No, ma'am."

"So, you are thirteen now," Marie smiled benevolently as she took up a comb thinking a change in subject was in order. The girl looked very under nourished and not just from her journey but a little stunted in her overall growth. *Lord, it was your mercy that she made it all the way back to Chartes Landing. One youngster all by herself, looking no more than ten? It is a miracle.* "and have you started your courses?" Marie asked easily as she gently worked with the child's hair.

"What courses, ma'am?" Martha looked up at her blankly.

"Oh… well… perhaps your ma-ma called it 'the Curse of Eve'? I generally refer to it as my 'monthly flow'… the Indians call it your 'moon time'...'"

Martha had no idea to what Marie was referring but at the mention of Indians she blanched as pale as a sheet.

"All is well," Marie said gently, patting her on the shoulder. "Not all Indians are evil, some have been my good friends."

"They ain't never gunna be my friends," Martha pronounced darkly.

Marie wondered that the Widow Carver...that is to say the second Madame Nicholet…had not prepared her daughter for the inevitable. But then, with so much else going on and Martha looking so flat-chested and young, it was possible her mother had lost track of her daughter's true age. Marie had learned what to expect from her older sisters but she had had "the talk" with both of her older daughters and had no qualms about giving such a lesson on basic biology to little Martha... but not tonight. Tonight the girl needed only to eat well and get tucked safely into a warm bed once her hair was dry.

When Jacques came home that evening, Martha was already fast asleep in the guest room of their imposing frame house. Marie greeted her handsome husband with a warm kiss saddened only by the news she knew she would have to convey. But she wanted him to eat first. There was a time when Jacques had called Francois his "right-hand," managing the lumber mill as he did and Marie knew the news would give her husband upset.

Izzy had already been given her supper and was asleep in the nursery. John, their first born, along with his brother, Richie, had arrived home from their day of mending fences to keep the cows out of the newly planted fields. Knowing their father insisted everyone make an effort to look "civilized" at the dinner table, they had both washed up and changed out of their work clothing.

Helen at seventeen and her sister Louise, just one year younger, had reached an age where no reminders to look their best were ever needed. Helen was being courted by Thor who took most of his evening meals by her side at Jacques' table and under Jacques' watchful eye. Both sisters always managed to look well-groomed and quite beautifully dainty and helpless despite being able to ride and shoot just as well as their older brothers. And when it came to asserting their wills, they were perhaps even stronger than their brothers.

Every time Jacques looked at Helen she was looking moon-goggled at Thor. Jacques would invariably look next at Louise and then, sighing to himself, wonder what muscle-bound cretin was lurking about the settlement entertaining plans to steal his second daughter away from his home. And there were times when Marie would catch him with a look and a smile and seem to read his mind. Often she would laugh and remind him that they still had little Isabelle, at least for a few more years.

"Caroline and Phillip will be joining us tonight," Marie announced pleasantly, as everyone gathered; she was always pleased to have all her children around her no matter the reason.

"What's the occasion?" John inquired as he walked up to his mother and gave her an affectionate kiss upon her cheek. With his blond curly hair and gracefully muscled physic, he remained a physical copy of his father even down to the small golden moustache except for being some twenty odd years younger.

Marie was saved from answering John's query with the arrival of Caroline and Phillip to the squeals of Jamie. This youngest son was still joyfully wallowing in the prospect of becoming an uncle and having someone to whom he could feel vastly superior. Izzy didn't count as she was his sister and still in the nursery and the thought had not yet occurred to Jamie that this nephew or niece would also be in the nursery for many years to come.

Everyone took their seat and after Grace was said the food, always presented proudly by Margot herself, began to make its rounds in large serving bowls.

"How far did you make it with the fence repair?" Jacques inquired of his eldest.

"Everything's been mended, Papa," John replied while shoveling mashed squash on his plate. Butternut squash kept especially well through the winter and Margot could create a dish using it along with cranberries and sugar that was nothing short of heavenly.

"Until the next time," Richie added rather flippantly while trading the hot biscuits he held for the gravy bowl.

Phillip looked at his mother as he accepted a platter of Margot's fried chicken. He knew from his wife that Marie had news to share but did not know exactly what.

"We have a guest under our roof tonight," Marie finally said, smoothing her napkin neatly upon her lap. From her end of the table, she spoke to her husband at the other end of the table but expected everyone else to listen. "A young girl came into the store today from the frontier; she was travel worn and bedraggled, half starved, and asking for me. Her name is Martha Carver."

Immediately Jacques recognized the sir-name of the Widow Carver who had married Nicholet.

"She has been bathed, dressed, fed, and put to bed; the poor thing was exhausted." Marie had everyone's undivided attention. "All of you save Jamie should remember Francois Nicholet who married the Widow Carver, a scant five years ago," she continued as heads nodded. "I am very sorry to say, the child did not have a pleasant story to tell." Marie proceeded to relay everything she knew to a room grown quiet. Even the clink of silverware against china had ceased. "It would seem she is now an orphan and in need of a home and family so I am hoping we can all agree to welcome her warmly into ours."

"How far did the child travel?" Jacques asked immediately.

"She was on an old plow horse and it sounded to me like five days perhaps," Marie replied. "How far could she have traveled do you think?"

"Depends on how straight a path she took," put in John.

"I think it's amazing that she found us at all," exclaimed Caroline. "All by herself!"

"I will go to the records office and see if there is information regarding what land Nicholet was planning to homestead," Jacques said thoughtfully. He had a very paternalistic attitude toward the settlement and everyone who lived in it or had lived in it.

"What is it you are thinking, Jacques?" Marie asked carefully as she felt her heart beat a little faster.

"We must go there without delay and see for ourselves what has happened. I will organize a party, an armed party, *mon cœur*, nothing for you to worry about. But we must know. There might be survivors and they might need our help." He could see the look of fear upon his wife's lovely face. "Or at the very least… we can give them a decent burial, *n'est-ce pas?*"

Marie swallowed her protest. There was no point. It was the honorable thing to do and her husband was, above all things, a man of honor. She just wished Richard Bonchance was there to accompany Jacques and watch over him for her but they had not seen him this winter.

There was no time to lose and Jacques began to gather volunteers that evening. After dinner it was still light outdoors as they met up in the stables. John was the first to make a case for being included. Pushing twenty, he was restless for some adventure in his life. Jacques knew his son was equally skilled with musket, sword, and thanks to Richard – bow and tomahawk as well. He was also an excellent horseman. Life in the settlement had been pleasantly peaceful but a young man needed real life challenges to test his mettle and so Jacques agreed it would be a good experience.

"Very well," he gave his consent. "Now ride out and spread the word to the mill crew, I am calling a special meeting at the mill in half an hour."

"Papa, you must let me come as well," Phillip said, excited at the prospect.

"Phillip, there are many challenges in this life. Right now your challenge is to accept *not* going but staying to care for your young wife. She is in a delicate condition and does not need the upset of worrying about what is happening to you at the hands of the Indians. No, you stay by her side and watch over her and your mama." Jacques saw his son's face go dark with disappointment but brighten again when he added, "Also, if William Boot decides to join us, I will need someone to manage the mill in our absence. It is an important responsibility, *n'est-ce pas?* Take it not lightly and remember good management is keeping a level head and watching out for your workers. In humility there is strength and never show favoritism."

"Yes, sir." Phillip knew argument was useless when his father spoke so decisively but the sting of being excluded was lessened by the prospect of managing the mill. He found himself looking forward to it.

"Now, join your brother in dividing the task of announcing a meeting."

"I wish to go as well, Mister Power," Thor volunteered. With his experience as a lumber-jack at the frontier from the time he was twelve until William had been persuaded to take over management of the mill, Jacques had little doubt Thor knew how to live rough.

"Can you handle a weapon?" Jacques asked.

"Of course," Thor nodded.

Jacques didn't question. This might give his daughter's suitor the opportunity to prove himself and his ability to take care of her.

"Very well." Jacques agreed. "Now, let us leave for the mill."

The men began to arrive at the mill looking surprised and concerned. Rumors were already flying. When everyone was present, Jacques explained the situation. William immediately volunteered as did nine other mill men; all had known and respected Nicholet. Those remaining assured Jacques they would keep the mill running and he announced Phillip would be the managing authority in the absence of both William and himself.

The next morning was Sunday, Jacques went to the settlement church and made his announcement. They were packing up to leave immediately if anyone wanted to join them, he said. Seven more men volunteered, among them the blacksmith who not only handled horses well but was especially skilled with a hunting knife. The man stood two heads shorter than Thor and William but was all muscle with a body like an iron anvil. Their numbers had swelled to twenty.

Twenty was a good size party, Jacques considered. It was unlikely they would be challenged by just any random raiding party and there had been no talk of all out war of which he was aware.

Everyone was responsible for his own rations, his own horse and weapons. Jacques thought it prudent to bring along several extra mounts. He now knew the general vicinity in which the Nicholets had intended on homesteading on the northern side of a branch feeding into the eastern side of the Delaware River. He didn't know how the child had managed it in only four or five days. And so they pushed westward.

As they rode the first day, they passed farm after farm, each one slowly waking to the new season. Jacques recognized where the old Indian village had been before the hurricane winds had destroyed it. Little was left as the forest was quick to reclaim deserted space. He pushed them onward to the site of the next village which the natives had abandoned to move farther west. On horseback they reached it before dark.

"This is where you were born," Jacques said to John as they tethered their horses and removed their saddles for the night.

"Here?" John looked around at the crumbling remnants of long houses.

"I believe that very spot is where the women's hut stood," Jacques pointed to an area now holding several pine saplings. "Believe me it was harder to reach without horses. Richard and I carried you and your ma-ma home in a litter like one might carry a fallen deer except your ma-ma sat looking the picture of a woodland queen on her throne."

John grinned. He had heard the story several times. The chief had been a bit smitten with his mother, he had been told, and didn't understand or like the fact that his father kept leaving her alone. But that was the life they had to live back then. Now, there was a crude road blazed that connected the farms with the settlement of Chartes Landing, a wide path upon which their herds of pigs and wagons of corn and other produce were driven to market.

They rose early the next morning and had breakfast in the saddle as Jacques continued to push while they had the benefit of the road, crude as it might be. He figured if they kept the pace, they would make it to the end of the road by sunset. He was right. As the farms began to thin, Jacques advised them to be as quiet as possible although a party of twenty does not pass through an area completely unnoticed. And he warned them to be extra watchful.

The next day they continued on. There was more forest now and one had to look very hard to catch evidence of any homesteads. Often it was a stack of rocks marking a property line or the glimpse of a cleared and plowed space. But houses or cabins were often hidden by trees, masked by ravines and hillocks. These were the folks who lived off the land and produced only for their own survival much as he, Marie, and Richard had done those first years. As yet, they had no cash crops or herds to bring to market but they had their own space on which to build, live, and raise a family. Something they most likely had not had before.

Jacques checked his compass as they pushed west by northwest, spreading out as every rider had to pick his own way through the untamed forest, searching to meet up with the Delaware River. They camped that night and were up before dawn to continue on. Finally, they reached a broad river. It was a formidable barrier with no bridge or ferry, Jacques could not imagine getting a wagon across without one or the other. It must be the Delaware, an impressive boundary between the New Jersey and Pennsylvania colonies. If Francois was to homestead on the eastern shore in Jersey, they knew it had to be close. They followed the river northward looking to run into its tributary. When they found it they crossed over and rode on. By mid-morning a shout drew Jacques' attention as one of the men ahead pointed. Jacques rode over and saw a fireplace and chimney standing within the still, ashy ruins of a burnt out cabin. Obviously, the owners had not been welcome in the neighborhood.

Jacques set his jaw and slowly approached. John was right behind him and Jacques did not try to shield his grown son from the reality of this life. They found the teenage boys tied to a tree with rawhide. They had been eviscerated, disemboweled – each with his penis cut off and shoved into his mouth. It was a harsh and brutal warning to others but it was more than that. Jacques knew such an act was a sign of total disrespect. Pure hatred. A hatred so palpable it seemed to hang in the air and drip from the surrounding trees.

Several of the men cut the boys down. Each rapidly decomposing body was wrapped in a blanket. Others began to dig two graves. The rest of the men continued to search, there was no sign of the mother and Jacques believed she most likely had been taken as a captive. But what of Francois? Jacques could not believe the man he had known would have run away but Indians did not take grown men as slaves, only women who were passive and young children who could be adopted and taught to live the Indian way. So where was Francois?

He heard Thor call out and looking over saw the young man gesturing at him. His father was standing by the well.

"There's something down there, Mister Power, sir, I heard something like a moan," the elder Boot said.

Jacques peered down into the well but could see nothing, then he, too, heard what sounded like a low moan.

"Francois? Is that you? Francois?" he yelled down the well. "Say something...anything! *Si tu peux m'entendre, parle!*" he shouted in French.

There was no response and then, another faint groan.

"Rope." Jacques turned to the others. "Who brought rope?" Three men scrambled to their horses and came back with coils of sturdy rope.

"I will go down, Mister Power," Thor volunteered.

"No-no, you and your father are much too large. I count on you to anchor the ropes, keep me from falling and pull me back up."

"No, Papa," John stayed his father with a hand. "Please allow me. I will go down. I will not say I am stronger but I am younger and perhaps a little more flexible, eh? And you will be up here to make sure I don't fail to come back up." He looked at his father intently, his eyes pleading for this opportunity and he saw Jacques give a nod of consent.

John immediately dropped his hat on the ground, stripped off his belt and sword, shucked his coat and pulled off his boots. Wrapping the end of one rope under his arms and around his chest with a secure knot, he took the second rope and in a moment of inspiration, he made a loop at the end in which he stuck his foot, much like a stirrup. The third rope end was lowered down with him for Francois. William and the blacksmith anchored one rope leveraging it around a nearby tree stump and let it out slowly. Jacques and Thor chose a second stump and did the same while several of the men awaited tension on the third. They had a young tree selected to assist them.

With the teams working together, John descended slowly. He noticed the well becoming more narrow as he progressed downward and marveled that Francois had been able to dig it out in the first place. Once he passed below the reach of the daylight and into shadow, John could finally make out the image of Francois below him.

"Just a few more feet," he called back up the well as he began to distinguish what he was looking at. Francois was caught on a very small protruding edge of rock and the dead bloated body of an Indian. The Indian was wedged in such a manner as to have saved the Frenchman from sinking into the water and drowning. The stink was unbearable.

John took the end of the third rope and with some effort, wrapped it around the smaller man's chest beneath his arms. John yanked three times on the rope and watched as it began to lift a delirious Nicholet. John worked to ease the man past his own body until Nicholet's dead weight swung freely. The team above continued to hoist and as Francois' feet began to disappear above him, John gave a yank to his own tether. He could feel his gorge rising as the smell nauseated him despite his efforts to breathe through his mouth. Jacques and the others began to slowly pull up John who was able to help by walking his feet up the wall, while the stones behind him bruised his back. Finally, breaking once again into the sunlight above ground and breathing fresh air was like exiting from a peculiarly cold and vile smelling Hell.

"Don't drink this water," he said with a grimace. "There's a dead and rotting Indian down there. Damn, the stink!" John growled and shook himself quickly putting on his boots. "They must have been fighting and went over the edge together. The Indian ended up wedged in, it gets much narrower as you go down… and he broke Francois' fall and kept him from sinking but..." John looked at his father, "He's been there for what? Ten, eleven days maybe? He had to have drunk the water and it's corrupted by that rotting body."

"No wonder they did what they done to his kids," said one of the mill men. "They couldn't get to him."

"And he took one of theirs with him," said Jacques. "That must have enraged them."

"Maybe it was their leader," suggested Thor.

"He was wearing one of those big, fancy breast plates made of bone and beads and quills," put in John and he shuddered again at the memory of the sight of that bloated body, the stench still in his nostrils.

"That usually indicates an important man," added Jacques who had visited with numerous tribes in his trading days. "Come, we must make a fire to warm Francois, build a travois to take him back, and see to the burial of the boys. I ask you all to pray for Nicholet for his fate is in the hands of God."

With the graves dug, they buried the boys. Jacques said a few words and John tried not to think of the brutality of their last moments alive.

"You did well, son," Jacques said privately to John. "It will help if you scrub the smell of corruption out of your shirt and hang it by the fire to dry before nightfall. We will stay here tonight.”

John was glad to strip off his shirt and using the water from his canteen and the bar of soap he had packed, he did his best to wash and rinse the stink away. As he worked however, he realized his breeches held the same odor and he was not ready to remove those. He hung his shirt to dry, the taut muscles of his young torso reflecting the firelight in the growing dusk.

“It’s a lost cause,” he said quietly to his father, disgust evident in his voice. “I should have brought a change of clothes. Why didn’t I think of that?”

Jacques smiled. “Some lessons are learned by the experiences we have. I believe that is what they mean when they say ‘live and learn.’ Here,” he tossed John a clean pair of breeches. “See how these fit and I would not roll the other into your saddlebag.”

“What should I do with it?” John asked as he stripped his breeches from his lean body.

“I would put them under your saddle blanket until you get home. I do not think your horse will mind, he has his own scent, *n’est-ce pas?*”

It was getting late. They hunkered down to their suppers around several small fires. William and Thor joined Jacques and John as they watched over Francois.

“What about the woman, his wife?” William asked at last as nothing had been said about her fate.

“Yes, I know. It seems heartless to go back home now but we have no idea what tribe or clan this was or where we might find her. And although I have the most experience with Indians of anyone here...” Jacques grunted. “still I have no idea where to look and cannot speak their languages. I wish Richard Bonchance was here.”

“But we cannot leave her to be tortured,” Thor was visibly upset.

“I am quite certain she has been taken as a slave,” Jacques explained. “It is not good medicine to torture women; if they did not consider her of some value, they would have left her dead right here. Her life may be rough but no rougher than it was here at the frontier. She will survive if she has the will...”

“Papa, surely you don’t mean to just forget about her?” John asked quickly. His shirt had dried and he was glad to put it back on. The mosquitoes were out for blood.

“No-no, you do not allow me to finish. If she has the will she will survive until we can find someone knowledgeable enough to search for her and buy her back.”

“Buy her?! Do you think they would be willing to sell her?” William sounded surprised.

“Most likely that was the whole point in taking her. There is often a time period in which captives are left unharmed and unmolested, nothing is done to diminish their value while the captor awaits an offer of ransom. Only if none comes is the woman’s fate determined.”

“What fate?” John looked up from the hardtack he was removing from his saddlebag.

"If she is of childbearing age, someone will take her as a mate."

"Whether she wants it or not?" John scowled.

Jacques shrugged and nodded.

"And if she is beyond childbearing?"

"Then she is just a work slave."

"And if she can't work?" John persisted.

"If she cannot even work, to her captor she has no value. But Madame Nicholet has someone willing to ransom her. Right now my bigger concern is Francois and whether we can get him home for care without killing him."

The camp was sleeping. Jacques heard an owl hoot but to his ear it did not sound authentic.

"John!" he whispered sharply and taking his musket and sword, he rolled away from the fire and deeper into the shadows.

John awoke. Seeing what his father was doing, he took his own sword and scabbard, poked Thor in the leg and grabbing his musket rolled after his father. The elder Boot was already awake and alert.

In the dark of the underbrush the four men spread themselves belly down, each at a different compass point, peering into the night.

"Do you see them?" Jacques whispered very softly.

"Yah," William responded with a low growl.

"We must sound an alarm," John uttered just as Jacques drew a bead on an approaching native. The musket ball ripped through the man's chest and the sound of the discharge woke the rest of the camp.

It was a blinding skirmish, a typical strike-hard-fast-and-melt-away maneuver full of noise; the kind of attack for which the natives were known. It happened so quickly there was no time to reload muskets. Everyone got one shot, then knives and swords came into play. At one point, Jacques felt his head being lifted by his hair but his sword was longer than the arm holding him and he skewered his attacker. He felt warm blood soak him as the body fell against him. Then, just as suddenly it was over and the enemy disappeared into the dark. It was effective in keeping everyone agitated and guaranteed no one would get anymore sleep for the rest of the night.

"Who was on lookout duty?" Jacques asked as they doused what was left of their camp fires. By moonlight, he checked on all of the men, doing a count as he went. One of his mill workers had been grazed with a war club. One of the townsmen had an arrow in his shoulder and another a knife wound in his thigh. He tallied up seventeen men including himself which left the three who were on guard duty unaccounted for. Jacques felt more wet seeping into his shirt and discovered to his shocked amazement that he was bleeding from his left side. It was too dark to see much of anything but it burned and he pulled his coat more tightly around himself.

The men who had been posted as guards were found in the morning shot through with multiple arrows, throats cut. So – four wounded and three dead, not a bad night's work for the raiding party, Jacques thought grimly.

They did not know how many of the Indians they had wounded but morning also showed them three dead ones. If there were more, the bodies had been taken away. So they had inflicted as much damage as they had received. Since they were leaving now, hopefully they would not be attacked again.

"I want the decorative clothing removed," Jacques spoke in a commanding voice to cover the fact that he was shaking inside. He looked at the native he had shot and then at the one he had skewered with his sword. This had to be the one who cut him as he fell against him. He had never actually killed another human being before and he thought of Marie. Then he thought of his son. John seemed to be bearing up under the night's attack better than he. "Also, collect and save those arrows and the lances," Jacques continued. "Anything that will help a scout identify which tribe they come from, anything that will help us discover who has Madame Nicholet. We are going to need a second travois for the wounded."

With the morning light, the blood seeping into Jacques' clothing was evident as John looked over at his father and took note of the pallor of his face.

"Papa, come with me." John grabbed hold of Jacques and steered him to a tree stump. "Sit down, please. You did not tell me you were wounded. Let me see."

"It is not so bad," Jacques tried to protest. "A mere bee sting!"

"You've been bleeding all night! Mama's gunna have a fit when she sees this," his son teased to mask his concern as he discovered a long gaping slice down his father's side.

"Does it look bad?" Jacques asked anxiously. "I cannot see it but it does not feel so bad. Perhaps it will heal before we get home..."

"Yeahhh..." John shook his head from side to side noting bone had been laid bare in several spots. "I think I ought to pour some whiskey on it, like old Doc St. Claire used to do. I need to stitch this together."

Jacques nodded a tight lipped consent and rested his hand upon his musket to keep his arm out of John's way. He stiffened up like a board when he felt the fiery sting of the alcohol but prided himself on not making a sound although his breathing became very ragged. Finally he croaked, "Do the same to the others."

"Right, misery likes company, huh? Here - have a couple pulls on this flask. It's not your cognac but it's good enough for the purpose," John joked to distract his father as he tossed him the whiskey and opened a pouch he had taken from his saddle bag. He withdrew the necessary supplies and began sewing up the wound. "I may not have known enough to bring an extra pair of clothes but I did bring some essentials."

"Umph, I do not know which is the more painful, your needlework or swallowing this rot-gut." Jacques took another swig. "How do you know these things?" he asked, genuinely surprised at his son's skill.

"I'm not a little child anymore, Papa. I've seen things, I watch, I listen, I learn."

"So you do… and I am very proud of you. You fought well last night, *mon fils*, but this is something I might not share with your ma-ma."

"Right," John grinned again. He knew the only thing his father was truly afraid of was making his mother worry. "But good luck trying to hide this," he added, nodding toward the wound.

It took considerable time but once John had dressed his father's wound, he went on to the other wounded. The thigh wound had bled cleanly. John flushed it with whiskey while the fellow swore a litany of blue guaranteed to put a blush on the cheeks of the most jaded soldier. With that done, the stitches he required felt like butterfly kisses.

Next, John went to the arrow wound. To simply pull the arrow out would cause more muscle damage but it was not very deep. It would have been simpler if the arrow had gone all the way through exposing the barbed head on the backside. John gave a cup of whiskey to the man.

"Here, drink this fast," he insisted and his patient happily complied. Then, John again took pains to flush the site with whiskey. He didn't want to have to cut the arrow out so he patiently worked to remove it by slowly twisting it to allow the muscle fibers to clear the barbed edges with minimal damage. The swallowed whiskey had the desired affect. His patient still hurt but he didn't care. When the arrowhead finally did come out, the wound bled profusely but with pressure the bleeding finally stopped. John used the cleanest bit he could find of the fellow's shirt and bound up the shoulder. He put the fellow's coat back on and fashioned a sling.

"That's going to be really sore, you can expect it but watch for any redness or sign of pus. If you see such, the doctor will have to clean it out."

"Thanks, boyo, that's some mighty fine work you did."

"You're welcome… I'm sorry I don't know your name."

"Just call me Sweeney, and I'm thinkin' I should be able to mount a horse."

"I think you may be right, Sweeney," John smiled, "as long as you don't feel dizzy. I don't want you to break your neck now falling off your mount. I've spent too much time fixing you up."

Sweeney laughed good-naturedly.

Finally John faced the head wound. The mill man's name was Ethan and John wasn't sure what he could do for him. A strong swing with a war club could smash a skull and kill instantly. Fortunately, Ethan had ducked just in time and sustained only a glancing blow. But John had no idea if the man had been hit hard enough to crack his skull or not, and if so, what could be done for it.

"Ethan, when you were hit did you black out?"

"Naw."

"Did you see stars?"

"Yeah, fuckin' stars and it damn well hurt."

"Can I take a look?"

"Sure, Johnny, only charge you a penny," he laughed at his joke and then grimaced and clutched at his head.

"Just sit quiet for a moment," John soothed.

"I sure could use some of that whiskey ya got."

"Uh-hm," John responded while examining the wound. He dabbed whiskey gently over the split flesh and Ethan gave a shuddering gasp.

"I-I didn't mean there! I meant to drink!"

"I know. But I'm thinking we ought to try some water first and see how you do with that," John replied. "Does your head ache?"

"Only like there's a midget with a hammer banging inside me skull."

"Have you felt like puking?"

"A little, but I didn't."

"It's fine if you do but like a hangover it will probably make your head feel worse. I'll wrap a bandage just to keep it clean but you need to have Doc Ajax look at you when we get back."

Ethan nodded and leaned back against the tree with a grunt.

Above ground and away from the chill of the well, Francois' fever climbed and he was obviously badly dehydrated. He needed all the clean water they could get into him but once they forded the tributary and headed east, they knew they would pass no other rivers or creeks until they reached the abandon Indian village of John's birth.

Jacques advised everyone to drink deeply at the river, fill their canteens, and conserve their water while he asked for voluntary contributions for Francois and Ethan. Ethan had his own canteen but John was encouraging him to drink a half cup every thirty minutes. All were happy to share but travel homeward was much slower dragging the two travois.

Jacques would not admit to the pain of his side but he did recognize his own thirst. They had only traveled a day and a half and already his canteen was feeling quite light. It was the loss of blood, he told himself that was driving his thirst. As they plodded along, he saw the smoke of a cabin in the distance.

"John," he called to his son. "Have everyone condense the water supply to empty a few canteens. I know mine needs refilling. I am certain Ethan's does as well. Perhaps we could empty a few others. There is a homestead over in that direction. We can get refills."

Jacques told William to continue their slow pace on to the crude road while he detoured off with John and one of the younger men from the mill to seek out the cabin. They would take the empty canteens, fill them, and catch up to the others again.

Riding to a hillock, Jacques asked the young lumber-jack to climb a tree and sight the smoke again to give them direction. When he came back down he told

Jacques and John they looked to be two or three miles away. They rode on and eventually found themselves looking at a well-constructed cabin. John saw his father wince from the harder ride and took the initiative to call out a greeting as they brought their horses to a halt.

"Hello?" John called, wishing he had insisted his father stay with the other wounded and, if not on one of the slow moving travois, at least only walking his horse.

A woman came out cradling a musket in her arms as she wiped her hands on her apron. She was followed by a youngster who also had a musket in hand. She shaded her eyes as she looked at them waiting to hear what they wanted.

Jacques removed his hat and nodded from the saddle. "We have run out of water, madame, and it would be very much appreciated if we might fill our canteens at your well."

"Thems a lot of canteens," the woman observed distrustfully.

"Yes, madam. We are actually a party of twenty on the road heading back to Chartes Landing. We have several wounded and a very ill man, all who desperately need water. The ill man is Monsieur Nicholet from the Nicholet homestead, perhaps you knew them?" Jacques asked.

The woman shook her head.

"A family of five, they came out here to homestead about five years ago, man, wife, two sons and a daughter."

"That sounds like the Carver family, Ma," said the boy, "Pa got together a group to help them dig a well."

Jacques nodded his head in the affirmative.

"Oh, the Carvers," she said in sudden recognition. "Why'd you call 'em 'Nick-o-lay'?"

"Only the children's last name is Carver. It was a second marriage for both and I am most sorry to say the boys were slain in the Indian attack. The girl escaped and made it back to Chartes Landing which is how we knew what had happened. We came to see if anyone survived and were also attacked." He gestured to his blood stained attire. "We found Monsieur Nicholet at the bottom of his well, still alive but in a fever and I believe his wife has been carried off by the hostiles."

"Oh my," the woman uttered not unsympathetically. "My mister told 'em they was takin' a big chance living there."

"Why is that?" Jacques asked.

She shrugged. "Guess the injuns just decided the little river was far enough. No one whose gone north of it in these parts has ever made it. They get tired of the harassment and leave. Don't recall anyone ever getting killed though… until now." She looked at the lad who nodded his agreement. "Well, come on, I guess you best get yer canteens filled so you can be on yer way. I'll bring you a pitcher. Can't rightly fill canteens with a bucket."

"Thank you," Jacques spoke for them all, trying not to appear as weak as he felt.

The three men, each occupied with his own thoughts, said little as they rode back seeking to intersect the crude road again. The jostling of a trot was aggravating Jacques' side and causing him significant pain. He worked hard not to show it but John caught sight of a telltale grimace and insisted they slow down.

"Lloyd," John said to the lumberman when they reached the road, "take these canteens back to the group. Make sure Ethan keeps drinking his water. We'll be right behind you but my father needs to slow a bit."

Lloyd nodded his agreement. On the road one needed only to follow the deep ruts made by the slow moving travois and Lloyd urged his animal to a gallop.

For a short time Jacques did not argue as his son reached over and slowed both their horses to a walk.

"Papa, you should have stayed with the travois. No, you should be on a travois. You've lost too much blood."

"I am fine, son."

"No, you're not." *You don't always have to be the hero,* he thought but dare not say it. "It's like I told that Sweeney fella, it would be a damn shame if you survived your wound only to fall off your horse and break your neck."

Jacques chuckled softly. "Yes, yes, it would."

"I'm serious, Papa. Please, if you feel the least bit light headed say something, please."

"Worry not, *mon fils,* I will let you know when you must worry, *n'est-ce pas?* In truth, the gallop is less painful to endure than the trot, so after this gentle walk we can gallop again and catch-up."

Jacques kept going. In a short time, they were within sight of the rest of their party who received them with relief. Jacques knew his wound was bleeding again and he forced himself to drink more water.

He watched his son jump off his horse and check on the other wounded. Jacques reined up his horse nearby. He wanted to dismount but realized he did not trust himself to do so without falling. He was light-headed.

John finished caring for the wounded and came back over to his father. "How are you doing, Papa?"

"I think perhaps now you may worry," Jacques replied and saw his world begin to darken.

John yelled for help as he caught his father and eased him to the ground. Thor rushed over to assist. "He needs to go on a travois," John said. "He's lost way too much blood. Damn! I never should have let him ride for water." The head injury and the leg injury were sharing a travois. Francois was on one alone. "Mister Boot," John called up to Thor's father. The older man heard and dismounted.

"Yah, John, with what can I help?"

"Tell me what you'd advise. Papa has to go on a travois, he's lost too much blood but I don't want to put anyone next to Mister Nicholet, he smells too foul.

But I hate to take the time to build another travois. What should we do?"

"John, it take no time for so many to build one little sled," he gestured. "We make fast." He smiled encouragement to the younger man.

William signaled and everyone dismounted. Within thirty minutes they had a fresh travois put together and attached to Jacques' horse. When Jacques regained consciousness he accepted his fate but told his son that his only condition was that when they neared Chartes Landing, he would leave the travois and remount his horse.

"There is no way I am arriving within the sight of your ma-ma, blood stained and on my back."

At this John nodded and grinned. "Agreed." But for the rest of the trip back home, John took every opportunity to check his father's dressing and encourage him to drink water.

Chapter 21

Marie was consumed with worry but said nothing that was not positive as she kept busy in the store. Every day seemed more like twenty. It was always hardest to wait with nothing but wild imaginings to fill your mind. Martha said little but seemed happiest spending time around Margot and watching her prepare food. Marie felt so sorry for the child who hardly seemed like a child at all. Forced to grow up and leave her childhood behind, Marie thought sympathetically. Martha reminded her a little of her own childhood.

It took the rescue party more than twice as long to get back home as it had taken to find the homestead but Jacques was grateful for the slower pace. His side felt inflamed but he wasn't bleeding anymore since he'd moved to the travois. However, he was determined not to arrive back to the settlement like a casualty. He would not do that to Marie. Finally they reached the coast and the group rode into town. Jacques back on horseback as agreed upon. In a settlement the size of Chartes Landing such an arrival was hard to miss.

Marie saw them from the windows of her store and throwing all dignity aside, she raced out the door to meet Jacques. He saw her coming and got down stiffly from his horse to catch her up in his right arm, trying to hide the pain the movements caused him. He could not swing her around but he kissed her soundly and lingeringly upon the lips, keeping her to his right side.

Neighbors standing nearby looked away and muttered "They're French, you know," by way of explaining to each other their leading citizen's total disregard for the accepted mores concerning public displays of affection. A respectable Englishman kept his feelings better guarded and his more tender sentiments behind closed doors.

For one long moment the couple looked into each other's eyes knowing they did not need to say anything more personal to each other at that moment.

"We found Francois," Jacques said at last. "Only by the grace of God is he still alive but he has a high fever and has not eaten since the attack. I will tell you all about it later." Jacques indeed would tell his wife more later but he had no intention of sharing every gory detail.

"And John?" Marie asked.

"Right here, Mama," John said, coming up to give his mother a kiss on the cheek and receiving a huge motherly hug in return.

"The rest of the family?" she asked hesitantly.

Jacques shook his head. "I will talk to Martha," he volunteered. "And I must inform the families of the three that fell," he added without emphasis.

"Oh, Jacques, she already thought everyone was dead and cried her heart out. Then, when you all left, she began to hope again. Now, it will be another fresh wound."

"I know, I am sorry," he patted his wife's hand, standing with his left side away from her. "And Francois may yet die but we think her mother is alive and so, for now, Martha is not an orphan. This is on what we must focus."

"You think Madame Nicholet is alive? A captive?"

"I think so. The Indians may wish to ransom her."

Marie nodded. "Wait…" her eyes suddenly snapped back to Jacques'. "Did you just say the three that *fell?* They are dead?"

"Yes."

"So there was more fighting," she concluded and he could not deny it. "Oh, *mon Dieu!* You and John…" she turned to hide the tears in her eyes. Only then did she notice the wounded men riding in the travois and the dead men tied over their horses.

The town barber who was also the undertaker took charge of the dead while the wounded were brought to the Power home. Someone went for the town doctor.

Jane Sims was beside herself trying to prevent an onslaught of dirt invading the Power home. There were the actual wounded and then those who helped bring them indoors. They seemed oblivious to even a simple request to wipe their boots at the door. The families came in, wives and children, emotional, crying, wringing their hands. She could hardly deny them entry. But at the busybodies and just plain gawkers she put down her foot. If they didn't scrape their shoes thoroughly, they were not welcome inside the house.

Doctor Archibald Ajax was a younger man, not rigid in his thinking. He had never attended so prestigious a place of learning as the Parisian Medical Academy, but he prided himself on reading all the medical publications he could get his hands on. He gave no argument when Jacques insisted the men's wounds be cleaned with whiskey or some form of alcohol. And since they had all bled with such wounds, Ajax saw no point in bleeding them again except for Ethan Gates.

"With a head wound like this, bleeding is critical to relieve pressure on the brain," Ajax argued. "And a good physic, if the patient is conscious."

Jacques wavered. "As you wish," he finally consented, "but Monsieur Nicholet – no!"

To not bleed Nicholet flew in the face of all basic medical knowledge dating back to Aristotle and his writings on Humors. Bleeding out the evil humors was a time honored medical practice for fevers.

Jacques remained adamant.

"He has been down a well for almost two weeks with no food and only be-fouled water, I think he needs every drop of blood he has," Jacques pronounced and Doctor Ajax very reluctantly complied.

Marie with the help of Jane cut the filthy clothes from Francois' abused body. He had a multitude of scrapes and bruises – from the fighting or from the fall? They could not tell and it did not matter. More importantly there seemed to be no broken bones but was there anything broken within? Every small injury was cleaned with whiskey until his flesh lost the scent of rotting carrion and took on the smell of a tavern. Easier to nurse without clothing, they left him naked between clean linen with warm bricks at his feet and cool rags on his head.

Marie could not help but note the change in the robust man they had known for more than twenty years. Laid out on the bed, he looked so helpless and fragile. His hair had thinned and gone very gray and once his face was shaved the slackness of his skin became apparent. She thought he was a year or two or three younger than her Jacques but he looked more like he could be Jacques' father or even his grand-father. In her mind's eye she saw the happy, hopeful, healthy man who led his new family out to homestead on the frontier. It had taken barely five years to turn him into a broken old man. It had been far more difficult than he had imagined because the Indians did not want them there. But almost two weeks down a well had not snuffed out his life. And now? His step-sons were dead, his wife was a captive and his step-daughter... Unconsciously, Marie turned to look at the girl who sat hud-dled in the corner, silently watching.

Jacques lay in his bed mulling over the problems at hand and trying to ignore the discomfort of his left side. Richard would not return until the end of autumn, or longer, and there was no one within the small settlement of Chartes Landing who had any real experience with the native tribes. Suddenly he realized he might write to the nearest fort and see if their scouts could help. He was used to being so fiercely independent and self-sufficient that he had neglected to consider that for which he paid his taxes – the protection and assistance of the British king's men.

Under Doctor Ajax's advise Jacques had been bandaged very tightly to inhibit movement. "Son," Jacques said to Richie who sat keeping a wary eye on his fa-ther. "If I am not to leave this bed I will need the chamber pot before my bladder bursts." That detail attended to, Jacques next asked for his portable writing desk.

Fourteen year old Richie had been tasked with guard duty and was under orders to report directly to his mother if his father tried to leave his bed. The lad brought over the small lap sized leather writing desk and a new quill. Trying to find a more comfortable position, Jacques first shifted left to free up his writing hand and was rewarded by a sharp burning pain that was a reminder not to twist his torso. Shifting back hurt just as much. He discovered sitting up very straight was indeed the more, if not *comfortable* exactly, at least tolerable. He proceeded to compose a quick letter.

"Richie, I need for you to take this to the post bag down by the docks awaiting the first packet boat heading south to Delaware Bay."

Richie looked hesitantly at the letter and his father.

"You know the bags I mean; there are always two, one for the boat going north to New York Towne and one for the boat going south to the Delaware Bay. Do not confuse the two. This," Jacques waived the letter, "must go south." Rather then wait on a letter, Jacques would have jumped into a boat and simply gone to the fort in person but for Marie.

Richie nodded and took the letter but before he would leave, he called in his ten year old brother James. Obviously the pair had been established as a guard dog tag team.

Yesterday upon Jacques' arrival home Marie had insisted on helping him out of his bloody clothes, and discovering it was mostly his own blood he was wearing, she was now in high dudgeon over his lack of concern for himself. She had called in Ajax to appraise the wound. He had nothing to add to the work John had done but did recommend a stiff bandage re-enforced with metal stays and a very tight binding, much like a corset, to keep Jacques from constantly re-opening the wound. That accomplished, Marie had forced him to bed rest after several snifters of his favorite cognac and he had to admit the hours of quiet, uninterrupted sleep in a real bed had done wonders. Marie had her bed made up on the beautifully carved divan they had acquired several years ago. She sought not to disturb Jacques but he missed her in their bed and he knew she was in no temperament to see him leave again so quickly.

With the letter dispatched, Jacques wanted to seek out his wife. A little extra attention might sooth her sensibilities, he thought. After all, the time would come when he would most definitely need to go to negotiate with the captors in person. He didn't see young Jamie as being much of an obstacle but as soon as Jacques' foot hit the floor, Louise appeared, obviously the captain of the guard. He knew of only one person in the world who was a more charming and irresistible bully. This apple fell not far from that tree.

"What are you doing, Father?" Louise asked as she stood blocking his ability to stand up from the bed. She rarely called him "father" which set the tone for this particular conversation.

"I thought I would go to see your mother," he replied, feeling inexplicably like he had just been caught with his hands in the sweets jar.

"She is nursing Mister Nicholet while Doctor Ajax is out seeing his other patients and she says you are not to leave your bed," Louise said while lifting his feet
back into bed. She fluffed his pillows expertly and with a gentle hand pushed him
back against them. She straightened the sheet and coverlet over him and tucked
them tightly under the mattress, on both sides.

He looked up at the faces of his children staring down at him and felt pitifully
out numbered and very much like a cocooned caterpillar.

"How is Francois doing?" he asked, shifting the attention away from himself.

Louise shook her head. "Not well, his fever goes unchecked and the doctor in-
sists he should be bled." She fixed him with a calculating eye. "Perhaps…"

"What?" he frowned.

"Papa, I think Mister Nicholet is going to die no matter what we do. Perhaps it
would be better if you allowed the doctor to bleed him. If you do not, will he not
blame you for Mister Nicholet's death?"

The savvy little thing had a point although if someone did wish to blame him,
they could do so anyway, claiming he had waited too long to give his consent.

"Perhaps you are right," he said at last. "Tell your ma-ma I wish to see her as
soon as the doctor returns."

Louise nodded sweetly, kissed her father on the forehead and then placed a cool
hand on his brow. "You are also feeling feverish," she said with a frown of her
own.

He raised his right hand and pointed his index finger. "I am *not* to be bled, understand? I have lost more than enough blood already."

"Of course, Papa."

"Marie," Jacques, dressed in a colorful cotton banyan, called softly from the doorway into "the sick room" where they had put Francois. Jacques had finished a
breakfast tray she had brought to him. And after two and a half days in bed, he was
reasserting himself as head of the household. He was bored, sick of chicken soup
and sweetened aspic, and insisted on getting onto his feet, eating real food, and
seeing for himself how Francois was doing. His compromise with Marie was that
he would not go down the stairs until tomorrow. He found his compassionate wife
sitting close to the bed so she could keep changing out the cooling towel on the
fevered man's head. "How is he?"

"Not well. The doctor will be back shortly. I just sent him to the kitchen to get
some food; the poor man has not eaten since yesterday."

"And what of you?" Jacques asked as he came up behind her and began to massage her shoulders, proving there was nothing wrong with his hands or arms.

"I am fine." She leaned back against him, then sat up straight again. "No, I am
not fine. Why has this happened, Jacques? What has changed since we first came
to this place?"

"I am afraid you need only to look out of the window to answer that. Perhaps we here have not grown that much but from what I understand people are swarming into the Pennsylvania colony, not just Quakers but many others who seek religious freedom or just some acres to call their own. Philadelphia, the colony's main settlement, is reported to be growing more quickly than New York Towne. Remember your Indians friends who left as they felt themselves being crowded by all the new settlers, their hunting grounds being plowed into fields?"

"Yes, of course, they went farther west."

"Yes, they went farther west where I know other tribes already were living and hunting. They already have had to adjust and share hunting grounds and cultivation space but now white settlers are moving into those same lands farther west, cutting down more of the forests and plowing up more land. It would seem some tribe has drawn a line in the sand."

Marie twisted around to look up at her husband.

"We spoke to one of the homesteaders," he explained, "she said no one who has tried to cross that small tributary river has ever stayed. The Indians do not allow it. It sounds to me like they mean for the settlers to come no farther into their little corner of the world. Perhaps Francois should have heeded the warnings and come back to Chartes Landing."

"It just seems so unnecessary to fight, to kill… to die. There is so much land."

Jacques leaned down and kissed his wife's head. "I know, it seems like that." She nuzzled him then heard him inhale sharply.

"And what of you? How does your wound heal?" she asked, pulling open the banyan and lifting his shirt to uncover his bandaging. He had not put on his breeches and tried, in recognition of their lack of privacy, to keep his nether regions covered with his shirt tails.

"Not to worry. It is just tender and I twisted which I should not do."

"Let me see, Jacques. Let me see," she insisted and carefully but firmly undid his wrapping. "I cannot believe our son stitched you up. A very fine piece of embroidery." She looked up at him. "There is still a little bleeding but no pus. It is mending but do not get it wet just yet...which means stay out of boats, yes?"

How did she know what he had been thinking?

Jacques nodded an unspoken agreement and stood still as she redid his protective binding and pulled down his shirt, brushing it into place.

"Madame Power," Jacques whispered, "if you wish me not to rip open my stitches, you must keep your hands to yourself."

She smiled at that. "You are right, of course, I must have patience… as do you." She turned and removed the towel from Francois' forehead. Her smile disappeared. She could feel the heat in the cloth. "Oh, Jacques, he burns much too hot and nothing seems to help. I made a very strong willow bark tea. It did nothing. And he is weaker since the doctor bled him. I am afraid…."

Martha walked into the room and Jacques quickly closed his banyan. "He's going to die, ain't he?" she stated rather matter-of-factly.

Marie looked into the girl's eyes and suddenly any platitude sounded childish and patronizing. "I do not know," she answered truthfully, "but one should never give up hope."

"I'll be sorry to see him go. He was good to us. Ma will miss him a lot," she said placidly, then saying no more she went to the chair in the corner and sat there dry-eyed and watchful.

Jacques had two more chairs brought into the small room. It was a bit crowded but when the doctor returned there was a chair for each of them. And so they kept their vigil. Late that night Francois slipped away.

"He's gone," Ajax said softly as he checked once more for a pulse.

Martha immediately left her chair without a word and went to her room.

"He told me if he had not met the Widow Carver, he would have been happy to stay here and run the mill," Jacques said to no one in particular.

"But he was such a sad and lonely man until he met her," Marie reminded her husband.

"It seems he was a man destined to never be truly happy for long." And Jacques considered not for the first time how bountifully and truly blessed he was. Both he and Francois had remained true to their spiritual beliefs and been forced to flee their homes but whereas he had been blessed with so much happiness, Francois had suffered so much tragedy. And there was no understanding the *why*.

Marie said a silent prayer and good-bye over Francois' body, then patting Jacques on the arm she murmured a good-night to both men with a pointed reminder that Jacques needed his rest.

Jacques kissed her hand and murmured he would not be long.

After she had left the room, Ajax spoke.

"Mister Power… do you know much about autopsy?"

"The meaning of the word escapes me," Jacques shook his head.

"I realize people can have very strong feelings about the practice, but there have been great strides made in medicine by being able to open a body up and look inside… oh, once they are dead of course. It provides learning for the physician which he can use in treating future patients."

Jacques found the very idea repugnant but said nothing, waiting for Ajax to continue.

"I will never be able to go to the best European schools of science and medicine where I understand such things are now being done rather routinely as a matter of course study and classwork. The Church has finally dropped its opposition to the practice. I'm not certain where they get their cadavers, ah... subjects... but here in the small communities of the colonies I would expect most families to strongly object to the idea."

"I think you are right," Jacques said evenly.

"But this circumstance might provide me with one of the few opportunities I may ever have to do an autopsy. To look inside Mister Nicholet and try to under-stand exactly what caused his death."

"A fever..."

"That is what we say but fever is only a symptom. What was the cause? He had no serious wounds that we could see. I suspect something was damaged inside and I would like to know what, if possible."

Jacques carefully rose from his chair and went over to the bed. He stared for a time at the face of Francois Nicholet. It no longer looked much like him at all. He pulled the sheet up over the body.

"Why do you tell me this?" he asked, turning to Ajax.

"I... well... you... I mean, the man has no family to ask or to object...

"Martha...?"

"She's just a child and isn't even his real daughter..."

"His wife...?"

"Is yet to be found and when she is or *if* she is, he will be long time buried by then, she would never need to know since although there is nothing wrong with it, the knowledge might make her uncomfortable."

"So you are asking *my* permission?" Jacques said looking quizzically at the young Englishman.

"Yes, I guess I am," Ajax met his gaze with an honest admission. "It is an un-comfortable issue but discomfort is usually the road to learning."

Jacques suddenly felt lead-footed as he stood looking between the doctor and Nicholet's remains. He was exhausted and could not think.

"Let me show you to a guest room so you can stretch out for a few hours and sleep. I must have time to think and will see you again in the morning."

Marie stirred when Jacques entered their bedroom. She pretended to be asleep but by the candle's light she watched him remove his banyan, every move calcu-lated to favor his wounded side. She guessed it bothered him much more than he admitted. He needed rest so badly, she thought, his own body was trying to heal amidst the demands of everyone else. He left his long shirt on and as he ap-proached the bed she raised the sheet to welcome him in beside her.

"You are awake?" Clearly surprised, he crawled in carefully. "And back in our bed, I see." Because of his grunts, she could not tell if he was pleased with that fact or not.

"Unless it pains you...?" she suggested. Perhaps he was hurting even more than she realized.

He shook his head. "I always sleep much better when you are at my side."

"Are you sure? I can move back to the divan.," she offered.

"No-no, please do not leave," he said quickly. In the candlelight she thought he looked a little sad. "Only you should understand, I cannot... I mean I suppose I might but I do not think I should..."

"What?"

"... make love with you just yet... "

"Oh, Jacques, my sweet husband, just stretch yourself out, *mon amour*, and sleep," she whispered, stroking the side of his face with great tenderness. She could feel the rasp of his whiskers against her finger tips. "I think I might be just a little angry if you even tried, you know your wound has barely closed."

He did not argue. Instead she heard him sigh deeply and pop his toes in a stretch. "I admit this bed feels wonderful right now especially with you here where you should be." He squeezed her thigh and then he stretched out his right arm inviting her to cuddle up close to his unharmed side. "And so much better than our nights spent on the ground. I confess sleeping on the ground is not as easy as it was when I was twenty."

She chuckled softly in agreement then closed her eyes. "This has been much too long a day for you, my love. I allow you to leave the bed and you stay up for fifteen hours straight. Tomorrow, you must stay in bed until the sun is high in the sky," she murmured and kissed him softly, her right arm laying lightly upon his chest.

If only I could, mon cœur, *but tomorrow morning I must decide what is to be done with Francois' body.*

Within thirty seconds they were both sound asleep.

The next morning Jacques slept later than usual and awoke to the disappointment of an empty bed beside him. Marie was already about her day. He felt strong enough, however, to slip on his breeches although boots were currently out of the question and so he slipped his feet into something Marie had brought to him called *mules,* a hard heeled slip-on with no back. The chief advantage being, he did not have to bend over to put them on. The disadvantage being that he felt damned insecure navigating down the stairs.

When he reached the breakfast room he found John still with his food.

"Son?" Jacques nodded as he walked a little stiffly into the room, grateful to find no one else around.

"Good morning, Papa. You appear to be feeling better."

"Good morning. And yes, I am fine but if these bindings make me feel anything like a woman feels wearing her corset, it is a complete puzzlement to me why they do."

John chuckled.

"I want you to bring your breakfast to my study," Jacques said as he lost no time going to the buffet filled with food being kept warm by small candles under chafing dishes. He filled a plate with scrambled eggs, bacon, a generous stack of blueberry hot cakes, some cheese and slices of melon. He put the plate on a tray, poured a large mug of hot coffee, went back and grabbed a serving of butter along with a fresh muffin, a small pitcher of warm maple syrup and tableware with a napkin. Picking the heavy tray up he winced only slightly and led the way to his study. The tray went onto his desk and he immediately turned back to close the door behind John.

"What is it?" John asked, feeling equal parts surprise, confusion, and apprehension.

"Sit down," Jacques invited and pointed to a spot on the desk across from him. "Put your plate there and pull the chair up."

John did as told and waited.

"Eat-eat-eat," Jacques waved at his son's plate, "while it is still warm. And be grateful for *real* food," he added with a smile.

The coffee was hot and Jacques could only manage a few sips before he said, "I have… a problem? No-no-no." he shook his head, rejecting that description. "A dilemma?" he raised his shoulders, "not really that either. A… situation? Yes, it is most definitely a situation and perhaps a moral dilemma which could lead to a problem."

John had never see his father quite like this before. His father was a man admirably well grounded and confident in himself and his moral compass, so sure in his definitions of right and wrong. He was never confused about which was the honorable path or the proper course of action.

"You have heard that Francois died last night?" Jacques asked, his finely arched eyebrows lifted and gathered in sadness.

"Yes, Jane told me. I think the doc is still here... sleeping."

Jacques nodded his head as he chewed his first mouthful of bacon in many days. "He was exhausted. And you… you truly surprised me in how well you took over the role of field doctor. Have you been reading our anatomy books?"

"Some."

"And have you heard of something called *autopsy?*" he asked while pouring syrup over his hot cakes.

"I believe it is the practice of opening up the corpse in an effort to determine the cause of death."

Jacques nodded as he sucked spilled syrup from his finger. "Exactly. And what do you think of such a practice?"

"Well, Papa, it's been going on amidst the aristocracy for generations, hasn't it? Whenever a noble or monarch is suspected of being poisoned, the physicians open him up and examine his organs. But the hypocrisy is that the Church was against it for purposes of learning about diseases. It was permissible to open up a wealthy aristocrat to see if his wife had been feeding him arsenic but it wasn't acceptable to open up an anonymous cadaver to teach young doctors what our internal anatomy really looks like so they could better treat wounds or diagnose disease."

"Mmm… And what if the cadaver is not so anonymous? What if it is your mother or your sister or..."

"Ajax wants to autopsy Nicholet!" The words jumped from John's mouth.

"You are really very quick," Jacques said, shaking a finger at his eldest son. "So what do you think of that?" John was quiet for a moment. "His stepdaughter is living in our home, do not forget."

John made a face as though a child, and a stepchild at that, could have no bearing.

"And his wife is out there," Jacques gestured broadly, "somewhere waiting to be ransomed."

John actually snorted. "We're going to need to have his remains buried long before she makes it back. It's getting warmer every day and we all rot in the end. She won't even know the difference."

"You sound like Ajax."

"I only mean that if it is going to be upsetting to her then perhaps it's better not to tell her. There would be no purpose in it."

"So you think I should give him permission?"

"What I think, sir, is that there will come a day when doing autopsies on the dead to learn more about disease and advance medical knowledge will be common place and people will not see it as wicked or a violation. After all, Papa, does the Bible not tell us our bodies are just vessels of clay, from dust we come, to dust we return? Isn't it our whole teaching that our souls leave our bodies behind to return to the Lord? So what possible harm is there in discovering how these bodies failed?"

For a moment Jacques sat motionlessly looking at his son and it was in that moment that he realized John may look just like his younger self but this eldest son was indeed his own individual, uniquely fashioned and a copy of no one. And the future now belonged to him.

Later that morning Jacques quietly told Doctor Ajax to proceed. Nicholet's body was transported to the doctor's make-shift lab. John attended him and learned. Three days later with no one else being the wiser, the body was sewn back up, dressed and, with a short service attended by most of the mill workers, buried in the church yard.

Two weeks later, Jacques' knife wound was completely closed. Ajax removed the stitches and pronounced Jacques healed enough to travel but with the caviat to exercise care and good judgment. "No fox hunts," he admonished as a bit of English humor.

It was time to leave.

Jacques had received word back from the fort telling him to either bring three good horses or be prepared to buy them to use as ransom. It was the going rate for a white woman.

Chapter 22

Penelope Richmond sat demurely in the shade of the apple tree. It was the same apple tree she used to climb as a child. She giggled remembering the skinned knees and the torn skirts and her nanny scolding. But that was long ago. Their nanny had left after Grandfather Witherspoon died. As a child, she had never understood that. Now she realized her grandfather must have been paying the nanny. After all, their mother had been delivered of four children in the first five years of marriage. Penelope had been the sixth and there had been seven more after her. But wasn't thirteen an unlucky number? Truth to tell, they had never really been thirteen. Six of her siblings lay in the church yard. Three had died as infants, two by illness and the sixth by a dreadful accident. But she was grown now and she poured tea for her two very best friends as they all chattered about this boy and that.

Penelope had learned to pour tea very gracefully and prided herself on not spilling a drop. They weren't rich and she had only one good tea dress but they weren't exactly poor either. Grandfather Witherspoon had left a sum of money to her mother. Da was a very respected vicar and often waxed on about the sins of avarice and covetousness. Penelope did not envy anyone their good fortune but she did hope to marry a handsome, well positioned man someday. One who could give her a nice house which she would cheerfully fill with babies just like her mother and make into a lovely home.

"So who have you set your cap for, Penelope? Anyone we know?" Beatrix Cummings had such a persistent way of coaxing information out of a body. "Tell us, there must be someone."

Penelope blushed. "Da says I may not even think of marriage until I am sixteen."

"But you'll be sixteen in less than a year," Emily Owens teased. "You should begin window shopping as I have."

"Oh, Em, I cannot be that bold."

"You need to go to dances," Beatrix advised. She was already sixteen and her father was an officer in the King's army. "I danced with the most handsome captain last week but he hasn't worked up the courage to come courting… yet." She giggled convulsively.

"Oh, do be careful, Bea. Mum says solders can be very," Penelope paused and took a long breath, "unpredictable."

"I know. They are always getting orders to do this or do that or go here or there and they must go of course and break plans." Beatrix reached for a little tea cake. "I do believe in all my life, my father has been away from home more than he has been at home."

"If I should marry a military man, I would insist on an understanding," Penelope offered demurely. "If he professes to love me then he must take me with him wherever he is posted."

"But what if he was sent to the jungles of Africa? Or the wilds of America with native Indians wanting to take your scalp?" Emily asked, her eyes round at the thought.

"Why, I should go with him, of course, and he and all his men would keep me safe."

"I think mother actually enjoys the time alone," Beatrix said with an air of sophistication. "She need not consult Father about anything and can do as she pleases while he is gone."

"But then whatever is the point of getting married?" Penelope questioned.

"Why to have children of course!" Beatrix replied and giggled knowing full well exactly how those children came into being, thanks to her cousin Daniel. It also seemed a much better motivation for marriage than just spawning another brat.

"Yes… children," Penelope sighed. "My very own children..." and suddenly she went stiff.

Blue Wing looked at the white woman sitting in the dirt making weird gestures and talking to herself.

"She crazy in head," she muttered to Little Buck's Mother. "She hear voices that are not there but hears not our voices."

Little Buck's Mother nodded, not looking up from her quill work. "She is bad medicine. I told Little Buck to give her back to the white men before she calls evil spirits to us."

"What he say?"

"He want ransom. I say no amount of ransom is worth bringing evil spirits into our village."

"We should end her."

"No-no, cannot. Must not. Now she here and if we end her, evil spirits within will leap to another of our village. Best to give her back and let white men deal with her."

"Why would they give ransom and bring her back into their village? I think they must be laughing at us for taking her away. They no longer are responsible for her." Blue Wing kicked a dirt clot toward the white woman. "We must feed her and she do no work."

"Sit down, Blue Wing, sit with back to her and think of other things," Little Buck's Mother invited, gesturing to a spot across from her. "I welcome your company."

§

Penelope Richmond met Second Lieutenant Samuel Carver a week after her sixteenth birthday when she accompanied Beatrix to a post dance. The girls were under the protective wing of Colonel Cummings. Three months later the banns were posted and in due time the young couple was married. Vicar Richmond was pleased to have another daughter married off and out of the house.

Thanks to the Colonel's influence the young couple enjoyed a full year without change while Penelope gave birth to their first child, a son, and she discovered having babies wasn't as easy as her mother always made it seem. Then, with baby Ezra in tow, they were off to North America, the Colonies, and a fort on the border with the French territories. When Ezra was two, his brother Michael was born. Penelope was discovering life on the frontier had its challenges.

Two years later, heavily pregnant and distressed with the heat of the Mississippi delta basin, Penelope persuaded newly promoted Captain Carver to apply for a posting farther north. The Delaware Bay sounded pleasant. They transferred and Martha was born. It was a very rustic post, however, barely a fort at all. Competition with the French had created a certain *joie de vivre* at the last post despite the mosquitoes and oppressive heat. The officers invited each other over for dances and holiday parties, quite civilized actually, and Penelope found herself regretting their latest move. True, it was cooler but so much cruder. Keeping order within the native populations was their chief order of business and there were no parties.

Martha was five years old when Captain Samuel Carver returned from a policing action strapped across the back of his horse. Penelope was bewildered and devastated. She lost the baby she was carrying and when she had recovered she was politely told she must move on.

Move where?

There was no question of going back to England unless her parents sent her passage. Her widow's benefits were totally inadequate. By the time she paid off all their debts, she had barely enough money to book passage on a packet boat going up the eastern coastline.

While on the packet boat, the captain and a few of the other passengers shared their opinions of possible new homes. New York Towne was busy, dirty, and filled with crime. Boston was even bigger and more expensive to live in… and it would cost more money to reach. Chartes Landing, however, said the captain, was a quiet, peaceful little community. They had never had any Indian problems, sailors did not make it a port of call, and because of the lumber mill and logging interests it was populated with many big, healthy, single men. Penelope began to perk up.

With her children in tow, she walked from one end of the settlement to the other. Choices for employment were limited. There was no market for housekeepers, the only such position known was up at the big house and it had been quite solidly filled for many years. The same could be said for a position as governess.

She was loathed to become a tavern wench, Da would disown her. She had no skills as a butcher or baker or candlestick maker but when she happened upon the seamstress' shop she bargained her services to sew hems and straight seams and other such less skilled and more tedious tasks.

The seamstress gave her a lead to a cheap room that would accept her children if she would help clean up after the evening meal each night. Before nightfall, Penelope and her three reasons for living, ages ten, eight and five, were safely tucked up in a large four poster bed just off the kitchen of a logger's home. Martha found playmates amongst the logger's children and Ezra and Michael found ways to make a penny here and there to help their mother.

Penelope could finally write home for now she had a return address to send to her parents. It took over five months to hear back and when she did it shook her world yet again.

Mum was dead.

Penelope's stomach felt like she had been dropped from a great height. There was a hollowness and a light-headed feeling while her stomach leaped toward her mouth. She broke into a fine sweat. Of course Penelope knew that everybody dies but she had never even once considered the possibility of her mother not being there. Like the sky is or the ocean is, Mum just is… or was. Always there and taken for granted. Penelope felt more alone than she had ever felt before.

She read the date again. Over a year ago! Why hadn't her Da written to tell her long before this? How could he not tell her? He should have written while Samuel was alive and could have given her comfort. They might have been given Compassionate Leave, gone back to England… why everything might have been so different... might have turned out for the better. Samuel might never have died. Oh, why had Da not written to her before?

The next paragraph held more revelation. Barely a respectable six months after putting her mother into the ground, Vicar Richmond had married again. A widow… a young widow... a *very* young widow… younger than Penelope herself! And she brought her own two children to the marriage (as well as her rich old husband's money, no doubt, knowing Da).

He concluded by writing that since he was still in the process of trying to empty the "nest" of the first flock while accepting that he was also starting a second family, he was in no position to encourage her to come home. *Encourage?!* He didn't know the meaning of the word.

Penelope was shaking. She let the letter drop to the floor and with weakened knees she sought out the logger's wife to beg a medicinal shot of whiskey. She had never had hard spirits before but she felt the time had come.

The logger's wife took one look at Penelope, trembling, pale as a death mask, and unfocused, and knew instantly that if anyone in this life ever needed a good stiff drink, it was the Widow Carver.

Time passed and Penelope leaned hard upon her sons to see her through each day. They were her bedrock of stability, her encouragement, her laughter, and her hope. Her children gave her the will to get up each day and sew long hours until her head ached and her fingers felt numb.

Most everyone within the logging community knew when her year of mourning was over and soon several likely prospects came courting. At twenty-seven she was still a very attractive woman. Slowly she narrowed down the possibilities to Francois Nicholet, a gentle man with a good job and dreams of establishing a farm on the frontier, with land to pass along to their children. The children liked him, she liked him and when he proposed marriage, she said yes.

§

Jacques took both of his older sons with him on the packet boat going to the fort at the mouth of the Delaware River along with their mounts and three additional mares of excellent quality. There they met the scout, Trainer, who had written to Jacques… or at least he had signed the letter.

The man was obviously part Indian with high cheek bones, black eyes, and a swarthy complexion but he spoke English like any mountain man. In a way he reminded them of Richard. With his buckskins and beads, and an animal skin hat over his grizzled brown and gray hair he stood out from the uniforms who were stationed at the fort. He had no patience with ceremony and could be equally critical of white and Indian.

"You got what they call the five nations: the Mohawk, Oneida, Cayuga, Seneca, and Onondaga." At this point he spit his tobacco juice off to the side. "They joined together as the Iroquois alliance 'n' have things pretty much settled between themselves as to whose territory is where. 'N' they got their neighbors the Susquehannock. Ain't none of them any shrinkin' violets, don't ya know. Tough, mean bastards if ya git on the wrong side of 'em." (spit)

"Well then, along comes the Pennacook, Massachset, Narragansett, Pequot, Mohican, Montauk, Monacan and Lanappe or what cha call Delaware. All who used t'be right happy living along the coast, don't ya know, but now what's left of 'em come pushin' in trying to git away from the white man 'n' his diseases." (spit) "It all makes fer too many trying t'claim the same land. They themselves are agriculture based, don't ya know, 'n' there's only so much game 'n' when the trees get chopped down 'n' the land gets plowed up 'n' fenced, the game goes away. Now you add in all these new white folk coming along 'n' yeah, by damn, things is gittin' a might bit hot 'n' tight." (spit)

"Some friends of ours tried to homestead just east of the Delaware River to the north," explained Jacques. "From what I understand they were harassed and finally, brutally attacked. That is when Madame Nicholet was taken."

"Ain't no fightin' that's purdy, Mister Power. I think ya know that." He fixed Jacques with a squinty gaze.

Jacques nodded. "I have some arrows, some bead work we took off the fallen."

The scout took the arrows and twisted them in his fingers.

"Kinda unusual to kill off yer best prospect for ransom, you sure they're lookin' for ransom?" (spit)

"There was an incident," Jacques explained. "I do not believe they planned to kill but everyone ended up dead except the daughter who escaped. And the wife disappeared. I am sure the wife was taken. Can you tell us where to look?"

"Well, this here is a Susquehannock arrow right enough, 'n' it looks to hold the marking of the Turtle clan. Yup… here again on that beading, see it? So that's where we need t' look."

"I am sorry Monsieur Trainer…"

"Just 'Trainer'" (spit)

"As you wish, but how do we go about contacting this… clan?" Jacques asked in honest ignorance.

"Oh, I got my ways, don't you fret. You 'n' yer boys jist sit tight."

"Very well, Monsi… ah, very well, Trainer. I thank you."

"Well, don't thank me yet. We got a ways to go." He grinned displaying a set of horribly stained teeth.

The scout lumbered off leaving Jacques, John, and Phillip on their own. The three corralled their horses where hay and water was available, sought the hospitality of the fort which was crude housing, and bought supper from a vendor selling stew by the bowl, bread by the loaf, and beer by the tankard.

Trainer put the word out via his personal communications network and he didn't expect it to take long for word to come back regarding a white woman to trade.

Jacques and his sons were out at the corral. They had been spending a great deal of time brushing their horses and so spoiling them with attention that their coats shined like mirrors in the sunlight. The Power trio had the time and there was little else for them to do as they waited.

"Mister Power," Trainer called as he approached the corral. "Some'm's fishy." It was only a few days since they had talked but the earth had turned hard and dry so little dust puffs could be noticed at every step.

"What do you mean?" John was first to reply. He tossed the curry brush to his brother.

"Word come back way too fast 'n' they already want t' meet us a couple miles up river."

"But this is good, is it not?" Jacques was more than ready to head back home, into Marie's arms and his own soft bed. Nothing about this could happen "too fast" for him.

"It's a mite too good," Trainer grumbled suspiciously. "Too easy, too good t'be true, like they say."

"How so?" asked Phillip.

Jacques watched Trainer who was chewing his tobacco again. It was an unquestionably disgusting habit. The scout scratched his chest and spat.

"Some'm's going on," he said with a suspicious frown. "Usually takes a week to hear back, 'n' that's jist fer starters. There's always a bunch of hem-hawing 'bout where t'meet, when t'meet, dickerin' over price which always seems t'end up bein' three horses but it's got t'be dickered for as part of this little dance… this time, slam, bam – bring the horses 'n' meet us blah-blah! I'm tellin' ya, some'm's not right."

"Like what?" Jacques frowned.

"Like maybe she's feelin' poorly 'n' they're afeared she's gunna up 'n' dee on 'em," he said bluntly.

Jacques thought immediately of little Martha. The girl was expecting him to bring her mother home to her but what if Madame Nicholet did not make it home?

"If you are right…" Jacques realized that the woman had undoubtedly witnessed what had been done to her sons. He could only imagine the horror it would be for any parent to see. His stomach knotted as he thought of his own sons tortured in such a manner. "We will take two horses."

"What?" John looked at his father.

"What are you thinking, Papa?" asked Phillip.

"I think Trainer is right. I think Madame Nicholet is ill, she could be dying and they are rushing to get rid of her before they have nothing to trade. If I think about it more I will bring only one horse. After what they did, they deserve only a hangman's rope. Come, let us go." Jacques began to saddle his horse, outrage, indignation, and helplessness coursing through his veins.

"I got an idee," the wily scout looked to Jacques before turning to spit again. "I'll ride one o'them horses bareback so's they think we're only bringing one. If they take it, they take it. If they balk I'll slip off 'n' give 'em t'second."

"If they take just one horse," Jacques said darkly, "then we know something is very wrong with Madame Nicholet."

They rode a rough road running along the river until they spotted the group up ahead, three braves sitting on their ponies, one holding a tether tied to a white woman's neck but her hands were free.

Jacques held a white flag of truce. Trainer, holding the reins of one of the saddle-less horses, sat upon the second and walked his horse slowly toward the Indians while leading the other horse behind him. Jacques and his sons stayed where they were. Little Buck mirrored the action with Penelope, walking the woman toward Trainer. As they got close, Little Buck dropped her tether and kicked his horse to action. He grabbed the reins from Trainer's hand and pulled up and around urging both the trade horse and his own pony to gallop back to the waiting braves who all took off and disappeared within seconds.

It was all a little difficult to understand for from where he was sitting, Jacques thought Madame Nicholet looked perfectly fine.

John rode up and jumped down from the saddle. He took the rawhide from Madame Nicholet's neck and set her up on his horse. She seemed happy, cheerful, and even a little flirtatious on the ride back to the fort. She said nothing about her experience with the Indians, didn't seem to be grieving for her sons. It was damned eerie. And what little she did say made no sense at all.

When they arrived back at the fort, Jacques told Trainer to keep the mount he was riding as a "thank you" for his help and services. The scout was obviously pleased and shook Jacques' hand in parting.

On the packet boat home, all three men tried to understand what was going on with Madame Nicholet. She didn't seem to recognize her name nor that she had been married. The name Carver also meant nothing to her and Jacques was beginning to have grave misgivings about the upcoming meeting with her own daughter.

As soon as they arrived at Chartes Landing, Jacques sent Phillip to find Doctor Ajax. "After that go home to see your wife," he encouraged with a small smile and Phillip nodded in appreciation.

Jacques and John rode home with the woman who insisted on being called "Miss Richmond."

At the house, she introduced herself to Marie as Penelope Richmond and spoke of her father, the Vicar, and her mother. When Martha came into the room Penelope's face lit up in a huge smile as she rushed to hug "Tulip," her favorite little sister.

"Have they sent you to fetch me? I'm late I know. I'm so sorry. I got myself lost and turned about in the forest. I hope father isn't angry. These nice gentlemen found me and here I am."

"Mum?" Martha looked at her mother, startled and confused.

"Mum sent you? Oh, I hope she isn't upset with me too."

Marie served up tea as they waited for Doctor Ajax. Fortunately, it was not a long wait as avoiding confusing subject matter grew increasingly difficult. Penelope displayed the very best of manners although she was obviously very hungry. The tea cakes, cold cuts and biscuits were a tremendous hit and eating filled the voids in the conversation.

"Miss Richmond, I'm Doctor Ajax," the young doctor introduced himself upon his arrival. "If you've finished with your tea, I'm going to ask you to join me in the other room so I may examine you just to make certain you didn't hurt yourself." She and Martha obediently followed him and he guided them to the privacy of the library.

After a thorough exam, Ajax sent her off with "Tulip" to seek out Marie and freshen up. He found Jacques and John waiting for him in Jacques' study.

"I hope you do not mind that I have invited John to join us," Jacques said. "As you know he has shown a remarkable interest in the healing arts."

"Of course," Ajax nodded and accepted a glass of cognac as he settled into one of Jacques' big wing backed chairs.

"She's a bit under nourished," Ajax said as Jacques sat down behind his desk and pointed John to the other chair. "But there is no sign of torture or trauma. Physically, there is nothing wrong with the lady but she firmly believes she is just fifteen, a young virgin who is still living with her parents. A time in her life before she was ever married."

John listened attentively.

"We have so little understanding of the mind," Ajax added sadly. "All I can say is she seems happy but she keeps saying she wants to go home. When I asked her where home is she gave me the name of a community in southern England."

"It was the same for us. I think she witnessed what was done to her sons and the shock was too much," Jacques said grimly. He had not shared those gruesome details with anyone but to Ajax he now described how they had found the Carver boys.

"Good lord!" the doctor gasped.

"Is it possible her mind has taken her back to a time before there was anything in her life to be connected with her sons… as a way of living with or I should say *forgetting* what she saw?" John suggested.

Ajax looked at John for a moment and then at Jacques. "That is most perceptive of you, John. It is as good a theory as any. The more I study medicine, the more I see, the more I believe anything is possible. By all accounts she was devoted to those children, I cannot imagine… I mean… such a ghastly… the horror..." He couldn't finish his sentences but took a bolstering gulp of his brandy.

"I read that there are more than twice as many women committed to asylums as men," John spoke softly.

"That is understandable, they have such delicate sensibilities," nodded Ajax.

"They also have husbands, brothers, and guardians who find it expedient to put them under lock and key," said Jacques. He had no desire to open up another debate but it was his experience that women were capable of enduring a great deal. His own wife and his mother were both excellent examples.

John looked at his father.

Ajax shrugged a little and shook his head slowly. "We still know so little of what the mind is capable of doing. If we touch a burning hot iron, we recoil faster than we can think. Our body wants to preserve itself. It makes sense to me that the mind could also recoil, unbidden... as a protection."

"But when we lose touch with reality is that not when we say one is truly insane?" Jacques offered.

"We label people 'sane' or 'insane,' we call them 'normal' or 'abnormal' but what does it really mean? I think John's theory has great merit. Penelope witnesses something so horrifying her mind cannot live with it. So instead, it chooses to live in a much happier time but a time with nothing to remind her of the children she has lost. And to accomplish this, she has lost more than fifteen years of her life. I believe it is still in there," Ajax tapped his own head, "but will she ever let it back out? I do not know. Would not any of us if facing truly unbearable things not choose to forget in favor of a happier time?" Ajax stared at his glass.

"We might wish to but we do not," Jacques responded.

"Ahh, but do we not hear the elderly say they remember only the good times?"

"I think that is more a figure of speech, Doctor. More brandy?" Jacques held up the decanter.

"Thank you." Ajax set his glass on the desk. "Just a touch and you are right, of course. This… this… condition is not normal and so I cannot believe it is healthy. Someday a reckoning may come. It is as if her mind has closed a door on all that pain but someday that door may suddenly burst open."

"What do you recommend, Doctor?" Jacques ran his hand through his hair. It was getting late and he was tired. "I do not believe she is dangerous, do you?"

"Oh, no, quite the opposite, she is possibly happier than she has been in a very long time but she isn't capable of dealing with the real world. She must be looked after. She keeps asking to go home, and home to her is her little town in England and her parents' house. Apparently she has a large family who can take care of her once she arrives. And Martha is old enough to see them safely back… Martha," he sighed as if just remembering the girl. "Poor child, she has lost everyone in her family even her mother but has now a 'new sister' she must look after. How odd that must seem. I will talk to the child. I understand she and Marie have established a good relationship, perhaps Marie can join us. Martha is going to have to understand that right now it is best to humor her mother and play along with her 'make believe' world… so to speak."

"I am certain Marie will be happy to help in anyway she can," Jacques nodded. "You need only ask her."

"Oh…" Ajax looked at Jacques and then at John as if expecting Jacques to speak for his wife and to her about the request. "Yes, quite."

"Meanwhile, I am certain she would tell you Martha and her mother may both stay with us while I send to discover when the next ship going directly to England is to leave New York Towne. The packet captain can find out for me, I am certain. I am more than happy to pay their passage and provide enough to see them home. I will entrust it to Martha." He shook his head. "She's such a little thing but she has become the parent."

"Indeed."

As Jacques waited for news on ship schedules, Marie generously arranged a new and complete wardrobe for both Penelope and Martha. As the women busied themselves with fittings and selecting necessary accoutrements, Jacques saw to the mill.

Phillip had done an admirable job running things in Boot's absence. And yet he stepped back into his role as an ordinary mill worker without any resentment upon William's return. Daily, Phillip applied himself with single-minded diligence. It gave Jacques pause. Before his very eyes, Phillip had made remarkable strides in gaining maturity. And what of John? He was capable of so much more than digging in posts and mending fences.

Jacques and Marie accompanied the odd mother-daughter pair with their new luggage on the packet boat ride to New York Towne and saw them safely aboard a barque bound for Southampton. Jacques gave Martha a letter to deliver to her grandfather attesting to the particulars of their situation and he entrusted her with a purse, more than adequate to cover their needs in making their way home from port.

As the couple stood at the docks, waving a good-bye, Marie looked at the little face waving back at them and was reminded of herself at that age. At thirteen she had been a drudge working in Bouchet's tavern and the world had seemed so big and cold… and hostile. She wondered how it felt to Martha. This child had done no wrong, her mother had done no wrong either. But they had lost everyone and everything on this side of the ocean and her mother was no longer right in the head. Marie was glad they had family to which they could return.

"Jacques, when was the last time you wrote to your parents?" Marie asked as Jacques reserved space on the packet boat and paid for their passage to return to Chartes Landing the next day.

He sighed. "You are correct to remind me, *ma chérie*, they are due a letter." He kissed her hand which she had slipped into the crook of his arm. They proceeded to walk toward their favorite inn. "But there is so much that has happened that I cannot write about, *n'est-ce pas?* It would worry them unnecessarily."

"Just hearing from you means everything to them and the children are always a good subject," she smiled.

"Yes-yes, they are. Phillip is really maturing. I think marriage was the best thing to happen to him."

Marie couldn't help but chuckle. "It often is just what a man needs," she said and then she remembered Francois and sobered. "I hope John finds a good woman."

"Speaking of John, he has shown an amazing aptitude for medicine. It is as if he has an instinct… a natural talent we would be remiss to not encourage."

"Encourage in what way?" Marie's own instinct told her she might not be happy with the answer.

"I… that is to say *we* should send him off to school." He looked down at his wife but her bonnet hid her face. "What would you think of that?"

Marie was quiet as they continued to walk in the mild spring air. Jacques waited patiently until at last she spoke. "You know how I feel about my children, Jacques. After you, they are my whole world and…" she looked up at him fiercely, "I would admit this to no one but you… mother's are not supposed to have favorites but I think John holds a very special place in my heart and I know not if it is because he is the eldest or because he looks so very much like you, my precious husband."

Jacques swallowed and smiled indulgently. "I share your guilt, my darling, I think Louise could get me to do to anything and I know it is because she is you all over again."

Marie saw the warmth in his eyes and felt a flush come to her cheeks.

"Still," she continued, "I want always what is best for all my children. So to answer your question… I think we should ask John what he wants to do. And if it is to become a doctor then by all means he should receive the proper education."

They had arrived at The Pork 'n' Porridge where they always stayed if they could get a room. It had doubled in size over the past few years and become much more plush. Hank and George were now managing the place together. Under doctor's advice, Henry Thompkins had retired to the peace of vegetable gardening but his wife still called the shots in the kitchen employing a wooden spoon to rap the knuckles of anyone who dared to try to deviate from her tried and true recipes.

"How hungry are you?" Jacques asked quietly as he stood with their room key in his hand. Marie was very familiar with the look she saw in his eyes.

"How healed are you?"

"As good as new."

"I did not bring my tea."

"I am prepared."

"Dinner can wait."

They climbed the stairs and made their way down the carpeted hall passing a table set out with candle holders and candles. Marie lit a candle at the wall sconce as Jacques unlocked the door to their room. Once inside, Jacques locked the door and rapidly threw off his coat and pulled off his boots as Marie set the candle and holder on the mantle, removed her cape and bonnet and unloosed her hair. Turning to his wife, Jacques began to remove each piece of her clothing with exaggerated care until she stood in only her thin shift and he saw again the girl rising from the river like a sea nymph, the cloth of her shift wet and transparent and clinging to her every curve.

Marie set about removing the rest of Jacques' clothing. She loosed his cravat and pulled it slowly from around his neck; unbuttoning his waistcoat, one large button at a time. Finally, she eased it gently from his arms. The belt came off next. Pulling up his shirt from within his breeches, she managed to pull it over his head and off his arms, revealing the long, new scar running down his side. She traced down its very pink length with her finger tips.

"Oh, my love, when I think of what could have been... how close you came... what might have happened... everything inside me turns to water and I cannot breathe," she confessed softly.

Standing there in only his breeches, he felt her kiss her way along the bumpy ridge of newly knitted flesh until she reached its bottom. He was aware of her moist tongue as it traveled upward and over the slightly numb disfigurement, her warm breath a balm to his drawn flesh until the air cooled his skin in the wake of her path.

She saw the hairs stand up on his body, a golden pilosity on his chest and arms, and she gently dragged her nails up his biceps and down his chest caressing his pectorals, strong and solid beneath her fingers. Lingeringly she kissed the flesh over his beating heart. Catching a nipple in her teeth, she held it while worrying the tip with her tongue.

"Ohhh, God," he groaned softly, burying his fingers in her mass of loosened hair. "I have missed you so, *mon cœur*."

He felt her warm hands undo the laces of his breeches; slowly they slipped inside, caressing his flesh as they went until her fingers dug into the hard muscles of his buttocks. He shivered as his breeches dropped to the floor.

Marie could feel her own moisture dampening the inside of her thighs.

"I...must...have you," her voice had turned husky and urgent.

"I will get a skin," he whispered, starting to reach.

"No. Your hand… now…" she raised the hem of her shift. "The other... in my mouth..."

She stood close, undulating against him, pressing into him, while Jacques' free hand caressed the silky, slippery inside of her sensitive lower lip, full and flushed with passion, her heated breath coming in quick little gasps until with a muffled cry she sighed.

"Only an appetizer," she breathed teasingly into his ear. "Now you may get a skin." Slipping off her shift, she stood patiently. "Are you ready to enjoy the main course, *mon amour?*" She smiled provocatively.

His blood throbbed through his extremities as protectively sheathed, he came up behind her and pulled her shoulders toward him so he could reach the sensitive spot on her neck just under her ear. "Very ready," he whispered and felt her tremble and quake beneath his kiss. "I want you this way to start."

"To start," she echoed.

He smiled at that and slowly caressed her hips and the perfection of her derrière. He sought her entrance and heard her gasp.

"Go slow and deep and hard," she urged softly. "Please, Jacques, I have such a hunger for you tonight I beg to be completely glutted."

With single-minded concentration, Jacques was beyond the ability to speak for a considerable time as they took their pleasure with each other in a variety of ways, sharing repeated ecstasies.

Much later they lay side by side totally exhausted, drenched in sweat and struggling to reestablish normal breathing. The room smelled pungently of sex, fresh sweat, Marie's perfume and Jacques' cologne with faint whiffs of cooked food drifting up from the floor below.

"I am as weak as a kitten." The words seemed to fall from her mouth; she made the effort to lick her parched lips.

"How many times was that?" Jacques reached for the small jug of water laced with wine at the side of the bed, handing it first to Marie. "Four or was it five? My darling, I thought you would never stop. It was truly amazing!"

She drank deeply and gave the jug back to him. "I was not of a mind to keep count," she gasped, "but it has rung me dry. You, my love, are the one who is amazing."

"And so," he grinned proudly, "have you been sufficiently 'glutted'?" He drank deeply from the jug himself.

"Very, very much so," she smiled lazily "I am drained and feel so incredibly relaxed and at peace. But I think my toes are permanently curled. I know my thighs are humming. You are quite remarkable, my husband, you always have been, you always know exactly what to do to drive me wild with both desire and satisfaction. And you, too, had several servings, *n'est-ce pas?*

He nodded and chuckled quietly.

"What?" she asked.

"I was just thinking… it is a very good thing most men are not capable of multiple times or nothing would ever get done in this world. It is one surfeit with which it is impossible to become bored."

She laughed. "A surfeit you have certainly mastered..."

"It took me some years."

"... and yet you continue to achieve so many other things outside the bedroom."

"But you do not know what temptation I fight."

She looked at him in puzzlement. "What temptation do you fight? If there is something more you wish, you must let me know."

"The temptation to simply stay like this in bed with you forever. And let the world be damned. *Mon Dieu*, woman, by now you were supposed to be wrinkled and sag a little, after all you are soon to be a grandmother, and you have had seven… no, eight babies. You should at least be plump... fat even… so I would not lust for you every time I look at you."

"Oh, Jacques, stop," she giggled. "Someday undoubtedly I will have wrinkles. And what if I do become fat, what then? Would you find another lover?"

"Perhaps," he teased. "if you became really, really fat. I always enjoy having you on top but if you became too fat, you would hammer me flat." He laughed and stroked the softness of her cheek and chin. "But wrinkles matter not. What we share is far too special to be changed by a few wrinkles." Much more seriously, he asked, "Marie, have I told you of late how very, very much I love you?"

"Oh, my darling," she continued to caress him. "You cannot possibly love me more than I love you. It is such a fullness in my heart, at times I think it will burst."

"It frightens me sometimes," he said quietly, "I have come to doubt my ability to continue life without you."

In response to this, she was quiet. A tear filled her eye.

"I feel that way as well," she said very softly. "And so... perhaps... you can understand how terrifying it was to see that you had come so very close to… death."

He said nothing but continued to look at her in the candlelight. "I never want to cause you pain but a man must protect those he loves, his family, his friends, those who are weaker... or he is not a man worthy of your regard."

"I know."

She stretched beside him then, slowly like a cat, the thin sheen on her body reflecting the candlelight. "I have not felt this wanton and driven since my pregnancies but," she fixed him with a look, "I cannot be, no, seriously, I cannot. I had my monthly flow just before you returned and as you know we have not made love since... until now."

Jacques carefully removed his final sheathing, then reached out to pull the sheet over them against the evening chill. He gathered her to him.

Marie sighed. "I cannot believe that once I thought making love simply meant allowing you to have your way with me."

He smiled. "Instead you have learned to have your way with me."

She chuckled softly.

"I cannot believe I once thought of you as just a pleasant little peasant girl who needed my protection."

"That is all I was back then," she turned so they were face to face, "and if I had not begged you to take me with you to the New World…?"

"I remember how much I admired your courage."

"But then, you would have shipped me off to New France."

"No…"

"Do you not remember? You offered to pay my way to go where you said it would be easier for me because they spoke French."

"Did I? I was very blind."

She nodded agreement. "How different our lives might have been. It hurt me even then, you know, to think that you could send me off and never see me again."

"That would have been… I cannot believe I was so thick." They were quiet for a moment as the sounds of boisterous talking filled the hall outside their door. It diminished, footsteps muffled by the carpeting. "I think Richard would have followed you." She said nothing. "I am certain he was in love with you even then."

"Jacques," she reached up stroking through his hair. "Richard loves us both, he is like a big brother. As such I love him dearly and am so grateful that you have had him as a good friend to partner with in this new world, but I could never think of him like this. My heart and my desires have always been only for you."

"That is what he once said to me."

"He is right." She turned to settle up against him.

After another brief silence, he asked, "Do you feel like getting dressed and going down for supper?"

"Not at all," she replied softly. "What about you?"

"No," he chuckled, "in truth, I am so completely spent I do not think I could navigate the stairway."

"How is your side?" she asked with concern.

"It is not my side that bothers me, woman; it is a wife, of whom I still cannot get enough." He pulled her in close to him and kissed her repeatedly on every surface he could conveniently reach.

At that she smiled, loving the shower of kisses and the comforting feel of his hands holding her. "Tomorrow morning is soon enough for food," she sighed, feeling very safe, cherished, and protected, and she promptly fell asleep.

Phillip and Caroline moved to the big house and into *Grand-père's* wing just before the baby arrived and Marie was very grateful. The return of her second son and a new baby in the house helped her combat the sense of loss created by John's leaving that autumn. They had seen him off on one of Dufee's last ships of the year bound for France. And she had experienced an overwhelming sense of dread and fear, anxiety that she would never see her eldest son again.

When she and Jacques had first spoken of sending John to school she had thought *in the colonies* but apparently there was no medical school on this side of the vast ocean. How could she have known? Doctors picked up their education and training very informally, it would seem, by reading and working side by side with another doctor. Hoping they helped more people than they hurt. Even England was sending their best and brightest to the Continent for a more profound and formal medical education. And ironically, most of the oldest, best reputed medical schools of renown were in France.

Marie marveled that her husband could so calmly speak of sending their son into the very country from which Jacques himself had barely escaped.

"He is an American, my darling, born in the English colonies with papers proving he is a British subject. There is nothing to worry about. He speaks English like an American colonialist but he has the advantage of also being beautifully fluent *en française*."

Marie was not reassured.

"Of course, he must call upon his grandparents," Jacques smiled with enthusiasm. "Can you imagine how overjoyed my mother and father will be to see him? How old was he when they left?"

"Ten or eleven," Marie replied rather tonelessly.

"Can you just imagine?! They will not recognize him."

"Of course they will! He looks exactly like you, Jacques! Do you not realize your enemies will become his enemies?!"

Jacques pulled her onto his lap and began kissing her hands. "You are a mother bird who frets as her babies leave the nest. Do not worry, *mon amour*, Pa-pa would not let anything happen to John and if he is to learn anything, he will be spending most of his time with his studies, *n'est-ce pas?* My enemies are long dead." He took her chin and turned her face toward his. "Marie," he said softly, "you must not remain upset. He is a young man going out into the world, the same age I was when I told my own mother good-bye. But there is a great difference, *mon cœur*, you have other children to fuss over and our son can always return to us."

The tears began to roll down her cheeks. "I know, Jacques, I know," she wrapped her arms around his neck. "When I think of what your poor mother suffered, I know I am being selfish and childish and I love you so much for loving me anyway." She tucked her face against his neck in shame.

"Always, my darling, always."

"Now I know exactly how painful it was for your mother. She is truly an amazing woman. And you should write her a little everyday."

He smiled at that but did not disagree. He really should write to his parents much more often than he did, he thought, and resolved to do so. He patted and pet Marie until he heard her sigh and felt her relax. She had such a tender heart. A heart full of caring and giving and empathy for others. And when she loved, she loved so unselfishly and completely.

They remained contentedly sitting, wrapped in each other's arms, for some time.

Chapter 23

Marie joked with Jane that God made the earth of dirt to give women something to do. It came in two forms either mud or dust and after a woman spent her whole life battling it, the final insult came when she died and they stuck her in the ground and threw dirt on top of her. The children thought that was very funny but Jane barely cracked a smile.

At the store, Lyndyn also thought it was very funny and laughed uproariously the first time he heard it until he discovered that Marie did not really consider chasing dirt a job only for women. Keeping the shelves and merchandise clean and dust free and the floors swept out and scrubbed was a steady, necessary chore for any shopkeeper, man or woman, and years ago she had established a routine. Starting at one end of the store all the shelves and goods were cleaned up and polished in an on-going process whenever business was slow. And inevitably, by the time the job was finished it would be time to start all over again. It was a good system and she taught it to every apprentice.

One drizzly day in late autumn, Marie was applying herself to this very task. She had given Lyndyn the day off. He was fighting an early head cold and she had encouraged him to seek a visit to the Boot's steam house. Business was slow and so, she also had sent Caroline home to spend time with her baby.

The inside lanterns were lit to counter the gloom of the day and alone in the store, Marie was busily moving a display of dishes. Suddenly, she heard a low, resonating voice ask, "Madame Marie?"

Startled, she jumped almost dropping a dish and spun around to find herself face to face with a very tall, dark, and exceptionally handsome young stranger.

"Oh...I am sorry," she apologized. "I did not hear you come in." She looked quickly at the door to assure herself that the bell was indeed still there and it was. "Yes, yes, I am Madame Power. What can I help you with?"

The man standing before her was so devoid of facial and body hair she thought he was perhaps still in his teens, and dressed very oddly but very cleanly in a combination of buckskins and broadcloth. His linen shirt was opened widely at the throat and she could see a bead and shell necklace within lying against his broad, hairless chest. He had a sword and scabbard hanging at his waist but also a tomahawk thrust into his belt. His black wavy hair was neatly clubbed under a tricorner hat which he removed as he made her a leg in a courtly bow.

"*Je suis Raphaël Michael Sebastian et c'est un honneur de vous rencontrer,*" he said in perfect French with a grin as broad as his face and full of very white, straight teeth.

Marie continued to stare. His cheekbones were nothing short of extraordinary and his eyes had an almost hypnotic quality. If she were twenty-five years younger and had never met Jacques, she was certain she would be swooning at his feet. As it was, she had her moment of fluster.

"Ahh," she cleared her throat. "*je suis désolé* ..ahh, *je...*" at that moment Marie decided to re-awaken the mature adult in her. After all, she was old enough to be the boy's mother. "What I am trying to say, young man, is you are very good-looking but I have no idea who you are. How do you know my name? I know full well if I had ever seen you before I would not have forgotten."

"*Je suis le fils de mon père,*" he continued to grin.

"*Oui* and just who is your *père?*"

"That would be me," replied a very familiar voice and Richard Bonchance stepped out from the shadows.

"Richard!" Marie gasped and accepted his bear hug embrace.

Richard and Raphael were both laughing.

"It is a game we play from time to time. Sneaking up on beautiful, unsuspecting women," Richard teased.

"You were so quiet. However did you get in without my hearing?" Marie asked in bewilderment.

"You left your back door open!" Richard replied and roared with laughter again.

"Oh." Marie clutched her chest in fun. "You almost gave me a heart attack. Shame on you. And now we must switch back to English, yes?"

Richard shrugged his large shoulders in tacit agreement. "Raphael has not had as much exposure to English and I am not the best one to be teaching but he is bright, he will catch on." Turning to his son he added more slowly, "This is the best *maîtresse d'anglais* around, she taught me when I knew nothing. If you are lucky she will do the same for you."

Raphael nodded rather gallantly.

"Oh, shush, Richard, that is not really true." She looked at Raphael and also spoke more slowly. "He had lessons on the ship coming here and I had to catch up."

It had been a very long time since they had last seen Richard and, indeed, once again there would be much to catch up on. Marie decided to close the store. The idea that Richard had brought home a son still had not fully taken hold.

As she drove them to the house in her buggy, Marie told Richard of Phillip's marriage and new baby, and Thor courting Helen, and most recently, John going to Europe to study medicine. Details would have to come later as the house loomed ahead.

"Did you stop by the mill?" she asked.

"No, we could not wait to surprise you. And we spent a good amount of time becoming properly civilized again. I should say *me…* Raphael is always very civilized. When his mother died I took him to some nuns I know and they raised him."

"Oh. I am sorry to hear that. I mean about his mother. Is he Catholic then?"

"It was a long time ago but she was a very beautiful French girl and no, the nuns, they understood I did not wish him indoctrinated with their rituals."

"Well, it is perhaps just as well that you skipped the mill. Jacques has been working with the apple crop so much of late, he might not have been at the mill today at all. In fact, he may already be home."

The buggy had barely stopped when Raphael leapt out to help Marie down. Taking her by the waist, she sailed to the ground as though of no more weight than a feather. Richard meanwhile slowly and stiffly got down on his own.

"Oh..*merci, monsieur*," she acknowledged, feeling the strength of Raphael's young shoulders beneath her hands.

"*C'est un plaisir, madame*," he replied cavalierly.

"Richard," she said rapidly in English, "this boy has been raised with far too much charm and here I am walking him into a house filled with women."

Richard grinned.

When the three walked in the door, Jane was right there and she and Richard went through their usual bit of flirtatious silliness. He telling her how she had not aged a minute in his absence and was more attractive than ever and she giggling like a young maiden and telling him how well he looked. And when he introduced Raphael, Jane all but melted on the spot.

Marie had the opportunity to observe Richard more closely and realized, in truth, he did not look terribly well. He was moving very stiffly and was in obvious discomfort. All the years of wandering, sleeping on the ground, and wintering in the snows were exacting their dues.

They found that Jacques was indeed home and after introductions she excused herself and went to confer with Margot concerning dinner. Marie wanted something a little special to mark the occasion. For it truly was an occasion. It was not everyday that they had the privilege of being introduced to a child of Richard. And such a child. Richard had been a very decent looking young man in his youth but to have sired such a spectacular looking son, the mother must have been truly extraordinary which led Marie to speculate on just what kind of secret, double life Richard had been leading all these years… and who had the lady been?

Later, as they gathered in the drawing room awaiting the call to dinner, chatter was running high and the volumes were increasing. Phillip introduced Richard to Caroline, Thor and Helen were introduced to Raphael, as were Phillip and Caroline, and Richie and Jamie were tickled to see Uncle Richard and meet his son.

Then, Louise walked into the room.

Marie saw it as plainly as the Biblical hand writing on the wall. Louise took one look at the tall, dark, and stunningly handsome young stranger and was shot through by Cupid's arrow. In turning to look at Raphael, Marie saw that he had just been immobilized by the very same dart.

Marie spent the rest of the evening watching her daughter and Richard's son. The conversations swirled around them, they smiled, they nodded, they said the polite thing but Marie knew they really didn't have an interest in any of it. All their interest was in each other. It was sweet in a way, she thought, but it was also highly flammable. With Phillip, Caroline and the baby in *Grand-père's* suite there was no mandating the boy stay downstairs. The best she could arrange was for Raphael to share a room with his father but once Richard had liberally imbibed in Jacques' cognac she was certain the boy could come and go as he wished with his father being none the wiser. Helen and Louise still shared a room but they were sisters. Who knows how many times Louise had turned a blind eye to Thor and Helen, and Helen could not be expected to play guard dog to Louise.

Dessert was served and Marie had begun speculating on the feasibility of taking up the challenge herself and sleeping in the girls' doorway when she realized she could never get away with that without Jacques knowing. She remembered her sworn oath to always take Jacques into her confidence and never keep secrets from him again. Very well then, she must find a way to tell Jacques without inflaming his paternal instincts.

After dinner, the young people took over the drawing room. Caroline was playing the clavichord and Phillip was accompanying her on the violin. Richie enjoyed playing the violin as well when no one was telling him he had to play. Jamie had a small triangle with which to keep the beat when he could not manage the music on his recorder. Thor and Helen led the dancing and Louise and Raphael followed step. The Sims were there tapping time, even Margot had come in from the kitchen to enjoy the music and was prancing around with Isabelle, who had been allowed to stay up as a special treat. The adult and child sought to mimic the steps of the others.

Marie watched with a beneficent smile upon her face but she saw the charged lightning whenever Raphael and Louise touched. *Mon Dieu!* She glanced about the room. Was she the only one who could see it? It was so obvious! And Marie knew if this daughter was anything like her mother, she could be in Raphael's arms before the night was over… unless...

It was time to talk to the fathers.

Marie slipped away and went to Jacques' study. She knocked as a courtesy, she couldn't have heard a response anyway, and then, she opened the door.

"Marie… what is it my darling? Is everything well?" Jacques stood up smiling, Richard never made it up from his chair.

She closed the door after herself and signed for them to sit as she took a seat.

"At the moment, everyone is amused, but before the evening grows later I do need to talk with both of you." She had their attention. "We have been very blessed to have some beautiful children," she began, "and they are healthy and strong and intelligent. Everything a parent could desire, is this not so?"

"Yes-yes," Jacques and Richard both nodded.

"Well, gentlemen, what is the most natural thing in the world when healthy, strong, and beautiful children grow up?" She looked pointedly at each of them but neither seemed to take the hint. "When Thor came to you asking permission to court Helen, I know you had some words and set some boundaries in the expectations for his behavior." She looked at Richard. "Raphael comes into our home as the son of a beloved friend and I am certain courting was never even a consideration but you are here now and in case it has escape your attention, Louise and Raphael cannot keep their eyes or hands off one another."

Jacques almost upset his drink as he jumped to his feet.

"Jacques, please sit," she put a calming hand upon her husband's arm. "Nothing improper has happened as of yet, but I am surprised neither of you noticed at dinner. It is important to know when there are sparks flying near the dry tinder, yes?"

"It does not surprise me," Richard said calmly. "Louise is…

Please do not say she is like me, Marie silently prayed.

"…very charming and quite irresistible."

Marie nodded. "And Raphael is devastatingly gorgeous, with the manners of a prince-ling. I think he has quite swept her completely off her feet."

"It is best that she be reminded to stay *on* her feet, *n'est-ce pas?*" Jacques strained to stay calm. "Marie, perhaps you had best talk to your daughters again and Richard… ?"

"Rest assured, I will talk to my son before the night is over. But I want you both to know, he is a very good boy… much better than we ever were," he added looking at Jacques. "And he has never had a sweetheart before. He actually has been quite sheltered, growing up with the nuns."

Marie nodded and stood, signing them both to keep their seats. "I guess we have our work cut out for us but for now, I am going back and enjoying the music."

When the door closed behind her, cutting back the sounds of the merry-making, Jacques and Richard were alone in the quiet once again.

"When I think of all the things we did, all the experiences we had before we were even Rafe's age, I wonder if I have done my son a wrong forcing him to live like a monk."

"We also were very lucky we did not catch some terrible disease."

"*Oui,*" Richard shook his head with a guilty grin. "So, tell me… my son and your daughter, would it be such a terrible thing?"

"I do not want him sowing his wild oats with my daughter!" Jacques was incensed.

"Of course not! I speak of something much more permanent… and acceptable. Two virgins would have a lot to explore with each other..."

Jacques grimaced and scowled, "Ehhh, for God's sake, Richard, do not speak like that! I do not want to hear it!"

Richard smiled but refrained from anymore obvious references to carnal knowledge. "We have been friends all our lives, as close as any brothers but such a match would actually make us family," he suggested mildly, "would it be so bad?"

"Mmmm I suppose that depends… he is educated?"

Richard nodded. "The nuns did well by him. Oh, he does not speak English so well but he will learn."

"And what does he want to do with his life?"

"What does any twenty year old want to do? He seeks adventure, challenge, a purpose." Richard slumped back in his chair. "Truth to tell, I could not have carried on the past three years without him. I have no women anymore, Jacques, I nursed the last one into the grave four years ago. I picked up Rafe at the convent three years ago and he has been at my side ever since. He loves me." Richard was tearful. "God love him, he loves his pa-pa and I love him. He is all I have in this world."

This was a Richard Jacques had never seen before and he didn't know quite what to say.

"And you have us. You must know Marie and I love you, Richard. We are family. I admit to being a little jealous sometime back but I have moved beyond that. You are always welcome here. This is your home."

"I know, I know, but you and Marie have each other... while Rafe? He is my blood!"

"What about the others?" Jacques could not stop himself from finally asking.

"There are no others… well, there were but you must understand how it is, Jacques, children belong to the mother and her tribe. The mothers moved on or died, the tribe takes over and while you are not a stranger, you do not have a strong relationship with your own children. Quite honestly, you can never be certain they *are* your children. And now, they are all grown and scattered. But Raphael was different. His mother was a white woman."

Jacques poured them each another cognac. He did not say that he thought a strong relationship was difficult to develop with a father who went from woman to woman and was always away. "It sounds like you need to retire from the wandering life, *n'est-ce pas?*"

"True. I am older than my years, *mon ami*. The life takes its revenge as you grow older. My knees, my hips, shoulders, hands," he held up his hand slightly misshaped by arthritis. "I cannot lift what I used to, I cannot hike like I used to, I look pathetic getting in and out of a canoe, and trying to seat a horse is almost impossible. In the wilderness I am now useless. Nothing but wolf bait."

Jacques forced a chuckle. "I do not believe it, now you are playing upon my sympathies. You just want to retire, so retire, you have worked hard enough. Go sit in the Boot's steam house and melt your bones! Meanwhile, we still must discuss whether I want your son to court my daughter."

"You need someone to continue making the rounds of the trading posts. Someone you can trust, someone who has the allegiance of family. I have taught him everything I know. He has made the trek with me for three years now."

"But Louise may not want an absentee husband."

"If Louise is half the woman her ma-ma is, she will cope until he can train up someone who you can trust to continue the work. Rafe needs to find an apprentice, yes?"

"And you tell me in three years, he has never spent time with the Indian girls who are thrown at you?" Jacques arched his brow in disbelief.

"Damn me if he does not remind me of you! The nuns did one hell of a job on him. He is almost prudish about casual relations." Richard cleared his throat. "And it goes without saying that he is my only heir. He will inherit a small fortune."

Jacques gestured dismissively. "You would have to die first and I expect you to be around a long time yet, *mon ami*. You will stop making these brutal treks and you will have Marie to watch over you. She soon will have you comfortable and eating right."

Richard smiled fondly. "She can be a little tyrant, can she not?"

"And so can Louise. Your Raphael had best watch himself."

Richard laughed again, his good humor restored.

"Hmm," Jacques muttered and sat thinking for a time, his forefinger smoothing his mustache. "Well, here we are, we have them courted, engaged, wedded, bedded, and domesticated and we do not even know if they are going to like each other beyond a momentary attraction. 'What fools men be.'"

"What?"

"Never mind."

Marie's mother instinct was unfailingly correct and she was grateful she was able to speak to both girls together without seeming painfully obvious about her concerns for Louise's discretion and chastity.

"Men love the challenge, the chase, the pursuit… but when the prize is captured too quickly, the challenge is gone. A young man may press so very sweetly, or even desperately, to get under a girl's skirts but often once they do, they lose interest."

"How long did you make father pursue you?" Louise asked boldly, in almost a challenge of her own.

"Things were very different for us. Our circumstances were rather… mmm, unusual. Your father and I knew each other… and not in the Biblical way," she raised her finger to their giggles. "We were friends over a very long time, many years. In fact, he was my best friend. And so we became very well acquainted with each other and we shared our hopes and dreams for the future. When we decided to embark on a business venture together, we came here. The three of us. We lived in the same cabin, but not in the same bed mind you. Your father was very chivalrous and protective of me and your Uncle Richard was there as well. Neither of them kissed me or touched me… I mean familiarly. They were very respectful and your father showed a great deal of restraint but over the years we were falling in love. And we did not kiss… or anything else... until the night we exchanged our wedding vows."

"When did you know you loved Papa," Helen asked as she sat slowly brushing her long hair.

"Quite honestly, I can barely remember a time when I did not love your pa-pa. He was always my knight-in-shining-armor. In France, he used to come into the tavern I was working in. He was always so kind and polite to me even though I was just a silly little serving girl and he was the son of the duke. And he was generous and chivalrous. I learned these things about him before he ever had any interest in me sexually so I knew they were real. Not something he pretended to impress me."

"That is how I feel about Thor," Helen sighed. "When he came to our nursery, we were only children but he was the eldest and he was never mean to me or to any of us. He was always kind even when our brothers teased us."

"Kindness and virtue are not the worst things with which to start a serious relationship," Marie smiled. "Just remember, my darlings, men value virtue. They may say they do not but they all do. They all want to know a woman is capable of saying 'no' to other men, so we must say 'no' to them as well until marriage. It is after the wedding that they value an adventurous spirit in the bedroom not before."

"But when one gets these feelings, like nothing else will satisfy them...what is one to do?" Louise asked.

"Those are the exact feelings you must put a damper on," Marie said quickly, "lock them away and do not let them out until your wedding night. If you do not control them, they will control you… and that can be very dangerous. A woman always stands to lose so much more than a man – her virginity, her lover's respect, her reputation, her parents' trust, and she may well gain a child she is unprepared to raise. Many men are not inclined to take on the responsibility of a family and so they are less inclined to marriage. If their desires and lusts for a good woman are satisfied without a wedding, why would they want to marry? And once satisfied are they not free to move on to the novelty of another?"

She left them then, her beautiful and spirited daughters, so fresh and new and full of promise. Neither of them had ever known a true moment of pain and she prayed a mother's desire that they never would but she knew this was an unreasonable expectation. Life was wonderment and pain, blessing and sorrow, and the best one could hope for was that the blessings would be great and the sorrows small.

Saying "Good-night" Marie planted a motherly kiss upon each smooth, sweet-smelling forehead. She knew they would think about everything she had said. They might not want to agree but in the end, they did want to make their beloved Papa proud of them.

§

"You do not pick flowers in another man's garden." Richard said. "It is dishonorable."

"What is it you are trying to tell me, *mon père?*" Raphael pulled his shirt off over his head and Richard seeing the hard, lean muscles of his son's torso was reminded of the days when he himself had no belly flab.

They were in the guest bedroom, standing opposite each other on either side of the large four poster bed. Raphael reached for his nightshirt and slipped it on.

Richard sighed deeply. He had no experience at this sort of thing and was very uncomfortable. *Encouraging someone to enjoy sex and trying to discourage someone from even thinking about it were such totally different things. Like hot and cold, good and bad, sweet and bitter, night and day. Enough of that,* he chided himself. *How delicately must I put this? Or how strongly?*

Richard cleared his throat and started again.

"Jacques and I have been friends since we were children back in France… you understand this?"

"Of course, I think you could say it in English and I would understand," Raphael gave Richard a cheeky grin.

"I noticed you seemed quite taken with his daughter."

"Louise," he sighed and suddenly Richard saw it. The boy looked as if he had lost his senses.

"*Oui-oui*, Louise. And what exactly is it you think when you look at her?"

At this Raphael blushed and turned away, sitting down on the bed and pulling off his boots.

"Hmm… *Oui*, well, I think she thinks similar things about you. You are young, you are good-looking, you have a pleasing temperament, good manners, why would she not think similar things? The fact is, you are of an age to pay court to a young woman. Did the nuns tell you what *paying court* means?"

"We read stories of knights who paid tribute to their ladies fair with tokens of courtly love like writing poems and doing good deeds." Raphael looked up at Richard, then stood and dropped his buckskin breeches, picked them up from off the floor, folded them neatly, and placed them on the chair.

"*Oui,* well, in real life in our times it is not exactly like that but… but similar. First of all, today one does not set about paying court to a young lady unless one has serious intentions towards her." Richard settled himself into the bed with a groan, leaning himself against his pillows and pulling the sheet and blanket up to his chest. He had ceased sleeping naked and always wore a long night shirt; tonight it was flannel and he kept on his stockings. At this time of year, he could never be too warm. "A nice girl, a good girl is never to be trifled with or forced to do anything she does not desire. Do you understand what I mean when I say 'serious intentions'?

"Perhaps, Pa-pa, you should tell me," Raphael climbed into his side of the bed but was not nearly so quick to pull up the blanket.

"It generally means, the boy intends to get to know the young lady better with a view toward perhaps proposing marriage. You do know what proposing marriage means?" Richard almost growled.

Raphael grinned, "*Oui,* Pa-pa."

"So when a young man decides he is ready to marry and he meets a young lady that he is attracted to and who he thinks might make a good wife, he asks her father if he may pay court. Meaning spending a lot of time with her...ah, chaperoned time...so the two can really get to know each other much better and he can decide if she is indeed someone with whom he wants to share his life. Someone with whom he is willing to stand before God and an entire church and vow that he will love and honor, protect and cherish for the rest of his life until death parts them." Richard looked again at Raphael. "It is a very serious vow."

"Why must he ask her pa-pa?"

"Because this is a sign of respect; one does not try to pay court if the girl's father is against it."

Raphael thought about this for a moment. "Did you ask permission to pay court to *ma mere?*"

"*Oui,* of course," Richard lied. He wished he knew how much Rafe remembered of his mother.

"You said 'chaperoned time', why must it be chaperoned?"

If there had not been a chill in the room, Richard would have broken into a sweat. This was far more difficult than he had expected. "*Mon fils,* correct me if I am wrong but when you look at Louise you are thinking lustful thoughts, *n'est-ce pas?*"

At this Raphael blushed scarlet beneath his smooth dusky complexion.

"It is fine," Richard punched him playfully on the upper arm. "It is perfectly normal when looking at a pretty girl, as long as you do not act upon those thoughts and the chaperon, you see, is there to insure that you do not."

Raphael turned to look straight at his father. "She does something to me. I feel things I have never felt before and I want to take her into my arms and shower her with kisses and touch her all over her body. I feel I must hold her and I feel a pressure down here." He patted himself. "Is this love?"

"No," Richard replied earnestly, "that is what we call *physical attraction.* And your body wants to bury itself inside the woman where you will plant your seed and create another human being. Frankly, a man can feel the desire to do this with any woman but it is not love."

"I never felt this with the Indians."

"No?" He shrugged. "Well, not every woman inspires a man to lust."

"Then tell me, what is love?"

Richard thought of all the years he had loved Marie. "Ahh, love," he sighed. "Love is wanting that woman so strongly you think you might die and yet accepting that you cannot have her if she does not feel the same. Love is doing anything and everything you can to see her happy, to protect her, to be willing to die for her. And if you truly love a woman… as you come to know her and realize that what she wants is completely the opposite of what you want, true love will stand aside rather than make her miserable in the future and it will bear her and your rival for her affections no ill will."

Raphael was staring at his father. "Pa-pa, who did you love like this?"

"It does not matter, *mon fils*, it was a lifetime ago." Richard pulled his covers closer. "But understand, it is easy to love all the good things about your lady, but can you overlook everything that might irritate you? Can you forgive her no matter what she does? Does she return your love? And can you stay true to her and forsake all others? If you can say *yes* to all that, then fight for that love – it is the most precious thing I know. Now lie down and go to sleep, the morning comes quickly."

"*Bon soir*, Pa-pa."

For a long time they both lay very still and very quiet but with too many thoughts to sleep.

The Raphael who sought out a private audience with Jacques the next morning was a very different Raphael than anyone had seen the day before. He was very serious and rather humble and Jacques could tell he was trying his best not to appear nervous. Taking pity, Jacques did try to put the boy somewhat at ease but not too much for he knew what Raphael was about.

"I come to seek your permission, monsieur, to court with your daughter Louise."

"You mean to court my daughter?" Jacques said sternly.

"*Oui, oui,* is that not what I said?"

"You said with… no 'with', you do not court with – you court."

"*Oui-oui.*" The boy nodded.

"And how does she feel about that?"

"Oh, I know not, monsieur. I have not dared to speak to her until I have spoken to you."

Score one point. "That is good thinking. How old are you?" Jacques queried.

"I am twenty years, monsieur."

"My Louise only turned sixteen this summer."

"She is very mature for her age."

Not the kind of thing a father wants to hear. "You are a guest in my home but this does not mean you are allowed free access to my daughter. *Comprenez vous?* If you wish to leave the immediate premises with her, you will ask for permission, *comprenez?* And someone will go with you. You will treat her always with respect and keep a decent distance between you..." at this he actually glowered. "*comprenez?*"

"Oh, *oui*, monsieur, a chaperon is required, is this not so?"

"Absolutely. And you will never go into her bedroom."

"No, monsieur."

"And she is not to go into yours."

"No, monsieur."

"I charge you with the responsibility of keeping these rules. Louise is barely more than a child. And know this, if you violate her, I will take my hunting knife to your *couilles – comprenez?*"

Raphael gulped involuntarily. "*Oui*, monsieur."

"Since we now understand each other – do you still wish to court my Louise?"

Raphael looked Jacques straight in the eye. "*Oui*, monsieur, very much."

"Very well. I give you permission to respectfully court my daughter."

Raphael rose and bowed low. He walked out of Jacques' study a very happy if somewhat shaken young man.

Jacques remained seated for a few minutes. "Well, now at least," he said aloud to the ink pot on his desk, "I know the identity of the muscle-bound cretin. And just where he is lurking."

Chapter 24

Through the rest of autumn and onset of winter, the elders around the beautiful young man and the lovely young girl watched the romance bloom. The young couple's peer group sought to assist anyway they could. Helen and Thor were starting to make plans for their own wedding which was set for the first Saturday after Helen's eighteenth birthday. And Caroline and Phillip whose wedding had been very quick and very quiet, enjoyed the planning vicariously.

There had just been an early winter storm and the new day broke clear and sunny. The snow was deep and the sun was making it perfect for packing into snowballs, making snowmen, and building forts. It beckoned to the young people and soon they were all outside.

The mill was closed because of the storm so Jacques had stayed home. He stood, looking out the window of his study, his door standing open, his desk, a mess of papers through which he had no desire to look. He did not feel like working. He was watching the children. He loved it best when they were wrapped in layers of clothing and one could barely distinguish who they were much less how old they were. They were playing. Throwing snowballs at each other, laughing, falling down to make snow angels, rolling in the snow. He knew Raphael and Louise were taking advantage of the situation for padded body contact and he could only smile. He had been very hard on the boy, but that was a father's job. If Raphael was man enough to withstand the threats and frowns of a stern father, then maybe he was man enough to take care of Jacques' little girl.

Thor had proved his courage when they went to the Nicholet homestead. Jacques had no doubts that Thor could provide for and take care of his own family and he had known Thor Boot all the boy's life. But Raphael was still a question mark. Who was this handsome, charming, and mysterious young man who if he married Louise could quite literally take off with her to anywhere. The laws of their world gave a husband the right to beat his wife, to claim ownership of all her property, to lock her away… no, the husbands for his daughters must be men who would never do such things no matter how provoked they might be. It spoke to their character, their moral compass, their deepest beliefs, and humanity.

Phillip had challenged Raphael to a wrestling match which had ended in a dead heat, proving he knew how to use his body strength. Jacques had challenged Raphael to a fencing match and discovered his skills were only mediocre but with a tomahawk he had a deadly aim. He could not shoot as well as Louise and Helen but he could pull a tight bow and release a powerful arrow. Undoubtedly Richard had set him on the path of learning those skills. Something of a surprise considering he had spent most of his life in a convent being raised by a pack of nuns who had undoubtedly fawned and petted on him constantly. Well, they had given him superb manners. He certainly had not learned those from Richard. But manners did not put bread on the table, nor did they defend one's home and family.

Twenty – that was John's age. It was the age he and Richard had been when they had arrived in the colonies. Now it seemed so young but then…? Then, he had been a man with his own fate in his hands. John was only twenty, and he too now had his fate in his hands.

Jacques turned slightly. He could hear Richard's cane-assisted gait coming down the hall. Doctor Ajax had suggested the cane. They had invited him to dinner and, honestly put, they had trapped Richard into an examination. Between the torn muscles and tendons that had never been properly treated the time he caught his foot in a trap and the arthritis he admitted to, Ajax recommended a cane, minor doses of laudanum and some specific exercises. The laudanum they did not mention to Marie.

Jacques thought for a moment. It was now five years since Richard reportedly had bound up the stairs to burst in on the little witch and save Marie's life. Jacques was so concerned about the men his daughters married being able to protect them and he had almost lost his Marie, failing to protect her from what was happening right before his nose. Jacques still felt a degree of guilt. He would never completely forgive himself but Richard had been able to leap up the stairs like a deer - only five or so years ago. And now? Now, on his worst days he could barely walk.

"Richard, come in and have a seat by the fire," Jacques invited when his old friend finally reached his study door. "Today is a day for us to sit by the fire and for the children to play in the snow. I have been watching them. They could be seven or eight or nine again. Where goes the time?"

"It flies," Richard grunted as he sat in one of the wing backed chairs. "And the older I get, the more I discover I regret. Generally, it is not what I have done but what I have *not* done that bothers me."

"Oh, yes? And what do you regret today?" Jacques asked lightly as he poured a glass of wine, skipped the water and handed it to Richard.

He took the glass with a nod of thanks. "I regret not bringing Raphael here long ago. He should have been in your nursery just as the Boot children were. I should have brought him when we lost his mother. And now, Jacques, I want to tell you all about it. It is only right… before your daughter and he become too close. I have wrestled with this and have concluded that it is my duty to tell you."

"Tell us what, Richard?" Marie was standing in the doorway.

"Oh, Marie, I did not see you there. I am sorry. I was talking to Jacques, I do not think our conversation is for a lady's ears."

"To the contrary!" Marie walked in, closed the door, and promptly sat down in the other wing backed chair. "If this is about the young man who one day may very well become my son through marriage I think I have every right to know everything. After all these years, you know full well there is no story so shocking that I cannot take it in stride."

Richard looked at Jacques.

"You heard her, *mon ami*, she makes her point and my wife usually wins her arguments."

"Very well," he drained his glass and held it forward for a refill. He cleared his throat. "Raphael's mother's people were settled on the Quebec frontier many years ago. They were among the first push by King Louis to send farmers over. But as I understand it, they were not really farmers. They were debtors who saw the opportunity to escape their debts, nothing more. So they hunted some, lived off the land, and made corn liquor which they traded to the Indians. The household consisted of the man and his wife, his father and brother, plus the couple had three sons and a daughter of their own.

"Apparently the daughter was a wild young thing who had developed a weakness for alcohol. She stole a jug of liquor one night and ran out into the forest where she found a young buck and some of his friends who were more than happy to help her drink it. They… well, Marie, I do not think I have to say it. Nine months later she has a half-breed baby and does not know or care who the father is or what tribe he is from. The story is there were several Huron, a neighboring Ojibwa, and a renegade Cherokee at the party, any of whom could have been the father." Richard looked down at his glass. "My money is on the Cherokee, I hear they are a pretty people.

"A few years later the wife dies and sometime after that the old man dies. After just so much time of being isolated and without a woman, the daughter's own father rapes her, and his brother does the same and they share her. She ends up pregnant once again only this time it is by one of her own kin. In her sober moments, she must have struggled with this reality. Some say she was drunk and slipped, others say she purposely jumped off the top of a waterfall. Either way, they found her body several days later, down stream.

"By now the little girl is maybe about six or seven years old, the mother and grandmother are both dead and since she is only a half-breed which to these..." Richard halted unable to find the right words to express what he thought of these men. "... they considered her something less than a person, so the man and his brother begin using her. Then the boys figure why should they be left out? And the poor child grows up with all five of her kin using her without shame or mercy.

"When she got her courses she, too, became pregnant. And she died giving birth to Marianna who was a quarter Indian and three-quarter the product of incest. That pack of degenerates did not know what to do with a baby so they gave her to the church who found someone to care for her, at least for a time.

"When I first came upon Marianna she was perhaps fifteen. Barefoot and half naked, she was sleeping under a cover of leaves for warmth and not three feet from one of my bear traps. If she had lain down just three feet over, it would have crushed the life from her."

Richard's voice changed from the anger he had felt for the abuse of a child to softness as he was lost in a more pleasant memory.

"Marianna was the most exotically beautiful creature I have ever seen but she was like a wild thing one must tame and gentle, but of which one can never feel completely certain. Of course, I assumed she had run away from something and I brought her home to my hut. My woman did not like it but it was what I chose to do. We fed her and clothed her and slowly she began to trust… a little, like a wild horse that has never been broken. I never touched her but my woman was not happy and we fought continually over the next several years. Then one night about twenty-one years ago, after another huge fight in which my woman stormed off, Marianna came to my bed freely of her own choice and I poured myself into her.

Raphael was the result."

Jacques and Marie remained silent trying to digest the story they had just heard. Finally, Marie spoke. "What happened to Marianna?"

"The night we had together, I could tell she was not a virgin but she never talked about her life. I do not know if the church gave her back to her rotten family or if someone else abused her but... she was a good mother," Richard nodded his head, tears in his eyes. "She did well with Raphael, and she said she loved the name I gave him but she never talked much beyond cooing his name to him. She had what the doctors would say was a surfeit of melancholic humors. Although my woman never returned, Marianna never came to me again. But she stayed in my hut and took care of her baby. Then one day when Raphael was only three, she killed herself. She did it quickly by jumping off a steep overhang."

"Oh, Richard," Marie gasped. "I am so sorry."

"I think she had waited for me to return because she had not wanted to leave little Rafe all alone." And with that Richard broke down and sobbed.

Marie looked at Jacques. She got up and went to Richard and while sitting on the arm of the chair she gathered him to her and held him. Jacques nodded with compassion.

"How did you learn all this, about her family I mean?" he asked after a few minutes.

Richard straightened, wiping his eyes on his sleeve while Marie continued to gently rub his back. Jacques offered him a handkerchief and Richard blew his nose.

"One of the sons made confession," Richard growled at last. "He was dying and wanted absolution for his part in the whole abomination. The priest knew I had taken in Marianna and he came and told me."

"Is that not breaking some kind of sacred trust?" Jacques asked.

"It is, but he was so revolted, he forgave himself."

"So Raphael is an eighth part Indian," Marie said softly as she moved back to her chair. "That is where he gets those beautiful cheek bones and soft, permanent tan."

"But he does not know," Richard quickly interjected. "I have never told him."

"But why not?" Marie asked in surprise.

"Because it would serve no purpose, Marie, except to possibly make him miserable." He saw the incomprehension in her face. "There are people who would spit at him if they knew and if he and Louise get married, they would spit at them both."

"They would not dare," Marie said indignantly.

"Perhaps not in Chartes Landing because of you and Jacques, at least not to their face. But behind their back, even here, people would ridicule. Find excuses to not allow their children to play with Rafe's children. And in New York Towne or Boston, the doors of better society would be permanently closed to them and their children, and even their children's children. Jacques, you know this is true."

Marie looked at Jacques and he nodded sadly. "It is true, even though he is only one-eighth, he is a *half-breed* to them. And we must consider, if he and Louise should marry," he cleared his throat, still uncomfortable with the thought, "their offspring would be one-sixteenth, nothing at all but still there would be those who would whisper and point fingers and avoid them."

The room was quiet until a snowball hit the window and the three looked over. There stood Louise, waving her mitten covered hand at them, laughing.

Marie and Jacques smiled and waved back.

"Thank you for telling us, Richard. It is right that we should know," Marie said softly. "And perhaps you are right, perhaps it is better that they do not know for now but still it is information they really should know... someday."

"When?" Richard grunted.

"Perhaps when the last one of us is about to die," she said quietly and left the study to arrange for hot chocolate to be served when everyone came back indoors.

Spring of 1712 brought more disturbing rumors of war all along the frontiers of the colonies. So it was with mixed emotions that Jacques planned to send Raphael back out to the trading posts along the Saint Lawrence River. He had grown to like the boy, despite the almost hypnotic hold he seemed to have over Louise but Jacques also saw this break as an opportunity for his daughter to gain back her senses. Perhaps absence would cool things down a bit. There were, after all, other suitors available within their settlement. He did not want his daughter jumping willy-nilly into anything. She was only sixteen. She should be enjoying her youth and freedom from household responsibilities.

Meanwhile, there was a wedding for Helen and Thor in the making. Jacques escorted his women to New York Towne on a shopping expedition while Richard accompanied Raphael to stock up for his trek. New York was changing. The old Wingate Emporium was now only one of several such stores to choose from and it was no longer the most attractive. Master Wingate had passed and before she died, his widow Abigail had sold the store including home and stock to Samuel Cooper who purchased it with the aid of a loan from the town's leading bank.

The last time Marie had been inside she had been aghast at the condition of the merchandise. The shelves were dusty, stock was depleted, and prices had risen without reason. A slave was there sullenly waiting on customers and Samuel's wife, a rather slatternly overweight young woman in a dirty apron had been overseeing things but did not seem to know where anything was located. Marie had made a token order only because Samuel knew the business she had always done with the Wingates. Now she steered everyone on to a newer establishment which she had found to be run much more efficiently and which was willing to bargain price considering the volume of business the Powers and their associates brought with them.

Richard assisted Raphael in supplying himself with trading goods for his trek up the Hudson and into the Great Lakes region. The young man's attentions were terribly distracted by the presence of Louise but Jacques and Marie could hardly have left her at home considering she, too, was involved in the wedding planning. When Richard was finished, Jacques signed for the cost of the supplies and arranged for delivery at dawn the next morning to the western docks where they had moored Richard's boat.

Taking Marie aside Jacques asked, "Do you want me to take Rafe and Richard elsewhere so Louise keeps her mind on your planning?"

Marie knew what he meant. "I think that might be an excellent idea. We could meet you at The Pork 'n' Porridge for dinner."

"Let us make a new memory by trying a new establishment. We will scout it out and come back for you."

"Very well," she smiled as he kissed her hand in farewell.

Marie left her own supply list with the owner and promised to return. Then she took her daughters out onto the street. Passing a large window, Helen was taken by a silk dress on display.

"Oh, mother, it's beautiful!"

Marie and Louise stopped to look. The dress began white around the neckline and shoulders, then the sleeves poofing one out of another gradually darkened from the palest lavender, to lavender, to dark lavender and with the aid of satin ribbons to finally be edged in dark purple. Meanwhile the dress itself did much the same. Marie marveled at how it had been constructed although it seemed to her a bit heavy or perhaps matronly. The craftsmanship was most excellent but somehow a purple dress for a young girl's wedding just didn't seem fitting unless she was royalty.

"You don't like it." Helen said in disappointment.

"It is… very unusual," Marie said looking up at a sign saying *Miss Lilly's* with an arrow directing foot traffic to the upper floor via an outdoor staircase. "it is just that I am not certain purple is an appropriate color for a wedding. But why do we not go up and see what else Miss Lilly has to offer," she smiled at her oldest daughter.

The three proceeded up the stairs and Marie opened the door causing a bell to jingle. They stepped into a room that was comfortably roomy with mirrors hung about making it appear even larger. It offered several chairs for seating.

A petite lady quickly appeared from within. "May I help you?" she smiled her greeting as she looked at each of them and Marie detected a French accent.

"My daughter was attracted to the dress in the window," Marie smiled warmly. "She is planning her wedding but somehow I feel the purple is perhaps too strong for a young maiden."

"Ahh, and when may I ask is the wedding to take place?"

"This summer," bubbled Helen. "The dress is so unusual, wherever did you get the design."

"The design is mine, mademoiselle, I am a *maîtresse couturière*," she replied proudly, perhaps even a trifle haughtily.

Helen and Louise did not understand but Marie did, only because she had read of them in connection with the fashion plates she often received.

"Mademoiselle Lilly is a fashion *designer* of the Women's Guild in Paris," Marie explained, she looked at Miss Lilly for confirmation. "A very prestigious honor, you are to be congratulated."

The woman looked pleased to be thus recognized.

"So tell us, Miss Lilly, what would you design for my daughter Helen to wear when she marries her tall, strong husband-to-be?" Marie asked lightly. "Could you give us some ideas?"

Jacques asked Brother Robert who was now Pastor Robert of the Huguenot Church of New York, if, as a special favor, he would come to Chartes Landing and perform the wedding service. Pastor Robert was pleased and honored to agree but before they parted company he passed along a warning.

"My friends, please take care on the streets after dark," he said, speaking quietly in French. "It would be wise not to even be out after dark. You have perhaps noticed the growing population of slaves?"

"Yes, we passed by the slave market. I have always found the practice disturbing," Jacques nodded. "I remember when we first came here, there were not nearly so many. Now everywhere I look, I see them."

Pastor Robert nodded. "It is an evil practice for which we must expect a reckoning someday. I hear things. My parishioners hear things. Bits and pieces overheard here and there. There is a great deal of unrest and unhappiness within a certain element undoubtedly nurtured by unnecessary cruelties. I have seen it myself, and I have seen the hatred in the faces of the slaves when they think no one is watching. It is not a good situation."

"Do you really think it is that volatile?" Richard asked with grave concern while fingering the knife in his belt.

"I know you are not often in our town, I just would not wish to see you caught unaware," the preacher said with a frown.

"I suppose sooner or later one must expect something to happen," said Jacques, looking around to ensure there was no one around to hear even their French, his hand resting on his foil. "I thank you for your words of caution."

"Good day, *mes amis*. Let me mark the wedding date on my calendar so I do not forget."

The trio left the Huguenot church and Jacques hired a sedan chair for Richard's sake. Two large black males picked up the chair with Richard's weight in it quite easily and a small mulatto male collected the fee for what remained of the afternoon. Richard was grateful to get off his damaged leg and Jacques and Raphael easily kept pace with the bearers.

"That was not pleasant to hear," Richard said as they were on their way. "I feel like we should get back to the women."

"Yes-yes, but there is just one more thing I must do." When they arrived at their next destination, Richard and Raphael remained with the chair while Jacques sought a personal gift for the young bride as well as one for her mother. At the best jewelry house in town he found a perfectly matched and well sized string of pearls for both of them.

The jeweler gave Jacques a recommendation for a new inn. The newest in town with a well reputed dining room. The men returned to the agreed upon meeting place and it was not long before Marie and her daughters arrived.

"Well, my darling," Jacques greeting his wife warmly. "Did you get all your shopping done? I do not see many packages." He took what few they had and gave them all to Raphael to carry. With the young man's arms thus occupied, he couldn't very well have them all over Jacques' daughter, now could he?

"Oh, Papa," Helen gushed. "We met the most marvelous seamstress..."

"Much more than a seamstress, she is a true artist..." Louise burst in.

"A dress designer," Marie explain more calmly. "A Huguenot woman who was a distinguished member of the Dressmakers Guild in Paris. I think our daughter will have a most exciting dress. All the measurements have been taken. I have ordered up a dress for myself and one for Louise as well. The woman shall mail a choice of original designs and we can choose and return for a fitting."

The men all nodded pleasantly.

"You could wear rags and you would all be beautiful," Richard declared with good humor.

"My sentiments exactly," smiled Jacques.

"Absolutely." Raphael looked over at Louise.

Jacques led them on to the new inn, a splendid establishment, a full three and a half stories high. The lobby had two chandeliers, plush carpets and potted plants. He booked a suite consisting of two bedrooms and a small sitting room offering a view from the third floor. This for the girls, Marie and himself. Richard and Raphael took a room on the ground floor for the sake of Richard's leg. The fourth or "half" floor was tucked under the sloping Mansard roof line and these were the smallest and cheapest rooms with far fewer windows.

The dining room was very elegant and the ladies wished to freshen up before eating so Jacques made reservations for later.

The women could not wait to inspect the rooms and were very pleased with everything they found. They also discovered their sitting room and each bedroom opened out onto a private balcony over-looking the street.

"It's so much fun to watch the people," Louise stood at the railing wishing Rafe was with her.

"It's so much better being above the dirt and noise of the rabble," Helen agreed.

"It is lovely, Jacques," Marie smiled, "although I must admit feeling a twinge of guilt at not seeing the Thompkins at The Pork 'n' Porridge."

He walked out and wrapped his arms around her from behind, holding her to him. "We have been very faithful patrons, *ma chérie*, but even faithful patrons deserve to see what new experiences the world has to offer, um?" He nuzzled her neck.

"They hosted our wedding," Marie said to her daughters. "Careful, do not lean so on the railing. The party was very... I believe *spontaneous* is the word. And everyone staying at the inn or even eating at the inn joined in on the celebration. And we danced and danced. Your father had to dance with every matron and wallflower, they all wanted to dance with the handsome, charming bridegroom," she laughed. "And I had to dance with all the men who asked me."

"Which was every man in town," Jacques added with a smile.

"I cannot believe how much it has changed," Marie said as she watched the traffic below. "Everything is becoming so crowded, so cramped. Why do people not spread out more? Remember when you used to walk me back to the Van Hootenaugs every Sunday?"

"Of course."

She watched the street for a time and then shivered despite Jacques' warm embrace. "I do not believe I could stand to live here anymore." She turned. "Come girls, let us fix our hair. It is time to go down to supper."

The party of six dined very leisurely that evening. Jacques was most interested in their selection of wines. Richard was happy with whatever Jacques chose. Helen kept revisiting their discovery of the Parisian seamstress and Louise and Raphael only had eyes for each other. Marie thought about tomorrow when they would say good-bye to Raphael until autumn and understood exactly how her second daughter felt.

They retired at a reasonable hour. Everyone had had a busy day and Raphael would be leaving very early in the morning. The rooms were warm as all the heat within the hotel rose upward. Marie had asked Jacques if he thought leaving the balcony doors open for circulation would be safe. Being on the third floor he assured her was very safe. She went to the girls' room and opened their balcony door as well and leaving the bedroom doors ajar created a noticeable movement of fresh air.

In the middle of the night, Jacques awoke to the sounds of shouting in the street and he could swear he had heard musket fire in the distance. Going out to the balcony he saw people running, some white, some black, more shouting, yelling. He looked northward and saw flames leaping up from a burning building.

Marie, wrapped in a shawl, came out to join him. "What is it, Jacques?"

"I am not certain but I can see there is a fire."

"Where?"

"Over there," he pointed northeast. "It appears like someone's home."

There was a growing din of shouting back and forth, cursing, weeping, footfalls, chasing. They saw soldiers marching double-time up from the Battery. Every black out on the street, free or slave, was arrested amidst angry shouts and sounds of more weeping. Jacques *had* detected musket fire and he heard it again.

"Whatever is it, Mother?" Helen's voice was heard as she stepped out onto the balcony from her room, her sister right behind her.

"Get back inside," Jacques said sternly.

"But..."

"Inside," he affirmed, "And you too, my darling," he said more gently to Marie. "We will all stay inside," Jacques was remembering Pastor Robert's warning. "and lock the doors to the balcony. It is cool enough. Go back to bed."

The girls obeyed their father as did Marie who turned to him in the privacy of their bedroom. "It is impossible to think of sleep." She pulled aside the curtain and peered out the window just as a scream penetrated the night. "Oh, *mon Dieu,* what was that?!"

"Marie, please," Jacques pulled his wife away from the windows. He thought of closing the draperies but decided against it. Keeping an eye out for fires in a crowded town made of wood was a prudent idea. "I can go downstairs and inquire..."

Just then his daughters came rushing out of their room and burst into their parents' room.

"Don't leave us, Papa!" "Don't go! Don't go!" They both threw their arms around him, clinging like burrs.

"Well, I can see there is no hope for sleep," Jacques said in weary resignation as he patted them both. Marie turned to hide a smile before speaking.

"Girls, go get dressed. It is not far from dawn. Make yourselves presentable, pack your valises and perhaps your father will invite Rafe to come up for breakfast?"

"What about Uncle Richard?" asked Louise who knew him to be a very lenient chaperon.

"Richard should not suffer the stairs. He and your father can find out what exactly is happening, yes?" she looked at Jacques. "And perhaps find breakfast downstairs while he has ours sent up...?"

"An excellent idea," he nodded, "now, if you girls will leave me so I may dress."

They left to return to their own room and Marie shut the door to their room before turning to her husband with a smile. "Now, are you not glad I packed you a nightshirt?"

After breakfast, the inn manager announced that everyone planning to leave was to have another day in their room without charge. The authorities wanted everyone off the streets and indoors as a type of martial law was invoked. No one was being allowed in or out of the town while door to door searches continued. The adults took it in stride, as long as everyone was safe nothing else mattered. Louise and Raphael couldn't have been more pleased with the reprieve to their parting and Helen wouldn't have minded if she would have been allowed to shop.

By the next morning the town's activities were returning to normal. But the air was rife with rumors. Some said 30 had been arrested, some said 50 and Marie even heard one person exclaim it was 100. The message seemed to be that the authorities had matters well in hand. However, despite the tears that came to Louise's eyes, Jacques insisted his ladies remain within the shelter of the inn while he and Richard alone went with Raphael to the west dock where Richard's boat was moored. They must see to the delivery of Rafe's supplies and he must be on his way without distractions. As Jacques and Richard saw Raphael off they cautioned him to steer well to the middle of the Hudson lest any runaway slaves be lurking along the river banks and attempt to swim out and take over his boat.

The packet boat which went south all the way to points in the Delaware Bay was so packed with passengers, Jacques, Marie, Richard and the girls had to wait yet one more day before making their way home. The boats allowed no black passengers amidst a continuing plethora of rumors and contradictory stories. And it would take weeks of trials for the whole story to sort itself out in what was subsequently called *The New York Towne Slave Rebellion of 1712*.

The official word was that because the slaves within the more crowded urban centers had more frequent contact with each other than on the vast plantations of the south, they had more opportunities to plot and plan mischief, vengeance, and rebellion against grievances, real and imagined. With a population of around 7000 people of which approximately 1000 were slaves, New York Towne was no exception. Once the trials were over the official story was that a small group of thirty to fifty colonial born slaves, feeding off of each other's complaints and miseries, formulated a plan and instigated a rebellion drawing in many of those slaves only recently come to the New York shores.

Setting fire to the outhouse of the home of Peter Van Tilburgh on Maiden Lane located at the outskirts of town was the signal by which all slaves were supposed to take up guns, axes, knives, whatever lethal weapon they could and proceed to kill any and all whites to be found. When the white population came out of their homes alarmed by the fire, the armed slaves shot into the gathering crowd, killing nine whites and injuring six more. Panic ensued, and men ran for the Battery to report to Governor Robert Hunter who sent in the militia. Upon seeing the armed soldiers coming, the rioters took off into a wooded swamp.

The militia along with armed by-standers swept the town looking for rioters. Some of the guilty commit suicide rather than face the punishment awaiting them. Approximately forty were brought to trial, eighteen were acquitted, a few more were pardoned while those found guilty were executed. And the end result was harsher slave codes, a growing toleration for more severe punishments, the forbidding of even free blacks from owning firearms, and the imposing of stricter limitations on social contact with other slaves. How strictly these codes were enforced and how severely violators were punished was always up to the individual slave holder.

Jacques read the newspaper reports to the family at the breakfast table and Marie re-affirmed that she had no desire to ever live in New York Towne again.

"You will take notice, children," she said rather proudly, "your pa-pa has managed to discourage anyone from bringing slaves into our settlement."

In the weeks to come before Helen's wedding, Marie confirmed her suspicions that the talented dress designer they had met, who was no youngster, had been forced to leave a very lucrative trade with a very prestigious clientele. A highly honored member of one of the only women's guilds in France, she had been protected for a time by patrons who were loathed to see anything happen to her. She had hidden her beliefs and even went to Masses but finally she grew ill under the strain. When the opportunity arose, she fled to England where she reestablished herself successfully for a number of years until she lost almost everything in an unfortunate liaison with a charming but unscrupulous and often cruel man. She sought to put an ocean between them when she took what remained of her personal wealth which was only her jewels and disappeared to the wilderness of the colonies. Establishing a small shoppe in New York Towne, she was determined to begin again.

The designs Miss Lilly sent to Marie were stunning, each more beautiful than the one before. Helen had a very difficult time deciding and the gown created for her wedding was unlike anything anyone had ever seen. Elegant beyond words yet so light and fluid as to capture the wondrous grace of youth. It was hardly a dress to be hidden in a small lumber and farm community but deserved to be shown off in the most sophisticated ballrooms of London or Paris. Miss Lilly had put her best talents into it in appreciation of the warm patronage of Madame Power and yet the gifted woman made certain it did not rob the spotlight from the young bride-to-be herself. Helen loved it and when she put it on, she felt the closest to a queen as she thought she would ever feel.

It was a lovely late spring day and Marie had just asked Jane to order up a tea cart from Margot and serve it outside. She spotted Richard sitting out in the backyard looking rather like a turtle basking in the sun.

"Jane, please add two shots of Monsieur Power's good cognac to that tray... on the side."

"Yes, ma'am," Jane replied and bobbed on her way.

Marie slipped out of the back door.

"Are you asleep?" she asked very softly as she approached the reclining man sitting in a wooden chaise lounge propped by pillows.

Richard opened his eyes and gave her a huge smile reminiscent of the old

Richard of yesteryear. "No, Marie, I am too young to take naps."

"It is a beautiful day," she offered.

"Yes, it is," he nodded agreeably.

"How is your leg today?"

His smile went crooked. "Ahh, and we were doing so well. We actually managed two exchanges before we got to my leg."

"I am sorry, Richard, I did not mean..."

"No-no, it is reality and I must live with it. It is thoughtful of you to ask. I just get so tired of being defined by my leg. I am the same age as your husband and look how he goes, he never stops. I try not to envy, Marie, although there is so much to envy him for," he said, not looking at her. "But I think myself a very small person to envy him for his good health."

Margot appeared with the tea cart.

"Ah, thank you, Margot. Oh, this looks lovely!" She looked at the woman and gave her a well deserved smile of appreciation. "Richard, will you join me for some tea and these wonderful pastries?"

Richard was about to decline when he saw her lift a shot glass and toss the contents into the teacup before she added any tea. "Now that kind of tea I will have," he grinned again.

She poured the tea and gave him his cup, then poured one for herself without the cognac. "So what do you think about all day, Richard."

He shrugged. "I think of Rafe, I think of the upcoming wedding and the next one to come. That will be Rafe's." He took a generous gulp of his tea. "They have such a passion for each other, do they not? My Raphael and your Louise. It is so pure. It reminds me of you and Jacques. But it is a hard life, being gone more than half the year from each other. He will not be here when she has his babies, when she is ill, when she is lonely for a man. Jacques was. From the time you had children, he has always been here for you."

"That is very true," she nodded.

"I hope to persuade Rafe to give up the treks once the babies come. Hopefully, there is something else he can be happy doing that will keep him closer to home. I will remind him, he does not want to end up like me."

"When I was in so much pain, you brought in Ingrid and Master Wang to help me. Why do you not do this for you?" she frowned momentarily.

"Because I am old and injured and you were young and not injured, just pulled apart."

She snorted softly. "Oh, come now, Richard. Be reasonable, I have no doubt the needles could help you as well as the massage."

Richard sat up a little straighter and looked at Marie. "The needles would have to be applied daily for a time, perhaps forever. Even if I could find someone, no Chinaman wants to come here to live..." he saw her begin to speak and added, "and I do not wish to leave again."

She closed her mouth and offered him a fresh cream puff. He took it and popped it into his mouth in one bite. He emptied his tea cup in several swallows.

"Would you like another?" she asked.

He held out his cup. "You are truly spoiling me. What have I done to deserve such attention?"

"Be not silly." She took his cup, emptied the second shot of cognac into it and added a little hot tea. "You are the dearest friend and you should know as much by now. I am aware that you have done much for Jacques and I certainly know how much you have done for me. There is nothing Jacques and I would not do to ease your suffering."

He sighed. "Well, soon I hope to have grandchildren and they will distract me, eh? Perhaps I just have too much time to think about myself."

"Perhaps," she smiled and sipped her tea. "And perhaps we shall get you a regular appointment with Madame Ingrid."

With the natural sensitivity that women are often blessed with, Marie noticed a growing mood overshadowing her usually positive, optimistic, and cheerful husband. He was saying little but Marie had the feeling it was connected with the upcoming wedding. One late morning she walked by his study and seeing the door open she observed Jacques just sitting motionless and staring off into space. She entered and sat on his lap.

"What is it, my much loved husband, that weighs so heavily upon your mind?" she asked as she threaded her fingertips through his curls.

"Nothing, nothing," he flushed, "you just caught me daydreaming."

"Ah, so," her finger traced down his cheek and stroked his moustache. "Remember when you made me swear never to hide anything from you again? That is a path that runs both ways, is it not?"

He looked into her face and those warm eyes full of feeling. "Of course." She did not look away and it compelled him to say more. "I was just thinking, the children are growing up so quickly."

That did not seem to bother you with John and Phillip, she thought but wisely did not say.

"Yes, but think how fortunate we are. I expect we will get a letter soon from John and Phillip works right here with you. Helen will be married soon but she moves only a mile or so away into the beautiful house Thor has built for them. Helen needs to become mistress of her own home," she added thoughtfully. "It is her temperament but I have no doubt we will see her all the time. And since Thor works for you, he is not going to move her away from us." She smiled and kissed him lightly on the lips. "I can think of many parents who are not as blessed as us."

"You are right," Jacques conceded but still the smile did not come.

"And I have wanted to speak with you about Louise." She felt him tense. So there was the real problem, just as she suspected. "It would be denying reality to not accept that sooner or later she and Raphael will marry."

Jacques said nothing.

"And if Rafe is going to continue doing the trading treks, I do not want her left alone for more than half of each year. So, I would like to propose that we invite them to live with us. She will have company while he is gone. She will have help with the babies to come..."

Jacques visibly perked up. "Should I add onto the house, do you think?"

"At the moment I do not think that is necessary. By the time Louise marries, Phillip and Caroline will be moved into their new house. Louise and Rafe can stay in *Grand-père's* suite, can they not? And since our nursery is growing empty, they can fill it. We have plenty of room."

"Do you think they will agree?"

"I cannot imagine they would not. We can allow Louise to do whatever she likes to decorate the suite to her liking. It certainly gives them the privacy they would like and she would not be alone every spring, summer, and fall. I know how sad that is, my love."

"That is an excellent idea! Oh, Marie, not only are you beautiful and fruitful, but you are also very wise. How did I come to be so blessed?!" He gave her an exuberant kiss and squeeze. "I love you, my darling!"

She smiled, happy to see his change in spirits.

"Now," he exclaimed, "is it not time for lunch?"

Chapter 25

Spring 1713

Jacques came home early after meeting Dufee's ship in the harbor. Jamie was doing his lessons under the watchful eye of Sarah who was rocking his niece, Charity. Little Charity was teething and in bad temper. Jamie was working out the conjugation of a Latin verb on his slate board when he caught sight of his father riding up the drive.

"Papa's home!" he said and flew out of the room, slate and chalk tossed aside. The young boy rushed downstairs hoping for some target practice but his usual expression of delight in greeting his father faded as the lad looked at the unusually somber man. His father's face had a strange unfocused appearance beneath his head of hair now equally gold and silver. And his shoulders seemed to sag and Papa's shoulders never sagged.

Rather mechanically, Jacques walked passed his youngest son to his study and sat down in his favorite wing backed chair before the hearth. He made no expression but stared blankly into the small fire Sims had just begun in the fireplace.

Then, as if only just realizing his son was standing nearby, he told Jamie to go immediately and fetch his mother from her store.

Jamie pulled on his coat against the cold air and ran as fast as his legs would carry him, down the drive and down the hill to the street that led to the emporium.

"Mother… Mother," he cried out as he opened the door to the store. Instantly, Marie knew something was amiss. "Papa says you are to come home at once."

"What has happened?" she asked grabbing her fur cloak, the same beautiful gray fur Jacques had given her the night he had proposed marriage. She had others but it was still her favorite.

"I don't know, Mama, but he looks… different."

Marie left the store knowing Caroline and Lyndon could lock up. It was not usual for her Jacques to come home early and bid her urgent presence. She had not taken the buggy and so, on foot she half ran all the way home as rapidly as her clothing would allow.

She rushed in the door completely out of breath. She was perspiring and threw her cloak off into Jane's waiting arms, hurrying to his study. "Jacques? Are you ill? What is wrong?" she called out. Her first look at him told her something terrible had happened. Her heart leapt in her chest and seemed to lodge itself painfully inside her throat. She was trying very hard to remember to breathe. Something had happened to John, was all she could think, he had been studying in Paris and staying at one of his grandfather's city mansions but they had received a letter only a week ago saying he was moving on and going to observe the work being done in Switzerland. Had he been arrested at the border for trying to leave and thrown into that horrible prison they called the Bastille?

Jacques took the hand she had placed on his shoulder and drew her even nearer. Saying nothing, he put his arms around her hips and buried his face in her skirts, weeping against her belly as her hands caressed and held him. She refused to ask the question because she so feared the answer.

Jamie was frightened.

Marie looked up and saw their youngest son standing there watching. "Go look after your little sister and please shut the door as you leave." She did not speak harshly but in a tone that was not to be refused and there was a tremor in her voice.

Jamie shut the door to his father's study as he had been told and stood very quietly, listening. He heard his father continue to cry. He heard his mother soothing him. He heard whispers, low talking. As hard as he tried, however, he could not make out a single word. Then, it grew very quiet, he heard more low murmurs. After a long time he heard his papa blow his nose several times. Floor boards creaked. Afraid of being discovered, Jamie quickly left the hall and went outdoors.

That evening everyone was gathered together. Caroline and Phillip were home from their respective jobs. Caroline was now over the sickness stage of her second pregnancy. Marie had sent a message to the new Boot household requesting Helen and Thor join them for dinner to hear important news. The newly-weds arrived very curious. Helen was nursing their new infant Thomas and Thor was most solicitous and proud.

Raphael had returned from his first solo trek in the company of Indian guides. Far from cooling their passions, the separation had caused him and Louise to burn so much hotter that Jacques had agreed to a New Year's Day wedding. They were the even newer newly-weds and Louise had just shared that she believed she would be having their first child in November when Raphael, who had just left again for the long trek into the north, returned.

Richard was proud and content. There was something poetic about his son marrying Marie's daughter and the prospect of his blood finally being mingled with hers… but of this he never spoke. He had made mention of building his own little house but Marie would not hear of it. If Raphael was to be a fur trader, absent more than half the year than he and Louise were to continue living in the big house so she would not be alone, Marie said. After the wedding and a two month honeymoon to themselves in the apartment over the store, they had moved into *Grandpère's* suite just before Rafe had to prepare to leave again. By then, Phillip, Caroline, and Charity had moved into their own home, a stone's throw away. And whatever would Richard do all alone by himself? Marie had asked.

Young Richie was now sixteen and discontent with everything. He was shorter and smaller than his older brothers and bored with the idea of farming. The mill held no attraction and he vacillated between wanting to become a lumber-jack, wanting to go trade trekking with Raphael, and wanting to moodily avoid everyone. Marie had learned to roll her eyes, take a deep breath, and be grateful that Jamie and Izzy were still children at their lessons.

Isabelle was six and a half going on seven-teen, quite the precocious little lady, and more than a bit spoiled with Jacques very comfortably wrapped around her little finger. She was now allowed to dine with the family at supper although the other children had had to reach the greater age of twelve before gaining such a consistent privilege. Marie understood; Jacques was simply compensating for the loss of his other daughters. Not that Jacques would ever really lose his daughters but he was no longer the only man in their lives.

The one person missing other than Raphael was John.

The dining room was the largest room in the whole house. Margot had brought all the hot food to the sideboard and was ready to begin serving as soon as the Master gave the usual blessing but instead, Jamie saw his father take a small glass of brandy and quickly gulp down a portion of it before he spoke.

Jacques cleared his throat. "Tonight, I have something of grave importance to share with you," he began very seriously as he stood at the head of his table. "I have waited so we could all be together." His face had lost none of its youthful handsomeness but had mellowed with mature distinction that was now strained but composed; only the redness of his eyes and huskiness of his voice betrayed his emotions.

Jamie looked away from his father and at all the faces up and down the table. Everyone was turned toward Papa and had become absolutely quiet, their eyes watching him intently, everyone except Mama who was looking down sadly into her lap.

"Today, I received a letter from my father's attorneys. It was a long time coming due to winter weather." He cleared his throat again. "Jean-Philippe, *Duc du Pouvoir*, my father and your *grand-père*, has passed away. May God give his soul rest."

Little gasps could be heard all around the table. The older children all remembered their grandparents quite well and frequent reference to them had kept their memories alive.

"They write that he went quietly in his sleep. It was his heart." Jacques stopped to take another sip of brandy as though steeling himself for the next. "Three days later, almost to the hour, his beloved wife and *duchesse*, my mother and your *grand-mère*, followed him. God rest her soul." There was a catch in Jacques' voice then. "I have been told she also went quietly having expressed the desire to live no more on this earth without her beloved husband." He paused and cleared his throat again.

"Those of you who are old enough to be aware of the political conditions and affairs of state will understand why his properties have all been passed on to his sister's son, my cousin, Henri-Richard, *Comte du Tullielle*, who, being Catholic, is the only heir the law of France allows, and thus, he is now the new *Duc du Pouvoir*.

The entire room was still, not a whisper, not a breath was heard.

"Lest you think my father had forgotten us, I assure you he did not. First, I would remind my sons to hold tight to the signet ring each of you has. It bears the *Pouvoir* coat of arms. Pass it and our proud name on to your children. *Pouvoir*, Power... it is our name in this, the New World.

"Second, I have learned that my father made very special arrangements to have a considerable sum of money put into the hands of Swiss bankers in my name. It is his departing gift which comes with wishes for me to use it to buy land here, land for the family, land for each of you to have from this time forth."

Jacques walked to the mantle to look at the miniature likenesses of his parents. The little portraits set side by side. He had brought them with him from France twenty-seven years ago. Raising his brandy glass in a salute, he said, "God bless them both and may they enjoy happiness together in Paradise!"

Emptying the vessel, he threw the glass forcefully into the hearth. The sound of shattering glass was soon multiplied as everyone came closer and, one by one, did the same, the young ones with their well-watered wine. It was the only tribute they knew to give to the loved ones who had died and were buried an ocean away. The grave had severed their link to the Old World forever. They are now, for better or worse and forevermore, a family of the New World.

Epilogue

In August 1776, two days after his sixteenth birthday, James Power III enlisted as a private in the New Jersey militia. His mother, the daughter of an English gentleman farmer, cried bitter tears. They lived a good life on a pleasant farm in the New Jersey countryside and she saw no reason for her son to fight in this war against King George. Their community was bitterly divided on the issue. James' father, James Power II, a gentleman farmer himself, was involved in local politics and understood his son's zeal. It was only because of a weak heart condition that this grandson of Jacques and Marie did not accept a commission of his own.

In late February 1778, young James' family received a letter from General George Washington. Penned by the General's own hand, the letter offered sincerest condolences and praises for the young Corporal Power, who had lost his life honorably in the service of his country and the performance of his duty. James had died of dysentery at Valley Forge.

The next Sunday in his hometown, a memorial service was held in young James' honor and all the surviving family attended. His younger brother, Charles, looking stiffly serious in a new black suit of clothes, nodded quietly to a multitude of cousins, aunts and uncles as they entered the church. His mother, ashen faced behind her black veils, clung to her husband's arm. And Grandpa Jamie, now seventy-eight years old and the last remaining member of his generation and the only one of his peers to have lived long enough to know his adult grandchildren, watched the whole proceeding. Locked onto his smallest finger by an arthritic knuckle was a heavy gold ring which he had planned to leave his namesake one day.

The old man watched his first born son fight back tears and stand staunchly at his wife's side. Old Jamie was suddenly reminded of another day many, many years ago, and yet, not so terribly long ago, when he had watched his own father struggling to fight back tears while announcing to the family the death of his own father and mother on the family estates in France.

It was far easier, reflected old Jamie, deep in thought as he twisted the ring round and round on his finger, yes, far easier to live through the passing of one's grandfather than to endure the passing of one's grand*son,* especially one who had beat the odds and survived to adulthood. The former was God's natural law - to be born, to live, to grow old and to die. The latter was the world turned suddenly upside down. Old Jamie jerked his head and cocked it to one side to listen. He could have sworn he heard the sound of glass shattering.

Suggested Book Club Discussion Questions

1. In Book 1, *The Huguenot*, after Marie kills her attacker she says she thinks it has changed her. How do we see Marie's character changing in Book 2?

2. Do you think Donald Sims should have told on Renée and Thor?

3. Discuss the theme "Building the Dream" in relation to:

Jacques	William Boot	The Wingates
Marie	Francois Nicholet	The Thompkins
Richard	The Sims	Lyndyn Peterson
Brother Robert		

4. Jacques was ready to call out Richard, his best friend, in a duel. It is sometimes difficult for us to understand why a man in the 17th or 18th century was willing to face death in a duel on "the field of honor." Do you think we have lost this sense or feeling about "honor" today?

5. How many places can you find where Marie tries to tell Jacques of her fear to have more children?

6. Does desiring physical punishment to "wipe the slate clean" seem unusual? What are the pros and cons?

7. What do you think might happen when Martha and her mother arrive back in England?

8. In Chapter 23 (page 287 in printed book) Richard defines love to Raphael. Do you still think this is applicable in modern day? Explain.

Jacques and his entire family think his mother, the *Duchesse du Pouvoir,* is dead... but is she?

Read her heart-rending story in: *The Huguenot and **The Tower of Constance**,* a historic prison on the southern coast of France where many a Huguenot woman was sent to die just because she was a Protestant.

The following is an excerpt from:

The Huguenot
and
The Tower of Constance
an ebook novella
by
D.C. Force

They traveled for several days. It had been especially slow going in the more hilly terrain. The grades were steep and they had changed animals more frequently. As they approached the coast, the land flattened out. The roads felt sandy and smoother.

It was almost nightfall, and Hélène was aware of a change. There was a dampness in the air and the smell of salt seas. Stretching around to peer out the window she saw that they were approaching a town and a huge, massive tower sat at the corner of the town wall. And at its top sat a little tower, perhaps two more stories high with an iron works at its top.

Having left the softer, sandy dirt of the open road, the horses' hoofs rang out, echoing against stone pavement. The sound reverberated as they passed through what she thought must be a very thick stone gateway in an equally thick stone wall. Then the wagon stopped and rough voices commanded they make haste in climbing out. Every woman struggled with stiffness and soreness while some suffered painfully aching joints. One woman fell and skinned her hands bloody. Their guards did not care.

They had arrived in Aigues Mortes.

The stone courtyard was ablaze with the late afternoon sun. A large woman who hardly seemed a woman and had a large ring of keys knotted about her girth came out to meet the wagon and began to mock and jeer at them. In her hand she held a thin stick of hickory which she waved about to great effect.

"So these are the latest little doves." Her eyes moved rapidly and seemed to take in everyone everywhere all at the same moment. "My, what a lively crowd. Are you sure they have a pulse?" she asked of no one in particular. "By the looks of them half will be dead before the month is over. Come – come. Move along, move along, step quickly and line up over here."

The women drew up into a line as quickly as they could.

"My name is Madame Marta. You will not speak to me unless you are spoken to. I am not your mother, nor your sister, nor your kindly auntie. I am not your confessor or your friend, do you understand? I am your jailer. I am the authority that from this moment on decides when you eat and if you eat, when you sleep and when you move your bowels, do you understand? Obey my rules and we will get along, try to disobey my rules and your life here will be very short."

With her stick she pointed to the gate. "I hope you all took a good look at the world out there before you came inside our gates." She snickered cruelly. "That is the last time you will see that world if you are here for life and most of you are. And even if you are not, chances are you will die in here before your sentence is up."

Madame Marta began to walk slowly down the line staring down at each woman like a drill sergeant inspecting his platoon. When she came to Hélène she stopped.

"Lift your skirts!" she barked.

Hélène looked at the woman with unabashed confusion.

"Are you deaf? Lift your skirts!" She lashed out with her stick and whipped Hélène's arm.

Startled, Hélène reached down and lifted her skirts an inch or two from the ground."Higher!" Madame Marta snapped and whipped her arm again.

Hélène raised her skirts a few inches more.

"To your knees!" the jailer cried impatiently.

Hélène felt the blood burn her cheeks as she raised her skirts exposing her feet, ankles and calves.

"I thought so," Madame Marta said smugly. "Those dainty little shoes will not last a month. Better get your hands on some good sturdy wooden sabots or come winter you will be barefoot and your pretty little toes will turn black with frost bite and fall off." Several women gave an audible gasp, one a groan and another began quietly weeping.

"The same goes for the rest of you," she raised her voice to address the entire line, "who think you are too good to wear peasant shoes. They are the only shoes that will last here." And she raised her own skirts just enough to show off her wooden shoes. She continued down the line, taking her time, enjoying making the women uncomfortable under her scrutiny.

She paused at an older matron with a protruding belly and using the stick, she gave her belly a poke. "What is this, are you hiding something or are you pregnant?" she asked with mocking accusation.

"No, madame," came a muffled reply. "I am too fat."

"Worry not, we will melt that off your bones," Madame Marta replied harshly and continued on, finally pausing in front of a very pretty young woman of nineteen or twenty. "What's this?" With her stick she lifted the linen *fichu* from the girl's neck exposing the tops of her healthy young breasts. "Is this any way for a modest Christian girl to dress? Why not unlace your bodice right now and give the guards a really good look?!"

Hélène saw color flush over the girl until she was as red as a beet and appeared totally and completely mortified and humiliated.

"They will be happy to keep you busy on cold winter nights, eh? Are your nipples pink or wine rose?" Madame Marta asked as she poked at her breast with her stick as though to pry up her nipple from within her corset. The girl was on the very brink of tears trying to fend the stick away. Marta flicked the switch across the girl's bare flesh. "I asked you a question. Now is when you speak."

"I-I am not sure, madame. Pink … I think," she replied weakly.

"So you stare at your breasts, do you? And what else do you do, eh? Do you take your hand and put it between your legs, eh?" She laughed again thoroughly enjoying the girl's discomfort.

"Marta!" A commanding male voice called down from a window overhead in the building opposite the tower. "It is late. Move them along."

The laughter ceased immediately. "Follow me, my little princesses."

Meanwhile…

What is Marie and Jacques' son John doing in Europe?

Look for the third full length novel in the Huguenot series to be released in 2020.

The Huguenot
and

The Heathen

by
D.C. Force

visit the author's website at
www.DCFORCE.com

www.ingramcontent.com/pod-product-compliance
Lightning Source LLC
Chambersburg PA
CBHW020924110726
47900CB00001B/287